Stocking Fillers

Fillers

EDITED BY
LORI PERKINS

BLACK
LACE

Contents

1 3 5 7 9 10 8 6 4 2

First published in the US by Ravenous Romance as
Merry SeXmas: an Anthology (2008) and *The 12 Days of Christmas* (2009)
First published in the United Kingdom in 2012 by
Black Lace Books, an imprint of Ebury Publishing
A Random House Group Company

Addresses for companies within the Random House Group
can be found at www.randomhouse.co.uk

A CIP catalogue record for this book is available from the British Library

The Random House Group Limited supports The Forest
Stewardship Council (FSC®), the leading international forest
certification organisation. Our books carrying the FSC label are
printed on FSC® certified paper. FSC is the only forest certification
scheme endorsed by the leading environmental organisations,
including Greenpeace. Our paper procurement policy can be found at:
www.randomhouse.co.uk/environment

Printed and bound by CPI Group (UK) Ltd, Croydon, CR0 4YY

ISBN: 9780352346810

To buy books by your favourite authors and register for offers, visit
www.blacklace.co.uk

A Partridge in a
Pear Tree

by Dahlia Schweitzer

It was Sarah's first Christmas. It was also her first winter in Vermont. She'd been raised Jewish and, as such, had never been much interested in the privileges and responsibilities of Christianity. Mass and Easter she didn't care much about, and Lent was certainly not on her radar, but Christmas had always made her jealous of her classmates and neighbors who got to install large evergreens in their living rooms. She loved the smell of the trees, the warm twinkling of the lights, and the seductive smell of the holiday cookies.

From Thanksgiving until New Year's, Sarah was a Christian-by-proxy. Always too loyal to her faith to celebrate Christmas directly, she made sure to be invited to as many Christmas parties as she could find, and whenever possible, she would offer to help decorate friends' trees, and she was always available to climb ladders in order to drape lights over gutters. In December, she was as supportive a friend as she could be to those who celebrated her favorite holiday.

Until she moved to Vermont.

She'd only been there a few weeks, so she didn't have any

friends yet. The job she'd moved for, which was supposed to start December 1, had been postponed to January 2, so she was unexpectedly left with a month that offered little responsibility beyond the occasional trip to the mall. She'd bought a shower curtain; she'd bought a mop—there simply wasn't much left to do. She hiked a lot. She joined the local library and became a regular, going through a book every day or two. She read everything Sidney Sheldon had ever written. Then she sampled Michael Crichton. And Michael Connolly. Then Mary Higgins Clark. (They were near each other alphabetically).

It didn't matter what she did; nothing could fill up her time. She took long showers after her long walks. She baked. She stared out the windows at the gorgeous Vermont landscape. She was glad she'd moved there; she liked the idea of starting over, conceptually at least, and she loved the crisp winter air, but nothing could fill the persistent vacancy created by her solitude.

During one of her trips to the mall, while seeking out a new hairdryer, she stumbled into the holiday section—which by no means implies it was somehow concealed, inconveniently inaccessible to the general public. Quite the opposite: the holiday section dominated, sprawling over aisles, spilling out over and above the confines of the shelf space. Until then, Sarah had managed persistently to avoid the glut of Christmas paraphernalia. She'd set up her menorah and she was determined to be devout for another year, especially in her solitude. She had no excuses for being a by-proxy-Christian. She actually liked being Jewish and loved Passover. She wished there were more Jews in Vermont.

So every time she went on one of her regular shopping expeditions, she would do her best to turn away from the mistletoe and the endless strands of lights, from the wreaths and the stuffed Santas, the wind-up reindeer and the adorably embroidered stockings. She was good. She was committed to her menorah.

Well, she was committed until the hairdryer escapade, and then she could resist no more. Emerging from the small appliance section, heading towards the cashier, it was suddenly there, and she was suddenly in it. It was a Christmas overdose. Bombarded on all sides, she just stood and stared. Pivoting in a circle like a wind-up doll, she studied the red, green, and fake-snow-white consumer excess on all sides. Even she had to admit it was a bit much. There was a certain mockery to the extravagant need to market all aspects of the holiday, and she was relieved she didn't feel the need to buy everything.

In fact, she left quite safely, carrying only a box of ornaments, two long strands of lights, and a very cute, petite Christmas tree.

Sarah was going to have her very first tree, and she was going to decorate it herself. This was Vermont, after all, a place of opportunity, where no one knew her and, more importantly, where no one knew her Jewishness. No one would ask why a Jew, who was happy being a Jew, would want a tree. God, she was convinced, would look the other way. It was Christmas, after all.

She felt giddy by the time she got home. She'd been unable to restrain herself from repeatedly glancing over her shoulder at the precious possessions in her back seat. She couldn't quite believe she'd done it, and she couldn't believe it had taken her this long. After all, what was a tree? It was décor; it was interior design. It was the holiday spirit. It wasn't like she was laying baby Jesus out on her welcome mat. This was just a bit of greenery, some color, and a little soft lighting. Unable to stop smiling, she practically sailed through her front door, the tree tucked under one arm, the plastic bag under the other.

It wasn't until she'd deposited everything in front of the fireplace that she realized she'd forgotten the hair dryer. She'd abandoned it somewhere between the ornaments and the lighting. Sarah laughed. She didn't care. She could buy a hair dryer anytime, but this was Christmas. It was the only time when she could buy a tree, bedeck it with lights and glittering globes, and feel part of something large—and a little bit naughty.

She assembled the tree to the right of her fireplace, hanging the various ornaments evenly throughout. She had bought two strands of holiday lights, one for the living room for internal holiday cheer, and the other to be draped around the bushes beside her front door for obvious external holiday cheer.

It was when she was outside, trying to determine exactly how to festoon her bushes with lights, that she first heard the bird. Not gifted with the best ability to determine sound direction, it took Sarah a moment and several glances about to figure out where the chirping was coming from. She lived beside a huge wooded expanse, but the cold weather had stripped the trees of their leaves, so it didn't take long to spot the distinctive red beak and black stripe of her favorite partridge. Many a recent morning Sarah had sat on her front porch, wrapped in a blanket, nursing a tea, and watching her partridge fly about the trees. He would never get close enough when she was outside, but if she left the odd piece of bread out as an offering, he'd always swoop by as soon as she'd stepped back indoors.

She also spied on him often from the anonymity of her kitchen window, watching him trot around the hardening icy ground, soaring into the trees whenever the forest belched an unexpected and startling sound. Some mornings, when she read the paper in bed, she could hear his calls resonate among the trees. A kindred spirit of a sort, he seemed as alone as she was; she never spotted him with another bird. Seeing him always made her feel a little less alone and a little more like she was at home.

Sarah nodded in his direction now, displaying the results of her lighting artistry as if the little partridge cared about her holiday decorations. She turned to duck back inside to gather a few scraps of bread to leave for her feathered friend just as the sound of the shotgun shattered the silence of the Vermont countryside like an explosion. If she'd still been in civilization, she'd have assumed it was a car backfiring. But in her new remote surroundings, she knew there wasn't a car nearby. It was definitely a shotgun, and it was way too close.

Whirling around, she raced towards the outskirts of the woods. The blast had been so loud, the hunter could not have been far. She looked desperately for her partridge, but he was nowhere to be found and she sighed with relief. She couldn't see him in the trees nor could she spot his bloody carcass on the ground. Either the hunter hadn't aimed for her bird, or he'd missed. Regardless, she knew she had to get rid of the hunter. Parts of the woods permitted hunting, but the area adjacent to her house was off limits. It was too residential. The problem was that most hunters weren't aware of that; the change in zone wasn't clearly marked, and as her house was one of only a few, it was hard to determine this was now a residential area.

Luckily, the hunter was wearing the requisite orange vest and it didn't take long for her to spot him in the thicket. She waved and shouted as she ran in his direction. He turned impatiently to determine the cause of the commotion, lowering his shotgun so it pointed at the ground.

"You're not allowed to shoot here," she panted, struggling to catch her breath.

He simply stared at her, a slight grin on his face.

"Why's that?" he asked.

Taking control of her breathing, she stood up straighter to face the man, and was startled to discover that the hunter was extraordinarily good-looking—well, in a rugged, chiseled, Vermont kind of way. Feeling even more discombobulated, she took a deep breath before speaking.

"This is considered a residential part of the woods. I live"—she pointed over her shoulder—"just over there. I know it's not clearly marked, but you're not supposed to be hunting over here."

As if amused, the hunter grinned even more and leaned towards her. It was only when he leaned over that she realized how tall he was. He had to have been at least six-foot-four. But this was hardly the time to flirt.

Apparently, the hunter felt differently. A flirtatious note to his voice, he leaned in further, his face inches to hers, and said, "I'm terribly sorry for the mix-up. Will you ever forgive me?"

"What were you hunting?" she asked, suddenly suspicious and alarmed. Second guessing her earlier search of the snow, she realized that just because she hadn't seen any blood it didn't mean her partridge was safe.

"I was hunting a bird," he said matter-of-factly. "A partridge. Small little bugger."

She could feel the blood escape from her face and knew she must have gone ghostly pale.

"What? What is it?" He grabbed her shoulder with his arm, suddenly concerned.

"That's my partridge," she stammered. "Well, not mine, but mine. You know. Did you hit it?"

He shook his head. "No, the little beast flew off when he heard me coming. He's somewhere over there." He gestured towards the horizon. "Haven't a clue where, though. You say he's yours?"

She paused. She wanted to be precise. "I don't own him, but we have an understanding. We share bread. I like to listen to him. Do you know what I mean?" Sarah realized she was being anything but precise and worse, probably sounded crazy.

The hunter nodded. "I do. And I apologize. I'm glad I didn't hit him, and I apologize for coming close. I promise to turn around, walk away, and never come back. I'll leave you and your partridge in peace."

True to his word, the hunter pivoted with a closing nod of the head and began to make his way back through the woods.

"Wait!" Sarah called.

He turned and looked at her.

"Do you think . . . would you mind . . . it's just that you're so tall . . ."

"What do you need, ma'am?" he said, with the finesse of a firefighter prepared to rescue a cat from a tree.

"It's just my Christmas lights. They're not high enough. I can't get them on the gutter, and I just moved here, so I don't have a ladder. Do you think you could . . . ?" Sarah's voice trailed off. She was embarrassed. She didn't like to ask for help. She was always the one doing the helping. This role reversal felt foreign to her.

Clearly, the man was used to such requests. He smiled obligingly, gestured her onwards with his arm, and told her to lead the way.

Feeling a little bewildered by the recent turn of events, but also convinced it was somehow part of the Christmas spirit, Sarah did just that.

It wasn't until they got back to her house that it occurred to her she didn't know his name, and she turned to him, her mouth just beginning to form the words, when he reached out his right hand to shake hers. One step ahead of her, he said, "Will."

She closed her mouth, smiling at their silent communication, and shook his hand. It was surprisingly warm, considering the chilly Vermont winter air. "Sarah."

They held each other's hands for a moment, the surroundings completely still in that way that only happens when snow lines the ground and the trees are bare. The heat of their bodies flowed through their fingers and, for a minute, Sarah forgot about the lights and about Christmas. She even forgot about her partridge.

As he released her hand, she snapped back to her senses. With a slight cringe, she asked him to rest his gun in a remote corner of the porch. Then she explained exactly how the lights should hang. With Will's height, it took him mere moments to drape the lights along, his long, lean arms never hesitating as they reached first one gutter corner, then another, and then, in what seemed like only a moment, all was perfect and Sarah smiled. Somehow, even with the shotgun, it had still ended up being perfect.

"Would you like some cider?" she asked. "A beer, maybe?"

The hunter grinned. "Sure. That sounds great."

Sarah slid past him, past the porch bench where she'd sat

many a morning watching her partridge dart in and out of trees and around her house, past the silent shotgun in the corner, and turned the handle on door to the house. As the heat from inside washed over the front of her, she became acutely aware of a different kind of heat behind her. She looked over her shoulder to find Will close behind. Too close? Maybe, but she was surprisingly comforted by his presence.

In the kitchen, Sarah stuck her head into the fridge and grabbed the cider. As she pulled a pot from beneath the stove to warm it, she watched out of the corner of her eye as Will lifted one foot and expertly unlaced a boot with one hand before unlacing the opposite, then stepping out of them both. The musky scent of his wool socks wafted through the kitchen.

"Forgive me," he said. Was there a twinkle in his eyes? "I should have done that at the door." Startled, Sarah realized she was still wearing her own boots and she bent to clumsily unlace them as she turned the knob on the stove and the short click, click, click was quickly replaced by the whoosh of the igniting burner under the cider.

She nervously smiled at the hunter, who stood nearby, absently scratching at the stubble on his chin. She stepped out of her own boots, kicked them aside, and turned to grab a wooden spoon, stirring the cider on the stove.

Suddenly, Sarah felt that heat behind her again and simultaneously a hand snaked around her waist. She froze as Will's hand grabbed gently at the wooden spoon just above hers. "You're still wearing your jacket," he said quietly, seductively. "Let me stir the cider . . . get comfortable." She turned to him, chest to chest, and stared up into his eyes.

"Cups are there," she said, waving to a rack on the wall

without breaking her gaze. Her hand, just below his on the spoon, lingered for a moment longer than it might have. She ducked under his arm and shed her coat. Will reached for two cups and ladled cider into each. Silently they sipped and stared at one another.

After draining his mug, the hunter deposited it on the counter and moved to stand directly in front of Sarah as she leaned against the kitchen sink, his hips only a few inches from hers. The electricity between them sparked, denser than actual flesh.

She felt drunk on the cider, even though it was non-alcoholic. She continued to stare at his face, the face of the man who had almost killed her partridge and who had absolutely violated her woods, and she knew she yearned to see him naked. That, with a hunger intensified by weeks of solitude, she wanted his hands all over her body, to feel his sheer physicality against her and inside her.

As if he could read her mind, he slowly unzipped his vest, letting it fall to the floor, never letting his eyes leave hers. She smiled at him and lifted her sweater over her head, dropping it on top of his vest. His grin broadening, he followed suit, his sweater quickly joining hers on the floor. It took about thirty seconds until they were both topless, and another thirty until they were fully naked.

It gave her a second's pause to think she'd literally met this man barely an hour before, but only a second—and then her hunger for the touch of another body, for the feel of his skin beneath her fingers took over, and he was matching her every second of the way.

The two of them devoured each other. His teeth ran along her shoulders, gnawing on the bone as it rubbed against the flesh, his tongue tracing the lines of her neck while her lips surrounded his nipples, feeling them grow harder, stiffer in her mouth as her hand made its way across the expanse of his ribcage, his taut stomach, until it reached its destination. He was so engorged that she marveled at the definition of veins across skin, at the way she could barely wrap her hand around him, could barely tame his manhood. The subsequent moan that came from the center of his being sent shivers down her spine.

It wasn't enough to touch him; she wanted to taste him. She sank to her knees and ran her hands up his toned and athletic thighs. She licked his hips, and his pelvis, and slid her tongue across each thigh, relishing the salty sweetness of his skin before making her way between his legs.

She slid his cock against the roof of her mouth. He was so hard, so large, so stretched tightly against his own skin, that he barely fit inside of her. She let him slide as far down her throat as she could stand, knowing by the pressure of his hand against her head that he wanted more than she could give him, so she wrapped the fingers of her right hand against the base of his cock, giving herself an extra two inches of space. She started moving back and forth, hand and mouth in perfect precision, her tongue licking the length of his cock, her throat tickling its head.

She slowly picked up speed, drawing him out as long as she could, echoing the beating of the blood in his veins, her other hand cupping his balls, the warm wetness of her slick saliva spreading all over his tight, hot skin. So hypnotized was she by the act of maintaining rhythm, she didn't even notice the wetness leaking out of her until he wrenched her up, hands grasping her triceps, practically hoisting her to his level. He grinned at her again and she realized how much she was aching for him.

She thought she couldn't possibly want him any more than she already did, but then she felt him slip his cock along the edge of her pussy and against her clit and the desire rose up inside her like an inferno. Suddenly she felt that if he didn't split her in two right then, right there, she might combust on her own, exploding in a bonfire of her own making.

"Want me to go inside?" he asked, that damn grin still painting his face.

"Oh God, yes, yes, please," she begged, her arms wrapped around his body, pulling him in close, her head against the broad expanse of chest and sternum.

"Look at me."

She looked up at him, her eyes locking on his as he ran his cock again along the outside edge of her pussy, against her clit, and then, drawing a sharp breath, sank inside her. Together their moans were so loud, Sarah couldn't differentiate between Will's and her own, they matched so perfectly in volume and intensity. She pressed herself to him further, crazed by lust and desire. All she cared about was getting him inside her as deeply as possible.

Curving against her, he moved in and out—slowly at first, but it was clear neither of them had much patience for pacing. Deeper and faster, he shoved her against the edge of the kitchen sink so hard she had to grip it with her hands to keep from sliding over the edge and landing ass first in the deep basin, legs in the air. He pressed against her, pushing against the kitchen sink, and she bucked back against him until simultaneously they both came in a damp, hot, sweaty mess.

The room was nearly silent with the exception of their gulping and panting as they struggled to catch their breath. Sarah collapsed against the hunter's chest, his cock still throbbing and spasming inside of her.

From outside, a faint singing. She heard it first and smiled.

"Friend of yours?" Will asked. Sarah turned to see the partridge perched on the tree branch just outside her window.

It was December 14 and Christmas was coming.

Two Turtledoves
by Lisa Lane

Melinda lay across the sofa completely naked, trying different poses. She tried lying on her back, propped up against her elbows, stretching one long, shapely leg across its length, and artfully bending the other. She tried lying on her side, one leg bent over the other, her head resting on her hands. Finally, she decided to wait for him on her stomach, her knees bent and her legs crossed over her, her chin balancing on her fists. She had finished two cups of eggnog during the last hour while playing around with the last of the Christmas decorations and getting dinner started, and the alcohol had finally begun to hit her.

A CD of traditional Christmas songs played softly from the bedroom and the smell of cinnamon from the scented pine cones she'd placed around the house now mingled with the pine smell emanating from the elaborately decorated tree. Bows and garlands adorned every door, and a sprig of mistletoe hung in the living room right above her spot on the sofa. She had timed dinner so it would be ready just about an hour after Brent was due home from work.

He was late.

Melinda stood up, stretched, poured herself another cup

of eggnog, then returned to the sofa, ready to resume her pose should she hear the front door open. She sipped the spiced drink slowly, not wanting to trade in her comfortable buzz for a full-on state of drunkenness.

He would be home any minute.

Any second, now . . .

She waited patiently, not moving from the sofa as the minutes passed. Five. Fifteen. Thirty.

She finished her drink and closed her eyes for a moment of rest, the long day finally catching up with her. She had gotten up early with Brent, fixed him a nice pancake breakfast, then had spent the rest of the day running errands and decorating the house. She had planned the evening perfectly in her mind: Brent would come home to find her naked on the sofa, ready to greet him. He would find the mistletoe and they would kiss, and then they would make love in the living room before sitting down to a delicious and lovingly prepared meal.

The third eggnog had been a mistake, she realized too late, and her body craved a nap more than anything else.

She lingered in that half-sleep state, her thoughts drifting back to her plans for the perfect evening. She played out every detail in her mind. The front door would open, and then quickly close, the soft sound of snow sneaking in with the momentary draft. Brent would walk into the living room, pleasantly surprised to find Melinda in her pose.

She would sit slowly and seductively upright. "I've been waiting for you."

"It smells like Christmas in here," he would say, meeting her on the sofa as he spotted the mistletoe.

Sitting beside her, he would take her into his arms, then offer her a passionate and loving kiss. His arms would run along her body, feeling her and enjoying her, as she loosened his tie and unbuttoned his shirt. She would expose his firm, strong chest, and then remove the shirt and tug at his pants.

She would shift to her back as he climbed over her, his hands moving down below, feeling that she was hot and wet, overwhelmed with her desire to feel him enter her. His cock would be swollen and hard, its base thick and its head perfectly defined, and he would hold it just out of her reach, teasing and testing her.

As he dipped down, brushing up against her, he would steal another kiss. His chest would be warm and firm, and he would taste sweet as their tongues met and played against one another. The room would heat up as they pressed their bodies together and she would spread her legs around him. Then he would slide into her, their eyes meeting as their breath escaped them both for a brief moment. She'd bring her hips up to meet his, and together they would rock and sway in unison, grinding into one another, savoring one another.

The pleasure between them would swell, filling her and enveloping him. Their lips would meet again frantically, and they'd thrust into each other with growing intensity, hungry for more. They'd begin to build together, their pace quickening with their shared gratification.

"I love you," he would say, his words penetrating her mind, and his breath tantalizing the last of her senses.

"I love you, too," she would respond breathlessly.

As her fingernails ran down his back, scratching him slightly, she'd find his hard, round ass and take him into her hands, driving him harder and deeper inside of her.

Finally, he would groan, "I want to come inside you."

"I want to feel you come." And with the orgasm a split second away—

Melinda jumped with a start, immediately waking as the oven timer sounded.

Dazed, she glanced around and got her bearings. He still wasn't home. *What was keeping him?*

Melinda hurried to the kitchen to remove the bird from the oven and mash the potatoes. The tile was cool against her bare feet, somewhat sobering to her as she padded toward the oven.

Where was he?

It was just the two of them. Their families were scattered across the country and their finances too tight to allow for travel, so she'd roasted a small stuffed chicken and made just enough mashed potatoes to see them both through one round of leftovers. It was a tradition they'd started only a few years back, but already they had made it their own. He opted to work longer hours at Christmas, the extra pay justification to spoil her for just one day. Melinda was happy to take the time preparing for his return, planning every detail, doing what she could to make the evening special. Brent delighted in finding some way, without going beyond his means, to outdo the years before. They would be married ten years in January, but the spark between them remained bright, their efforts to keep it that way reciprocal.

She drained the potatoes in the sink, the hot steam rushing over her body as she poured the boiling water down the drain. Another wave of heat washed over her as she moved the chicken from the oven to the cool stovetop. She mashed the potatoes and emptied the stuffing, rushing to complete her presentation in time to return to her pose.

A combination of worry and anger slowly began to fill her. Brent should have been home by now. She knew rationally that he was caught in traffic, or perhaps even out buying a last-minute present for her, but she couldn't help but resent whatever circumstance was behind his tardiness. Instead of posing seductively, with dinner hot from the oven—instead of the night playing out just as it had in her mind—she was fitting aluminum foil over dinner and scrubbing chicken grease off her hands.

She heard the front door open and shut precisely as she wrapped the last fold of aluminum foil over the chicken. She froze for a moment, trying to decide whether she was going to express her worry or her anger, then struck a pose as she heard him near. She would hear his excuse before she decided which emotion to unleash.

She took a step back with a giggle as Brent stepped in, dressed in a Santa costume complete with a stuffed stomach, white wig, and fake beard. He carried a vented cardboard box from a pet store, carefully using both hands.

"Merry Christmas," he said with a deep and jovial Santa voice. He smiled at the sight of her naked body, but held character. "Have you been naughty this year or nice?"

"Incredibly naughty," she said, still laughing. "Do I still get my present?"

"Only if you show Santa how nice you can be," he said, cracking a smile and handing her the box.

She peeked through the top, seeing two scared birds huddling and ready to spring. She shut the box before she could get a good look, thwarting their unwanted escape, but from what she could tell, they looked like doves. "You bought me a pair of doves?"

"Turtledoves," he said. "Ho, ho, ho!"

"That would explain the partridge in a pear tree you brought home last night," she joked.

"You don't like them? Well, Santa could take them back."

She smiled. "Two turtledoves. That's very sweet." She gave him a hug, his suit soft against her bare skin.

"Their cage is in the living room," he said, peeking under the foil. "Dinner's ready?"

She nodded.

"Were you planning on eating it naked?"

She nodded again. "Only if you keep on the Santa suit."

"Deal." He gently plucked the box from her, giving her a quick peck on the lips. "I'll get the birds set up in their cage while you serve us dinner."

"Sounds good."

He walked out with the box, looking clumsy but adorable in his big black boots. Touched and amused by his effort, she moved to the stove with two plates, hoping their dinner would still be hot.

The chicken steamed as she removed the foil, but the potatoes were already beginning to turn cold. She decided to make a quick gravy, already resigned to the idea of reheating the potatoes when she was done, and she quickly threw a piece of foil over the pan as she heard Brent yell from the other room.

"Heads up! The birds got loose!"

She heard the frantic flapping of wings and a nervous purr coming her way as one of the doves, then the other, flew into the kitchen. She grabbed helplessly at thin air trying to catch one, but missed miserably and sent it out of the room. She gasped as the other dove suddenly landed in the mashed potatoes. The bird looked around for a moment, stupefied, as it sank into the lukewarm mass, its little feet kicking in a futile attempt to keep from sinking even deeper.

Melinda dove toward the bowl, horrified when the bird leaped out, sending potatoes in all directions with another flap of its wings. She turned as the bird flew out the way it had come in, just missing Brent's head as he entered the room. He noticed the bits of mashed potato splattered across her chest.

"I don't think you'll want to eat the potatoes," she said. She set the bowl aside and removed the foil from the chicken and stuffing, then turned off the burner with a disgusted flick of her wrist. She dug a fork into the stuffing, and lifted it to her lips for a taste. "Stuffing's cold," she said, pouting.

Brent gently pulled the fork from her hand, stealing a taste for himself. "Still tastes good."

"We should track down the birds."

"They're not going anywhere." He gave her another kiss. "I'm starved. Let's eat. We can worry about the birds when we're done."

Melinda nodded, feeling hungry herself, and began serving them separate plates, but Brent stopped her. He plucked a piece of chicken from the pan, using his fingers, and moved it to her mouth.

She ate the piece with a smile, and then picked a bit of chicken out herself and held it out to him. He offered her another.

She moved to the stuffing, taking a small mass of it in her hand, and moving it to his mouth. He did the same, playfully smearing a bit of it on her face.

She giggled. "This isn't wedding cake!"

"No?" he asked, smearing another small handful across her lips.

She sank her hand into the bowl, then pressed a handful of stuffing into his face, covering his fake moustache and catching bits of it in the beard. With a laugh, she backed off as she saw him reach for another handful.

She retreated to the bowl of mashed potatoes, then quickly flung a hefty handful in his direction. She missed, only to find him suddenly tossing stuffing her way. A small amount of it landed in her hair, and another quick handful left bits of seasoned bread crumbs across her chest.

"I hope you're planning on cleaning up this mess!" she said, laughing.

He responded by flinging another handful of stuffing her way.

She tossed the last of the potatoes at him and they splattered across his coat. He saw that she was out of ammunition, and charged toward her with another handful of stuffing. "What are you going to do now?"

She dodged as the stuffing became airborne and he retaliated by smearing his greasy hand across her face.

"Yuck!" She gagged.

He moved to her face, and playfully licked her nose.

"So, are you going to help me clean up?" she asked.

"Some of it," he said, moving to her lips and playfully flicking his tongue over them. "Santa's still hungry."

He pulled down the fake beard, and began to lick the bits of potato and stuffing from her chest.

"How do they taste?" she asked.

"They taste good." He continued to lick her, moving to one of her nipples, teasing it with his tongue. He sucked on it, letting it go hard in his mouth, and then he moved to the other, caressing it with his lips and teasing it to hardness.

He ran his lips up her chest, moving them up her neck, down the curve of her jaw, and then to her lips. They kissed passionately, and she pressed tightly against his padded jacket, wrapping her arms around him. He caressed her back, his hands slowly making their way down to the thin curve of her ass.

They both jumped at the sound of a loud crash in the living room.

Instinctively, Brent sprinted into the living room, Melinda hot on his heels, knowing already that one of the birds had knocked over the vase. A bird flew past them and disappeared down the hall leading to the bedroom. The other was nowhere to be seen. The vase had stood on a small table by the door but now lay in several pieces on the ground, a bouquet of dried wildflowers in disarray beside it. Across the room stood the Christmas tree, and beneath it sat a dozen wrapped presents. A flannel red sack sat on the floor beside the gifts, and just to the side of the tree stood a large birdcage.

Melinda and Brent ignored the broken vase for the moment, opting instead to find and catch both birds before doing anything else. They hurried together toward the bedroom.

One of the birds stood on the bed. She was a pretty little bird with a mottled brown body. She walked in tiny steps, her head bobbing up and down, calling to her partner: *"Trrrrr! Trrrrr!"*

The other bird answered and they realized he too was in the room, high up on the curtain rod. His feathers were darker than hers and his body a beautiful shade of blue. He watched, unwilling to leave his vantage point, staring as Melinda and Brent attempted to corner the female.

But she deftly jumped high into the air and joined her partner on the curtain rod. They cooed back and forth, inching toward one another. It was as if they both felt the need to repeat to the other, in their own little language: *"I'm okay. Are you okay?"*

"I'm okay. Are you okay?

"Now what do we do?" Melinda asked.

Brent leaped toward the birds, waving his hands. "Ho, ho, ho!"

Both birds flew off with a horrified wail, rising over his head and skillfully avoiding his attempts to snatch them from the air. In an instant, they were out of the room.

"Smooth!" she laughed and the pair headed back into the main part of the house.

They returned to the living room, seeing nothing at first, but they turned as they heard the birds call to one another, once more.

"I'm okay. Are you okay? Trrrrr! Trrrrr! I'm okay. Are you okay?"

Melinda, Brent just behind her, hurried into the dining room and found the birds on the dinner table. They struggled to step over the lacy tablecloth, their tiny claws snagging the fine material as they walked.

"You grab the male, and I'll get the female," Melinda murmured as if the birds might understand the plan should she say it any louder. "On three."

Brent nodded.

"One . . . two . . . oh shit!" Melinda cringed back, realizing she stood naked in front of the uncovered dining room picture windows, the bright light in the room leaving little to the imagination for anyone who might be standing on the street outside.

Melinda jumped back into the hallway. "Did anyone see me?"

Brent turned to the windows, feeling his body go flush

beneath the heavy jacket and fake beard. "I don't think so." He turned out the dining room light, and then peeked out. "I don't see anyone."

They both laughed, overtaken by the thought of neighbors seeing the two of them through the window, one of them stark naked and the other dressed as Santa. It was both embarrassing and exhilarating.

Melinda peeked past the wall, the light from the other room spilling over and offering just enough for her to see a faint outline of the two birds. "Can doves see in the dark?"

"I don't think so."

"What should I do?" she asked, dismayed at the thought of getting dressed just to catch a bird.

"Hurry up and grab yours, and run back to the living room!"

"Okay . . . are you ready?"

"Just give me the word."

"Now!" Melinda said and each gently grabbed a bird and expertly released their tiny claws from the tablecloth.

They returned the docile birds to the living room, and then carefully placed them into their cage. They took a moment to admire the two willful creatures, watching them huddle up against one another, comforting in one another's safety and well-being with another long string of soft, purring sounds.

Melinda pointed to the other presents beneath the tree. "Where did all of these come from?"

"Santa," Brent said with a chuckle.

"Oh, that's right," Melinda said, smiling.

"So, where were we?" he asked, pulling her close.

"You didn't see the mistletoe."

He looked around, spotting it over the sofa. A grin peeked past his fake beard as he slowly backed her toward it. They tumbled together onto the sofa, beneath the hanging icon. She landed safely on his soft, stuffed stomach.

Their lips met, and she kissed him through his fake beard, the wiry white hair tickling her face. She giggled.

"What's so funny?"

"I never thought I'd be making out with Santa!" she said.

"No?" He rubbed up against her, getting hard. "You're turning Santa on."

She felt him, her face going red as she slid to the floor and unbuttoned his pants. He sat back, relaxing, as she revealed his erect cock and wrapped her mouth around it. She closed her eyes, licking the shaft and sucking as she pulled back, taking the base of it in one hand.

He moaned lightly as she twisted and rubbed, enjoying the balance of his hard, solid mass and its soft skin against her tongue. It was warm and slightly salty, and she breathed heavily as she serviced it with her mouth, caressing him with long, loving strokes.

Gently, he nudged her further down as he joined her on the floor and slowly turned on her, making his way to her moist pussy with his tongue. The fake beard was soft against her shaved skin, and a shiver ran through her as he tickled her clit with tender kisses and quick laps. She spread her legs, prompting him to enter her further with his tongue, and she sucked harder as he rolled and licked the hard, spongy spot inside her.

They knew each other's bodies well, knowing just the right spots on which to concentrate, each building the other's excitement with equal skill and fervor. They increased their intensity together, moaning and writhing in ecstasy, moving as if in a slow, passionate dance. They followed one another's lead, their moves growing stronger and deeper, reveling in the gift they each gave, and relishing in the sensations running through their bodies.

She felt him go even harder as he paused, moaning loudly and exhaling passionately as he came in her mouth. The jizz was thick and salty, and she continued to suck until he cried out, the sensation overwhelming, and pulled away.

"You're an animal," he said, and then moved to finish her.

She rolled on to her back, the fake whiskers tickling her as he went in deep. He caressed her body, and then found her hands with his, clasping them together, licking and rousing her selflessly and enthusiastically. She felt her body tense as she moved toward climax, her legs spreading wider, her hands clenching.

She let out a loud cry, the release coming quickly and intensely, her muscles turning into jelly and relaxing as he collapsed at her side. They both breathed heavily, hearts racing, as they lay beside one another on the cool floor catching their breath.

"How was that?" he asked.

She thought about the night she had planned, and how differently it had turned out. She glanced over at the doves, now silently cuddled up against one another, and turned back to her husband, who lay in a wrinkled, food-spattered Santa suit. She smiled contentedly. "Perfect."

Three French Hens

by Cameo Brown

Clucked

Mirelle studied the ardent expression of the young man beneath her—Mark or Dark or Dork or something was his name—watching his desperate need inch toward tortured ecstasy as he neared climax.

She straddled his waist, falling forward to stroke his smooth chest as he clutched her breasts, enjoying the way he submitted to her desire in order to satisfy his own. He gave her his finger to suck and she drew it in, just as she would a hot, hard cock needing relief. She suckled it.

His gasp turned into a moan.

She lifted herself against Mark's engorged cock, the first inklings of her orgasm tickling her clit and eliciting another thick stream of cream from her pussy. Mirelle tightened her ass as he pumped into her, his eyes closed, moaning.

She rocked with him, thrusting up and down, her nails now digging at his flesh, leaving red, angry marks. He didn't seem to care.

Her pussy spasmed, biting his solid length as it penetrated her soft folds, scalding hot from the exquisite friction their union produced, and he spurted inside her, showering her eager eternal womb with his warm jism, its energy pouring into her.

This is the part she loved, the part preserving the sanctity of her immortality.

His essence washed over her.

"Oh God! Oh God! Oh God!" he shouted, bucking beneath her.

"No, silly mortal, god-*dess*," she corrected, her orgasm looming. What would it matter? He would remember nothing of their encounter anyway.

His thoughts and memories flowed through her ichor. His wants and needs swamped her intellect and her mind floated away into oblivion.

Everything he was or ever would be dissolved into her being, and she fell into the dark abyss of his humanity, reveling in her ability to return from the depths of ultimate knowledge, immune to the bonds of uncertainty keeping so many humans hostage there.

She came.

Sparks showered her brain. The sudden release of tension combined with the serene rawness of his cock penetrating her created a high of pure bliss, a hit stronger than any drug. She rode him wildly, forcing him to offer more than she knew he had to give. Forcing him to please her thoroughly and completely.

She didn't let him relax until she'd milked every last drop of pleasure from his prick. Only then did she allow the human, his job finished, to fade into a deep, forgetful slumber. When he awoke, he'd only remember he'd visited their diner, The Hen's Tooth Grille, and nothing more.

Mick would wake in the same booth in which she'd

seduced him, the one where he'd sat all evening nursing sweet tea and a broken heart after his girlfriend—Pailey, Jailey, or something—jilted him and went back to apologize to her ex-roommate, or some such nonsense. Mirelle didn't pay much attention to what came out of his mouth. She much preferred watching what grew in his lap.

Mirelle's climax ebbed, bringing with it flashes of the young man's life. Her pussy stopped fluttering on his cock as they rolled by like a series of movie clips.

Alarming visions flitted across the back of Mirelle's eyes, growing more and more disturbing. Her eyes snapped open.

"Sisters! Come at once!" she barked and slid off the man beneath her, who snored already, and charged into the communal living area joining their three boudoirs.

Martine was the first to appear: naked, giggling, and slapping away the groping hands of her amour. He grinned like a fool and smacked her ass as she stumbled into the living room. She glanced back and waved at her lover with her fingertips, blowing him a kiss. He pointed to his dripping erection with both index fingers and mouthed, "Hurry."

Minette showed up a second later, her hand between her legs and her eyes half closed. She stumbled toward them, stopping every couple of steps to massage her depths a little more and grunt, pleasuring herself along the way. Minette fell into Martine's arms, her release imminent.

"Uh. Uh huh. Uh huh! Uh! Uh! *Oui! Oui! Oui!* Oooo la la!"

Minette slumped against Martine, a languid, peaceful smile replacing the earnest concentration darkening her features just moments before. Martine kissed the top of her sister's head, giggling.

"Are you quite done?"

Minette removed her hand from her pussy, sighing, and wiped it off on her nude hip. She nodded, her reddish curls bobbing like an erect penis on a marathon runner as mischief oozed from her sparkling green eyes.

"Sisters, you remember Robert Waldridge?"

"Rob? I could never forget such a man," Martine said, flirting, and placed her hand over her heart, even though there were no men around to appreciate the effort.

"Robby!" Minette squealed, jumping up and down and clapping in front of her perky breasts.

Mirelle glanced at her sister's heaving bosoms and noticed their nipples pebbled as much as hers, Martine's pink and Minette's dark brown. Good, now she had their undivided attention.

"I've gained knowledge," she continued, lifting and opening her thigh so her sisters could see the evidence of her and Murk's activities. She beckoned to them. "Come see for your lovely selves."

Martine and Minette touched Mark's creamy, dripping come. Minette held it up, rubbing it between her index finger and thumb. She sniffed it as her pale, divine skin absorbed its knowledge, and wrinkled her nose. Martine plopped a glob into her mouth, sucking it off her finger.

"Oooh," she cried, screwing up her pretty face. "This man is a fool and a dolt. Why do you fuck him, Mirelle?"

Mirelle rolled her eyes. As if mental capacity was ever a consideration when it came to fucking. Sometimes her sisters amazed her—how many years had they been alive? Suddenly, unshed tears brightened Minette's emerald orbs.

"Oh no, Mirelle! Our Robby is going to make a terrible mistake!"

Martine's chocolate-brown eyes widened as Mark's come

opened his secrets to her and the truth unfolded before her as well.

"What do we do, Mirelle? We can't let anything so horrible happen to our Rob!"

Mirelle nodded. Much better. Now they were all of the same mind, and, being skilled in the ways of love, she knew exactly what to do.

"Sisters, it's time for a cruise to the Caribbean."

Bella Raye Noringer stood outside the Port of Miami and stared at the colossal ship, the *Sea Empress*, wondering if she weren't about to make the biggest mistake of her life. Though she'd let a porter take her luggage, she didn't have to get on the ship, she told herself. She could still call this whole trip off.

When she and Mark planned this Christmas holiday, she'd thought it would end with a romantic proposal on a beach somewhere far away from the dismal Chicago weather. She never thought she'd be standing here alone, trying to decide whether to take a trip planned for two as one.

Finding him in bed with Hailey six months ago certainly limited her choices from "going with Mark" to "going or eat the cost of the trip." Canceling meant losing a great deal of money—money she didn't have.

Over the last few weeks, she'd convinced herself she needed a vacation and a chance to rebuild her self-esteem by strutting her stuff in front of as many single, horny men as she could find. Now the time had come to board the ship alone, and she didn't know if she had the courage.

"You know, *mon ami*," a soft, feminine voice startled Bella. "Beautiful women always get what they want, and you are so very beautiful . . ."

Bella's jaw dropped. A gorgeous blond woman with ocean-blue eyes positioned herself beside her. Vivacious with golden waves cascading out of a silky blue scarf and down her shoulders, the woman's countenance could only be described as regal.

Smartly dressed in tight blue jeans, a red blouse with a sailor collar showing off her voluptuous curves, and deck shoes, she looked every bit the typical rich trophy wife, except her beauty was natural and her red-lipped smile sincere. She captivated Bella.

"So very beautiful," the vision said, her voice like rich, smooth caramel.

She leaned over and kissed Bella on the cheek before sauntering away. Bella watched her retreating form, following the swaying hips until she noticed the woman walked toward a man in the crowd. A very familiar man. Her heart pounded and her thighs clenched. It was the sexual threat himself—her brother's best friend.

Rob Waldridge.

Her breathing quickened. What was he doing here? Did he know about her and Mark? He'd probably offer her a hanky and pat her on her head, which is not where she wanted him to pat her. Her nipples hardened. Just looking at him made her think naughty thoughts, but it wasn't her fault. Not really.

Hunky Rob Waldridge, with a solidly muscled six-foot-two frame, dark brown hair, and incredible hazel eyes, had fed her deepest fantasies for years. Since their teens, she'd heard rumors about Rob's creativity and prowess in the bedroom. Nothing specific, just enough to pique her curiosity. And she was more than a little curious.

How many times had she masturbated to visions of what

she thought he might do to his women? It wasn't like she'd ever know, though. To him she was nothing more than his best friend's younger sister.

After years of hope and frustration, at twenty-eight, Bella had decided waiting on Rob to notice she had tits and a nice ass—if she did say so herself—qualified her as certifiably insane. Mark came along at the right time, and Rob had faded into a distant, sexy memory. Until now.

Jealousy poked at her, but she dismissed it. How could she begrudge anyone's happiness simply because it evaded her? The woman's words rang in her ears.

Beautiful women always get what they want.

What did she want? Maybe on this trip she'd find out. Adjusting her satchel and her attitude, Bella headed toward customs and whatever lay ahead.

Firm, creamy tits magically appeared in Rob Waldridge's field of vision as he straightened from plucking the lacy handkerchief from the ground. He blinked in surprise.

He tried hard to look the other way, but not too hard. For some reason, these breasts seemed to want his attention, or maybe he only hoped they did. Only a second before, he'd stooped to help an elderly lady retrieve her wayward accessory, and now he couldn't take his eyes off the magnificent cleavage bouncing gently in his face with every breath of the owner.

"Rob, aren't you glad to see us?"

A flirtatious giggle followed the wispy words spoken in a delicate French accent, and Rob's gaze immediately snapped up to find ebony eyes dancing with mischief.

"Martine," he breathed, taken by her mortal beauty as always.

From the velvety black bob framing her heart-shaped face to dainty toenails polished in a baby-pink hue, Martine oozed feminine charm.

As taught, Rob reached for her hand and she extended it with an elegant swish so he could kiss it. She rewarded him with an impish smile before yanking him to her and crushing his lips with hers, kissing him breathless. So much for dainty and feminine.

"Robby!"

A squeal, equally accented with a French lilt, interrupted their interlude. Rob broke the kiss and inhaled, trying to get some air to his oxygen-starved brain. Martine sometimes didn't realize her own strength.

"Robby, Robby, Robby!"

Rob took the opportunity to extricate himself from Martine's snug embrace just in time to catch Minette, who launched herself at him in a burst of exuberance.

Minette's arms circled his neck and her legs captured him around the waist. Martine patted her hair into place as Minette rained tiny kisses all over Rob's face.

"Robert," a silky voice intoned behind him, and he turned around, Minette still attached, to find Mirelle grinning at him.

Minette released their kiss, dropping her head to his shoulder with a contented sigh, and he set her on the ground. Once steady, the petite beauty ran over to Martine and hugged her sister. They giggled and waved at him.

Mirelle placed her hands on either side of his face and gave him a peck on each cheek, then placed her full, red lips against his. With a mew, Mirelle stepped back and fanned herself with a graceful, well-manicured hand.

"We've taught you well, Robert," Mirelle complimented,

her sisters nodding. "You always were a good student."

"And you three always know how to say hello with such flair."

Mirelle strolled over to Martine and Minette and situated her statuesque form behind her curvy and petite sisters, respectively. They all beamed appreciatively at him.

Uh-oh. He was fucked. Or about to be.

"Ladies," Rob warned, but it was no use. The batting of eyelashes had begun in earnest.

"Oh, Robby, please don't make us go. I want to ride on the big boat," Minette begged, her lip already puckered in a practiced pout.

"I want to ride on the men who ride on the big boat," Martine added, blowing him a kiss and winking.

"Sisters, sisters, I think Robert knows us too well to believe we have only his best interests at heart. Is this not true, my dove?"

Rob nodded.

"Robert, my sisters and I are here to help you, to pay our debt to you so we can stop worrying about your happiness," Mirelle explained.

Martine and Minette nodded with so much enthusiasm, Minette's breast popped out of her bright green halter top. She scolded it in French and tucked it back in, but it peeked out the edge of the lucky material. Rob shook his head.

"You don't owe me anything. You gave me etiquette lessons, remember? And I wrote a nice little story about your average, ordinary diner, no matter what the locals say about it."

"But we do," Mirelle continued. "You refuse to succumb to our charms because you will have to forget us. None of the others care."

"Because none of the others know they're going to forget. I do. You guys should be more careful when an investigative journalist starts asking questions. Now, why are you really here, ladies?"

"We're here to keep you from making the biggest mistake of your life."

Rob blinked, taken aback. So they knew his plan and came to stop him before he made a terrible mistake? Shit. Bella couldn't be a mistake. Rob wanted her too much.

The last year had been tough. He'd watched his best friend's younger sister and the drip she dated, Mark, get closer and closer. He knew they had to be fucking, and it drove him crazy.

He pictured her writhing beneath the creep and wanted to rip his head off. He thought he'd blown it until he heard about the break-up. He booked passage on the *Sea Empress* and planned on surprising her. Beyond that, he had no idea what to do.

"I think I can take care of myself," he said, trying to process it all.

Mirelle's eyes narrowed as if she were addressing the dumbest man on Earth, and perhaps she was. She nodded over her shoulder at something behind her. "So you can take care of that?"

Rob followed her gaze and went cold. Bella, his Bella, hurried toward the door to customs, her short chestnut waves blowing in the wind, as she jostled through the crowd with her satchel. He hardened instantly.

Her yellow halter dress highlighted her best assets, setting off the elegant curve of her hips and the softness of her tummy, not to mention her round, firm breasts. Even at this distance, she took his breath away.

His stomach dropped a second later. Bella stopped, looking around as if someone called her name. From somewhere to her left, Mark burst through the crowd, and, as Rob scowled helplessly, he pulled a surprised Bella aside. She stared at Mark, her head tilted as if she didn't believe what she saw, and Rob's gut twisted.

Mark dropped to his knee and placed her hand to his chest. Rob couldn't hear what he said, but from the crowd's reaction, he guessed Mark was proposing.

Rob grabbed the handle of his carry-on and headed the opposite direction, away from the three goddesses and the vision of the woman whom he wanted, giving herself to some idiot. For the second time.

Mirelle, Minette, and Martine, tits jiggling and hips wiggling, hustled in front of him, blocking his path. He glanced at each of them in turn.

"You are in our favor, Robert," Mirelle said. "You truly care for us. We want you to be happy. You want her, do you not, Robert?"

Robert met Mirelle's gaze, and he marveled at the wisdom glittering in the depths of her blue eyes.

"Then go get her before it's too late, *mon cher*."

With Mirelle, Martine, and Minette cheering him on, he headed toward Bella and the opportunity to show her just how good they could be together.

Bella still couldn't believe Mark had the nerve to put her on the spot like this. How could she have ever thought she loved this conniving asshole? If he thought he'd get a yes by putting her on display, he was fishing off the wrong pier.

She had just opened her mouth to tell him to fuck off when Rob Waldridge stepped through the crowd, his tight jeans and fitted T-shirt showing off his incredible physique. Mark continued to talk, but Bella couldn't hear anything except the rush of blood in her ears.

Rob stared at her, his eyes roving up and down her body as if she wore no clothing at all. Heat rose in her cheeks and the flutters in her stomach inched lower. Her panties grew tighter and wetter.

He had a hard-on. She saw it, and he knew she saw it. He shifted his weight and for the first time since she'd known him, she realized how well hung he really was. Already some of the rumors were true. Her pussy twitched.

"Get on the ship, Bella," Rob commanded, his deep sexy rumble leaving no room for argument, but she tried anyway.

"I—I . . . Mark's proposing," she stammered, hoping no one in the crowd noticed the tips of her breasts pebbling under Rob's intense scrutiny.

"Get on the ship, Bella," Rob repeated, and made a swooping gesture.

For reasons she couldn't explain, Bella yanked her hand from Mark's and shoved her way through the crowd, leaving him open-mouthed. Rob followed. The heat from his body and his male scent intoxicated her. Her skin tingled. She walked in a daze.

Once aboard, he only spoke four words, and the flutters planted themselves firmly in her moist cunt, begging for attention.

"Your room or mine?"

The tiny hallway on deck 4 didn't allow for much distance between two people, and Rob made the most of it. He kept his hand on Bella's lower back, guiding her to his cabin. Her submission to his commands surprised him, and he liked it.

A click of the OceanKey later, with all extraneous items having landed in various spots on the floor, Rob pinned Bella to the back of the stateroom door. He crushed her full, pink lips with his, urging them apart so he could explore the warm wetness within. She obliged, and his tongue probed hers. Bella tasted of rich chocolate, a delectable treat, and he set about devouring her.

He moved his body against hers, letting her feel his erection. She stared at him wide-eyed as the smell of her desire drifted up between them. Her cheeks turned pink.

"So you belong to Mark?" he said, running his hands up and down her body.

"No. I belong to no man," she said, leaning into his touch.

"You're in my room. You belong to me now. You understand?"

Bella nodded, trembling. He lifted the hem of her dress and slid his hand between her thighs, massaging the damp material covering her mons. She was hot and wet. Rob stepped back and licked his lips, deciding where to begin.

In one swift move, Rob reached behind her and tugged the halter tie loose. The cloth puddled at Bella's feet. Holding his gaze, she shimmied out of her panties, and he nearly exploded.

Rob drank in the sight of her. Soft, curvy, exquisite. Her breasts were just the right size, not too big or too small, with dusky brown nipples pointed directly at him.

Her soft tummy accentuated the flare of her round hips. The juncture of her thighs sported a honey-colored patch full enough to suggest she didn't wax, but she didn't need to. Nature had blessed her with a glorious, inviting mons that awakened a primal mating urge inside him.

A garden of delights awaited the man lucky enough to

find himself between her legs, and he had a sudden urge to plant some seed.

He reached behind her and locked the door.

Bella watched as Rob made his way across the room. His confident stride and the way his muscles rippled and flexed as he thoughtlessly tossed his T-shirt on the loveseat sent delicious heat flowing through her body. Crisp brown hair covered his chest and formed a line dipping into his waistband, mesmerizing her.

His jeans and briefs joined the T-shirt a moment later. He stood, gloriously naked, his large erection dripping and pointing at her from a patch of thick, wiry brown hair.

He wanted her. Her pussy swelled with longing.

Rob dug through his bag, searching for something. He held up a silky red scarf and yanked on its opposite ends, as if testing it.

"Come to me, Bella."

She obeyed, and Rob turned her away from him and brought the scarf around in front of her. Catching the other end in his hand, he lifted it to her eyes and gently tied it in place.

Rob stroked her back, kissing and nipping her neck. He rubbed his cock against her ass, and she tingled all over. The sensations, made even more powerful by her lack of sight, overwhelmed her. She leaned against him.

"No," he said, his voice husky with desire. "Stand up."

Rob moved in front of her. He suckled one nipple, then the other, causing the tips to ache with need. His lips burned her skin, tracing a path from her breasts to her navel and lower. When his tongue invaded her pussy, caressing her clit, she gasped and grabbed his shoulders for support.

"You taste good, Bella. I could eat your pussy all night long, you know that?"

Bella was nearly speechless, lost in ecstasy.

"I want . . ."

Rob interrupted her. "No, Bella, this isn't about what you want. It's about what I want. Do you know what I want?"

"No," Bella whispered.

"Then I'll show you."

Something soft touched her shoulder. Another scarf, maybe? Whatever it was, Rob let it drift across her breasts. He crossed her hands in front of her and laid the material across her wrists, teasing her with the coolness and texture. He wrapped her wrists and tied them tight.

Bella winced, the unaccustomed pressure suddenly frightening and uncomfortable. Rob slid a finger under the binding and moved it back and forth. Bella relaxed.

Rob picked her up and carried her a few steps, setting her down gently. The floor-length curtain separating the bed from the loveseat tickled her back.

"Lift your arms," Rob commanded, and Bella obeyed.

Rob moved her bound hands around above her head, adjusting the material on something. The warmth of his body and the moist skin of his cock bumping into her as he worked produced an ache inside her.

When she tried to drop her arms, she couldn't. She balanced there, naked, blindfolded, bound. Totally exposed. Rob could do whatever he wanted with her and she couldn't stop him. She didn't want to stop him.

"Bella, I'm going to fuck you senseless. You understand?"

Bella's voice refused to work, so she tried to nod even though it wasn't easy with her arms over her head. Her pussy throbbed. She was so swollen and so ready to be fucked. He knew it, but made her say it anyway.

"Do you want me to?"

Bella licked her lips and nodded. "Yes," she managed to whisper. "Fuck me hard, Rob."

Rob started at her ankle and licked his way up her calf to her thigh. His wet tongue caressed her skin, enticing goosebumps the closer he came to her pussy. He licked her inner thighs, adding his wetness to hers, and gripped her soft ass.

His rough fingers massaged her cheeks as he rubbed his face in her mound. Rob spread her legs and feasted on her, sucking her clit and licking her folds until she squirmed, the exquisite pleasure almost too much to bear.

The tension building for years now morphed into the beginning of a desperate need for immediate release. When Rob's hot tongue slipped inside her tight opening, teasing her, she thrust her hips forward, needing more.

"Fuck me, please, Rob," Bella begged. "I can't take any more."

"I'll fuck you when I'm ready, and I'm not ready yet."

Rob wound his arm around Bella's waist, steadying her and penetrating her with one finger. He waited for her body to accept it before pushing even deeper.

He rubbed her pussy, adding pressure to her most sensitive spot. Her pleasure built and built. He brought her to the edge and she lifted herself to him. Rob pushed two fingers into her tight hole, stretching her and filling her.

He thrust gently, moving in and out, settling into a steady rhythm, stroking her and filling her as she moved her hips back and forth. Her pussy spasmed, grasping at his fingers.

Suddenly, everything stopped. She panted, naked and

titillated. She wasn't the only one. With the room silent, she could hear his breathing, as heavy as hers. Without warning, he swept her up into his arms with a feral moan and unhooked her wrists.

A moment of weightlessness later, Bella found herself bouncing on the mattress. She barely got her bearings before Rob mounted her. He crawled up her body, positioning himself between her legs, and pressed his swollen cock against her dripping opening.

She placed her wrists behind his head and lifted her hips to take him in. With one thrust, Rob planted himself firmly inside her, sunken to the base. He stopped long enough to kiss her, letting her taste her own flavor, and it set her on fire. She tasted good, she thought. She tasted like a woman. Like a woman who wanted a man. And Rob was that man.

Rob rode her hard, pushing deep and pulling out. His cock took up where his fingers left off, and the delicious friction brought Bella to the precipice again, ready to fall into a swirling pool of sensation the next time he entered her.

Everything went white. Waves of ecstasy emanated from her pussy and spread throughout her entire body. Tiny sparkles of light glittered in her brain, floating behind her eyelids and filtering through the white-hot bliss enveloping her soul. She screamed when she came, and continued to scream as her rapture ebbed and flowed along with Rob's increased pounding.

Just when she thought she could catch a breath, Rob tensed and erupted with a howl, filling her with his warm jism and bathing her pussy with his come. He slid in and out of her so easily, reveling in his climax as he held her tightly beneath him.

He continued to ride his orgasm, pumping what seemed

like gallons of himself inside her, letting her feel his release as much as he did, holding her hips as close to him as he could. After several seconds, he slowed, pushing his cock deep inside her one last time. He buried his face in her neck.

Bella wanted to feather his body with light caresses, but her hands were tied. All she could do was hold him to her as he lay on top of her, breathing heavily and grunting satisfaction. Bella, her body humming, took a chance and kissed his hair. He stiffened and stilled, and, for a moment, Bella feared she'd done something wrong.

His lips found hers and told her otherwise. They kissed for an eternity, feeding off the intimacy of the act until Rob broke away and swore.

"Damn, woman."

Bella laughed and thought she heard Rob chuckle. He rolled to her side and settled her against him.

"Rob?"

"Yes, Bella?"

"When are you going to untie me and let me go?"

"Never."

This holiday was shaping up to be the best one ever and the ship hadn't even left the dock yet. How did that happen?

"Rob?"

"Yes, Bella," he murmured in a seductive, sleepy tone.

"Merry Christmas."

Days later, Mirelle leaned out over the railing on the highest deck of the ship, Minette beside her with her head on her sister's shoulder. They watched Robert and Bella walk down the gangplank, arms around each other, smiling. Martine, otherwise engaged in activities of a carnal nature with a waiter from the Good Ship Lollipop restaurant, depended on their narration to keep her informed as her amour pummeled her from behind.

"Oh uh *oui* yes *oui oui*!" she cried. "What are they doing now?"

"Robert gathered her in his arms and is kissing her breathless."

"Ooh, how sweet. Oh, right there!"

"Now they're waving at us."

"Wave—uh huh uh uh uh—for me," Martine panted. "Oooo la la la la!"

Mirelle waved while Minette applauded the waiter's performance. He fell over, his flaccid cock smacking his thigh. He was snoring before he hit the ground.

Martine suddenly stiffened.

"Sisters!" she cried. "I have gained knowledge."

Mirelle and Minette grinned at each other, and the three French hens, being skilled in the ways of love, knew exactly what to do.

Four Calling Birds

by Isabel Roman

Chapter One

Lark Summers strode across the American University campus, bundled against the frigid Washington December air. She took a moment to admire the Christmas tree in the center of the courtyard, but for only a moment. She didn't want to be late for her favorite professor—er, meeting. Her cell phone chirped and she frantically fumbled through her bag so as not to miss the call.

"What are you going to do?" her excited friend asked. "Are you going to do it? I hope you're absolutely sure he's not gay!"

"He's not gay," Lark sighed, tired of this question. "And yes. I intend to tonight."

"I knew you would," Paige Nightingale crowed. "Are you going to set it up like we planned?"

"Absolutely," she said, laughing. "We spent all night on this, as well as a bottle of very good vodka. But," she added, opening the door to the Economics Department with her one free hand, "I might add in a few surprises of my own."

"Yum," Nightingale said. "We're going to want all the nasty details tomorrow."

"Speaking of details, Nightingale," Lark lowered her voice. "Are you going to take our advice and invite Adam to dinner?"

"Yes," she all but purred. "I have a very special menu planned."

"Let me guess. You're on it."

"Of course! What kind of seduction would it be if I wasn't the main course?"

Laughing again, Lark glanced down the hall to Professor Turner's door. She'd stopped just around the corner.

"I've got to go," Lark said. Her heart sped at the thought of seeing Seth Turner again. She'd wanted him from the moment she'd walked into the doctorate program and no matter what she'd done, it hadn't been enough to grab his attention.

She would be graduating with her Ph.D. in international economics next week. It was now or never.

"Good luck!"

Yeah, Lark thought as she muted her phone's ringer. She was going to need luck. Knocking on the door, she smiled her sultriest smile when it opened. Seth blinked at her, his beautiful grey eyes registering surprise.

"Ms. Summers." He smiled back and stood. "I'm a bit surprised by this meeting request. I'm no longer your professor. Do you need a reference already?"

Lark handed him the small square envelope, her smile never slipping. "I knew it would take an engraved invitation to get you to notice me outside the classroom." Poor man. He looked stunned. But something flashed in his eyes. Acknowledgement? Arousal? Both?

Lark hoped it was both.

"I've always noticed you," he murmured.

Heart leaping at his words, Lark waited for his response. He read the single paper quickly. Accustomed as she was to watching his beautiful hands, she didn't miss his fingers twitching on her invitation. Dragging her eyes back to his, she tried to remember to breathe.

"Would you like me to respond promptly?"

"Yes," she whispered, the word sounding breathless to her own ears.

He leaned down, eyes locked with hers, lips too far away for her liking. "I'll be there."

Paige Nightingale looked down at her phone as it chirped.

"Ice cream!" Megan Cardinal-Walsh said. "You both eat ice cream and then go down on him. You'll blow his eyes out of his sockets."

"Thanks for the visual, Cardinal," Paige mumbled as Christmas music blasted from the store's speakers. "But I'm way ahead of you—one carton of plain vanilla already in the basket."

And one of double chocolate mint swirl, just in case the whole thing backfired.

"Did you get my package?" she asked.

"You mean the one from the Pink Pussycat?" Cardinal said. "Oh, yes, I got it—and have had a helluva time hiding it from Ethan."

Paige snorted. "Only until tonight. I know you're nervous, but we're all behind you."

"I know," her friend sighed. "It'd be easier if I knew Ethan would be home tonight. And yes," she quickly added, "I told him I wanted him here no later than seven."

"It'll be fine," Paige began but Cardinal cut her off.

"I have to put the finishing touches on everything," she said. "Have fun with your neighbor!"

Paige hung up and looked at the phone for a moment, concerned. But this was the weekend they'd planned for months. Bolstering each other's confidences, arranging each detail right down to perfection. Oh, she'd have fun seducing Adam Forrester. She just wondered what took her so long to realize what a hunk he was.

Megan Cardinal-Walsh glanced around the kitchen and living room, making sure it looked the same as always. She wanted to surprise him, so she'd set everything up in their bedroom. Smoothing her hand down her business skirt, she could faintly feel the sexy lingerie through the material.

The Christmas-red silk felt decadent against her skin. She'd almost forgotten what it was like to seduce her husband. Between jobs and social lives, they hadn't had much time for sex.

When her cell phone rang, she was afraid it was Ethan calling to tell her he was working late again. But no. "Robin?"

"What'd you get in the Pink Pussycat box?"

"Never you mind that, Eva Robin," Megan laughed. "Did you set everything up just as we discussed?"

"Yes, yes," Robin said. "Lingerie, check. Candles, check. Blindfold, check."

"If you don't get a ring from him by Christmas," Megan advised, "dump him."

"Yeah," Robin said but didn't sound convincing to Megan's ears. "Have you heard from Nightingale and Lark?"

"I talked to Nightingale. She's setting up her own

seduction. Haven't heard a peep from Lark. We'll have to see how she does with her professor later."

"Have fun tonight," Robin said and hung up.

Megan looked around the bedroom once more, nervously glancing at the clock.

Eva Robin puttered around Alex's apartment. She much preferred his Georgetown place to hers. It had a better view. Plus, her roommate Lark was planning her own seduction, and needed the privacy. She'd taken a half day from her paralegal job to set up this scene.

Cardinal wanted Eva to break up with her boyfriend if he didn't propose. Eva loved Alex Parker, wanted to spend the rest of her life with him. Hell, she'd even stopped going to her childhood dentist and switched to his practice. If that wasn't love, what was?

Of course, it could have something to do with the quick sex they had whenever she visited.

Lately, it'd always been quickies. Tonight was going to be different.

Alex hadn't bothered with a Christmas tree this year, so she'd spent the afternoon decorating the small one she'd purchased, stringing it with white garland. Dinner was on the table, candles lightly scented the room, and she was already dressed. The stilettos hurt her feet, but she ignored the pain in favor of the scene.

The key sounded in the lock, and Eva turned toward the door. Alex walked in, carrying a bag of Chinese food. Then he looked up and saw her.

The bag dropped to the floor.

Chapter Two

"Baby?"

Eva smiled. This was exactly the reaction she'd hoped for when she'd purchased the black lace bra-and-panty set. The garter belt was a suggestion from Lark and, judging by Alex's reaction, a damn fine one, too. Taking her time, she walked across the floor, swaying her hips as seductively as she could. Alex continued to blink at her, silent.

"Thought I'd give you an early Christmas treat," she purred.

With one finger, she traced his jaw, closing his mouth. Trailing a hand along his neck, she moved behind him and slipped the coat off his broad shoulders. She kicked the takeout bag into the hallway and latched the door closed behind her. Alex didn't look like a dentist. He was tall and strong, his short dark hair falling over equally dark eyes.

"This," he managed, turning his head to watch her, "is more than a treat."

"Are you hungry?" she asked, dancing her fingers down his arm to his hand. She walked backwards, easily guiding him to the dining room.

"Yes," he said.

In one smooth movement, he pulled her to him and kissed her. His impatience thrilled her, and her already wet core ached for him. They continued to walk backward, and Eva felt the edge of the couch bump her legs.

Alex guided her down to the cushions, hands under her hips to tug off her flimsy panties.

"Dear God," he rasped.

"Do you—" Before she finished, his mouth was on her

carefully groomed, hairless pussy. "Oh!" she cried, arching into him.

His tongue swirled around her clit, and she hitched her breath with every swipe. Inserting one finger into her, he moved it in and out, teasing her with the light touch. Withdrawing, he moved his talented tongue over her outer lips, licking the moisture that seeped from inside her.

Eva opened her legs further, hips jerking against him. Spreading her wide, his tongue delved into her.

"Please," she begged, "Alex, please."

"Have you been wet for me all day?" he murmured, kissing his way up her body to her lips.

"Yes," she cried when his fingers played over her once again. "Deeper," she pleaded. "Put your fingers in me deeper."

He complied instantly and thrust two fingers into her. She arched off the couch. Forcing her eyes open, she saw his gaze, black with passion, steady on hers. His control was almost gone, and she reveled in it.

"Yes, oh, Alex, yes!"

"Come for me, Eva," he whispered.

She did, shattering beneath him as his fingers continued their quick thrusting. Heart pounding in her chest, she opened her eyes. Alex kneeled naked before her.

Sitting up, she reached forward to help him. Climbing atop him, the carpet a soft scratch on her knees, she whispered, "I want your cock in my mouth."

"Yes," he groaned as Eva slipped her lips over his erection.

Moving her tongue over him, she relaxed her throat. Her fingers dug into his ass, squeezing the cheeks as she moved up until only the tip of him remained in her eager mouth. Alex groaned, fingers tangling in her hair, guiding her harder along his cock. Eva took his balls in her hand as she lowered her head again.

"Baby," he moaned, "I need to be inside you."

He flipped her over and thrust into her. Wrapping her legs around his hips, Eva met each pounding drive, lost in sensation. His fingers glided down her bare sex, one fingernail, then two and three scraping over her clit.

She came, shouting his name as she rocked against him, mindless to everything but the pleasure he gave her. Eva felt him come, the weight of him a warm comfort atop her. But then he moved, and she was afraid her carefully planned seduction was for naught.

"I was going to wait," Alex whispered as he rummaged through his clothing. "Carried this with me for a month now."

He opened the small box, and it took her a moment to register the diamond ring nestled within. Blinking, she looked up at him.

"I love you," he whispered, lips soft against hers. "Marry me?"

"Yes," she said, and kissed him.

He placed the ring on her finger and lifted her from the floor, carrying her to the bedroom where she had planned to actually seduce him. She'd have to call everyone later, let them know the good news. But that could wait. Alex laid her on the bed, mouth closing around her breast. Her three closest friends would definitely understand.

Chapter Three

"Honey," Megan said, putting the dishes into the sink. "Before you watch the game, can you change our closet light bulb? I can't reach it."

"Sure," Ethan said, setting his beer on the counter and following her up the stairs.

He went straight to the closet, and she followed, opening her blouse. Slipping her hands around his front, she kissed the back of his neck.

"You know how I always promise to punish you when you don't do something I want?" she asked.

Ethan chuckled, tightening the bulb she'd only loosened. "Promises, promises."

She backed up to the bed, and watched him turn. Letting her blouse drop to the floor, she picked up the handcuffs. "It's more than a promise tonight."

Her husband stood before her, stunned. Stepping slowly toward her, eyes never leaving hers, his voice was husky. "What's this?"

"I have a handsome husband whom I don't have often enough. So," she said, fingers grazing his cheek. "I thought I'd take this opportunity to chain him to our bed."

"This is a new side of you," he whispered, lips grazing hers. "I like it."

He circled her, grabbing her ass through her skirt. Swatting his hands away, she offered a playful smile over her shoulder. "Not tonight," she said and pushed him onto the bed.

"Tonight," Megan whispered, climbing over him and straddling him. She brought her lips a breath from his. "Tonight, I'm in charge. Tonight, you're going to do exactly what I say."

"Yes, Mistress," Ethan replied, blue eyes dark with desire.

She could feel his cock hard against her core, and wanted nothing more than to feel him inside her. However, she had other plans for her husband. Unbuckling his belt, she quickly slid it from his pants, steadily watching him as she did so.

"Tonight," she said, "you're mine."

She made quick work of his clothing, and soon had him handcuffed to the headboard. At the end of the bed, Megan stripped off her work clothes and stood before him. She watched his cock swell, lobbing drunkenly back and forth, and she felt a rush of feminine power.

Running her hands over her breasts, she tugged the white bows directly over her nipples. Ethan's breath caught in his throat. Smiling at his reaction, she crawled onto the bed, wet and ready for him.

"You know," she whispered, tongue peeking out to lick the top of his cock. "I wore these all day."

He grunted, and she watched as his eyes darkened further, this time with jealousy. Closing her lips over his cock, she bobbed her head for a moment, just enough to tease.

"I was wet for you all day," she added, sitting on his thighs. Playing with the white bows, she pulled and twisted her nipples, moaning with every bolt of electricity that went straight to her clit. Drawing her legs up, she flattened her feet on the bed and presented him with the view of her crotchless panties.

"You've worn that all day?" he demanded, voice hoarse.

"Yes," she whispered, slipping a finger into her dripping sex. "And have thought of nothing but fucking you."

"Let me taste you," he demanded, straining against the handcuffs. "I need to taste you."

"You need to taste me . . . what?" she demanded.

"I need to taste you, Mistress!"

Smiling, she slid up his hard body and opened her legs for him. She moaned as his tongue skimmed her outer lips, plunging into her moist opening, and she arched against him. He had the most talented mouth.

After a moment, she reluctantly moved away and turned to lie atop him. Rocking her hips against his cock, she kissed him slowly, tasting herself on his lips. Kissing down his chest, she bit his nipples, shuddering in need as he groaned for her. Pleading and demanding more.

"What do you say, Ethan?" she murmured against his mouth.

"Please," he whispered, hips rising to meet hers.

Guiding him into her, she didn't move. Her blood pumped hot just beneath her skin and flesh, demanding she meet his need pulsating just below her, but still she didn't. Ethan growled, arms struggling with his restraints. Megan watched him, forcing herself not to move. His hips jerked upwards.

"Naughty boy," she purred, smacking his thigh.

Lifting up and rocking down, she moved. Each stroke deliberate. Stretching forward, she rose until his cock almost slipped out, wanting to savor each inch of him. Slamming down hard, she gasped when he filled her.

Faster, Megan rode him, unable to take her own teasing. She found her clit, rolling the small nub between her fingers as her body brought them both to orgasm.

Collapsing on top of him, she kissed his sweaty neck.

"This is indeed a Merry Christmas," he murmured. "Now unlock me so I can have my way with you."

Megan laughed and did just that, reminding herself to thank her friends for giving her the courage and the means to do this. But then Ethan's hands were on her, flipping her on her belly as he kissed the back of her neck. Shivering, Megan forgot all about her friends, and only felt desire.

Five Golden Rings
by Brandi Woodlawn

Mistress says I've been a very good slave this year. So good, in fact, that I'm almost sad to see 2008 go. It's been a year of awakenings. A year where I've learned things about myself, about my body, things that I should've figured out by now. After thirty-five years, I thought I knew who I was. But then I met Mistress and realized just how much I didn't know.

I didn't know it was possible for me to love a woman. Women aren't supposed to love other women, at least not where I come from. I played that game, conforming to what others said I was supposed to be, all my life. Being subservient isn't hard for me; in fact, it's always felt "right" to me. I have a deep compassion for humanity, a deep desire to serve others. But at the same time, I had a problem with conformity and I was consumed with guilt. Guilt over trying to be something I wasn't.

Once I realized that my guilt stemmed from suppressing the desire to be with a woman, and that there was nothing wrong with that desire, my life changed for the better. When I met Mistress, my doubts and misplaced guilt disappeared and were quickly replaced with hunger. And even though I am her slave now, for the first time in my life, I finally feel free.

Mistress opened up a whole new world to me. At first I was not an eager student. I thought I knew everything about being a woman. I'd been walking around in a woman's skin—surely that would count for something. But when it came to discerning what brought a woman pleasure, well, I knew nothing because everything I'd been taught up to that point had come from two sources, my parents and my church—both of whose mantras could be boiled down to three words: "Good. Girls. Don't."

While I knew the names of my various body parts, I didn't want to say them out loud. Vagina, clitoris, breasts, nipples. They sounded so . . . clinical. But it was better than the euphemistic alternatives. Pussy, clit, tits, berries. Those just made me blush. A habit Mistress would break.

"Again," Mistress commanded.

"Pussy," I said.

"Touch it," she said.

I put my hands between my legs.

"Next," she said.

"Clit," I said.

"Touch it," she repeated the order.

I spread my lips apart and shuddered as my index finger made contact. I felt my neck burn.

She swatted me with the riding crop. "There's nothing wrong with exploring your body," she explained. "How are you supposed to tell me what you want if you can't bring yourself to say the words?"

"I'm sorry," I said.

She swatted me again. The welt on my ass stung.

"Don't apologize."

"Yes, Mistress."

"This isn't about punishment," she said. "It's behavior

modification. You're learning good behavior. Now, it's time for your reward."

My heart swelled with pride. Even though I'd failed by blushing, I was getting better at vocalizing my desires.

"Tell me what you want."

"I want to make you come," I said. And I did. I was thankful for the progress we'd made. I felt great and I wanted to make her feel great too.

"I don't know if you are ready for that yet."

I hung my head and fought back the sadness.

"I want you," she told me. "But in order for the experience to be satisfying for me, I think we need to work on getting you reacquainted with yourself first."

I nodded.

"When was the last time you came?"

I blushed again. "I don't know . . . a few months ago."

"By yourself? Or with a man?"

"A man."

"When was the last time by yourself?"

"Longer," I said.

"Why?"

"I never thought it was right to squander an orgasm."

"What's that supposed to mean?"

"If I had one by myself, then I might not be able to have one later."

"So you stockpiled your orgasms?" she asked. "Saved them up for your partners?"

"Yes."

"I'd say that was kind of you if I didn't think that was the most ridiculous thing I'd ever heard." She laughed, but it was the kind of laugh that indicated disgust.

I almost apologized but caught myself.

"You're the one who's going to come," she said. "First, you'll do it yourself. And then, I'll make you."

"I don't think that will work." I hesitated.

She swatted me again with a harder blow.

"Ouch," I said.

"Just who do you think is in charge here?"

"You are, Mistress."

My self-induced orgasm was a long time coming, perhaps due to nerves. It felt awkward to be watched. No one had ever wanted to watch me before. Mistress sat in an armchair she'd made me push into the corner closest to the bed. When I was done, she said, "What were you thinking about while you masturbated?"

I didn't know what I feared more, telling her my thoughts or being caught in a lie. I opted for truth.

"I was thinking about having an orgasm as quickly as possible so this would be over," I said.

"That's what I thought," she said. "You looked like you were thinking too much."

"What was I supposed to think about?"

"Moments," she said.

"I don't understand."

"You need to stop worrying about the destination and start enjoying the ride."

"I did enjoy the ride."

"No," she said. "You enjoyed the orgasm, but not how you got there."

"I don't see what the difference is."

"You will."

She got up from the chair and joined me on the bed. She straddled me, hips aligned over mine, and rocked back, supporting her weight on her heels. Her bra and panties were black, just like her hair, which was pulled back in a ponytail high atop her head.

"What do you see?" she said.

"You, the bed, the chair, the drapes."

"What about the dresser? Can you see that?"

I turned my head to the left. "Yes."

"Tell me everything about it."

"It's made of dark wood. Not cherry, something cheaper that's been stained. It has three small drawers on the first row. You put your white socks in the left compartment, your underwear in the middle, and your colored socks on the right."

She leaned forward and began kissing my neck. She kissed from my shoulder up to my ear and said, "What else?"

"It has three larger drawers underneath the small ones," I continued softly. "You put your T-shirts in the top, your pants in the middle and heavier clothes like sweaters in the bottom."

She kissed her way down to my breasts. She flicked my right nipple with her tongue. "What else?" she said. Then she drew my nipple into her mouth and sucked.

It was getting harder to focus. I felt a tingling between my legs and squirmed.

"What else?" she asked again.

I took a deep breath and exhaled. "The middle drawer is missing a handle and the bottom drawer has a big gouge in it."

She kissed her way down my stomach and repositioned herself. She parted my thighs, spreading my legs wide and sat on her haunches between them. I felt exposed.

"Enough with the dresser," she said. "Now, tell me about what you smell."

I inhaled.

"The candle," I said, slowly. "It smells like Christmas. Evergreen and holly?"

"Good," she said. She leaned down and began kissing my thigh, working her way up the right side, down the left, and back again.

It tickled and I laughed uncontrollably. She stopped.

"Smell anything else?"

I was wet and the faint odor of my arousal was barely detectable. "Me," I said. "A little."

"Would you like to know how you taste?"

I nodded.

She slid a finger inside me, withdrew it, and held it to my lips. The scent was stronger now, a heady musk. I licked her finger and noticed the scent did not quite match the taste. It was salty, but not bitter. Not at all like what I was expecting— not at all like a man.

She kissed me. The taste of my sex was still faint on my lips.

"You taste good," she said. "I want to taste you some more."

As she moved back and buried her face between my legs, her ponytail brushed against my thigh. I felt the goose bumps rising, not just where her hair had touched, but all the way down to my knee.

Her tongue moved in circles around my clit. She flicked it gently with her tongue and I began to moan. The candles burned and the scent of Christmas filled my nostrils. I noticed the floral print on the drapes was not only azaleas but hydrangeas, as well. I was thinking about that as I felt my thighs begin to shake and I lay helpless as the tidal wave of pleasure crashed down on me.

Mistress backed away, then crawled over my leg and snuggled up next to me.

"What were you thinking about this time?"

My body still quivered and I gulped as currents of electricity coursed through me. "Evergreen, azaleas . . ."

"The coming orgasm?"

"No. What you were doing felt amazing. But the end sneaked up on me."

She laughed, but this time it was hearty, no disgust. "It's nice when that happens, isn't it?"

"Yes."

"That's what I meant about enjoying the ride."

"Mistress?"

"Yes?"

"When do I get to take you for the ride?"

"Not tonight," she cooed into my ear. "But soon."

My training had only just begun. Once I'd learned to not overthink things and enjoy the moments, Mistress rewarded me with many orgasms. I longed to return the favor but she continued to deny my requests.

"I don't understand why I can't do this for you," I said.

"It's not that you can't. It's that I don't want you to. Not now."

"Why not?"

"I have a kink of my own," she said. "I'm your Mistress. But I have other lovers."

"I know," I said. Mistress had told me of the others before our relationship had crossed over to intimacy. I hadn't met any of them, nor did I expect to. I'd learned to enjoy our time together. Whatever happened when we weren't didn't change or diminish the feelings I had for her, though her lack of interest in allowing me to provide her pleasure was beginning to spark jealousy.

"When you deny my requests and then reference the others, it makes me feel . . ."

"Unimportant?"

"Yes," I said. "If they provide you pleasure, why do you need me?"

"Maybe if I explain the kink, it will make more sense. Do you want to know?"

I was surprised she would reveal this to me. "Yes."

"I am Mistress to you. But I have a Master." I stared at her in silence and after a moment she continued. "There are things he's taught me, things I can do only for him or only with his permission."

"You are only allowed to get off if he says it's okay?"

"Yes. He's taught me how to control my orgasms. He can make me come just by telling me to . . . without ever touching me."

My eyes widened in disbelief. "I've never heard of such a thing."

"I doubted him when he told me about it too," she said. "If I hadn't actually experienced it, I probably wouldn't have believed it was possible."

"What do you get out of this? Is it more intense?"

"Not always," she said. "The best part is learning how to enjoy being aroused, that not every interaction has to end in orgasm. Sometimes it's more intense when the time between orgasms stretches. But when you give control of your body over to someone else, the bond between you becomes stronger. It's a form of intimacy enhancement. Some people find it appealing. Some don't. It's not for everyone."

I was intrigued. The thought of coming without being

touched, coming on command—I had to know if I could do it too.

"Mistress, can you teach me?" I begged.

"I don't know." She hesitated. "I'm still learning myself."

"What you don't know we could learn together," I said.

She smiled mischievously and simply said, "Okay."

Around noon the next day my cell phone rang. "Hello?" I said.

"Are you ready for your first lesson?"

"Mistress?" I whispered. She'd never called me during work hours before. I was happy to hear her voice but concerned my co-workers might be listening in. My eyes scanned the office and determined no one had even looked up.

"Are you ready?" she asked again.

"Yes."

"Go into the bathroom. Once you're in a stall, I want you to stimulate yourself until you are about to come but don't . . . stop just before. When you get home from work, finish what you started."

Instinctively, I began to protest, but I heard a click as the call went dead and I realized she was gone. Doing what she'd asked at work wasn't going to be easy. What if someone walked in and heard me? Butterflies fluttered in my stomach at the thought. But if I didn't do it, Mistress would be disappointed and I would be punished. I didn't want to disappoint her.

I left the office and took the elevator down to the second floor. The optometrist that had offices on the floor was closed between Christmas and New Year's, which meant the bathrooms should be unoccupied.

I pushed the bathroom door open. The room still smelled

of pine floor cleaner and it was apparent that no one had been in there all day. The toilet seats in each of the stalls were flipped up from being cleaned the night before, but none of them had been flushed and the water was still bright blue with cleaning fluid. I breathed a cautious sigh of relief, hoping it decreased my chances of being caught.

I chose the stall farthest from the door, and turned the latch behind me as I slipped inside. I kicked off my heels and squirmed out of my pantyhose and underwear. I stuffed them into my purse and slipped back into my heels. If someone did walk in, they'd see my feet and with shoes on; nothing would appear out of the ordinary at first glance.

Masturbating in a public restroom is not sexy. I was thankful for the memory of the moments Mistress and I had shared far away from there. I thought about the azaleas and hydrangeas on the drapes in her bedroom. The sweet scent of her freshly shampooed hair. I thought about the way her black bra pushed her breasts up and the way they sagged slightly without it. I thought about the scar above her left eyebrow and wondered how she had gotten it. I thought about how I loved her and all the while I touched myself. My finger alternated between stroking my labia and gently circling my clit. I started to feel a slight tingle and I didn't want to stop. A few more minutes and I'd be satisfied. I forced the thought from my mind. The whole point of the lesson was to learn about delayed gratification. And as much as I wanted to come right then and there, I wanted more to please Mistress.

I abruptly dressed, washed up, and splashed cold water on my face before heading back to my desk. The afternoon passed slowly. Somehow, filing the third-quarter sales reports didn't seem as important as it had when the day began. I continued to work but was acutely aware I was moving a bit slower than usual. My mind kept wandering back to thoughts of going home and finishing the job I'd begun in the restroom.

On the drive home my thoughts consumed me. The tingling between my legs spread like fire. My neck flushed and my nipples were hard. At home I hastily dropped my briefcase, keys, and purse by the front door. I absently closed it behind me and rushed upstairs to my bedroom.

The light on my answering machine blinked. I pressed the play button.

Mistress said, "I hope you had a good afternoon at work. If you've been good, make yourself come. If you've been bad . . ."

The riding crop cracked against something hard, something that wasn't flesh.

". . . call me."

The answering machine beeped and then clicked.

The message was over, but I played it again. Hearing the lilt in her voice when she spoke of being good or bad made me yearn for her presence.

I'd been good, so I made myself come. And although I hadn't been bad, I called her anyway.

"Mistress?"

"Were you bad?"

"No," I said. "I did what you asked."

"Good," she replied.

"It was wonderful," I said. "When can we do it again?"

"Patience, my sweet. You have other lessons to learn."

Mistress handed me a small box wrapped in Christmas paper and adorned with a green bow.

"What's this?" I asked.

"Some people believe in the twelve days of Christmas."

"Christmas is over," I said, slightly embarrassed. "I don't have anything else for you."

"Just open it," she said.

I tore the paper aside and removed the lid. Inside, I found a small purple vibrator ribbed with five gold rings.

"It's not really a Christmas gift," she said. "You'll need it for our next lesson. But when I saw it in the store, it made me think of the song. I couldn't resist."

"It's cute," I said. I took it out of the box and admired it. It was smaller and lighter than many of Mistress's other toys. "But I thought vibrators were meant to bring on orgasm faster. Sort of counteracts the kink, doesn't it?"

"No," she said. "This is how you're going to learn about control."

"I don't understand," I replied.

"Don't worry, you will."

I knelt naked before her.

"Insert the vibrator and use your muscles to hold it in," Mistress said. "Like doing a Kegel."

I complied. It *was* like doing a Kegel, only harder.

She turned the vibrator on low. The first ring glowed. "Release it when you feel like you are going to come."

I didn't last long and came before I let it slide out. I expected Mistress to be disappointed, but she wasn't. She praised me for trying.

"Learning to do this is not easy," she said. "You'll get the hang of it, with practice."

I nodded.

"I want you to practice every day until you can hold it in for five minutes on low without coming."

"Yes, Mistress," I said and felt the goose bumps crawl up my arms.

After months of practice, I was able to hold the vibe on higher settings and for longer periods of time. There were times when I failed, but those times were decreasing in frequency. With each ring's illumination, I became better at controlling my body and mastering my responses.

When I reached the fifth ring, Mistress allowed me to have orgasms with the vibe and talked me through it. Sometimes she told me to hold it back, then give me permission to come. Sometimes she'd tell me to stop completely and not allow me to reach orgasm. Sometimes she'd demand I come immediately. Before long, my body had been trained not only to be stimulated by her or the vibe, but also by her voice.

One day late in the year, Mistress said I was ready to begin work on the final lesson: coming upon command, without physical stimulation but by her voice alone. We'd been practicing for months, building up to this moment. Even though I wanted it to happen, part of me still didn't believe that it was actually possible.

"You've been working so hard. I'm proud of you," Mistress cooed.

I was lying on her bed, fully clothed, remembering the first time I'd come in that room. I was thinking it was almost Christmas again. This year, the burning candle did not smell of evergreen and holly, but instead of cinnamon and nutmeg. The scent of eggnog so was strong, I could almost taste it.

"Do you want to come for me?"

"Yes, Mistress."

"Are you wet?"

I squirmed. I was. "Yes," I said.

She took the vibe out of the box and held it up. The five gold rings sparkled in the candlelight.

I squirmed again. Looking at it made me want it. Looking at her, smiling a wicked smile, made me want her. I ached for them both.

She turned the vibe on. The sound of its buzzing created a prickly, tingling heat which ran up my thighs before settling between them.

I moaned.

"You want the toy?"

I thought of shepherds and wise men following the North Star. The glowing rings were my beacons reminding me once again that I hadn't reached my destination.

"Yes," I whispered.

She turned it off. "Come for me and you can have it."

Something stirred deep inside of me. My body was responding to her command. As I rode the wave through the endorphin rush, I felt the contractions in my vagina.

"Oh."

I bucked my hips and shuddered in release. Once it was over, I began to cry. Even though it was a shared experience Mistress and I had been working towards, I had never been sure we'd ever really get there.

"What's wrong?" Mistress asked. She lay down next to me and wiped the tears from my cheeks.

"You did it," I said. "It really worked."

"I know," she said. "And watching it was wonderful. I am proud of you." She kissed my cheeks and my forehead.

I sobbed.

"Did it scare you?"

I nodded.

"The first time it happened to me, I was scared too."

"Why?" I tried helplessly to choke back the tears.

"It's not easy to give someone else that kind of control over your body."

"That's not what I'm afraid of," I said, sobbing.

She brushed my hair back and tucked it behind my ear. "What scares you?"

"We've reached the goal. I'm not a challenge anymore."

"Ah, you're wondering if I'll tire of you."

"Will you?"

"This is only the beginning," she said. "There are lots of other things we can work towards."

"Like what?" I said.

She pulled a sex toy catalog off of the dresser. "I still have to get you a Christmas present." She flipped through the pages while singing, "On the sixth day of Christmas . . ."

"Finding a vibrator with five gold rings was a fluke," I said. "You don't really think you're going to find something with six geese on it in there, do you?"

She stopped at page eighty-seven. "What do you think?"

I looked at the picture she pointed to. The Extreme Goose: a toy shaped like a goose head and neck photographed next to a grown man's arm.

"You really should see the look on your face right now," she said, laughing.

"I think you're going to have find a new favorite Christmas song."

"Don't be so quick to judge," she said. "After all, you didn't think you could handle coming on command."

"But that looks . . . painful," I said.

"It would be if you tried it right now. But think of all the fun we could have working our way up to it."

"Our way?"

"It wouldn't be fair to ask you to try something I wasn't willing to do myself," she said.

"Hm . . . I don't know," I said.

"Well, you have time to think it over," she said. "Even if I ordered it now, it won't get here until the new year."

She winked, then smiled that wicked smile.

A New Year's challenge. How could I resist?

Six Geese a' Laying

by Katy Sirls

The sun was just disappearing below the horizon through the tiny square window, casting hues of dull orange and pink over the vast expanse of sky, when the public address system broke the drone of the engines to announce that the plane was beginning its descent. With a small gasp, Stacia eagerly peered out her window to take in the expanse of New England below. Somewhere down there, only minutes away now, he was awaiting her arrival.

It had been too long. Three months, to be exact. Three months without seeing his face, without feeling his touch, his kisses, three months without him inside of her . . .

Stacia fought back the familiar pang of heartache that came with thoughts of him. She reminded herself that only moments from now they would be together again, in each other's arms. She shifted restlessly in her seat, as if her continuous movement would push the plane to its destination faster.

Now that she was so close to being back in her home country and with the man she loved, she honestly couldn't comprehend how she originally thought she was going to last six months. The decision to come home from France three months earlier than expected had been hers and hers alone, but she'd known Luke would be thrilled with the news.

I have a Christmas present for you, she had written seductively in her fancy handwriting, wanting to wait for his response before telling him she would be home in time for Christmas. And when she did tell him, she made sure to include that simply thinking about his "present" made her wet. And it did too—three months was a long time to build anticipation for what she planned to do to him upon her return.

Stacia unbuckled her seatbelt before the cabin lights flickered on. She was on her feet before she was supposed to be, and grabbing her luggage from the overhead compartment. The passengers around her glared in annoyance, and a flight attendant motioned for her to remain in her seat, but Stacia was hardly aware of them. There was only one person she was thinking about.

Once she was off the plane and through customs, Stacia fought her way through the crowds of people, looking for the face she hadn't seen in too long. The handsome, tanned face framed by glistening dark waves. She looked around her and saw myriad people, but not the one she was looking for. She almost called out his name despite herself—but then heard her own name, being called excitedly from across the room.

"Stacia!"

She spun in the direction of the voice, and all at once she saw him. Luke. Running towards her, skirting his way around people blocking him, a broad grin lighting up his face. Even from a distance, she could see how his blue eyes glittered with the happiness he felt at seeing her. Stacia immediately dropped her bags and ran towards him as well. When they met, he swept her up in a tight embrace.

It was just as Stacia had envisioned it. His arms were tight around her, his body against hers in the way she had missed every single day that she was in France. His face was in her hair, softly kissing her neck, then kissing her lips, and for just a moment it was as if they were the only two people in the airport. She savored the taste of his lips, his tongue, against her own.

"I missed you," he whispered softly, his mouth playing gently over her ear.

"I missed you, too," she replied. She pulled away to look into his eyes, and laughed lightly. "Let's never take a three-month hiatus again."

His expression told her he wholeheartedly agreed. "Let's just get through Christmas," he told her, running a hand through her hair. "Then we can go to New York together, just like we planned."

She sighed happily at the thought, wrapping her arms around him again and leaning her head against his chest. It had been his idea to spend Christmas with his family in Sunderland before heading up to New York, and as much as she was looking forward to getting settled, she had to admit she was looking forward to seeing the farm Luke grew up on. She was eager to arrive in his hometown, most likely lit up with Christmas lights and smelling of apple and pumpkin pies cooking in the homey little restaurants.

Luke picked up her bags, and together they walked through the frigid New England winter out to his car. The majority of the drive was spent talking about the various things they had missed in each other's lives during their time apart. While the conversation was interesting enough, Stacia's mind was elsewhere. As she watched him drive, she wondered if he was aware of how she was feeling, how she wanted him right then and there, and if he felt the same way.

Simply looking at his body, his toned chest and arms only slightly hidden by his sweater, made her hot.

As if to test how Luke was feeling at that moment, Stacia reached over and put a hand on his leg. Then, slowly, she began to move it up until it rested on the unmistakable hardness that told her he was indeed feeling as hot for her as she was for him. Through the shroud his pants created, she lightly stroked his cock and heard him exhale slowly at the long-awaited sensation of her touch. She thought about the pleasant surprise she could give him if she were to unzip his pants and take his cock into her mouth. She thought about all the familiar places along his shaft, the veins stretching up to meet the ridge of his cock head, where she could run her tongue and tease him into a wild frenzy. But she ultimately rejected the idea, deciding instead he would have to wait with her until the moment when they could both release the sexual anticipation steadily growing inside them.

The sky was dark but lit with stars when they arrived in Sunderland. Stacia took immediate pleasure at the cozy sight of children playing in the snow, couples walking hand in hand with presumably peppermint- or gingerbread-flavored hot chocolate, and colorful lights woven into various trees. Luke took the scenic route through town, heading for his family's farm near the Connecticut River, where they would spend the holiday.

When they pulled up in front of the picturesque farmhouse, Stacia couldn't help but smile at the plastic Santa Claus figure, lit from inside, perched on the roof. As she got out of the car, she saw thin wisps of smoke coming from the chimney, disappearing into the night air, and in the distance she could see the flowing river. Still, the calm beauty of the house's exterior didn't compare to the inside, where they were greeted by warmth, the delicious smell of meats and breads wafting into the front hall, and the sounds of *I'll Be Home For Christmas* playing softly in the background.

"I hope you're hungry," Luke said with an amused smile, referring to the large meal his mother had prepared for their arrival. Stacia didn't have a chance to answer as the two of them were instantly surrounded by Luke's family: his parents, grandparents, and five siblings. As they all sat down to dinner, Stacia found herself engaged in conversation, but that didn't stop her from exchanging glances with Luke across the table.

She could read those eyes too, and knew exactly what he was thinking: he wanted desperately to be alone with her. But dinner and the machinations of "catching up" with the family dragged onward and it was more than a few hours before they were able to sneak out onto the front porch. They sat together on the porch swing, breathing in the refreshing but chilly night air, and hoping it would be at least a few minutes before they were discovered by someone wanting to play a board game or bake Christmas cookies or reminisce about Luke's younger years on the farm.

"It's so nice out here," Stacia commented, gazing at the stars above them. "If I had been you, growing up on this farm, I might have been tempted to stay forever."

"That's easy to say when you *didn't* grow up here." Luke laughed. "Besides, there's only one part of the farm I've ever actually enjoyed taking care of. It's *my* area."

"Really?" Stacia's eyebrows went up in interest. "And just what area do you consider to be 'yours'?"

Luke opened his mouth to answer, but stopped. He cocked his head to one side and his eyes narrowed as he considered how to answer her. Finally, he stood up and offered his hand to her. "Come on. I'll show you."

Stacia smiled, but looked around doubtfully. "Now? It's so dark out."

"The moon is bright," he reminded her. "We'll be fine."

Stacia reached out and took his hand in her own. She had been waiting so long to feel his touch again that feeling their palms pressed together, their fingers intertwined, made her body tingle.

They walked for a few minutes in the direction of the river until Luke stopped before an area that appeared to be a rather large chicken coop. As they neared it, Stacia could make out the forms of birds, some of them walking slowly over the grass, and some of them on the ground sleeping. Geese. Six geese.

"You take care of them?" Stacia asked, stepping up to the fence and leaning over slightly.

"Yeah. No one else really does," Luke answered, looking at the geese warmly.

"How come?"

Luke grinned at her. "Because the geese like me. They've been mine since I was a boy. They don't respond well to anyone else."

Stacia reached her hand out to the nearest goose, who promptly snapped his beak at her. As she yanked her hand back, Luke laughed good-naturedly. "I told you." As if to prove his point, he reached out and lightly scratched the head of the same goose. "They actually mean a lot to me. They're the one reason I was sorry to leave the farm."

"Don't they fly away?"

"Sometimes they fly down to the river," Luke said, pointing, "but they always come back. And, as an added bonus, we get goose eggs from time to time."

As Stacia watched, three other geese realized Luke was at

the fence and waddled over. He ran his hand over each one of them, fondly petting them as if they were cats or dogs. As he did so, Stacia reached out and put her hand on his shoulder, lightly touching the fabric of his shirt. She could only just feel the form of his body underneath.

At her touch, Luke lifted his head and turned to look at her. His eyes, tender and intense at the same time, bore into hers. Stacia wondered what he saw there. Could he see that she wanted, so badly, to wrap her other arm around him—to feel his chest, grab his ass, grasp at his cock? She felt her breath catch in her throat as he slowly leaned in closer to her. She closed her eyes as his head came in next to her own, and she felt his breath on her neck. A light shiver ran through her body as his lips brushed ever so softly down her neck and onto her shoulder.

"I've missed this," she breathed, her hands moving over the muscles in his chest and arms.

Luke lifted his head and smiled playfully. "What? This?" He slid his hands beneath her shirt, using one to rub her back and the other to clutch at her breasts. Then the hand on her back slowly slid down, into her pants, until it was resting on her ass. "Or this?"

Stacia bit her lower lip. The sensation of his touch was so close to the sweet spot between her legs, it was already growing wet in anticipation. "You're getting closer," she murmured.

She shivered at the tickling sensation as he dragged his fingers lightly away from her breasts and down her stomach. He paused for a moment before sliding them past her waistband and down to her clit, where he began rubbing slowly. He leaned in again to kiss her, gently whispering, "I *know* you've missed this."

Breathing heavily, Stacia could only nod in agreement. She felt him suddenly slide two fingers into her, and her heart began to race. She saw the outline of his hard cock, hidden behind his pants, and all at once she wanted him. She wanted—*needed*—that cock inside her. Her hands dashed madly for his zipper, ready to take his pants down and pull his cock towards her.

The hand that had been clutching her ass reached out though, and stopped her. He offered a mischievous smile as he artfully kept her from reaching his cock. With his fingers still inside of her, searching for her G-spot, she didn't put up much of a fight either.

Stacia eyed him. Her breath in ragged gasps, she reminded him, "This is supposed to be my present to you. How is that going to work out if your cock is hidden away?"

Luke laughed and said teasingly, "You want to make love to me right here? In front of the geese? In the snow?"

Stacia glanced over at the geese and burst into laughter at their inquisitive, watchful gazes. "That's not fair," she complained, though her voice revealed her good humor. She put her arms around Luke's neck. "I thought I was going to get lucky."

This time it was Luke's turn to start laughing. "I hope not," he said. "That could have been bad."

"Huh?" Stacia furrowed her brow in confusion.

Luke pointed behind her. Stacia spun around to see Luke's two sisters prancing through the snow, heading in their direction. They laughed together as they ran, and hardly paid attention to Luke and Stacia in the distance, but Stacia blushed at the thought of what could have happened if they had carried on the way she had wanted to.

"Shit." She giggled under her breath just as Luke quickly

withdrew his hand from her pants. They did their best to act like they had spent the entire time playing with the geese.

Luke's sisters, they found out a moment later, had come to fetch Stacia. The baking of Christmas cookies, a female tradition in the family, was about to take place, and they wanted to make sure she was included.

Stacia looked forlornly at Luke. "I guess you're meant to get my present a little later on," she said quietly and allowed herself to be led back to the house.

In truth, Stacia was much more disappointed than she let on. She had been so hot, so ready for the feeling of having Luke's body at one with her own, and being pulled away so abruptly left those emotions raw and hungry. Luke could see it in her eyes and she could read his face as they walked through the field. It told her, *I'm sorry*. And it said even more clearly, *I'll make it up to you*.

For the next few hours, as she rolled dough and mixed icing with red and green food coloring, she held on to the remnants of Luke's touch. She thought about his hand on her ass, his fingers inside of her, and managed to retain the tingling sensation she always felt when she was turned on. She began to wonder just how easy it was going to be getting away from the myriad people who lived in the house.

Once the cookies were baked, frosted, decorated, and put on display on an ancient heirloom Christmas platter, Stacia headed to the guest room to change her clothes. Her black sweater was covered with so much flour it was barely recognizable. She decided it would be a good time to put her pajamas on and settle in for the rest of the night.

Before she had a chance to rummage around in her suitcase, though, her eyes landed on a peculiar object resting near her pillow. It was shaped like an egg, and as Stacia curiously took it in her hands, she noticed it had been lightly dusted with red glitter. The weight and feel of it confirmed it was, in fact, an egg. It was bigger than a regular chicken's egg, though: a goose egg? It had a small red bow stuck to its top, and a small note attached to the bottom.

Eagerly, she tore the note from the egg and opened it. "Done baking? Meet me outside near the big oak tree," it said.

Her heart leapt, and she smiled gleefully to herself. Not even conscious anymore of the flour covering her clothes, she hopped off the bed and made her way as casually as she could outside. The porch was quiet and the night was clear. Her feet carried her as fast as they could down the steps and around the house to the oak tree, the largest tree on the property. As she approached, she looked for Luke but didn't see him. She stood in confusion for a moment, then circled the entire tree slowly.

She had almost made a complete circle when she spotted a glistening green object, right at eye level, sitting in a branch. Stacia immediately knew it was another egg. This one was wrapped in glittering green wrapping paper and tied with thin red ribbon. Like the last one, it had a note attached.

"Don't you want to know what you're getting for Christmas? Come find me by the garden shed."

Stacia thought about his rock-hard cock and immediately headed for the shed, which sat perilously close to the house. As she drew nearer, she didn't see Luke and began a careful search of the area until she found her third egg. It had a sprig of mistletoe taped to it and, like the others, had a note attached— but this one had something more. Rather than simply sitting in the snow, this egg had a makeshift bed: Luke's sweater.

Stacia thought about Luke, potentially waiting for her somewhere with no shirt on, his nipples hard like glass in the cold night air, his sexy, toned pecs and stomach bare for her to see . . . and touch . . .

She enthusiastically ripped the note open.

"I want you. Come down to the chicken coop."

As she ran towards the chicken coop, she grew even more excited at what she would find there. It was another egg, sitting atop Luke's carefully folded pants, alongside another note that instructed her to meet him by the geese.

Stacia half expected Luke to be there waiting for her, but he wasn't. Instead, there was a fifth goose egg, bigger than any of the others had been. She was hardly able to focus on the egg itself, though, as her eyes were glued to what was lying next to it. Luke's boxer shorts sat on top of the fresh snow. Stacia snatched her newest note and opened it to see where this wild goose chase would lead her next.

"You want my cock?" it said. "Come and get it. I'm down by the river."

Thinking about his cock, and how much she wanted it deep inside her, Stacia instantly took off in the direction of the river. She trotted through the farm for a little while, and it wasn't long before she could hear the sound of the river in the distance. She reached the water's edge and instantly spotted the small campfire further along down the bank. She made out a shape next to it. Not a goose egg, not a letter, but *him*. Luke. He stood in the cool night air, his waves blowing in the breeze, his body completely naked and the shadows of the flames dancing along his skin. One hand was stretched out towards her, holding the last goose egg. But it was his cock that caught her eye. It was standing hard and ready, waiting for her . . . and as she drew closer, feeling the warmth from the fire, she saw he had wrapped a small red ribbon around it.

"Merry Christmas," he said softly.

She smiled and gently took the egg from him. "What's all this?" she whispered. "You stole my present idea!"

"I knew what you wanted," he explained with a light shrug of his shoulders. "So here it is."

Stacia could feel herself growing wet and swollen in expectation of what she would do with her "present." Slowly, she took the ribbon off of his thick cock. Then, she backed away a few steps and began to slowly remove her own clothes, one article at a time. Luke had taken great pains, clearing the area and laying cozy down-filled sleeping bags in a circle around the fire. The setting was perfect, but she wanted to tease him as much as he had teased her with his game. When she was as naked as he was, she sat down on one of the sleeping bags and opened her legs slightly, beckoning him with her eyes.

An intensely excited expression washed over his face as she parted her legs. He moved over to her in a passionate, pulsating frenzy, and before she knew it he was on top of her, kissing her passionately, his hands exploring her breasts, her hair, her neck—everywhere except where she wanted to feel his touch. Her heart raced with desperation and the burning need to relieve the build-up of sexual excitement within her.

Slowly, she leaned back and wrapped her arms around him. She arched her back slightly, pressing her pelvis against his manhood in an attempt to show him just how much she wanted, needed, his body at one with her own. In response, he moved down and, all at once, entered her.

Stacia cried out as she felt the sensation of his cock filling her, rocking gently in and out of her. The tension that had built up within her from wanting him released itself, and she was overcome with pure ecstasy. As Luke moved his hips back and forth, he moved his mouth to her neck, kissing down to her chest until he came to her breast and gently rolled his tongue over a hard nipple.

She rocked in tempo with him, firmly grasping his ass in both hands and pulling him as far into herself as she could. Luke's mouth dropped open with pleasure, then he countered her action by transforming his gentle swaying motion into a series of hard, intense thrusts. The fire beside them roared, competing to release as much heat as they did with their passion.

As Luke continued to thrust into her, Stacia wrapped her legs around him and pulled his body close in to hers. Their stomachs touched, their chests met, his pecs against her breasts, and again their mouths locked in a kiss that was pure ardor and zeal for one another. Her hands moved over every part of his body they could reach, fully taking in the feel of his skin, his muscles. Every thrust of his cock into her moist cave sent waves of pleasure through her, a sensation she was thrilled to be able to feel again.

Just as Stacia felt herself climax, Luke paused, gasped, and impaled her with a particularly deep thrust. As they came together, their eyes met, burning with fierce desire. Her body shuddering, Stacia let her head fall back, and her gaze fell on the stars above, glittering and shimmering in striking beauty—just like Luke's eyes.

Luke withdrew from her slowly and wrapped a sleeping bag around them, trading passionate kisses. Lying there, Stacia sighed to herself.

"So," Luke said softly into her ear, "what did you think of your gift?"

"All I could ask for," Stacia responded. "What my true love gave to me."

Seven Swans a' Swimming

by Cecilia Tan

But anon her awful jubilant voice,
With a music strange and manifold,
Flow'd forth on a carol free and bold;
As when a mighty people rejoice
With shawms, and with cymbals, and harps of gold . . .

from *The Dying Swan* by Alfred Lord Tennyson

Robert. I didn't speak his name, but he turned as if he'd heard me. Perhaps he had. We old ones sometimes speak with the mind, and sometimes our kind can hear what is unspoken. Snow fell softly, like swan feathers through the evening air, the sky already dark but the London streets still bustling with light and noise and holiday shoppers. Swans were beloved of Apollo, it was said, sacred, and were seen flying over Delos when the god was born.

Robert was a god incarnate. It was half the reason I made him.

As he turned, his eyes had a moment of gold in them, like a cat's, then warmed with recognition as he focused on me. "Mirelle," he breathed, coming and taking my hands in his, mine bare, his gloved.

"It's Sarah, now," I said with a smile. But he had always been Robert, since his birth some six hundred years before. Compared to me he was practically a fledgling, but to anyone watching us meet on the cobblestoned sidewalk outside an apothecary shop, we were nothing more than two young lovebirds in our early twenties.

"First snow," he said with a boyish grin. There was a familiarity and ease borne of our long association. I had not seen him in fifty years, but he spoke as if we talked every day. "Lovely, isn't it?" He blinked as a few flakes clung to his lashes.

"Yes," I said, unable to keep from returning his smile. It had been fifty years, and I wanted very much to kiss him, like young lovers in the snow.

But the kiss I wanted was with warm lips, a velvet tongue. If we kissed now, it would be cold, but not because of the snow. I squeezed his fingers, the leather of his gloves squeaking as I did. "Hunt with me," I whispered.

He looked down shyly, his long lashes blinking again, and for a moment I thought he was going to deny me, to tell me he was bound to another now, or make some excuse. But no, he was merely taking in the moment, perhaps overcoming his reservations, before he looked up and said, "Yes."

We went to the bedsit I'd rented so I could dress in warmer clothes. Walking about snowy London in just a jumper, with no scarf or gloves, was bound to attract attention. And we did not want to attract attention. We wanted to be perfectly forgettable.

Vampires as old as we don't hunt often, and when we do, we do not have to kill. Especially not when we hunt for pleasure, as Robert and I were about to. There are strict rules we should adhere to, to prevent discovery. But in the modern age, it is so much more difficult to make a person disappear without a trace. Each choice had a risk. Commit murder and potentially draw the fear and attention of the populace. Leave a victim alive and risk discovery or recognition.

I hadn't planned to stay in London long anyway.

"Certainly not past Christmas," I told him, as I wrapped a pashmina around my neck. "There. How do I look?"

He swept his arms around my waist, twirling me like a princess at a ball. "Fabulous. As always."

I laughed and shook my head. "You know that isn't what I meant." It felt so good to flirt, though, to smile with ease.

I had buried my most recent lover in the summer. A sweet young Spaniard, he had loved me as fiercely and single-mindedly as a bull does a red cape. My feelings for him had not matched his in intensity, but he had not minded. He had loved me to drink his blood directly from his skin, to take it while he took me, rutting hard.

I had put a gold ring on him like one does on a black swan to keep him tame, although it was not his neck that I ringed.

"Let's go," I said, taking his hand and pulling him out the door before I could succumb to melancholy. "The city awaits."

He pulled me back into his arms. "Will you let me choose?"

I rested my forehead against his. "If you like."

"Male or female?"

I narrowed my eyes. "I didn't think you'd like a male."

His eyeslashes fluttered, but he was too bloodless to blush. "Only for you," he whispered. "If that's what you want."

I grinned. Yes, I preferred male victims the way I preferred male lovers, although the sweet taste of a maiden was not foreign to me. And I was intrigued that Robert might be tempted, for my sake, to . . . experiment. "Yes," I said, squeezing him, "that's what I want."

There was no hurry in us. Hunting together was a singular pleasure, and I would no more rush to consummate the bite than I would intercourse. We began at Harrod's, playing at being a young couple, looking at clothes and jewelry and knickknacks even as we looked at the people. He joked that he should buy me a diamond, that we could surely send some salesman over the moon with the immense stone he would choose. Robert's family had been rich even six centuries ago, and careful management of his investments had made him only more so in this day and age.

He seemed almost wistful as I led him away from the counter, or perhaps that was me, and I saw myself in him. But it was only moments before we were laughing again.

"What about that one?" I whispered to him, as we followed a young man through the shoe department who seemed to be alone.

"Hm, maybe . . ." he answered, and we separated to stalk him a bit more.

He led us on a seemingly aimless path through the store, stopping and picking up items from time to time, but never staying in any one department for long.

To me, he seemed incredibly lonely.

Robert met me at the bottom of an escalator and watched our quarry go up. He shook his head at me. "He'll be trouble," he said, as he steered me away from the moving staircase.

"Oh? Why?"

"Shoplifting," he said with a mischievous grin. "Weren't you watching him?"

"I was trying to get a read on his head," I said, "not watching his hands."

"He'll have security on him soon, if he doesn't already." He hopped onto the downward escalator and I joined him. "Let's move on."

We rode the Tube for a bit, but the crowds were still fairly thick, and so it was difficult to cull one sheep from the herd. I was still in no rush. We sat on a bench near a busker with a guitar, singing a haunting but unfamiliar song.

"Seen anyone else lately?" he said casually, as he leaned against the wall and crossed his ankles.

"Not really." I shrugged. "You know I like to go south during the summer." With Javier, it had been Spain that drew me when the days in Britain and further north grew long. Decades before, Venice had been my destination. I had even returned to Greece from time to time, though I had never again returned to the tiny isle where I had been born.

I still remember my maker's face. He was the first man I had ever seen with blond hair, bleached that way by the sun while spending his days aboard a ship, then forever that color, though the life ahead of him was eternal night. He was a hydrographer, or he had been before he was turned, and his work mapping the seas had brought him not only into the clutches of a vampire in Egypt, but to the island where I grew up, ignorant of such things.

I remember his face perfectly. I remember, too, the way it felt when he entered me for the first time, breaching me deeply with one fluid thrust even as his fangs set my blood flowing. I remember utter bliss.

Oddly, I do not remember the name by which he called himself. Perhaps if I went back to speaking my native tongue, it might return to my mind. In more recent years, he has called himself Nikolai.

I could not help but ask. After all, Robert had brought up

the subject of mutual acquaintances. "Have you heard from Nik?"

I did not miss the slight perturbation in his look, though he smoothed it away quickly. Was it . . . jealousy? I could not tell. "I have seen him recently," he said with forced casualness. "He's still living in Paris."

"Still pretending to be a Russian who speaks imperfect French?"

Robert laughed. "Yes. Though by now, his French is better than most." He'd been living there for nearly a hundred years, as far as I knew. That was a long time for one of us to stay in one place. He must have had a very stable food supply, or mastered the chameleonic arts, a talent that sometimes came to the very old ones.

He had been everything to me. My first lover, my vampire maker, nigh unto a god. Zeus transformed into a swan to mate with the mortal maid Leda. But what I had not realized at the time was that he had only been a vampire for a year or so himself. His peripatetic ways aboard ship had severed him from his careless Egyptian maker, and he had known almost nothing of vampire rules and law. The fact that he had not fallen victim to the undeniable perils of his new life during his early, reckless days was a marvel to many.

"Tell him hello for me the next time you see him," I said, holding my emotions in check.

"I will," he replied quietly, his own tightly reined.

After a pause he said, "Let us go hear some music."

"Robert, we are hearing music."

He clucked his tongue. "I mean, besides an Underground busker. Come on. We'll likely find someone in the nightclubs. Would you like to go dancing?"

I made a noncommittal noise. "These days, what they call dancing . . ."

He ran his gloved hand over my sleeve. "I would enjoy dancing with you."

"Very well." I chuckled. "Take me dancing."

With the span of my life I had seen the rise of Western music, the modal music of the Renaissance and liturgy, the rise of classical music, the invention of the piano, and the spectacle of opera. I would never forget the shock that rooted me to my seat upon seeing Wagner's *Lohengrin*. For of course, that opera features a Swan Prince who arrives by boat. The resemblance to Nik ended there, but it was not the first time I had felt like a bolt from the blue had struck me, as if the reminder of my past were some kind of sign.

Classical was overtaken by so many other forms, big band and rock and roll and hip hop. It had been perhaps fifty years since people in Europe once again danced the way we had in the pre-Christian days, just moving our bodies to the music however we liked. Bacchanalia lived in disco, and in the twenty-first century a new generation of club-goers learned to free their souls.

Robert paid our way into a large, dark, noisy building, swirling with lights and pumping with a throb so palpable it could have been the very heart of London beating. We checked our coats and outerthings and made our way into the crowd. We were not as gaudily dressed as most, and I wondered whether he had bribed the bouncer or glamoured him. Still, we were not noticed much. The more brightly colored and exhibitionistic dancers drew the attention, and we danced in relative peace.

I could almost imagine I was beginning to sweat as I

moved my hips to the relentless beat. His hands fitted over my hips as we ground together so close that if we'd had body heat, I would have felt it.

Anticipation of feeding was sharpening into hunger, even as the pleasure of his company was quickening into arousal. I pulled him close by the collar, my voice in his ear for him alone in the din. "I want you."

"And I want you," he answered back, holding me close now, the heat of the bodies around us making it almost feel like it should. He moved against me ceaselessly, but he could not become erect without an infusion. "Let us see who we can find, shall we?"

He let me go and turned to scan the crowd of hundreds on the dance floor all around us.

Time was measured in four-beat bars, and I lost track of how many minutes passed while we each sized up the smorgasbord before us.

He scanned those at the edge of the crowd, those watching the bodies writhing, but not dancing themselves.

My eyes locked onto a blond boy coming toward me, his shirt tucked into the back pocket of his jeans as he stalked slow and pantherlike through the crowd, dancing, yet each step brought him closer to me.

I licked my lips, and the next thing I knew, he was dancing so close that I could feel the heat radiating from his bare skin. Out of the corner of my eye I saw the bit of color that had been his shirt fall from his pocket and disappear into the undertow of feet.

I wanted to touch him, to run my hands up and down his skin, to make his nipples stand up with the coolness of my fingers. I dared one touch, just a brush of my fingers over his chest, and he looked up with unbridled hunger in his eyes.

I glanced at Robert and found him watching. He gave an approving nod. I licked my lips again, and beckoned him closer with a twitch of my head. Now we'd find out if this incandescent little candle flame would flicker out if met with the prospect of the three of us together.

Robert came up behind him and we danced that way for a long minute, the boy sandwiched between us. I laughed at my own designation of him as a boy. He was certainly in his mid-twenties, and I got a feeling he might be older than he looked. Something about his eyes. Implacable, like a swan's. I reminded myself that he was to be a meal, perhaps a sex toy, and not more. Not one of my swans at all. Melancholy threatened to sweep through me, right there in the midst of the noise and energy of the dance floor.

Perhaps, I thought, I was finally tiring of eternal life. Even the early Christian mystics borrowed the pagan tales of swans and the afterlife. The Valkyries could turn into swans to bear the heroic dead to Valhalla. The Anglo-Saxons wrote in the Exeter Book of the swan being entwined with the metamorphosis of the soul after death. Pythagoras himself maintained that when great poets died, their souls were reborn in swans. Although the myth of the "swan song" is exactly that, only a myth, the romantic ideal of one final, soul-shattering performance prior to dying has been plumbed by all the great poets of English: Chaucer, Spenser, Shakespeare, Coleridge, and Tennyson.

Robert looked up at me suddenly, worry in his expression as he took in my woolgathering. He leaned close under pretense of kissing me. "We needn't kill him, if that's what you're worried about. He seems quite willing."

"I know," I said, pulling myself together. Now was not the time to contemplate either my own death or the deaths of my previous lovers. I would surely feel much better after a little blood. "Where shall we take him?"

"I have a hotel suite," Robert said and winked. He had clearly thought of everything.

In the taxicab to Claridge's, Robert urged me to play. I put my hand over the bulge in our quarry's trousers, and felt him hard with life. I rubbed him and he groaned, the bulge growing enticingly under my palm. Robert's hands circled under my jumper and pulled at my nipples. Unlike the men, I could muster some erect tissue without a fresh infusion, and I moaned softly, my fangs protruding nearly as much as the buds between Robert's fingers. In the back of my mind, I realized we had all left our coats behind at the club, but I was too taken with my two lovers to give it much thought.

Robert and I had not stayed lovers long, when we had been before. Not every maker had such a relationship with those he or she turned. In fact, I had only had two relationships with vampires before: Robert and, all the way back when I had been newly made, my own maker.

Robert was whispering in my ear, and I wondered if he truly could hear my thoughts. If he might have been listening to them all evening, since he had first caught the sound of his own name in my head. "You miss him still, don't you, Mirelle?"

I swallowed a lump in my throat, squeezing the denim and flesh in my grip. "Yes. Yes, I do." My longing for Nikolai, my rising arousal, and the undeniable tug of bloodlust made me strain toward the boy's neck.

But Robert held me back. "Not yet, Mirelle." He grazed my own neck with his teeth and I shivered in pleasure. "Almost there."

He did not lie. I found it likely he had picked the place we went dancing based on its proximity to the hotel. We bustled in a side entrance and into an elevator, Robert interposing himself between me and the boy, who seemed to catch on to the game and kept peeking at me from around him with "come hither" looks.

The moment the door closed behind us in the suite, Robert began stripping me out of my clothes. The boy slipped his jeans off easily, his slim hips showing the blue tracery of his veins under his skin. He lay back against a luxuriously large bed, placing himself at the center, like the pistil of a huge cream-colored flower.

I crawled over him, every bit of my attention taken up by the morsel in front of me, under me.

I felt Robert's weight on the bed behind me, but he did not touch. Just spoke. "Do you want him inside you? Scorching hot he'll feel just now . . ."

I nuzzled the boy's neck, intoxicated with the scent of fresh blood and the warmth of his skin. I rocked back and bent my head to his prick, slathering it until it was thoroughly wet.

They both made noises of surprise as I mounted him, neither of them quite believing, I suppose, that I would take Robert's dirty talk so seriously. But there he was, seated deep in me, and then I bent down to bite.

I knew just a bare moment before my fangs pierced him that all was not as it should be. But I had only that one moment to think—*he has no pulse!*—before my fangs and feeding instinct took over, and I bit into an enticing place.

His hardness surged inside me, thrusting up even as I tasted salt-sweetness, an ambrosial mixture of fresh human blood and a vampire's essence. For this was no human under me, in me, but a vampire who had fed so well and so recently that he felt in all ways alive.

His flavor was heartbreakingly familiar. *Nikolai* . . . I clung to him, still feeding, but tears begin to run down my cheeks.

"Yes." It was Robert speaking, still. "I hope you can forgive me for leading you on, Mir . . . er, Sarah." He finally remembered my current name. "But, well, Nik here has become such a chameleon, he . . . well . . ."

Nik couldn't speak for himself, not while I was sucking at the join of his neck and shoulder and rocking against him, not while the instinct to rut had never left his body and he was thrusting more vigorously into me with each passing second. He could only moan.

When at last I raised my head, running my teeth over my fangs, his appearance had changed, and he was as I remembered him all those years ago, more than a thousand, sun-bleached and tanned. His name returned to me, though my voice was no more than a whisper. "Arkadios!"

"Melité," he answered, nuzzling his nose in my hair and breathing deeply of my scent. "I never . . ."

But he did not finish his sentence, as a lustful sound took over his throat once more as I ground against him. Sex had not felt like this since—

I looked guiltily back at Robert and was surprised to find him perched on the edge of the bed, still fully clothed. He gave me a warm smile, his fangs showing as the scent of blood in the air was driving him close to the edge, too. He stood. "I'll leave you two to get reacquainted."

I could not protest, not for his nor for my own sake. Arkadios's thumbs fitted into the hollows of my hips and he thrust again, taking my attention wholly for himself. "Bite me again," he whispered, and I obliged, taking the other side of his neck this time, as the first of many orgasms to wrack me that night sent tremors through me.

It was only later, lying in the darkness of the December night with just the occasional hiss of a car going by or bursts of drunken Christmas caroling to break the stillness, that I began to cry. The melancholy that had bean threatening me all evening finally spilled over, now that I was sated and warm and reminded of how full life could be when spent in the company of someone I loved.

His fingers brushed at my cheeks and he held me tight until the fit passed like a summer storm. And then he tipped my head up to look at him. "You can tell me what's wrong, you know."

I shook my head, yet I spoke. "I think . . . it's time I put an end to my loneliness," I said in my misery, even as I was thinking that I would never get up the courage to go out to the desert or somewhere else where the sun would be inescapable.

"I agree," he said softly, and when I stiffened at that, he clucked his tongue. "I know we always talked past one another, but this is ridiculous." His tone sounded far from the angst-ridden one I expected. "Did I ever tell you why I made you?"

I shook my head, this time speechless.

"Because I could see even then that you were not made for the world of mortal men. Not in those days. It has taken all this time, a thousand years, for your sisters to finally catch up with you." He pressed a kiss, his lips still warm and supple, against my forehead. "And yet, none of them can match you."

My head was pillowed in the crook of his shoulder. "How many lovers have you had?"

"Thousands," he replied, his voice heavy. "And yet, none like you."

"Did you make others?"

"A few."

I was silent for a few moments. "Robert . . ."

"I know," he said. "And I know about your other swans. Robert helped me find you."

I bit my lip.

"He wants you to be happy, Melité."

"And you, what do you want, Arkadios?" I hadn't meant for it to come out so bitterly, but it was still so hard to believe that there was an end to this road other than bitterness and the evil that would come with it.

He hushed me with a gesture rather than arguing with me. Instead, he reached for something in the side table, and then turned back to me. He put a small velvet box into my hand.

I looked up at him.

"Swans are not the only creatures tamed by golden rings," he whispered, as I opened the box to reveal a pair of wedding rings.

"Oh, Arkadios . . ." I stared at the rings, then looked up to see the longing and apprehension in his eyes. He was afraid I would reject him. Robert's jokes about the engagement ring in Harrod's suddenly took on new meaning.

"Will you be mine forever?" I whispered, picking up the larger of the two rings.

"If you will be mine," he answered, taking up the other.

I answered that the only way that seemed appropriate: with a kiss.

Eight Maids a' Milking
by Jesse Blair Kensington

Last night, I dreamed of milk.

My most vivid dreams have always been about food.

Once, I had a dream about chocolate mousse swirling around my nipple. Another time, I dreamed Brad Pitt was spreading warm honey on my body. He lapped it off me until I awoke shivering in orgasm. I also once dreamed of spreading myself over a table of desserts while being fucked by a masked stranger.

In my dream of milk, first I become a ladle in a bathtub full of warm bubbly milk. Someone is using me for stirring. Then I am myself, a naked woman, and someone is pouring the milk over me. Her hands are beautiful, with clean, short nails, and long, distinctly feminine fingers. I struggle through the waterfall of milk to see her face, but as is the way of dreams, I can't at first.

She gently and slowly pours the white liquid over my breasts until my nipples become hard. She giggles—and I know who she is.

She is Arianna, one of the women I am here with for the three-day holiday baking retreat. The laughter spills out of her like a fountain. I love the sound of it.

In my dream, she reaches for one of my nipples and pulls it, twisting harder than I expect. I am flushed with excitement and embarrassment. A woman has never touched me like this before. I am strangely aroused and my body is so comforted by the frothy milk that I take pleasure in the stinging pain of her playful nipple teasing.

The next thing I know, she is in the bathtub with me. I see her face clearly now. Yes. She is Arianna, with long, dark hair, deep brown eyes, and lips shaped like a porcelain doll's, with a full, upturned mouth. So different than my blond, blue-eyed self. Her hair is now speckled with drops of white, thick milk and as she looks seductively at me, she kisses me, her tongue probing deeper and deeper into my mouth.

Tongue? No, wait, it's not a tongue, but a cock. It's hard and long and suddenly shooting its hot, salty offering into my mouth. As the shaft slides from my lips, I realize it is Sanj.

Sanj, the teacher, the baker extraordinaire, the man who insisted we milk the goddamned cows to use for our cream. I hated milking them, hated the smell of the animals, and afterwards my hands ached—all that squeezing and pulling.

But it had ultimately been worth it. I had never had milk straight from a cow, unpasteurized. In all my years of cooking and baking, this was delightfully new and raw, and I simply wanted more.

In my dream, I am still in the bathtub and Sanj lifts my chin gently after releasing himself from my mouth. Still in the milk, he wraps his brown body around my pale, freckled one. His skin glistens with the pearls of the white liquid. He whispers in my ear, something I understood in my dream, but couldn't remember when I later sat in class watching him stir the cream.

"You stop just when stiff peaks begin to form," he was

telling us. "Otherwise you will get butter." We are making pastry cream.

We were all intent on our own bowls of the smooth fluff. I glanced up and saw Arianna looking at me and felt embarrassed. There was something about the way she looked at me. Was she checking out my breasts? Christ, that dream was really messing with my head.

My eyes went back to the pastry cream. I stirred it gently and watched as the yellow mound became white, which is what I wanted. Sanj came up behind me.

"Nice rhythm you have there," he said.

I could feel his warm breath on the back of my neck, which made me involuntarily tingle. He reached over me to grab a towel and I was positive I felt his crotch brush my back.

"Thanks," I muttered.

"When you are finished, place plastic wrap tightly over the bowl and we will refrigerate it," Sanj said, his Indian accent present, but barely traceable.

He wasn't supposed to be here this weekend. We had all signed on for a weekend with Chef Ben DeFranco. But he had become sick just before and sent Sanj in his place. At first we were disappointed—then we got a look at him. Sarah had done some research on him. He was actually a doctor in India and baking was his passion. He was also a practitioner of tantric yoga—his family's heritage extended back more than a thousand years. They were members of this increasingly small sect in Northern India who still practiced the ancient art.

"Milk is sacred to the Hindu," Sanj announced. "In some parts of India, there is a belief that you must keep your cow happy because when you drink her milk, you are drinking her essence. Of course, you want to drink happiness."

"Lord Krishna is said to have appeared five thousand years ago as a cowherd, and is often described as *bala-gopala*, 'the child who protects the cows.' Another of Krishna's holy names, Govinda, means 'one who brings satisfaction to the cows.' Other scriptures identify the cow as the mother of all civilization, its milk nurturing the population."

"I can relate to that," Lydia said and laughed. Others joined in. Lydia had nursed three of her four children. One of them did not wean until she was three.

Sanj smiled and looked flustered. He went on as he helped Arianna with her stirring.

"Today, in heavily Hindu nations like India and Nepal, milk continues to hold a central place in religious rituals. And in honor of their exalted status, cows often roam free. Indeed, in some places, it is considered good luck to give one a snack, perhaps a bit of bread or fruit before breakfast. On the other hand, you can be sent to jail for injuring or killing a cow," he told us, which made us giggle.

Most of us grew up in the city and still lived there—Pittsburgh, to be exact. We had never seen a cow close up, let alone milked one. I, for one, did not care to do it again. Arianna was new to the group. Since high school, our baking circle got together every year to bake and exchange cookies for the holidays. There had been seven of us; now we were eight.

None of us was married—anymore. We'd seen each other through marriages, babies, divorces, and deaths. Now we were all single—whether widowed like myself, divorced, or just never married. We ranged in ages from our mid-thirties to late forties.

It was Lydia who'd entered us into the contest to travel to Vermont and spend the weekend baking with the chef. Usually, we made the same kind of cookies year after year.

Lydia made her poppy seed roll and I made poppy seed cakes. Janice made cherry squares; Karen made nut cups; Lucy made jelly rolls; Sarah, brownies; Marty, lady fingers; Jenna baked baklava; and Arianna made chocolate peanut butter balls last year, which was the first year she moved to Pittsburgh.

She was the youngest and certainly the most beautiful. If I told my shrink about my dream, I know what he'd say: "This does not suggest latent homosexuality. Arianna represents your younger self in your subconscious."

It was pretty bad when your relationship with your shrink was so close that you could fill in his sentences for him and diagnose yourself. But Dr. Jenkins had been a lifesaver for me when Dan died, and I wasn't about to change doctors.

Sanj was helping Sarah manage the plastic wrap and Lydia was cracking a joke. I was deep in the cream, looking at the swirls of it and remembering the way the milk felt in my dream—heavier than water, silky and smooth. I poked my finger in the white stuff and plunged it into my mouth.

"Annie," Sanj said and laughed. "You are breaking the rules."

But it was too late—my finger was in my mouth and I savored the sweet cream. "Sorry," I said and laughed.

"That Annie is a rebel," Karen commented.

"In oh so many ways," Jenna said and laughed.

"Hey, remember the time she danced topless on the bar?" Karen said.

"Okay guys," I said. "We don't need to go into my sordid past."

"Annie?" Sanj said. "I don't believe it."

They were mocking me. The truth was, of course, I was shy and mild-mannered— a typical accountant. I liked things to line up neatly in columns and rows, especially my life, but my life was not lining up so neatly. Dan wasn't supposed to die at thirty-eight. There was supposed to be time for children. I wasn't supposed to be alone at forty and I wasn't supposed to be unhappy in my career. It had always my dream to be a CPA. Yet here I was, and day after day I dreaded going to work. I had always fought the unpredictability and surprise of life, but somehow I was losing the battle.

"Okay," Sanj said, after we placed the pastry cream in the refrigerator. "While the cream is chilling, let's make the pastry."

As we mixed the pastry in our individual bowls, the room smelled of cold butter and flour.

"One of the tricks to good flaky pastry is to only touch the dough with your fingertips," Sanj said, reaching for my hand and guiding it over the dough. "Like Annie. Look at that, those beautiful fingers . . ."

I looked up at Sarah, who was right across the table from me. As our eyes met and she raised her brows, I felt the heat creeping up my face. Oh God. Was I blushing? Sarah, who still held my gaze, snickered.

I watched him poking at the fleshy dough and it returned me to my dream, reminded me of the way he folded back the lips of my vagina, the taste of his own cream still on my tongue. Those same brown fingers spreading me open. The image lingered in my mind as I watched him.

We placed our puffs of differing shapes in the oven. I wanted to make éclairs, and so did Lydia and Sarah. The others fashioned balls of dough for cream puffs. Jenna made beautiful little crescents.

"Snack time!" Jenna yelled but I didn't want a snack. I just wanted a drink of water and to sit down. I wandered into to the living room. A fire blazed in the fireplace and I could smell the scent of fresh pine from the Christmas tree in the corner. It was decorated in red ribbons and shiny balls and the fire shone in them. I was enjoying my solitary time with the tree and the fire when my friends started to trickle in with plates of fruit and bread and suddenly I was famished.

Sanj was still in the kitchen at the stove, stirring something that smelled of eggs, cinnamon, and nutmeg.

"Mmm," I said, piling grapes and brie onto my plate. "That smells heavenly." I walked up behind him and the intoxicating smell made me feel cozy, safe, and warm.

He turned to me and smiled. His smile was punctuated with deep dimples, one on each cheek. His eyes were deep and calm, oceans of tranquility.

"Annie," he breathed. I thought I saw a spark in his eyes. But it had been so long since I had even noticed another man, I wasn't sure.

"It's a treat for later. It needs to go in the fridge for a while. You call it boiled custard," he said.

"Boiled custard?"

"Yes," he said. I saw that he used a glass double boiler.

"My ex-mother-in-law made that every year for Christmas," I told him.

"Ex?" he said, turning back to the frothy mix.

"My husband passed away," I said.

"I am so sorry to hear that."

"It was five years ago. I guess I should be moving on," I said, something catching in my throat. I could not believe I was standing here at the stove with a total stranger, telling him this, holding back tears. It was the fucking custard. The smell of it seemed to grip me and hold me in place next to him, taking in his presence along with the memories flooding through me. It opened my wounds and laid them bare for him.

Sanj turned back to me. His eyes met mine and his free hand touched my cheek. He whispered something in another language. It made my heart race, though I had no idea what he'd just said.

"What?" I mumbled. "What did you say?"

"It's hard to translate, but it's something like: Such exquisite beauty trembles before such terrible pain. Let it go. Take my hand," he said, but it was still on my cheek, where it burned my skin. I felt as if I could drown in his eyes at that moment.

Sarah walked in and we jumped. "Oh geez, sorry," she said and promptly left the room.

Sanj, in his embarrassment, turned fully back to the stove. He lifted the cream-coated spoon. "Hand me that pitcher, please," he said to me as the women in the next room laughed.

"Your friends are laughing at us," he said as he poured the custard into the pitcher. He smiled.

I shrugged. Ripples of embarrassment shot through me. "I'm not worried about it."

"No." He placed the pitcher in the refrigerator, as the smell of baking pastry filled the room.

"Can I see you this evening?" he asked me after shutting the refrigerator door.

Me? I wanted to say. I must have been ten years older than this gorgeous hunk of a man. But something in me seemed to shed whatever concerns I had.

"You know, after dinner?" he said under his breath with a look of absolute hunger.

I was stunned, but found myself nodding my head yes.

When I walked back in the living room, the conversation abruptly stopped and all eyes were on me.

"Christ," I said, "what's wrong with you people?" I slipped down next to Arianna, who was drinking a glass of wine—her empty plate resting on her knees.

"What's going on?" Lydia asks. "Seems like he has the hots for you."

I shrugged. "I don't know."

"Annie," said Sarah and grinned. "I know what I saw. Sanj was touching you and looking at you with lust."

"Lust?" Arianna said. "Really?"

"Oh, she's embellishing. I was . . . we were talking . . . that's all," I told them. "Yes, his hand touched my face and yes, I'll never wash that side of my face again!" I tried to joke. There were a few nervous giggles, but nobody was biting. They knew me too well. Every one of them knew I had not been with a man since Dan had died. They knew I'd had one relationship and that I could not bring myself to have sex with him—which, of course, he very soon lost patience with. It was just too soon. He didn't want to hear it, so fuck him.

"Be careful," Arianna almost whispered to me.

"Yes, you know those tantric dudes—they do all kinds of funky shit with their dicks," Lydia said and we all laughed.

"Ladies!" Sanj called us back into the kitchen. He was pulling out the pastry. I grabbed a baking mitt and helped. The warmth from the oven was almost unbearable and I blinked several times against the heat.

The puffs were perfection, little brown balls all neatly aligned in a row. God, I don't know what I loved more, the perfect symmetry of my friends' creations or the delicious smell seductively rising from them. My éclairs turned out just right too, lightly browned and light as air. I marveled at them as they cooled on the rack. While we waited for our baked goods to cool, we filled our pastry bags with the cream. None of us had ever used one before and the process was a bit awkward.

The bag finally loaded, my pastry cooled, I gently squeezed the bulbous end and nestled the tip into a tiny hole in the éclair, watching as the cream began to ooze from the edges. By the tenth pastry, my hands were shaking slightly from the strength it took to force the creamy goo into the oblong pastry and the exhaustion of doing ten in a row. I realized it was time to reward myself with a lick of the thick custard, and so I edged my teeth over the end of a filled pastry and nibbled. I was almost sinfully delighted in my pastry—and nobody else seemed to notice.

Sanj appeared behind me. I felt him before I saw or even heard him. "Annie," he said. "Breaking the rules again?"

Startled, I jumped, smearing cream all over my face. I reached for a napkin. Lydia and Susan, nearest to me at that moment, both rolled their eyes and laughed.

"How could you not take a bite?" I said to defend myself. "It's such a temptation. I can't manage."

Sanj laughed. "You love food, don't you? Why are you an accountant? Why not a baker?"

In that moment, it was as if a veil had been lifted from my eyes. Why, indeed?

"She makes a lot of money," Sarah volunteered.

"Yes, but she could make money baking, as well. Have her own business," Sanj said.

"A new business is very risky," Sarah said to him.

"I like the idea," I announced suddenly. *What was I saying?* "I'm going to check into it."

I shot Sarah "the look," which I hoped would tell her to

mind her own business. The thought of having my own bake shop did somersaults and pirouettes in my mind. I held it there and played with it as I finished eating my éclair. I earned a good living and had substantial savings, had even paid the airfare for two of my less financially fortunate friends to be here. I loved being able to help them out. I couldn't deny that my salary would be difficult to leave behind . . . but happiness . . .

"Okay, ladies, we are finished for the day. See you at seven for dinner," Sanj said.

"What are you going to do?" Lydia was suddenly beside me. "We thought about going to this goat farm, checking it out."

"I need to have a shower and lie down," I told her.

"We aren't leaving for a while. We'll check in on you before we go," she said.

"Okay." I headed for my room.

Flour was everywhere—in my fingernails and hair, lightly dusting my eyelashes, even in my bra and panties. I slid them off and mindlessly tossed them in my laundry bag. Flecks of flour snowed down onto the brown, tiled floor. It was a mess. Type-A me would usually feel compelled to wipe it up, but not today. I felt lighter, unencumbered somehow.

A bakery—did I mean it? What would I name it? What kind of baked goods would I offer? What would my specialty be? Would they all line up perfectly on the display shelves? With every thought, I felt a sense of clarity and recognition. This was my dream all along—and I had not even known it.

I fell into my bed naked, parts of me flour speckled, like the first moments of a fresh fallen snow. My new self did not need a nightgown. I needed to be free. The cotton sheets felt so soothing on my skin and for a moment I wished I had brought my favorite vibrator with me. I rolled over onto my belly, spread my arms under the pillow, and closed my eyes.

A rapping at my door awakened me. How long had I been out? "Yes?" I said, slightly disoriented, thinking it must be Lydia gathering the ladies to go to the goat farm.

"Annie?" It was Sanj, his deep male voice and slight accent undeniable. My heart began to race. I was naked in my bed and a gorgeous hunk of a man stood no more than five feet away from me, with just a door between us. The old Annie would have remained silent, not responding, I mused.

I sat up in bed. "Yes," I replied, firmly—empowered.

"Would you like to come down for dinner?"

"Dinner?"

"Yes."

I glanced at my clock. It was seven. Where was everybody?

"Annie? Can I come in? I'm trying to talk to you through this door . . ."

"I'm in bed. I'm not dressed" is what I would have said if I were still the old Annie. But I was the new Annie, a naked baker surrounded by beautiful cotton sheets and a huge down comforter, lying on a brass bed made for at least two people. I took a deep breath. Butterflies crept into my stomach.

"Come in, Sanj." I sat up with the bedding pressed close to my chest.

"Are you okay?" He spoke into the dark room.

I flicked on the bedside table light. A glow spread across the room.

"Annie," Sanj said, his eyes meeting mine. "You are in bed."

"Yes, I guess I was more tired than I thought. Where is everybody?"

"They went to the goat farm. You were sleeping. They didn't want to wake you," he said.

"Shouldn't they be back soon?"

"They won't be. Since they left, we've gotten some snow." He walked to the window and pulled back the curtains. The lights from the building illuminated the winter wonderland beyond. There must have been two feet of snow on the ground.

I gasped.

He turned to look at me. "Annie, I must be honest with you," he said, walking toward the bed and sitting on the edge. 'I'm glad they are there and we are here. I've felt a pull toward you that I don't often feel. I am not like Ben."

I knew what he meant. I had read about Ben DeFranco's exploits with his students, as, I suspected, had a few of my overly optimistic girlfriends who had all too eagerly agreed to come to northern New England in December with me.

I reached for Sanj's face, which was a little rough by this point in the day, and leaned forward. His eyes glanced hungrily at my face and traveled to my covered beasts. The new Annie boldly let the covers fall away—and I watched the young man's face change as passion enveloped him. He pressed himself softly into me, and his mouth found mine, his tongue flicking against my own. His hands gently massaged my breasts, and my nipples became hard and alive.

I felt a hunger swell in me and pulled him closer, wrapped my legs around him firmly, and tore at his shirt until at last it was released from him, revealing a hairless, glistening brown chest with dark chocolate nipples. I ran my fingers over them, each one springing upward at my touch. His arms pressed me down—each one well muscled, the sinewy forearms on display. He lifted one arm first and then the next, guiding my fingers to his full lips and kissing them so gently, one at a time, it almost made me cry.

"Your hands," he breathed. "Your hands are so beautiful."

He ran his tongue along my wrist, slowly circled around the inside—a sigh escaped me. Such pleasure at my wrist—it astounded me as the need in me rose with my pulse. The moistness between my legs felt like a river of desire flowing from me.

Sanj pulled back and lay next to me. He looked at me. "*You* are beautiful. I . . . are you sure about this?"

I felt his cock hard against my hip pressing into me through his jeans. I knew he wanted me as much as I needed him.

"Are you sure you want . . . this?"

I place his hand between my legs. "Don't ask," I pleaded—no, *demanded*.

He audibly sucked in air as he felt my hot, wet slit. His baker's fingers, which expertly kneaded dough and braided intricate pastries, twirled and pressed my clit as his mouth found my nipples. I came hard and fast, bucking against his hand. Moans and cries of pleasure came from deep in my throat. I was so used to the cold, hard vibrator that I had forgotten what a warm, hungry hand could do for me.

"So ripe," Sanj said.

I reached for his cock, still in his pants. He grabbed for a condom, which was in his back pocket. His pants slid off, along with his boxers, and I gasped at the beauty of it—long, brown, and pulsing before me like a charmed cobra. I pressed the condom into the sheets next to me, ready to be used in a moment. I wanted him in my mouth first. I tongued the head of it and Sanj gasped, "Annie, oh . . ." I knew it would not be long as I took it in. I found my rhythm and sucked him until I felt his hot, salty bounty in the back of my throat.

I thought about what he'd said earlier about drinking

happiness and, I had to admit, I was happy. His hand at the back of my head—not forcing me to his throbbing member, but instead somehow holding onto me for comfort—quivered and shook as the post-orgasmic ecstasy washed over him, rendering him much like the mounds of dough we'd baked hours before. *How does this fit into his family's ancient tantric practice?* I wondered.

Sanj collapsed next to me. As he regained his senses, we tangled under the goose down comforter in a heap of sweat and stickiness and watched as the snow fell in big white fat flakes just beyond the window. I thought about Christmas, just around the corner, and the new year not far behind. I knew what the new year would hold for me and I was happy and content for the first time since Dan's passing.

"Your friends may be there all night." Sanj's words tore me away from my thoughts.

"That's fine with me," I whispered.

"Me too." He bent forward and kissed the nape of my neck. "Maybe they will get to milk the goats in the morning."

I smiled at the thought of my seven city-slicking girlfriends milking a bunch of stinky goats and reached for Sanj's cock, already beginning to rise again.

I had some milking of my own to do.

Nine Ladies Dancing

by Rhonda Leigh Jones

Grinning mischievously, Lisa brandished her makeup wheel at one of the Harper twins.

"Oh come on, Daniel. We can't just jump into a full dress rehearsal tomorrow night. At *least* let me put on your little red cheek circles."

The two ballet dancers stood in the theatre's large communal dressing room, which had tables and lighted mirrors on all four walls. Because it could be a madhouse when the entire company was there fighting for space and losing each other's applicators, Lisa had gotten there early and began pinning up her bright red hair. She hadn't known the Harper twins would be there early too.

Daniel lowered his head, but kept his eyes on her and grinned. He was the gentler of the two, the proverbial "good" twin, with soft brown eyes and hair that fell in golden ringlets. "You can put the whole *thing* on me if you want," he said. "Do you know how?"

Lisa nodded. At twenty-one, she was experiencing her first season as a professional ballet dancer, but this was definitely not her first *Nutcracker.* Since the age of ten, she'd had a fascination with stage makeup and had practiced on herself many times. She knew conservation was always the key to good stage makeup application.

"All right then," Daniel said. At twenty-eight, the Harper twins were veteran dancers and consummate professionals, when they weren't on the hunt for primitive pleasures. Lisa, of course, had heard a few stories from the older ballerinas, accompanied by whispers, giggles, and knowing glances, especially when she was around. But she was still innocent, and didn't know what men like this were capable of. Innocence was magical though, especially at Christmastime—especially during the *Nutcracker*—even though they weren't doing the "traditional" production.

The company was doing a darker piece based on the *Nutcracker* called *Jack and the Jester King*, about a young woman who receives a jack-in-the-box for Christmas. Upon discovering how lonely Jack is, she helps him return home to the Land of Harlequins. But the lecherous Jester King has his eye on her, and Jack has to fight for her hand.

The Harper twins, being the only men in the company at the time, were cast in the roles of Jack and the Jester King, with Daniel playing the part of the hero. Lisa, who'd had a crush on Daniel since joining the youth side of the company five years before, was thrilled to be dancing the part of Clara. It was exciting to come to rehearsals night after night and be manhandled by one brother, then rescued by the other.

Daniel, who had opted for an actual pair of tights tonight instead of sweats, pulled around one of the rolling chairs and sank into it, pressing the back against the dressing table so it wouldn't roll. He patted both of his muscular thighs with his hands. For a moment, Lisa forgot everything else, as her gaze followed the path of the beautiful, snaking veins up his arms. He had dancer's muscles, which meant his arms were larger and sexier than those of average slim guys, but they weren't too big. His shoulders were nicely rounded in the tank top he wore for rehearsal.

All of a sudden, Lisa felt extremely self-conscious.

"Losing your nerve?" he asked. He cocked his head at her and grinned.

She chuckled nervously and stepped to him, standing beside his chair and bending over his face. He looked up at her as she primly screwed the cap off of the white foundation. Daniel laughed and shook his head. "This isn't going to work," he said. "You're going to have to sit on me."

"*Sit* on you?" she exclaimed, trying not to let her eyes stray to the bulge in his tights. Ballet tights were so snug, there was always a bulge. You could practically tell whether a dancer shaved his balls with little more than a glance.

Daniel reached around and put his hand on her hip, guiding her against his leg. "Come on . . . be a good girl and hop on," he said. For a moment, she just looked at him with wide eyes. Even though Daniel was the "good" twin, he had quickly turned the tables on her little flirtation.

He waited patiently while she decided to do what he'd suggested, then let his arms fall to the side as he leaned his head back and closed his eyes. As she put the red circles on his cheeks, she felt grateful he had decided not to watch her, because her face had warmed so much she felt feverish.

Her friends, Paige and Sara, who had joined the professional side of the company when she had, would never let her live this down.

"It's funny that you're saving me from your brother in this production," she said when the circles were finished.

"Oh, really?" he asked, keeping his eyes closed. "Why is that?"

She shrugged. "I don't know. I just think the parts fit you."

He chuckled. "What if I didn't save you from him? What would you do then?"

Lisa thought it was a strange question. "You have to save me from him," she said. "It's in the script."

"Scripts can be changed." He wasn't smiling anymore.

Lisa furrowed her brow at him, wondering why he was teasing her like that. She swallowed, and shifted absently on him, accidentally pressing against his bulge. He gave a surprised groan. Lisa froze.

"I'm sorry," she said hurriedly. "Oh God—I didn't mean to do that." Mortified, she tried to stand. "I'd better start getting myself ready."

Daniel's hands moved more quickly than she would have anticipated. He held her hips firmly in place. "Nooo . . ." he said, drawing out the vowel. "You started this. You have to finish it. Besides, it's not like I minded."

He opened his eyes and smiled at her mischievously. She smiled back and began again to dab white paint on his forehead. This time, he watched her. She wondered if he could tell how turned on she was getting. It was all she could do not to rub herself against that bulge. The only thing that stopped her was that the thought embarrassed her too much, and the other dancers would be coming in soon.

Oh God, the other dancers! She couldn't let them see her like this. There were eight other women in this production—Paige and Sara, plus six other girls all in their twenties. Paige and Sara were the very ones she could trust to never let her live this down. She grabbed the makeup wheel and swiped her finger over the red. When she tried to apply it to Daniel's lips, he stuck out his tongue.

"Daniel," she scolded. "Come on. Everyone will be here soon."

"All right. I'll stop. Have your way with my lips." He grinned.

She slapped him lightly on the arm.

"I'd put you over my knee for that," said a male voice from the doorway.

Before she could turn around, Keith was behind her, leaning into her space, fitting his chin into the notch of her shoulder, almost pressing his face against hers. "If you do my brother," he said, "you have to do me."

Keith's voice had a harder edge than Daniel's. While Daniel softened his words by stroking the vowels, Keith hit the consonants hard and startlingly.

Lisa swallowed. She was glad when he moved away, but only because his presence made her body do things she couldn't control. It was more than just being turned on. She was a little afraid of him, and that made her want to fall down at his feet and beg him to do things to her. Things she didn't necessarily like. Beg him to take her to places she didn't necessarily want to go.

"I'm not *doing* you, Keith," she said when he pulled away. He looked at her from the corner of his eye and smirked. He kept his hair a little shorter than his brother's, in a layered, less boyish cut that still stuck out in some places with curls. Sometimes he even slicked it back.

"Of course you are," he said, making his voice coarse and harsh. "You just don't know it yet."

He had worn tights too—black to his brother's light grey—with a purple wife-beater.

Lisa swallowed. "What did he mean by that?" she whispered, looking away when Keith glanced at her and let the corner of his mouth twitch up with a hint of a self-satisfied little smile.

Daniel smiled warmly. "Don't worry about him. My eyes need their blue diamonds."

It wasn't long before the girls started fluttering in. Lisa was happy to see her blond and brunette best friends, Paige and Sara. Lisa was a redhead and the twins always teased them about being a "hot set," but Lisa had mostly ignored what the twins said.

Tonight, however, something felt different. For one thing, a worried scowl made Paige's forehead pucker.

"Milton isn't coming," she said, trotting over to Lisa for hugs.

"Why?" one of the other girls asked.

"Dog's sick. You know how he is about his 'widdle Foofie.'"

"What?" Lisa asked, nearing panic. "He can't just abandon us so close to opening night."

"It's no problem," Keith said. "We'll direct us. Won't we, Danny boy?" He had decided to wear his makeup too, and had most of the black eye-diamonds on. When he was finished, he'd have black lips as well, and white foundation.

He smacked his brother on the shoulder, smudging him with greasepaint. When Daniel looked up, Keith winked. Daniel turned back to the mirror, smiling to himself.

Something about the exchange made Lisa just a little uneasy.

When it was time for the eleven dancers to file out onto the stage, Daniel set up the music player near the back curtain while Keith walked around. "If I remember correctly, we were on the first Land of the Harlequins scene," he said.

Something about seeing him made up as the lecherous harlequin made Lisa shiver. She forgot to look away and wound up staring at him as he came near. He came so close, she could feel the heat radiating from his body. He kept his eyes on her as he passed.

Too late, she looked away.

"All right, everybody, listen up!" he said, his voice more commanding than Lisa had ever heard it before. "We're going to try a little something new. You know how Milton is all about playing it by ear when we're doing more modern routines? Well, I want us to do that tonight. No matter what happens, I don't want anyone breaking character. *No matter what happens.* Everybody got that?"

The older ballerinas started up with the knowing glances and giggles again. A few of them looked at Lisa, or her friends. Something weird was definitely going on, and she didn't appreciate being kept in the dark.

"Exactly how are you in charge here?" she asked Keith.

Paige nodded in agreement. Sara looked at her with wide eyes, her face framed by dark wisps of hair that had escaped her pins. The other ballerinas tittered even more.

Keith turned to her. There was something dangerous in his face, under the makeup. "We can talk about it in the back room if you want. Either way, rehearsal is going to happen tonight. If Milton walks through that door, he can have it. But until he does, *I'm* directing."

Lisa put her hands on her hips. "Talk in the back room? What does *that* mean?"

The dancers grew quiet, and watched her and Keith intently.

Daniel swept in and steered her away. "You don't really want to know."

"Why not?" she asked, forgetting to be thrilled that his body was touching hers.

"If you really want to know, I'll tell you later, but do what he says right now, okay?"

She pulled back to get a better look at him, studying his face to see if he was serious. He sure looked serious to her.

Keith turned back to the dancers. "We're going to start from Jack's and Clara's arrival in the harlequins' realm. He's happy to be home, she's in awe of the beauty, blah, blah, blah." He fluttered his hand in the air and turned to the newcomers. "Paige and Sara, of course, are her Soul and her Heart, so they're close by. As the little magical fairy creatures, the rest of you dance happily around them, and that's when I, the Jester King, notice her," he said, opening his eyes wide and placing his hand flat on his chest.

After the explanation, he took long strides to his place at the back of the stage, the dancer's muscles in his thighs bulging with every step. Clapping his hands twice, he called, "Let's do it!"

Lisa stared at him incredulously even as his brother, the official object of her crush, had his arm around her. She felt even more incredulous about the growing warmth between her legs than she did about Keith's arrogance. Trying not to think about it, she pulled away from Daniel and took her place near Paige and Sara. Daniel joined them. Keith turned on the music. Everyone waited.

To the piece that in a traditional *Nutcracker* would have been "The Dance of the Sugar Plum Fairy", Lisa adopted an expression of wonder and minced around the stage, pretending to look at this or that, while Daniel followed her with his face open in an exaggerated smile. As Jack, he got her attention from time to time, and spun her against him before something else caught her eye. It became a game between their characters, with Clara fleeing and Jack pursuing, each embrace becoming more intense and lasting longer.

In those moments, Lisa summoned her artistic professionalism to enable her to push her excitement aside and concentrate on getting into her character, while at the same time drawing from that excitement to make Clara's feelings for Jack real.

As her Heart and Soul, Paige and Sara followed her as though carrying an invisible train, making exaggerated movements of bliss, while the six magical fairy-creatures fluttered around them in a wide circle.

The rehearsal was odd, but beautiful. Lisa spun at the sound of the music and Daniel pulled her tightly against him, pressed his warm cheek against her ear and swayed them. The music softened, then darkened. Minor chords crept from the player, and Keith, the Jester King, turned around, mesmerized Lisa's character, and danced with her while Daniel's Jack stood by in anguish. Paige and Sara moved around him sympathetically, running their hands over his shoulders and giving him sad looks.

Keith's character handled Lisa's roughly. He spun her forcefully, holding her too tightly and too long, then let her escape before chasing her down again, a dark and twisted parody of her dance with Daniel, a human game of cat and mouse. Her favorite part was coming—the part where Jack would gather his courage and confront the Jester King, who would spin Clara away to be caught by Heart and Soul before clashing with her beloved. She had always found the fight between the two men, with all the leaping and posturing, almost unbearably animalistic and sexy.

Daniel approached with aggressive, sweeping motions

and Lisa tensed for the spin. Keith found her hand, but instead of flinging her from him, he pulled her tight. Daniel started to circle the other man, but stopped instead, and met his gaze. Even through her confusion, Lisa was struck by how gracefully he moved, and by the power of the unspoken communication that passed between the two brothers.

She knew it was about her.

"What's going . . . hey!" she heard Paige say, and saw her come to a full stop.

Keith's head snapped in her direction. "Don't break character!" he ordered. His head snapped back and Lisa felt the Jester King breathing against her shoulders and hardening against the small of her back. When she trembled, he squeezed her. Daniel looked down at her with an expression that was both kind and smoky, but somehow she knew he wasn't going to save her from his brother as he had during every other rehearsal. There was something almost apologetic in his eyes.

While the music boomed darkly on the stage, Paige trotted over toward Daniel, with Sara following close behind. "What are you *doing*? We don't have time for . . ."

Grinning mischievously, Daniel backed away and began dancing around Paige and Sara, while Keith continued to hold Lisa captive. Sara moved closer to Paige to escape him.

"Daniel . . . what are you *doing*?" Paige demanded.

Refusing to speak, he danced closer, herding the girls toward his brother, while Keith lowered his head and breathed in the scent of fear mixed with excitement from the side of Lisa's neck. She looked around at the others. The older girls now stood around watching, smiling and pointing as the brothers took control of the three newcomers.

"This is bullshit," Paige declared and turned to stalk away.

Daniel placed his body in front of hers. "Move!" she growled at him. He responded by running his gaze over her body, grinning and taking her head in his hands, and then kissing her while Lisa watched. Lisa's heart pounded even harder, partly from the horror of seeing her crush kiss one of her best friends, and partly because he was holding her captive—as though the story of *Jack and the Jester King* had actually come to life.

Paige pushed at Daniel's biceps. He responded by sliding an arm around her and grasping her rear, pulling her against him until she responded. Her surrender was palpable. She stopped pushing against him, and started moving in time with his swaying.

Sara stood by helplessly for a moment, then shot Lisa a questioning glance. Lisa couldn't do anything more than return the look while Keith's hand moved up, grazing its graceful fingers over her arm.

Daniel pulled away from his kiss with Paige, and turned her to face his brother, hooking an arm around her waist and extending his free hand to Sara, who widened her eyes at him before glancing back at Lisa.

But by that time, Keith's hand had made it up to Lisa's shoulder. He hooked his thumb into the thin fabric of her unitard and tugged. Brought back to reality, she tried to pull away, but he tightened his other arm around her. "Shh-shh-shh," he said, and bared her flesh.

Sara backed away, but by that time the older women had moved closer and clustered around her, herding her back toward the brothers. Lisa heard whispers of, "You're the lucky one," and "Don't worry. You'll like it," as they handed her friend over to Daniel, who no longer seemed as shy and innocent as he had earlier, but was still much less frightening than his brother by a long shot.

Lisa's stomach grew hot as she was fully confronted by the knowledge of who held her captive and who was pulling her clothing off her shoulders. "No," she gasped, wanting so badly to mean it.

"Yes," Keith whispered back. His hot breath seemed to scorch her ear. Her trembling had become uncontrollable. Now he would know just how afraid of him she actually was, that her brattiness was nothing more than a brave front, a protective shield.

The thin fabric moved down slowly, releasing her breasts. She moaned with the knowledge that she was no longer in control of her own body. Whatever happened here tonight, it would be at the whim of Keith and Daniel Harper. For tonight, she *was* Clara, only her Jack was complicit with the lecherous Jester King in her capture and ravishment.

Daniel watched her. There was something unsettling about seeing such a smoky look in his clown-doll face, and about the eyes of the older girls being on her and her friends. She felt like some kind of offering, and she was much more aroused than she thought she ought to be. All at once, it was too much. She pushed away from Keith, stumbling a little out of surprise that he let her go, and held her arms over her bare breasts.

Daniel let Paige come after her. The older girls came closer, surrounding the five of them, circling the group without touching, clustering whenever one of the three tried to make a break for it. Inside the circle, the men began to stalk the three girls. Still trying to hide her breasts, Lisa pressed against her friends, watching Keith with undisguised trepidation. In spite of the purple wife-beater and tights, the makeup made him look like a frightening apparition. It reminded her of *The Crow*. She watched him pass to her left; watched as his focus switched from her to Sara, who cringed back against her. Movement beside her startled her. It was Daniel. She looked up at him, unsure what was going to happen.

"What's going on?" she whispered.

Daniel gave her a half-smile. "Claiming. Now, no more talking," he said and placed a finger against his lips.

Lisa turned her body to the right so she could see how Paige was handling all this. Her expression was not the same as it had been before Daniel had kissed her. Her eyes were wide, but she didn't look as though she wanted to get away. If Paige felt fear, it looked as though she welcomed it.

That's how I feel, Lisa thought.

Someone was trembling, but she couldn't tell whether it was her, one of her friends, or all three of them.

When Keith returned to her, he stopped and looked down at her for a moment. With a smirk, he reached out to tug down her clothes and didn't stop until they were in a wad at her ankles.

Beside her, Sara whimpered. "Shh . . ." Daniel cooed, slipping her clothing over her shoulders as Keith had done with her.

"Hey," Keith murmured. "Over here."

Lisa looked at him obediently. She knew her eyes were green pools of fear and desire, but she let him see. He rocked back on his heels, nodded to himself, and grabbed her.

She felt herself fall and clutched at his arms, but he already had her, taking her to the floor, straddling her. God, he was beautiful. She trembled beneath him. She didn't understand what exactly was happening, how the twins were managing to control it, but she knew beyond a shadow of a doubt that she was going to be fucked.

Just a few feet away, Daniel was on top of Sara the same way, brushing her hair out of her face and planting little kisses on her cheeks and lips. The older women pressed in on them. They had Paige, who watched curiously as several sets of hands undressed her.

Keith guided Lisa's face back to him. "No," he said sternly. "Your attention belongs right here."

She studied his face, wondering what he was going to do next. He narrowed his eyes and flared his nostrils at her, then lowered his head to cover her mouth roughly with his. It was almost too much. She had never felt comfortable under his gaze and now he was holding her down to kiss her.

He pulled away abruptly and gave her a self-satisfied look, turning his head slightly to the side. "I've wanted you for a long time," he breathed. "But you . . . you always wanted my brother. Is it because he felt like the safe one? He's not, you know. He's just like me, only he's nicer about it. And tonight, he's going to fuck you just like I am. And your little friends too."

The certainty in his tone sent hot bolts through her stomach. "I . . . but . . ." was all she managed to utter.

He snickered and wound his hand in her hair.

"We're on stage," she was finally able to say. "What if someone sees us?"

"No one has a key except for staff."

"What if *they* see us?"

"Then they see us." He tightened his grip on her hair and lowered his lips to her neck as he pressed his tights-covered groin against her naked one, making her whimper. She was so wet for him she could hardly stand it. She could hear Sara moaning under Daniel, but Keith kept his fingers in her hair and wouldn't let her turn her head to see what was going on. She heard movement behind her, where Paige was, but she didn't know what was happening.

Paige grew quiet amid the cooing of the older girls, but Sara's moaning grew louder. Lisa wanted to know what Daniel was doing to her friend, and what her friend was doing with Daniel. She began to squirm in Keith's grasp, fighting against his weight and the pull of her hair.

Finally, he stopped and followed her gaze, then looked down at her. "You want to see what's going on?" he asked. "Fine."

Keith took his weight off of Lisa and roughly flipped her over on her stomach. She raised up on her elbows and looked around. To her left, Paige had her eyes closed in bliss as a few of the older girls tweaked and caressed her nude body. They had unfastened her long blond hair, and at least three of them had their hands in it. To Lisa's right, Daniel had his tights down and was sliding in and out of Sara slowly, while she moaned beneath him and watched him with large eyes. He didn't even look at Lisa.

A bright green condom wrapper lay near them like a piece of discarded confetti. It had no sooner dawned on her what she was looking at than she heard that telltale tearing sound behind her and the sharp smell of latex was in her nostrils, bringing back her earlier panic. Before she could react, however, Keith's weight was on her, pressing her stomach against the cold hardwood stage. He groaned long and loud as he slid the length of his erection easily into her slick opening, then settled his chest along her back and his mouth close to her ear.

"He doesn't want you," he whispered. "Not the way you want him to."

"What do you mean?" Lisa gasped, stinging from the words.

"He's not going to be your one and only boyfriend," he said, rocking his hips against her bottom. "We decided we wanted the three of you as a set, for the both of us. And we always get what we want."

Lisa's brain reeled with the information, but he thrust into her so hard she couldn't speak. "Oh my God," she finally managed to say as he filled her and pressed against her walls, forcing intense pleasure-pain into her body. Owning her.

"You," he said, nipping the back of her neck, "are so . . . mine . . ."

She surrendered as he fucked her, as he made her gasp and claw at the hard floor. The hot pressure in her gut became almost unbearable as her clit rubbed against the stage, spreading heat between her legs and exploding, making her helpless in the throes of ecstasy. She hadn't even realized she'd closed her eyes until she opened them again and saw Daniel looking at her intently through his clown makeup.

He pulled himself off Sara, who lay there with her eyes closed, snaking a hand between her legs. Daniel pulled off his used condom and handed it to one of the older girls, who made a show of taking it gingerly as he gave her a smack on the bottom. Then he kicked off his tights, pulled off his tank, and came over. His erection was huge and glistened with his own juices.

Keith pulled out and also undressed, meeting his brother's eyes as he walked over and accepted Paige as a gift from the older girls. He put his hand gently against Paige's cheek and brushed his lips against hers. Paige watched him, breathing heavily. Then he pulled away and pointed to the ground. She looked at him questioningly for a moment, then obeyed him, lying on the stage and opening herself. He gave her a lascivious smirk as he put on a fresh condom, stroking himself as he did so, and then he was on her, pounding into her in animal frenzy, making her arch and writhe.

Daniel straddled Lisa on his knees and flipped her over unceremoniously. Though the expression was softer than his brother's, there was still no mistaking the look of ownership in his eyes. It was a look she would have given anything to see just a few hours ago, a look she would have found sweet and romantic. Now it scared her, and forced painful shards of desire through her body. He wasted no time preparing himself and mounted her, shoving his cock in to the hilt, fucking her hard.

Daniel was the one who made her climax first, pounding into her, watching her reactions as he worked his hips. She threw back her head and gasped open-mouthed as though fighting for air. Grinning, he let himself come. She shut her eyes and rode the pleasure for a long time, listening to the grunting of her friends, and the cooing of the ballerinas as they began to make out with each other.

Eventually, she felt someone mount her again. It was Keith. He pressed his lips together and shoved his cock inside her, holding her wrists to the floor and fucking her furiously.

"Tell me you're mine," he said. There was a hard edge to his voice.

Lisa focused her eyes and looked at him.

"Tell me," he said through gritted teeth, pushing his cock into her hard, making her furrow her brow and groan.

"I'm yours," she whispered, and meant it.

He came with a satisfied smirk.

Late that night, they all returned to the dressing room as though from any other night's exertion onstage. No one said much while changing into street clothes. Lisa, Paige, and Sara gave each other questioning looks while the guys removed their makeup. The ballerinas left more quickly than usual. When Lisa and her friends tried to follow, Keith stopped what he was doing.

"And just where do you think you three are going?" His tone was teasing, but Lisa realized the intent was serious.

"Home?" Sara said.

"Nope," Keith replied, and went back to cleaning his face. "You're coming home with us tonight. Now that you belong to my brother and me, we want to fill you in on a few rules."

"I don't get it," Lisa said, her pulse hammering all over again.

"Oh, you will," Keith replied, smirking at Daniel, who smiled back. "You will."

Ten Lords a' Leaping

by Debra Hyde

What it is, I don't know, but once the presents get opened, everything about Christmas dulls. The lights on the tree seem to twinkle less, the empty space under the tree looks drab, even the eggnog loses its robust flavor. Maybe it's post-holiday letdown, but the day after Christmas, I'm one dull dude. I doubt that even a hot, naked Santa with a hard-on could perk me up.

This year was no exception. Even the freshly fallen snow seemed dingy this time around.

"I hate it when Christmas ends," I complained, staring out the window. "The days are short and cold and the nights long and dark."

"So much for merry and bright." Michael, my ever-mirthful lover, pointed out the obvious. His eyes narrowed. He was good at scrutiny, too. "It's the monotony of winter . . . and the monogamy."

The monotony of monogamy? "Since when?" I asked.

"The Christmas party at Chuck's, Eric. You've been testy and agitated ever since, and you and I both know why."

How could Michael say such a thing? I loved him. He was mercurial and fun, full of energy and enthusiasm, and never one to turn down a hot fuck from me. I could never tire of him.

One step ahead of me, he knew exactly what I was thinking. "I know you love me, bonehead. But enough with the denial."

"But—"

"But nothing. You could fuck me three ways to midnight every day until Lent and you'd still be restless. And it's time I did something about it."

I must've looked a bonehead at that point, stunned and speechless as I was. What did Michael mean? And what did monogamy have to do with it?

"I told people about this funk of yours and it turns out they're eager to relieve you of it."

"What?" I scoffed. "Visits from the ghosts of Christmas past?"

"More like the Twelve Days of Christmas. Except I can only afford one."

"Which one?" Michael grinned wickedly.

"Ten lords a' leaping."

Something leaped, all right. My cock. Maybe he was right; maybe I did need some variety. One thing was for sure: Michael was the gift that kept on giving. But still I was skeptical—we were going to throw away monogamy just like that? How would he feel? How would I feel? But still . . .

"So how's this going to work?"

Michael eagerly spilled the details. "Over the next twelve days, you will be reunited with a fuck buddy from your past. Maybe it'll be one guy, maybe you'll get tag-teamed. Anything goes—cocksucking, fucking, a little bondage and even discipline, maybe. You name it, you get to do it. The only proviso: latex barriers."

I was stunned and speechless. Then again, it's hard to talk with your jaw on the floor. Michael laughed, amused to see me so flabbergasted, and when I tried to respond, he waved me off.

"No complaints, Eric. And . . . no turning back. I've already made all the arrangements and these boys can't wait to get their hands on you. You game?"

The twinkle in Michael's eyes was irresistible, and I surrendered to it like a schoolgirl who finally got a smile from the local heartthrob. Game? You bet. I could hardly wait. That night, it took me forever to get to sleep, and when I finally did, it wasn't sugar plum fairies that danced in my head.

I was a bit agitated that Michael didn't rush his grand scheme into action. What a cock tease. Two days went by before I saw the first sign of his devious plan. I emerged from the shower to find a uniform laid out on our bed. Dark pants and a blazer, its handkerchief pocket emblazoned with a coat of arms I didn't recognize, a dress shirt and necktie, dark shoes and socks, and a tiny note that said only "Wear Me" attached to the collar all awaited me.

I didn't understand the nature of the suit until I stepped in front of the mirror to adjust the tie. I looked like a prep school boy.

Evidently, role play awaited me as well.

Michael approached me from behind, winding his arms under the blazer until his hands rested on my pecs. A gentle kiss on the back of my neck.

"God, you look hot."

I felt his hard cock pressed against my backside.

Michael murmured the compliment in my ear, his nose

nuzzling my hair. I wanted him right then and there, but he slapped my ass with a "Come on—can't be tardy!" and hurried me along.

My lover behind the wheel, we drove twenty minutes into the country—prep school country, that is. As we passed ominous iron gates and stately, brick dormitories, I knew which one we were heading to: The Norwich, home to many trust fund babies and scions. Which meant only one thing.

"Jack," I said.

Michael nodded.

Jack, onetime fuck buddy, taught at the prestigious academy. It didn't surprise me that Michael had put him first in line. Jack had, after all, played matchmaker between us. After he'd had his fill of both of us, that is.

Michael parked outside an old brownstone. We both stepped out of the car as he tossed me a backpack and a warning. "Don't be late."

The backpack felt weighted with books. Damn, he had thought of everything.

"Get going. Room 106."

I found the room without much trouble, but my stomach was filled with anticipation. I hadn't seen Jack in months, not since he'd taken a sabbatical and skipped town for a while. But when I entered the room, Jack was nowhere to be seen. In his place stood two "boys," men like me: Jack's boys. I remembered them from one of the holiday parties we'd attended. Uniformed and a good decade younger than I was, they seemed ready for some good old-fashioned schooling—but not without a little mischief first.

"You Eric?" one of them asked.

I nodded.

"We heard about you," the other shot. He was burly and sounded like trouble waiting to happen.

"Teacher's pet," the first one countered.

Correction: They were both looking for trouble. Burly slipped his cock through his school uniform zipper and began it. Like him, it was stout and thick—and hard in an instant. The other guy, Slim, laughed and followed suit, but upon unzipping, he lit up with an idea. "Hey, let's play a game!"

"What?" Burly asked.

Slim dug through his backpack, brought out a sandwich bag of graham crackers, and handed one to each of us.

"Let's see who can shoot their wad first onto a cracker!"

"You pervert," Burly hurled.

"That's right," Slim demurred. He took it as a compliment. "Come on, Eric. You game?"

That was twice I'd heard that question. Twice someone had enticed me with it. Who was I to refuse such kismet?

A good old-fashioned schoolboy circle jerk ensued. The three of us whacked off like madmen, fed off of a hunger for each other. The sounds of fists pumping our cocks, male groans and gasps, sweat filling the air, all drove us onward.

Then Burly teased me. "Eric the erect," he tossed off. "Man, would I like to drive it up your ass."

That's all it took. I came, gasping and sputtering. Jism shot from my cock, and it felt like a geyser, it was so intense. Somehow, I managed to hit the cracker. Euphoric, drifting in pleasure, I squeezed every drop from my cock.

Suddenly, the door crashed shut. The whole room reverberated. Books slammed against the desktop. A voice boomed.

"What the hell's going on in here?"

Jack, of course, and he was none too happy. He stood behind the desk, peering at us over his glasses.

"Three mischief-makers, I see."

His eyes bore into me.

"And one who's made more mischief than the rest." He leered. "Come up here, Master Eric."

I approached. He pointed to one end of the desk.

"Drop your drawers. Hands on the desk."

I assumed the position; he assessed it.

"Feet away from the desk. Legs apart. Stick your ass out."

Jack's orders rippled with confident authority, the kind that came with knowing no one in his right mind would dare question him.

"Young Master Stephen, why don't you get your mouth around that shriveled-up cock of his?"

Stephen, aka Slim, situated himself beneath me and sucked away. Still sensitive from my orgasm only moments before, I gasped at the feel of his mouth around me.

Jack stepped behind me. I felt his eyes staring hungrily at my ass. Was he going to take me? The thought made me ache with anticipation.

"Young Master Franklin, fetch me my paddle."

The order sent a shudder through me. My ass clenched; my cock lurched. A giggle tickled my cock—Stephen chuckling at my reaction.

Taking the paddle from his pupil, he placed a hand on my back to steady me and rested the paddle momentarily on my ass. "It's one thing to come into my classroom and find students up to no good," he began. "But when one of those students has his no-good all over a cracker? Well, that makes him the whipping boy."

The hardwood of maple wasn't my hard wood of choice,

and experience had taught me to dread its first strike. But Jack's dominance thrilled me and, as curious as the proverbial cat, I wanted to see where he would take me.

I felt another giggle between my legs as the paddle pulled away, swung, and met my sensitive cheeks with a deafening *thwack!* Its sting was every bit as fierce as I remembered, driving deep into my flesh and forcing my cock deeper into Master Stephen's mouth. His moan of delight mingled with my own moan of endurance. My cock swelled, ready for action.

The second blow came as soon as I had relaxed, sending another wave of pain into my flesh. Master Stephen wrapped his arms around my thighs, eager to swallow as much of me as possible. With the third strike, the pain melted away. Ecstasy. I had reached its threshold. On the fourth strike, I crossed it and entered into lust-soaked bliss.

I lost count of the swats after that. My only awareness rested in the mouth around my cock and a blazing desire for a blistered ass. Jack kept at me, pacing every move to keep me hanging in the limbo of bliss. He barked at me to fuck the face beneath me, then bellowed me to a halt when I neared orgasm. He commanded me to beg for cock—anyone's cock; yes, I'd take any cock, as many as he wanted—then laughed as he denied me. All the while, the paddle rained blow after blow upon the now-burning skin of my ass.

I squirmed in the delights of this agony, never certain I could take more, never sure I wanted it to end. But end it did, with a blow so mighty that it forced tears into my eyes.

Jack laughed as he stepped away, fully aware of where that last blow took me.

"Master Franklin, why don't you sheath up and punish this naughty boy's ass from the inside?"

I shuddered at the request. Jack's verbal blows took me places, too, it seemed. I glanced over at burly Frank. His leer told me said he'd been sitting there, stroking his rock-hard dick, just waiting for Jack's order. He placed the edge of a condom between his teeth and tore the wrapping open as he ripped it out of his mouth, never letting go of the weapon he'd primed between his legs. He spit the foil onto the floor, rolled the condom and squirted lube onto it without letting go. By the time Frank swaggered up to me, I wanted his cock with every fiber of my soul.

God, he was one hot bully. He could beat me up and steal my lunch money any day.

The tip of his cock stirred a moan from deep inside of me as it pressed its way into my tight outer ring. That moan escalated into a wailing cry as Franklin grabbed my red-hot ass with both hands. Pain came to life, bellowing against this intrusion like a sleeping dog provoked. But I loved it. I took every screaming inch of the dick and let it fuck me. I relished the sharp dig of fingernails in my searing flesh. I loved it all.

Jack watched our three-way, pleased with the work of wanton beauty he had orchestrated. Sensing his satisfaction, I wanted to give him a good show. I fucked Master Stephen's mouth, eager to unload myself; I pushed against Master Franklin's cock, urging him to rough me up and drive farther and deeper into me. I moaned and writhed, ripe for climax. And I wanted to give it all to Jack.

But Jack, without once breaking his stern gaze, picked up my jizz-soaked cracker, shoved it into my mouth, and turned his back on me. He left, abandoning me just as the pinnacle approached. Stunned, I wanted to call after him, but my mouth was filled with the spoils of my first orgasm. Master Stephen grabbed my balls. Master Franklin spread my ass cheeks wide. Overwhelmed, I came. Ecstasy spilled out of me in clenching spurts.

My climax started a chain reaction. Frank shoved his dick deep into me and bucked his way through orgasm, grunting with every thrust. Come splattered my legs—Master Stephen. He must've been jerking off the entire time.

And Jack missed every bit of it. I swallowed the cracker.

Afterwards, I sat outside on the steps, my backpack nestled between my legs, waiting for Michael. Jack didn't *need* my orgasm to validate his dominance, I realized. He probably got off more by leaving me dangling one last time. It made for a hot scene, but it left me aching. I needed soothing. I needed Michael.

With nothing more to do than wait, I opened the backpack and peeked inside. Books—paperbacks. I pulled them out one at a time to discover Michael had weighed it down with all kinds of schoolboy pornography. *Frat House Studs. Plebes and Paddles. Prep School Perverts. Professor Nutbuster.*

Jeez, Michael had thought of everything. When he pulled up, I climbed into the car, onto him, and covered him in grateful kisses.

Mornings later, I woke, Michael next me, angelic in slumber. Flat on his stomach, he slept with his arms crooked under his pillow, his head towards me. A beauty, his hair was cropped too short to greet me with sexy bed hair, but he always rose perfectly sculpted in lean, sinewy proportions. I drew a finger along his bicep, tracing its contours, swelling with love.

Michael flickered awake at my touch, a deep breath bringing him to life. He stretched in place and smiled.

"Morning," he whispered.

Overwhelmed with love, I said nothing. I gathered him into my arms, drew his body against mine, and kissed him. His lips met mine, soft and cushioned, his tongue following mine, following my lead like a perfect partner dancing. I caressed my way down his back to his ass and pulled his pelvis hard against mine. Our cocks mingled, things aroused by love but not yet hard with lust.

My hand on his ass, I ground my hips against Michael, my cock beckoning his. Love made me want him. But Michael broke our kiss and pulled back, his back arched and inviting. I trailed kisses down his neck and onto his chest, aiming to reach one of his taut, tiny nipples.

"No," Michael interrupted, his hands pushing me away.

"No? Oh, come on, baby," I pleaded. He was too gorgeous to let go of.

"You've got to save it."

"Save what."

Michael pointed to my throbbing cock. "That."

I stared at him in disbelief, ready to protest.

But he shook his head and claimed, "Three down, seven to go." Again, that wicked smile from days ago appeared. "Hope you have the stamina for it."

Slapping my ass, he rolled out of bed and bounced away into the bathroom, shutting the door behind him. I groaned, painfully thwarted, but when I heard the shower start, I followed, hoping I could catch him lathering up.

Except the door was locked. No way around it. I wasn't going to get any, that he'd made sure of. My cock, valiant just moments before, wilted in sorry rejection. I stood at the door, hang-dog dejected and pitiful, waiting for Michael and his promise of what was to come.

*

Michael pulled up outside of the Meathook, our lone leather club, well before the bar's official hours of business. Mystified, I opened my mouth to question, but he stopped me. "Private rental." My perplexity thawed into adoration. Like I said, Michael was the gift that kept on giving.

Inside, he ordered me to strip and stash my clothes in a locker. Naked except for my boots, I was about to ask "what now?" when someone stepped up from behind and wrestled me into a rough embrace. A Spandex hood slipped over my head, its ply thick enough that I saw nothing. My captor stepped back.

"Welcome back, boy." The voice was muffled, but I recognized its gruff, scratchy tenor: Aidan, the only man whom I had ever called Master. Astonished, I reached out, eager to touch him. My hand landed on his chest and was met with a pleasant chuckle.

"Glad to see you, too, boy. It's been a long time. But certain matters need attending."

A collar encircled my neck. A leash clicked into place. I shivered, staggered to return at last to Adian's hand, and I followed the tug of the leash as if born to it.

Voices met us in the large area that constituted the club's play space. Vaguely, I recognized them.

"Let's get this open," Aidan called. "I'll need your help getting him mounted."

"Sure enough."

"Can't wait!"

Oh yes, I recognized them all right. Bruce and Andrew.

"Let me get this latch," came a third voice. Oh, cripes— Caleb! I was being given over to a trio of rugby players, hooligans every one of them!

"Look, he knows. He knows who's going to dish it out!"

Robert, too?

"Serves him right, not showing up to any of our games."

And Simon!

"Some fan he is."

Five guys, every one of them an out-and-out bear. I was pumped.

I was led up three steps and guided into a pillory. I remembered the contraption from previous visits, a massive wooden wall of solid oak that held its victims in an incredibly strenuous position. You didn't kneel at this pillory; you sat in it, held in place by hands, knees, and head, with your ass hanging three feet off the ground. You were flesh waiting for punishment and damn if I wasn't finally its penitent.

It took some angling to set me up, but once the boards were locked in place and the steps were pushed out of the way, Aidan gave me over.

"Have at him, men," Aidan commanded. "And do it fast. He won't be able to hold that position long."

The group laughed. Bruce said something about a scrum. One of them manhandled my dangling cock and balls. God, I felt vulnerable. Propped in place by my limbs, my ass hung lower than the rest of my body. My cheeks felt so stretched, I could feel the air against my crack. I knew that every one of them could see my hole.

Someone readied me with lube. Fingers intruded, two, then three, slicking my fuck shaft. I gasped when they voided me.

"You want it, don't you?" Caleb challenged. I nodded, moaned, then begged outright when the tip of his cock began to tease my hole.

"Please, yes! Oh, please!" The hood magnified my voice.

Its sound rattled in my head like headphones turned up far too loud.

Caleb breeched me. My hole burned as it stretched to take his rubber-covered log of a cock. He held me by the ass cheeks, working his cock slowly until I took the length of him without resistance. Increasing his pace, he savored fucking me, moaning every time he pulled back. My tight hole was ecstasy to him.

Bruce barked at him to step off and stop hogging "the little fuck toy." I quivered as one cock left me and another took its place. Unlike Caleb, Bruce was a pig. Like a glutton at a table of food, he fucked me as if every thrust might be his last bite.

Until Andrew claimed a turn and slid his delicious cock into me. All muscle and fur, he was a connoisseur and, like Caleb, he relished every thrust.

By the time Robert and Simon completed the first round, I was oblivious to who had had me at any one time. One after another they plundered me, round-robin fuckers all. The pace increased and became ferocious. All finesse vanished. Men became ramming, rutting beasts and, hanging there, my limbs grew weak. I struggled to continue.

"Enough!" Aidan commanded.

Whatever cock had me slipped reluctantly out. Spent and numb, I didn't know whose it was until I heard Bruce mutter obscenely in my ear.

Without a cock propping me up, without a body against me, I sagged. Suddenly, I shook, my body too weak for the stocks.

"Hold him!"

Arms steadied me. "I gotcha." Bruce. I collapsed against him.

Aidan and the others worked like a pit crew, unlatching the pillory, returning the steps beneath me, and spotting me as Bruce carefully dragged me from the stocks. However piggish his fuck, thankfully his rescue was tender and attentive. Under Aidan's guidance, Bruce helped me onto a padded table. Gathered around me, everyone cuffed me into place, legs spread, arms at the side of the table. This would be my next trial.

Three plus five makes eight, I thought. *And Aidan will make nine.* There were ten lords a' leaping. Despite the blindfold, the homestretch was in sight, I wondered who Michael would save for the last.

Fingers brushed my nipples. Light caresses teased, then squeezed. Toying with me, Aidan spoke.

"You did well. Impressive."

Other voices faded, left. It was just Aidan and me now.

"You've become quite the bottom since our time together."

Bottom, yes. But submissive only once, to one man alone. Aidan, fifteen years my senior but all knowing and all commanding, immortal to me.

"Michael tells me you've been a stern and commanding husband," he continued. "Now, did I train you for that?"

I sighed. "No, sir. I'm sorry, sir."

Aidan chuckled. "Of course you are. That's why it would do no good to punish you for it."

He pinched my nipples just to prove it. I moaned loudly.

"Instead, we're going to have to work it out of you."

He grabbed my half-hard cock by the head and squeezed it. Hard. I lurched and cried out.

"But we're not talking some namby-pamby massage, you

know. No, we're talking something just a tad rougher than a happy ending."

Aidan abruptly slapped the length of my cock. Again, I lurched. But this time, my cock swelled to attention.

"Yeah, you need it rough all right."

Aidan grabbed my sack. His fingers circled where it met the base of my cock. He tugged until he had enough room to wind a length of string around it. His touch felt so deft, so familiar, so expert. I had to remind myself we hadn't played together in years. If I could only see his face.

But it was Michael's visage that came to me instead. My beautiful Michael. Love flooded me.

The string held me tight, its pressure a delicious sweet spot between my balls and my cock. My dick bobbed, eager for more. And, recovered from its exertion, my body came alive, ready to soak up every sensation. I felt destined for bliss.

A pinch, right at the base of my cock. Another one, right above it. I knew that sensation—clothespins! But tiny plastic ones that, unlike their nibbling wooden counterparts, bit like black flies in springtime. Each bite burned, then left throbbing pain in its wake.

Bliss would have to wait.

Aidan covered my cock in those nasty little things, lining them up in columns that covered the length of my hard, pulsating meat. Pain became delectable. Pervert nirvana—I had crossed that threshold yet again.

When the last clothespin had found its spot, something tickled me. The ends of string. But not the string around my balls. A zipper. Aidan had my cock in a zipper. The clothespins were connected to a length of string and he was going to pull them from my dick!

I whimpered, giving Aidan cause to laugh at me.

"So you know the pickle you're in! You always were a perceptive lad."

I felt his fingers toy with the ends of the string. Panic rose in me; I wanted to beg him not to do it. *No, please! Please, don't!* But he had been my master. Did I want to disgrace myself? No.

I took a deep breath. I braced myself.

And screamed through my hood as the clothespins ripped from my cock one by one.

It felt like an eternity, but I knew pulling a zipper was a lot like ripping off adhesive strip: it was over in blink. It took mere seconds for outright pain to dull into a sweet throbbing sensation.

But Aidan wasn't done with me yet. A thwack sounded and small stinging tresses kissed my cock, wrenching me from euphoria. A flogger specifically designed for the nether regions was now Aidan's weapon of choice and he lavished it upon me, lashing my dick until I cried out.

He stopped, letting me rest. But the moment my heaving breaths slowed and my whimpers faded, he resumed his assault. Three times he pushed me and three times he made me scream. But all extreme things must come to an end, and soon the flogger had finished its task.

Spent, I went limp. Exhausted, I thought I could take no more.

But hands jolted me alert. My cock, lube. Someone climbed onto the table, straddled me, and hovered over me.

Aidan? Never. He had always taken me from behind.

"Master?" I asked.

Hands gripped my head. Someone behind me, at the head of the table. A kiss came to rest on my forehead.

"Not your master," Aidan answered.

He rolled the hood from my head as the body above me sank onto my burning cock. Sight blurred, squinting against the return of light, I fought to see who had me now.

Michael. My dear, sweet Michael.

Aidan patted my cheek and, chuckling, left me in Michael's able hands. Neither master nor pig nor bear, Michael stroked himself as he rode me. He looked sweet and glad, but soon his expression would grow tight with urgency.

I ached to reach up and take him by the cock. Or grab his hips and drive myself into him. Or pinch his nipples until he shuddered. But I could do none of it, bound as I was. I could only let Michael ride me, let friction overtake me and lead me to ecstasy.

It didn't take long. I closed my eyes and cried out his name—"Michael! Michael, Michael, Michael!"—as I pumped myself empty.

Afterglow descended as my body relaxed, its exertions finally over. I opened my eyes and found Michael gracing me with that sweet smile of his.

"Season's greetings," he teased.

I laughed, a man reborn and no longer a Scrooge. Michael. What would I do without him? Michael, my tenth lord a' leaping.

Michael, my one and only.

Eleven Pipers Piping
by Heidi Champa

"Saving the best for last, are we?"

Before I could answer, James pulled me into the darkened bedroom. His body pressed me into the old wooden door. His knee settled between my legs, pushing up between my thighs. I could feel his hard cock resting against my belly, his breath hot in my ear. He was the last one. The last piper. It was hard to believe I had been with them all. It seemed so unlike me, so foreign to the woman I was the other three hundred sixty-four days of the year.

But on Christmas Eve, at this party, at this house, I turned into someone else.

James slid his tongue over my neck, capturing my earlobe in his hot mouth. My clothes were shedding like wrapping paper onto the floor, and before I realized it I was lying naked on the bed.

James undid his tie, the one I had given him three years before, with the picture of Santa on it. He grabbed my wrists and pulled them towards the wrought-iron bed frame. I didn't resist him. I couldn't have. He tied my hands tightly to the cool metal, his face hovering close to mine. He was close enough to kiss, his lips almost grazing my skin. But as

I struggled to reach his lips, he pulled back with a sly smile.

"I don't think so. Not yet. You made me wait this long, now you're going to have to wait a bit longer. Don't worry. I'll be back."

With that, he turned and walked out the door, locking it behind him. As I struggled against the silk, I felt my pussy tighten. A fresh wash of moisture coated my lips. The cool air from the old, drafty window caressed me and my nipples hardened. I could hear the party below me. The Christmas carols played the way they did every year, and the smell of cranberries and cookies filled the air. I tried to relax, to lie still. But, my mind kept wandering back to the party and all the things that had happened over the years.

I had never planned to have them all. I never set out to turn each Christmas Eve party into another sexual escapade. But that's what had happened. And now James. He was the last of the eleven, and the one whom I wanted the most. From the first moment I saw him, I knew I had to have him. I had to feel his mouth on me, feel his cock deep inside me. If I'd had my way, he would have been first on the list. But despite my best efforts, he made me wait—wait until all the others had been exhausted.

It only left me wanting him more and more each year. The others had been fun, but James was the one whom I had waited all these years for.

It had started several years before; a way to pass the time during Christmas break. The *Twelve Days of Christmas* show was a local tradition. Lots of students took part, especially ones like me who didn't have anywhere else to go over the holidays. I became part of the eleven pipers, partially by accident. Originally I had my heart set on being one of the dancing ladies but, sadly, it was not to be. I couldn't really play the instrument, at least not at first. But I faked my way through the early performances, learning as I went. The guys were so great, it felt so effortless. No drama like with all the dancing girls. It had been a blessing in disguise to become a piper.

As the years went on, our friendships grew and it soon became a huge part of my life. Even after school finished, the performances and the parties continued. The desire started to grow as well, the sexual tension building with each passing year. It soon became evident that some of the men were interested in a little more than eggnog and a friendly hug from me. At first, I resisted what had become so obvious, but it was becoming difficult to deny my own feelings. It was common knowledge that a lot of sex happened at the Christmas Eve parties. I was beginning to feel like the pipers were being left out.

That first year, I hadn't intended to begin our new tradition. I was just leaving the bathroom and I ran straight into Jason, a fellow piper. I thought he would just keep going right past me, but he didn't. He looked down at me, letting his hands fall gently on my shoulders. We stood there like that for a while, his eyes roaming over me. I felt myself getting hot, my whole body flushed with unexpected heat. Just the mere touch of his hands on me made me crazy. With surprising force, he pushed me back into the bathroom.

"Jason, what are you doing?"

He didn't answer; he just dropped his lips to mine. I let him kiss me, let his hands wrap around my back. I could barely breathe when he pulled back.

"Something I've wanted to do for a long time." He reached behind us and locked the bathroom door.

I thought it was just going to be a kiss. But as his mouth took mine again, the kiss quickly turned to a secret touch under my skirt, a slip of his hand into my panties. He seemed surprised to find me wet, and I was shocked at the speed of my own reaction. His finger pressed into my clit as his tongue continued to slide in and out of my mouth. I clutched at his shoulders, rocking my hips against him as the Christmas carols played gently, muted through the closed door.

He wasted no time working me into a frenzy; my orgasm was so close. We both ignored the footsteps in the hall and as his fingers rubbed against my clit, his middle finger slipped inside my wet cunt. I threw my head back as I came, my cries muffled by his hand over my mouth.

We looked at each other. I was still panting. I knew I had to return the favor to my friend. I couldn't just let that big, beautiful erection in his pants go to waste. Kneeling before him, I got no protest as I loosened his belt. And he said nothing as I slid his pants to the floor. I gave him one last look, one last chance to stop me. He never did. I slid my lips over his cock and he grabbed the counter for balance. I felt his whole body stiffen as the voices in the hall grew louder. As time was of the essence, I didn't mess around, pushing him deep into my throat with each stroke. The tile floor was cold under my knees; his hands wrapped roughly in my hair. It was a matter of seconds before I felt him swell and twitch under my tongue. His semen hit the back of my throat, hot and sticky. He was left to stop his own moans this time. As I stood, Jason stared at me in disbelief.

"Sorry. I didn't plan for that to happen. I just got carried away." His look was so apologetic, I wanted to hug him.

"No need to apologize, Jason. It was hot."

"I thought you would slap me when I kissed you."

"Not a chance."

"Well, I'd better get back. Merry Christmas." He kissed me on the cheek and walked out of the bathroom.

That was how it all started. The quickie in the bathroom with Jason set the stage for my yearly indiscretion. I wasn't sure if Jason had told everyone, or if it had opened a floodgate that was doomed to open anyway. Whatever the reason, every year had become another adventure. It had all led me here to this dark room, waiting for James to come back and finish it. My hands started to feel numb, but no matter how I moved them, I couldn't get any relief. I let my mind go again, trying to forget about the butterflies in my stomach that James had caused. I wondered what he was doing downstairs; if he was enjoying the thought of my torture.

After Jason, I had fixed my desires on Tom. I'm a bit embarrassed to say I wasn't subtle with him. But luckily for me, it worked like a charm. After we got through all the usual pleasantries and mingling, I had no trouble getting Tom alone. The host and hostess of the party lived in a monstrously large house with plenty of room for holiday mischief. We saw another couple heading off for their own misdeeds as we made our way down the dark hall. Tom pulled me into a small room decorated with flowers. I paid little attention as the heat of his mouth singed my throat. We were standing in the center of the room exploring each other when I heard a voice come from the darkest corner.

"It's about time, you two. I've been waiting forever."

My attention snapped to the left, and I saw Rob sitting in a chair in the corner. Rob was another piper. His face was mostly blocked by shadows, but I could see his hand opening his zipper. I looked back at Tom, but he was just smiling. Clearly, he had been in on the whole plan.

"Don't worry, Sarah. He just wants to watch. You don't mind, do you?"

"My girlfriend wouldn't like me taking part," Rob said.

I couldn't think of an answer. Did I mind? The "real me" would have. But the me who came to these parties, the me who had sucked off Jason the year before, didn't mind. I shook my head no, and allowed Tom to continue peeling off my clothes. We disrobed slowly, wanting to provide Rob with a decent show. I tried to ignore his presence, ignore what the extra set of eyes in the room was doing to my pussy. But I couldn't pretend it didn't get me hot. Tom dropped his head between my thighs, pulling my red thong panties to the side. I heard Rob get up from the chair and go to the window. He pulled the shade back, allowing the moonlight to come in and brighten the room.

"That's better. Now I can see your face, Sarah. And that beautiful pussy."

Rob was still standing, staring at us. His eyes watched intently as Tom dragged his tongue over my wet slit, my hips rolling to meet his probing fingers. He shifted uncomfortably, his cock clearly straining in his boxers. He sat down and pulled his cock out, and I watched him stroke himself to my pleasure.

I became so entranced by Rob's hand sliding up and down on his cock, I barely heard Tom tear open the condom package. He rolled it on and moved back above me, between my splayed thighs. My eyes moved back and forth between Tom and Rob, watching the two of them watching me. Tom guided his cock inside me, and I moaned into his shoulder. The Christmas carols played below us, filling the otherwise quiet room. I could hear Tom grunting above me, and Rob whimpering in the corner. I looked over at Rob and saw his cock moving in his hand. He caught me looking and smiled.

"Get on top, Sarah. I want to see you better."

My face burned hot as Tom lay back on the bed. I climbed on top of him, his cock right below my pussy. I eased down slowly, letting him slip inside inch by inch. I heard Rob and Tom gasp together, both taking in the sight of my pussy swallowing Tom's cock. I stopped when he was all the way inside, grinding my clit into his pelvis and tweaking my own nipples. I was into the show, feeling sexier and hotter than I ever had in my life. I started riding Tom, fucking him hard and fast. I grabbed his hand and pushed it to my clit, letting his fingers rub over my sensitive flesh. I could tell Rob and Tom were both close, their faces contorted in concentration. I leaned back, letting the light hit my body. I felt my orgasm creeping ever closer.

"Like what you see, boys?"

I never expected an answer, but I got one anyway. Rob gave one last tug on his cock and managed to choke off a wail as his come spurted out into a waiting tissue. Below me, Tom grabbed my hips, forcing me down onto his cock hard. I leaned forward, rubbing my clit against his undulating hips. The crest of my orgasm finally broke, and I cried out into his open mouth, my whole body shaking and trembling. With one last thrust, Tom came, his heavy breathing muffled by my desperate kisses.

The room again fell silent, filled only with our heavy breathing. I dressed quickly, leaving Tom and Rob to clean up. I went back to the party glowing and smelling of sex. No one seemed to notice. Except James. His look told me he knew what I had been up to. My pussy immediately felt empty again.

*

I tensed on the bed as I heard more voices in the hall. I wished I wasn't naked, wasn't exposed in this room at this moment. I tried to make out what the voices were saying, but I had no luck. It wasn't James. He was going to leave me here longer, to torture me even more. I was desperate to touch my aching cunt. I could feel the wet spot below me getting bigger, my arousal growing out of control. I couldn't stop the thoughts pouring into my head. All the things that had happened over the years were bubbling to the surface, filling the time until James put me out of my misery.

After Tom and Rob, I had sworn an oath to myself I would behave. I had managed to avoid temptation and keep myself upright the following year. I had even managed to avoid James, who was busy chatting to two of the dancing ladies. But my restless body couldn't help but wonder what was going on upstairs. I was certain there were shenanigans going on, and as I scanned the room I realized many of my fellow pipers seemed to be missing. Unable to control my curiosity for another moment, I sneaked up the stairs, walking the hall slowly. I listened for the familiar sounds of holiday fucking and when I wandered past the master suite, I was sure I heard Ian, one of my brethren, moaning. I stopped in my tracks and listened some more. There were more voices, all mixing together, and I decided to take a peek.

Pushing the door slowly, I let my eyes adjust to the darkness. Ian was in the room, standing near the dresser, his cock sliding in and out of Parker's mouth. Across the room, on the bed, Jake and David were wrapped around each other, kissing. I stood frozen for a moment, watching four of my piper buddies. I pushed the door open a little bit more and sneaked inside. No one seemed to notice my intrusion and if they did, they were too busy to stop me. I found a dark spot next to a chair and hunched down to take in the scene. Ian held Parker's head in his hands, pushing and pulling his cock in and out of his mouth. I heard Parker moan around Ian's cock, his hands grasping Ian's narrow hips. Ian, whose eyes had been on David and Jake, spotted me. I panicked, waiting for him to say something, but he just smiled at me.

On the bed, David and Jake had started jerking each other off, their mouths and tongues still intertwined. I tried to fight the urge to rub my own clit, but I couldn't stop myself any longer. I felt my heat through my pants, my pussy clearly wet and achy. I rubbed hard through the fabric, letting my fingers increase the heat in my pussy. David and Jake continued their rhythm, their hands moving in a brilliant tandem, choreographed to perfection. Ian thrust harder into Parker's mouth, his strangled breathing mingling perfectly with the rest of the moans filling the room. I tried to stay quiet as my pussy pulsed, but a few stray sounds were soon sneaking out of my mouth.

Needing to feel my own wetness, I let my hand dive into my panties. They were completely soaked. I pressed two fingers inside my cunt, my thumb rubbing over my swollen clit. Suddenly, everything in the room grew more intense. David and Jake were almost frantic in their movements, each straining to hold out longer to give the other more pleasure. And Ian moved so quickly that Parker was starting to have trouble keeping up. My own body was tensing to the point of no return. My senses were being overloaded, and I needed to come. Just then, I heard Jake crying out in the dark, his cock twitching and unloading all over David's hand. As if spurred on by his partner, David followed suit, his orgasm coming just as Jake's had finished. I started coming, my pussy clenching and pulsing as Ian came in Parker's mouth. I closed my eyes, listening to the sounds of pleasure filling the room, the Christmas carols drowned out by the sounds of ecstasy. I left quickly before anyone other than Ian discovered me. The party was still going on as normal, the action upstairs unnoticed.

I was beginning to think James was never coming back. It was growing more and more uncomfortable in the room. I was cold, my toes and fingers completely numb. Despite my restless pussy, all I could think about at the moment was the nice hot chocolate downstairs. I heard the door lock click, and saw James enter the room. My whole body relaxed as he approached the bed. He sat down next to me, the mattress bowing under his weight.

"How have you been, Sarah? Miss me?"

As he asked the question, his fingers traced over my stomach, teasing down to my pussy. I was sure he could feel the heat there without even touching me. He kept going, sliding a single finger between my slick lips, stopping just below my clit.

"Yes, James. I missed you."

"Seems like it. What were you thinking about up here? Was it Jason, perhaps? Or what about Tom and Rob?"

I opened my mouth to confess, but he covered my lips with his, his tongue probing deeply into my mouth. His finger left my cunt and moved up to my hard nipples. He moistened each one with his damp finger, the cool air making them even harder. "I know, you were thinking about Ian and the boys. He told me what a naughty girl you were, sneaking in there and watching like that. You liked it, didn't you?"

"Yes. I liked it."

"Did you touch yourself?"

"Yes."

As I answered, he sucked one taut nipple into his mouth. The heat was overwhelming, a stark contrast to the cool room. He sucked hard, grazing his teeth over my hard flesh without actually biting down. He toyed with the other nipple, his fingers teasing while his mouth tortured. I bucked my hips towards him, inviting him to touch me. But he ignored my silent pleas and continued his lazy teasing of my nipples.

He got up from the bed to shed his shirt and pants. I watched as he stood naked, his cock rising in the darkness. I was desperate to have him, and he knew it. He was going to make me wait, make me beg before he gave in. He sat down again, his hip resting next to mine. I waited for his next move, but he just looked at me, devouring me with his eyes.

"I know. You were thinking about Phil and Daniel, weren't you?"

I hadn't been, but as the words hit the air, my mind was shocked back to the scene from the year before. Daniel, Phil, and I had gotten tipsy on the cheap champagne at the party and managed to make it upstairs to an empty room. I shook my head at the thoughts coming through. James brought me back, with a finger teasing my clit.

"You didn't know it, but I was there. I saw the whole thing. You didn't even notice me, did you?"

"No."

This time, his finger slid all the way inside me; his palm rubbed gently over my hard clit. I tried to rub myself against him harder, but he kept pulling away from me. I moaned in disappointment as he smiled, enjoying my plight.

"I have to say, Sarah, I wasn't expecting you to fuck both of them at the same time. But you didn't hesitate for a moment. Tell me, who was better, Phil or Daniel?"

I couldn't answer. I was too focused on his finger teasing me, his words hitting me like a ton of bricks.

"Come on, Sarah, don't be shy. You can tell me. I know it all anyway. You think after watching you do that, we have any secrets?"

"I can't believe you know about them all. I can't believe they told you."

"Of course I do. We're all friends. And since I was the only one who hadn't yet had the pleasure of having you, the boys took it upon themselves to share with me. Were you trying to make me jealous, Sarah?"

"I wanted you. From the very beginning, I wanted you the most."

"I know. That's why I made you wait for it. I wanted you to come to me. I wanted to hear you ask for it. But you never did."

His one finger became two, pressing me open further. I cried out, squeezing my eyes shut against the flood of sensations between my legs.

"Open your eyes, Sarah. Look at me."

I did as he asked, staring up into his blue eyes. Even in the dark, they were sparkling. He pulled his fingers from my cunt and brought them to my mouth, making me suck them clean.

"Tell me, Sarah. Tell me how much you want me."

"I need you to fuck me, James. I can't wait anymore. I want it."

"Not good enough. But it's a start." He got up and moved down the bed. He pushed my thighs wide apart and settled between them. He opened my pussy, letting the cool air hit me. I shivered both from the cold and the feel of his fingers on me.

"So, Daniel and Phil tell me you taste good. Maybe I should find out for myself."

I felt his tongue slide up and down over my wet slit. His teasing strokes avoided my clit each time, despite my efforts to move him closer with my hips. He stayed one step ahead of me, making all my squirming worthless. Finally, he took pity on me and wrapped his lips around my clit. He sucked hard, drawing it into his mouth. Moaning into the darkness, I could again hear the Christmas carols filling the rooms below us. His fingers were back in my cunt, working in a steady rhythm with his tongue. I was practically weeping from the pleasure, my body unable to take much more. The noises from my throat were foreign even to my ears—the sounds of pure need.

"Now, there is a sound I didn't hear when Daniel and Phil were fucking you."

"James, please. I need you to fuck me. I need to come. I want you to fuck me. Please. I need you."

He moved up next to me again, letting my hands free from their bondage. I reached out for him, but he took my hands between his, rubbing them to warm them up. He moved over me, pressing my hands back to the mattress. I could feel his cock against my wet pussy. I tried to move him inside me, but again he evaded me.

"Say it again. Tell me, Sarah."

"I need you to fuck me, James. I can't take it longer. I need to feel your cock inside me. Fuck me. Please, fuck me."

His smile disappeared and his hands released mine. I don't know where the condom came from, or how he got it on so quickly, but the next thing I felt was his cock teasing me open. Slowly, so damned slowly, he slid inside me. I couldn't do anything but feel him; nothing else was getting through. All my senses were concentrated on his cock sliding into my cunt. Nothing I had imagined all these years could have prepared me for how it felt to finally have James inside of me.

"Was it worth the wait, Sarah?"

"Yes. Oh God, James. Yes."

I was babbling as he fucked me, my legs wrapped around his body. I moved with him, letting him take me, my body offering up no resistance. I knew I wouldn't last very long with my body so overloaded with sensation. With every slow, deliberate thrust, I could feel my body rushing closer and closer to orgasm. James grunted in my ear, his own pleasure evident, his cool exterior crumbling under the strain. I felt full, stretched; my whole body felt like it was pushed to its limit. James swiveled his hips, grinding my clit against him before thrusting into me harder and deeper.

"Come for me, Sarah. I want you to come."

Everything started to break apart, my mind falling to pieces as my body tightened under his weight. My pussy started to quake, pleasure bordering on pain shooting all through my body. I felt like I was being pulled apart by the joy of it all, his cock drawing every last ounce of feeling out of my body. I couldn't think or breathe. All I could do was come and it seemed like it would never stop, wave after wave coursing through me until I felt James drive into me harder, matching my climax with his own. It was so perfect, so sublime, I could hardly believe it was real.

Reality was slow to return. The last strains of *Silent Night* brought both of us back to Earth. James rolled from my body and lay next to me, his strong arms refusing to let me go.

"Oh God. Sarah. Tell me I won't have to wait another year for that."

"I think I'm done with Christmas Eve parties. Let's leave it to the next group of pipers."

"Sounds good to me."

He kissed me, just as *The Twelve Days of Christmas* began playing. Looking at the clock, I realized it was after midnight.

"Merry Christmas, James."

"Merry Christmas, Sarah."

Twelve Drummers Drumming

by C. Margery Kempe

"A ticket?" Gabriele asked, peering up from the envelope in her hands and cocking an eyebrow.

"Happy Christmas!" Nico grinned widely. When he noticed she only looked puzzled, he sighed. "For the concert today. My percussion ensemble!"

"Ah." Gabriele meant to say more, but she was stuck. "Thanks," she finally managed. "I'm sure it will be great."

If she had to be honest, all the percussion ensemble had done in the two months they'd been going out was ensure that Nico was never free on Thursdays. It continued to be girls' night out for her. However, when Gabriele stumbled home late, Nico was usually ready to help her finish the evening right. So she didn't completely mind the rehearsal sessions, but she couldn't really imagine a whole concert of nothing but drums.

Nico, however, was unable to hide his excitement. He grabbed her around the waist and lifted her up to twirl her in a circle. Once again, Gabriele marveled at the strength in his arms. Guess all that stick work was good for the biceps. "You're going to love it!"

Gabriele wasn't too sure, but when they headed over to

the performance hall, still giddy from their hasty lovemaking among the ribbons and wrapping paper of her tiny living room, she was more than willing to take it on faith. Nico's enthusiasm about everything was contagious. He saw her to her seat, gave her a big kiss, and then hopped up on stage and disappeared. Gabriele pulled out her mobile to do a little surreptitious texting while waiting, replying to her mother's queries about when they were going to get there for dinner and her best gal Zena's asking about Nico's gift.

The lights came down and the somewhat sparse crowd quieted. Gabriele watched as the curtains parted to reveal a stage lit with red and green, a tiny Charlie Brown-like Christmas tree at its center. A small boy stepped out from behind it, playing a simple tattoo on a toy drum. The audience applauded, including a few audible "awwws!" Gabriele smiled, too. The boy looked up expectantly. All at once, a thunderous assault began.

The drummers had arrived.

They entered the stage in two lines, one from each side. Gabriele saw Nico at the end of the line on the right. His face looked uncharacteristically serious, which made her smile. The two lines crossed and split, forming a rectangle as they continued to play. The thumping rhythm filled the air and even rattled the chair Gabriele sat in with its vibrations.

It was not an unpleasant feeling. Gabriele felt herself loosening up as she listened. The assault was not the violent cacophony she had anticipated, but more like a vigorous massage. As soon as the thought struck her, she smiled. This was much better than she'd expected. The drummers completed the opening song with a quick sequence of final beats and the crowd burst into enthusiastic applause, which Gabriele joined.

The second song began with a slow cadence echoing between two of the drummers, one of which was Nico, the other his friend Jonathan, a guy with the massive shoulders whom she'd met once or twice before. Gabriele found herself fascinated with the exchange. Gradually, additional beats and drummers were added until the hall rang with the pummeling of the drums. Her whole body thrummed in rhythm. She closed her eyes to better soak in the sensation. The seat buzzed underneath her, and her thighs pulsated along with each drumbeat. It was actually a bit delicious, Gabriele thought. She wiggled in her chair. "My my," she murmured as she quietly cleared her throat.

Gabriele looked around. There was no one sitting nearby. It was kind of dark in the audience, too. Feeling like a teenager, she moved her coat from the seat next to her onto her lap and slipped one hand beneath it. Her fingers strummed her thigh, feeling the beat concuss across the skin. Gabriele let her index finger slide down the seam of her jeans at her crotch and felt an electric thrill jump up from below.

She couldn't help letting her eyes swivel left and right and back again before letting her hand slip up once more to unbutton her trousers and slide the zipper down. She allowed her hand to wander down toward the massive heat rising from her groin. The hairs of her mound were itching with excitement. She tapped her clit, which sent a shiver up her belly.

I can't believe I'm doing this, Gabriele thought, letting her gaze sweep from side to side again, then closing her eyes as she gave in to the lure of the pounding rhythms. Her finger probed lower, finding honey flowing. She couldn't help a sigh as it slipped between her lips. The pounding of the drums echoed as vibrations in her skin and Gabriele enjoyed the sensation, keeping her finger still as the flesh vibrated around it. The beginnings of an orgasm were already gathering. She could feel the familiar tickle in her thighs.

Suddenly, the pounding reached a crescendo and stopped abruptly. Gabriele's eyes popped open with disappointment. She did not join in the applause, instead waiting impatiently for the music to begin again. On stage, the musicians had rolled out a large timpani. Gabriele grinned. Around the mammoth drum, four drummers waited, poised for the first beat. Behind it stood a redhaired woman, mallets in her hands. Without warning she deftly brought them down with a deep, loud boom that seemed to shake the room to its foundation. It was quickly followed with a rumbling roll across the broad surface of the giant kettle. Gabriele wiggled her finger and felt the drum roll repeat in the vibrations of her wet lips. It wasn't going to take much to make her come now, she thought as the four drummers added their pulse to the mix.

Even as the thought rose up, Gabriele could feel the mouth of her cunt pulsate with the same beat and she was coming, rocking to each thumping of the drum heads, her breath catching in the din of the auditorium, grateful that no one could hear, assuming that no one would see—or that they would mistake the source of her ecstasy. Gradually the reverberations inside her subsided. Surreptitiously, Gabriele rebuttoned her jeans, but she could not resist putting her finger to her other lips and tasting her wetness, sweet and tangy.

It was good, but it wasn't enough. As the thudding blows filled the air, Gabriele began to imagine another possibility for this Christmas afternoon. All kinds of presents, yes, that's what they needed. A private concert would be just the thing.

When the last of the applause for the last number faded away—it had been a wild ride of percussion and marimba as well as the drums—Gabriele got up and found her way backstage. Still feeling full of bliss and weak in the knees, she knew she had a silly grin plastered across her face, but it was the holidays. People were supposed to be in good moods.

She ran into the redhead who had played the timpani. "I'm looking for Nico. Have you seen him? By the way, I loved your performance. That was amazing."

The woman smiled. "Thanks so much. It's always a thrill to play that. My skin always vibrates for hours afterwards."

"Not a bad thing," said Gabriele, thinking of her own pleasure in the performance.

The redhead grinned. She seemed to share some of that pleasure in the pulsating beat. "No, not at all. One of the reasons I love to play."

"I'm beginning to understand that," Gabriele said, then followed the directions the woman offered to the green room, where Nico and Jonathan were stowing the last of the drums. Gabriele watched the play of muscles in his arms and back as Nico lifted a case back onto a high shelf. The tingle of her orgasm lingered, as if carried on the beats no longer audible in the hall.

"Hey, Gabriele," Nico called out when he finally saw her standing there admiring him. "We'll be done in no time at all. Just got to get these last few put away. This is Jonathan, by the way," he added, nodding to his companion.

"Yes, Jonathan, we've met before," Gabriele said, although she only had eyes for Nico. "Hey, before you put that last one away, can you show me how you play it? I mean—" Oh boy, did that sound stupid. How do you play? Hit drum with stick!

But Nico sensed she meant more. "You want to feel what it's like to play one? Sure! C'mere." Nico held the drum before him and looped a sort of strap around her shoulders. The big drum rested against her hips. Gabriele ran her hands around the edges, feeling the tautness of the head.

"Ready?" Nico asked as he picked up a pair of sticks. When she nodded, he brought them down, striking a glancing blow upon the drumhead in a quick repeating triplet pattern. Gabriele could feel the strikes echo through the drum and pulsate through her body. She closed her eyes to revel in the sensation. When Nico stopped after a long drum roll, she was disappointed, but she could tell that her skin was rosy with suppressed excitement.

It felt so good!

"Hey, I gotta get going," Jonathan offered after an awkward moment of silence as Nico's gaze took in the pink flush of her skin. She was afraid Jonathan saw it too, as he looked a little embarrassed as well, hiding a quick grin with a cough. He grabbed his big black bag and swung it over his shoulder.

"That's all right," Nico said quickly. "I'll take care of the rest."

Jonathan waved as he left the room, but neither of them noticed. "Shall I play a little more?" Nico asked her with a wicked grin.

"Yes, please," Gabriele answered, her voice an octave lower than usual, already wet between her legs and conscious of the weight of the drum, the pull of the harness over her shoulder and its pressure on her tender nipple.

Nico looked right into her eyes as he began to play the drum. At first the rhythm was simple and slow. In her head it sounded like "one potato, two potato," but the thump of the drum at her hips vibrated through her whole body. Nico's drumming picked up speed and each blow pounded her flesh as it beat the head of the drum. Without realizing it, Gabriele began to rock to the beat, enjoying the thrumming repeated by each nerve in her body.

"I didn't know you dug the rhythm so much, honey," Nico said, his eyes bright with excitement.

"Neither did I," Gabriele admitted. "Show me more."

"How does it make you feel, Gabriele?" Nico asked, moving closer as if to gauge her reactions more carefully.

"It makes me feel like I might come just from the throbbing of the beat," she said without hesitation. "Is that how you feel playing?"

Nico grinned again. "Sometimes, sometimes. Not as much as right now." He reached up to stroke her neck with his drumstick, flipping her hair away from her shoulders. Then he reached down to run his thumb across her very erect nipple. They both leaned over the drum to kiss, Nico thrusting his tongue into her mouth eagerly, burrowing his hands into her hair, but not letting go of the drumsticks.

"You wanna learn to play?" he asked when they finally came up for air.

"Uh huh," Gabriele said, not trusting her voice beyond those simple syllables. She reached up to caress her own breasts, feeling the nipples harden again. The throbbing in her clit was unbearably delicious, but she sensed Nico wanted to play a bit before he would satisfy her.

Nico tapped a little tattoo, but then walked around behind her. "Let me show you how it's done," he whispered in her ear, his voice husky. He slipped his arms around hers and snuggled up against her backside. He pressed tightly against her so she could feel the hardness of his erection.

This is turning him on as much as it is me, Gabriele thought and smiled to herself.

Before he started to play, he cupped her breasts, tilting the sticks to rub against her straining nipples. Gabriele groaned. The suspense was terrible, but she hoped it would last a while yet. Finally, Nico decided to let go of her breasts to tap out a bouncing rhythm, accompanying it with the grinding of his pelvis into her back. Gabriele rested her hands on the sides of the drum and let the pulsating strikes jut through her. Nico thrust against her from behind and the drum thrummed against her thighs like a second lover enveloping her in his embrace. Her whole body sang with pleasure.

Before long, Nico shifted both drumsticks to his left hand, continuing to play as he slipped his other hand down the front of her jeans, releasing the buttons as it headed south. A small squeak escaped from Gabriele's mouth, perhaps meant as a protest, but she could think of nothing but the relief that hand would bring to her swollen lips and pulsating clit. A charge went through her as his finger circled round the little fleshy button. Her legs trembled as his finger plunged into her wet cunt and she cried out, coming at once, with the beat still echoing in her nerves. Nico's hard dick pressed into her back. The drum thumped against his hand and her hips. Gabriele shuddered with the last pulse of her orgasm and sighed happily.

Nico pulled his hand out of her pants and reached to loosen his own zipper. "What if someone comes?" Gabriele whispered fiercely.

"Oh, someone's going to come all right," Nico rumbled in her ear and she felt her body stiffen with excitement. She heard the sound of his pants slipping to the floor, then his hot hands were easing down her jeans even as she thought, *we shouldn't do this, not here.* But her pants were down and he stepped forward to thrust his hot dick between her legs, sliding it back and forth just a little as if he were warming it up, although he was already on fire.

Then he started playing again. Gabriele gave up trying to guess his next move and surrendered herself to the rhythm. They swayed together as he drummed, each beat reverberating through the hard cock between her thighs. She had never experienced anything quite like it: the pounding of the beat, the throbbing between her thighs, the hunger that made her lips try to grasp at his length. Gabriele longed to have him inside, thumping her and not the drum skin, but he was determined to make her wait. He had a plan in mind. So she let the drum rock against her hips and his dick torture her clit, closing her eyes to enjoy the experience.

"I think I'm going to come anyway," she warned Nico, although this was clearly not his intention. He paused in his playing and began to slip out from between her legs, stopping only for a second to thrust up into her dripping cunt, making Gabriele gasp with surprise and pleasure. But it wasn't going to last. Nico withdrew just as suddenly and Gabriele staggered forward, led by the weight of the drum. Nico grabbed her around the waist to hold her up, his erection tucked into the crack of her ass.

"Now what, lover?" Gabriele asked in a voice barely above a whisper. She turned around to see Nico's grin. He stepped out of his pants and took her hand, pulling her to do the same, relieved her of the tenor drum, then led her over to the big kettle drum, which still sat in the middle of the room.

"Hug it," Nico said as he put down his drumsticks and picked up the big-tipped mallets for the kettle. Gabriele crouched down and stretched her arms around the drum as if she were hugging the instrument. Nico kept his eyes on her as he began to play. While the drum had been deafening in the auditorium, he played softly, gently rousing a rumbling thunder from the head of the drum that made Gabriele shiver and undulate at its side. Her whole body pulsated with the waves of sound. She began to think her flesh would never stop tingling from this aural massage.

Gabriele watched, fascinated, as Nico's erection waved like a conductor's baton. It was slick from her honey and looked beautiful. Nico's eyes were on her as he played, but his gaze seemed clouded, as if his thoughts were very far away. *What was he planning next?* Gabriele thought, hardly able to contain her excitement. There was a fine glow of sweat all over her body and she ached to have him inside of her, to put an end to this merciless pounding and get to the real thing.

Suddenly his gaze focused and his mouth opened slightly. Gabriele looked over her shoulder in the same direction and stood up abruptly. Jonathan was standing in the doorway and she was suddenly aware her ass had been obvious as she bent over to hug the kettle. She was grateful her long-tailed shirt covered it again as she stood up, but her cheeks flushed crimson anyway. Nico had hastily stopped his rhythmic play and silence hung in the room for a few beats.

Only then did Gabriele notice that Jonathan was holding a very stiff erection in his hand as he gazed at the two of them. She looked over at Nico, who seemed uncertain. There was no way she was going to pass up an opportunity like this, however. Turning back toward Jonathan, she said, "Why don't you join us?" He nodded slowly, as if in disbelief and walked toward them. He slid the bag off his shoulder and gave a crooked smile.

Happy Christmas to me, Gabriele thought.

"What shall I, um, do?" Jonathan asked, awkwardly fingering his cock and blushing some more. The two men looked at Gabriele. She took in Jonathan's wide shoulders and strong arms. They were a good match for Nico's.

"Play me," Gabriele said at last. The two of them looked at each other and grinned sheepishly. Nico handed the mallets to Jonathan and picked up the drumsticks again. Gabriele leaned over the kettle and spread her arms across its surface. After a moment, Nico and Jonathan began to play gently upon her.

Nico's sticks drummed across her back, tapping out a syncopation of admirable complexity and dexterous subtlety. He moved around her shoulder blades, circling them in a sort of figure eight, then moving up to play more gently along her spine up to the sensitive skin on her neck. Each strike ignited a sensational thrill and the percussion vibrated her skin. It was marvelous.

Meanwhile, Jonathan used the mallets to play her backside, rapping out a roll at the base of her spine, then careening off to the right cheek, then the left as he aimed steady but gentle blows in a speedy beat that shuddered down her legs and made her thrumming clit shudder with delight. Her whole body pulsated in the twin rhythms, different yet complementary, as the two musicians listened to one another's choices, picking up the sequence, innovating and then sending it back. She was the skin between them, their instrument of pleasure. Gabriele never suspected how deep the pull of the drum could go, how the beat of her heat increased with the pounding of the two of them.

As she lay there in otherworldly bliss, Gabriele was not at all surprised to suddenly feel Nico's dick at her lips. The vibrations shook through his erection as they did through all their flesh. She welcomed him in, luxuriating in the sensation of his sizzling heat as he thrust into her mouth, withdrawing to feel her lips tighten around him, to feel her tongue chase him as he slipped out, then thrusting into her once more with a groan. Amazingly, he never dropped the beat, but continued the tempo without pause.

"Can I?" Jonathan asked, his voice rough with passion and effort.

"Do you have protection?" Nico asked, which made Gabriele love him all the more. She didn't hear him answer, but he stopped playing and she peeked over to the side to see him fishing around in his bag, emerging triumphantly. As she sucked deeply on Nico's quivering cock, Gabriele heard Jonathan tear open the condom package.

In a moment she felt Jonathan's prick slide down the valley of cheeks, spreading cool lubricant across her ass as he headed toward her scorching wetness. He slipped forward, rubbing against her clit, which throbbed in welcome. But he backtracked and thrust inside her without warning. He was thicker than Nico and Gabriele felt a familiar tickle as he stretched the walls inside her. He had dropped the mallets and instead rested his hands on her hips as he began to thrust.

Gabriele was so scorched from the drumming that the orgasm came quickly and was followed by others as Jonathan continued doggedly thrusting inside her, feeling his way around. She cried out and Nico withdrew to watch her face as she came again and again. Suddenly Jonathan was there with her, shouting, "Oh yeah, oh yeah!" as he slapped against her ass in a frenzy, shooting inside her in a final percussive slam.

Nico dropped his sticks and grabbed his erection instead. "How about you play me now, Gab?" She looked up from the kettle and matched his silly grin. Jonathan withdrew slowly from her, saying, "Oh man, you are amazing, Gabriele."

Gabriele smiled at him and gave him a kiss on the cheek before turning her attention to Nico. She picked up the mallets Jonathan had dropped. "On the floor, buddy," she instructed Nico. He obeyed swiftly, his cock waving invitingly up at her. Gabriele wished briefly for a softer surface, but quickly dismissed the thought in her hunger for Nico. She straddled his body and slowly sank down upon him, making him groan with anticipation before she took his burning length inside her. Oh God, it felt good to have him inside at last. Gabriele tried to resist the urge to come at once and instead began to tap out a simple rhythm on his chest. Nico closed his eyes and enjoyed, awaiting her movements.

Slowly she began to undulate around his cock, still drumming on his chest gently and insistently. He began to moan and she gradually increased the speed of her gyrations and the beat on his chest. She could sense him stiffen inside her and knew it was time. Dropping the mallets, she grabbed his shoulders and propelled herself up and down as they both shouted aloud with joy, coming in waves of pleasure that Gabriele could feel down to her toes.

When they finally stopped bucking together, Gabriele was a bit lightheaded, but it was worth it. She had never felt a series of orgasms so intense. Looking over at Jonathan, she saw he had a semi and was stroking it thoughtfully. She looked down at Nico and he was dissolved in bliss. But she knew he could be ready to go again soon.

She reached for her bag and groped for her phone. Mom was just going to have to deal with her being late for Christmas dinner. There were still presents to unwrap, after all.

Red Bow
by Isabel Roman

One

December 13

Jessica Oberon pushed her blond hair off her forehead and searched once again for the file. It still wasn't on her desk.

"Tracy!" she called to her assistant. "If O'Brien still has that file, tell him it had better be on my desk in the next three minutes or it'll be his head!"

"Yes, ma'am," Tracy said from the open door of her office. "Chamberlain wants to see you when you have a moment, too."

Jessica slanted her brown eyes toward her assistant. "It's less than two weeks before Christmas. The advertising department is behind schedule. I have two people out sick and you're not looking too hot yourself. No. I don't have a minute."

Tracy nodded and sneezed. Jessica sighed and ran her fingers through her hair again. "Go home, Tracy," she said. "I don't want to be sick this Christmas." She went to see what the president of Chamberlain Advertising wanted.

Thirty minutes later, an armful of new client folders in her hands, Jessica reentered her office. Tracy had taken her advice and left for the day, which was just as well. Digging under her sink, Jessica found disinfectant wipes. She could not be sick for Christmas.

Turning from her chore, she noticed a cream-colored linen envelope tied with a red satin bow on her desk. Excitement skittered through her. Twelve days before Christmas and like clockwork, there it was.

It's been a year, lover. I've missed the taste of your body. I've missed your submission. Have you been a good girl? Room 801 of the St. Regis. 10 p.m. Don't be late.

Wetness pooled between her legs and she bit her lip to prevent a moan from escaping. She remembered last year very clearly. With her heart pounding in her chest and her knees weak at the thought of what he planned this year, Jessica slipped the note into her purse. But not before gliding the satin bow through her fingertips.

She had a lot of work to do before leaving this afternoon. Glancing at the clock, she saw it was still hours before their time together. How was she supposed to concentrate with his promise of seduction?

Arousal still thrumming through her veins, Jessica pulled into her garage and went to greet the chaos awaiting her. Her children, Julie and Sean, enveloped her in sticky hugs the second she walked through the door. It was always a race with them to see who got to her first. Falling to her knees, she kissed them both.

As they chattered about their days, Jessica guided them into the kitchen. Ellen, their live-in nanny and cook, stood at the stove stirring a delicious smelling pot of sauce.

"Has Kenneth called?" she asked, lifting Julie onto the island stool.

"Yes," Ellen nodded with an odd look in her direction. "He's working at the hospital late and isn't sure when he'll be home."

"Daddy always works late at Christmastime," Julie said.

"I know," she said and kissed her daughter's head. "Are you all packed?"

"Yup!" the girl chirped. "Can I go skiing with Grandma again this year?"

"Of course." Jessica smiled as she peeked around the corner at the too-quiet Sean. He was busy running a fire truck over the couch. "Grandma and Grandpa will be here any minute to take you to their house."

Jessica felt a momentary stab of guilt at leaving her children with the grandparents until Christmas Day, twelve whole days. She wasn't sure what she was doing was right, but couldn't help herself. He was a temptation to alluring to resist.

Just then the doorbell rang and both children ran to open it.

At two minutes to ten, Jessica stood before room 801 of the St. Regis. She hadn't changed out of her business suit, but had removed her panties and replaced her square-heeled shoes with stilettos.

Heart pounding with excitement, she slipped off her watch. As the minute hand moved closer to ten, she dropped it into her purse. With one last deep breath, she knocked on the door.

It swung open, the room dark and cool beyond the threshold.

"Take two steps in," a husky voice instructed. "Stay absolutely still."

Jessica did as instructed. The door closed and she felt him

behind her. His hands slid up her arms, loosening her fingers from her purse and removing her suit jacket. He undid the first buttons on her blouse, fingers a teasing touch on her sensitive skin.

A satin cloth slid around her neck, fluttering over the tops of her breasts. Drawing in a sharp breath, she fought to remain still.

"Good girl," he whispered in her ear.

Shuddering at his closeness, she waited as he took the cloth and tied it around her eyes. His lips were on her neck, as erotic as the satin on her breasts.

In the darkness of the blindfold, she felt him move around her. His fingers were smooth on her skin as he unbuttoned the rest of her blouse, the zipper of her skirt a harsh sound in the darkness.

The material pooled around her feet and she heard his sharp intake of breath.

"No panties?" His mouth was against her ear, tongue licking the outer shell. "Naughty girl."

She didn't answer, unsure if she should. His hand swatted her ass but she didn't yelp.

"What do you say, Jessica?"

"Yes, Master."

"Yes, Master, what?" he demanded. His hand was still on her ass, cool on the warm skin.

"Yes, Master," she said steadily, excitement tingling through her, "I am a naughty girl."

"So you are," he agreed, circling her.

She felt his lips on her neck, hands tracing the tops of her stockings. Slowly, too slowly for her liking, he moved along her body. Cupping her breasts, his fingers tugged her already-hard nipples.

"I see your body hasn't forgotten me," he said.

Though his voice was steady, she felt his cock pressed hard against her buttocks. She wanted to grind against it. Take him into her and assuage her aching body.

"No," Jessica managed. "Never."

Smoothing his palms over her breasts, he walked in front of her.

"I want you to remove my clothing," he instructed. "Don't touch me *except* to remove the clothing."

"Yes, Master," she whispered.

Jessica reached to where she knew his collar to be. Loosening his tie, she let it hang while her fingers slipped each button through its hole. She took her time, careful not to touch him, as he'd instructed, but eager to savor this. Though she wanted to run her hands over his chest, she resisted.

"I've missed you," she murmured as she gracefully knelt before him.

After untying his shoelaces, she slipped each shoe and sock off before reaching for his belt. Jessica slipped it around his waist, and dropped it on the floor behind her. Wishing she could see him, taste him, she quickly pulled down his slacks and boxers. His cock sprung free and slapped her on the cheek.

Turning toward the temptation, Jessica barely remembered she wasn't to touch him. Swallowing the impulse to ignore him and take his cock into her mouth, she sat back on her heels and desperately tried to ignore the throbbing wetness between her legs.

"With your tongue only," he said, "trace my cock. Don't use your hands."

Jessica moaned, but nodded. Her hands drifted down

her own body. Breath hitching, her tongue found his cock and circled the tip just as her fingers slid through her neatly trimmed pubic hair.

"Don't," he ordered, voice harsh. His fingers clasped around her jaw, just enough pressure to make his point. "Don't touch yourself, Jessica."

Whimpering, Jessica nodded and dug her fingers into her thighs. Closing her eyes behind the blindfold, she concentrated fully on him and soon lost herself in his taste. It'd been too long.

"Please me," he said. Fingers sliding along her scalp, he added, "And remember, Jessica. No touching."

"Yes, master." She nodded before taking his length into her mouth.

Relaxing her throat, she moved over him, taking him deeper and deeper. She thought she heard him moan, but couldn't be sure over the pounding of her heart and her own harsh breathing. Releasing him, she kissed his balls, taking one then the other into her mouth before moving back to his cock.

Feeling his fingers tighten on her head, Jessica moved faster, wanting him to come in her mouth.

He jerked her away, and she sobbed a displeased moan. "Kiss up my body," he ordered. "Use only your very talented mouth."

On legs weak from kneeling so long, her orgasm just out of reach, Jessica nodded. With one last lick on his cock, she moved to his hip, slowly mapping the planes and angles of his torso. Unsteady on her heels, nails digging into her palms, she sucked on his collarbone, nipped the soft spot between shoulder and neck.

His hands were hard on her body as he pulled her to him.

His mouth was hot on hers, and she kissed him back with equal fervor. He demanded from her, and Jessica was only too willing to comply.

Turning them, he walked her backwards until her knees hit the edge of the bed. He lifted her and and settled her on the sheets, spreading her legs wide. She shivered, moaning when his mouth left hers.

His hands were rough on her calves as he pushed her legs to her chest, and she felt the bed dip where he knelt before her. In one hard move, he entered her.

Crying out in pleasure, she shuddered beneath him. His fingers twined with hers, holding them at her sides. Oh, yes, this is what she'd fantasized about all day.

Suddenly, he stopped. Sobbing in need, she strained against him.

"Follow my instructions," he said from above her, "and this evening will be nothing but pleasure. Disobey me, and I'll be forced to discipline you."

"Yes," she managed. "Yes, Master."

"Remember," he said, mouth a breath from hers. "You are mine."

"Yes," she said again. "God, yes!"

He withdrew then, and pounded back into her body with enough force to move them across the bed. Mouth back on hers, he took and took, and all Jessica could do was hold on as she climbed higher. Suddenly, he released her hands; his fingers circled her clit and she shattered beneath him. Wave after delicious wave of orgasm rocked over her. She cried out, uncaring if anyone else in the hotel heard her.

"Mine," he repeated, and came as well.

Jessica automatically opened her eyes to see his handsome face contort but saw only blackness. He collapsed atop her, but she was careful not to wrap her arms around him no matter how much she wanted to.

"Good girl," he said at last and gently kissed her.

When she woke the next morning, thoroughly sated and sore from their activities, Jessica was alone. Fresh clothes were laid out for her, but her lover was nowhere to be found.

Sitting up, the sheet pooling around her waist, she stretched. That was when she noticed the bracelet. He only left her presents when he was pleased with her. The thin gold was tied into a bow around her wrist. Smiling, she turned it to the light from the open curtains.

That was when she noticed the letter. It sat on the nightstand, red bow tied crisply around the heavy linen paper.

You were a good girl last night, lover. Meet me in the men's dressing room of Saks at 1:30. You know the punishment for being late.

Two

Jessica hadn't the chance to stop home before going to Saks. She'd checked her cell phone messages from the hotel while eating breakfast in bed. Unfortunately, she was alone in that bed. Calling her children, she caught them before they went out to play in the snow. There was a message from Kenneth, too, confirming their dinner for tonight. When she returned her husband's call, all she got was his voicemail.

Rushing through the after-lunch crowd on a busy Saturday before Christmas, she headed straight for the men's department. Just outside the fitting room, she stopped. With twenty minutes before her deadline, she carefully watched the few men going in and out of the area. When she was sure no one else was in the fitting room, and the attendant had disappeared to put away unwanted clothes, Jessica made her move.

With seconds to spare, she slipped into the middle stall. He was already there. Locking the door behind her, she waited for his next instructions.

"Right on time," he said. Trapping her between his hard body and the flimsy door, he smiled wickedly down at her. "Very good."

In a lightening-quick move, his hands slipped up her skirt and tore off her panties. He shoved them in his pocket before pushing her onto the edge of the seat and kneeling before her.

His tongue was firm as he licked her, two fingers sliding into her. She arched against him, and he hooked her legs over his shoulders.

"Don't make a sound," he whispered. His fingers moved

steadily in and out of her, mouth pressing light kisses against hers. "Do you want to be discovered?"

Jessica shook her head. She looked into his dark eyes, which were nearly black with passion.

"Do you?" he asked, thumb pressing against her clit.

Biting her lip, Jessica stared at him. "No, Master," she breathed.

Her fingers curled around the edge of the cushioned seat, nails digging into the fabric. She pressed herself further into his hand. His thumbnail scraped her clit and she jerked against him, teeth once again biting into her lip.

"Good," he chuckled. "I don't want anyone else seeing you like this."

Then his mouth was back on her, sucking her nub, teeth scraping the sensitive bundle. Jessica clamped her teeth together in an effort not to scream. Rocking against him, she came. Shuddering, she continued to move as his fingers pumped in and out of her, teeth scraping her clit again and again.

Suddenly, he lifted her, seating himself on the bench and settling her over him. His pants were already undone and his grip around her waist was hard as he slammed her down, seating himself deep within her.

Jessica bit into his shoulder, desperately trying to stifle her moan. She didn't want to break his rules, afraid he'd stop.

"Quiet, darling," he admonished. "Not a sound."

Shaking her head against his shoulder, Jessica adjusted her knees on the cushion. His hands were rough on her as they moved, a pounding rhythm that had her once more biting his shoulder. She knew two things—the feel of her lover inside her, and the need for absolute silence.

His breathing was harsh, chest heaving, but he remained unnaturally quiet. Pushing her winter coat halfway down her arms, his hands tangled in her hair, yanking her head back. Mouth brutal as he kissed down her neck. Tears pricked her eyes, and she felt a bead of blood well on her lip.

With one hand, he wrenched open her blouse, buttons popping against the wall. Teeth closed over her nipples, and her breath shuddered.

"Come for me," he whispered.

He slammed into her once more, fingers on her clit. Teeth clenched tight, nails digging into his back, she rode out her orgasm in silence, shuddering around him as he continued to move within her.

Dropping her head onto his shoulder, she felt him come, the delicious sensation of his release. Vaguely, she heard him grunt.

His hands were gentle as they combed through her hair, lips unhurried as he kissed her. Jessica felt bruised, a wonderful sated feeling she relished.

"Ten more days with you," he said, "and we must wait another year before we can indulge like this."

"The years are longer and longer," she whispered against his shoulder.

"I know," he kissed the top of her head. "I know."

Carefully standing her on shaky legs, he fastened the two remaining buttons on her shirt. With a wry smirk, he pulled her coat over her, carefully slipping those buttons closed. Jessica leaned up to kiss him, soft and tender. Her fingers twined with his—she didn't want to let him go.

"Don't leave until I text you," he whispered with a final kiss, hard and quick. "If you get caught, you might have to miss tomorrow's rendezvous."

"I'll wait," she promised with a cocky smile. "But don't be late."

He chuckled and left the small room. Barely a minute later, her cell beeped. *Until tomorrow, lover.*

Jessica waited at the restaurant, sipping her wine. Kenneth was late. Christmas was always busy at the hospital, and she knew he took on more hours during the season to help them through it. While it was very nice of him, it interrupted the few times they could share a quiet meal together.

"Sorry I'm late, darling," Kenneth said, kissing her cheek.

"Busy day?" she asked, signaling the waitress.

He smiled ruefully, dark humor sparkling in his eyes. "The usual. One shooting, two knife wounds—one on a little old lady trying to carve her turkey."

"It's still days before Christmas," she chuckled. "Couldn't she wait?"

Kenneth shrugged as the waitress arrived. The young woman took their order, eyes lingering on Kenneth, and left. Jessica smirked at her husband. "Another admirer," she commented, raising her glass in a toast.

"What can I say?" He shrugged. "The smell of hospital gets them every time."

Jessica laughed but her eyes lingered on him. In his mid-thirties, Kenneth was tall, handsome, and had the most piercing brown eyes of anyone she knew. He carried himself well, confident in his every move. When he was with their children, he was the most popular daddy on the block.

"Are you scheduled every day until we leave for Vermont?" she asked.

He waited while the waitress delivered his beer before

answering. "I don't know," he admitted. "I may trade time with Morley."

"Good." She grinned.

They ate in relative silence, occasionally commenting on the season, their work, wondering if the weather forecast was right and it'd be a white Christmas.

"Ellen said something odd to me the other day," he began. His phone buzzed. Cutting himself off, Kenneth opened it and read the message. "It's the hospital. I have to go," he sighed. Rising, he dropped his napkin on the table. "Don't wait up," he whispered, lips lingering on her cheek.

"All right." She nodded. "Be safe."

Watching him leave, she signaled for the bill. Walking to her car in the frigid December winds, Jessica saw her letter on the dash. Feeling her spirits lift, she opened the door and climbed in. She started the car and she slipped the satin bow between her fingers, letting the anticipation build.

Three

Bundled against the blowing snow, Jessica stood before the door to the chalet. Vermont was gorgeous this time of year, even with the freezing winds. It was Christmas Eve, and tomorrow she'd go to her parents and spend the holiday with her husband and children. But tonight was for her. For them.

Meet me at the chalet. Wear your coat and the red stilettos. Nothing else.

The foyer was huge and welcoming, garlands decorated the banister and dripped from the chandelier. Turning left, she entered the great room, the only illumination coming from the decorated Christmas tree and roaring fire.

Wandering toward the tree, she noticed another note. Smiling, she plucked it from the branches and slowly opened it.

Remove your coat.

Shivering in anticipation, Jessica did so, letting the material slide to the floor. With the satin bow playing through her fingers, she walked around the couch. He was there, naked before her.

"You look beautiful, my pet," he murmured, gracefully standing.

"Thank you, Master." She smiled.

Excitement skittered through her, and she felt moisture seep from her core. A single finger traced her breast and she thought she'd come from that touch alone.

The warmth of his body seeped into her, causing her to shiver again. His cock hardened against her thigh. His hand swept along her hair, moving softly down her cheek.

"Close your eyes," he whispered, kissing her eyelids closed.

His mouth was on hers, the only part of him touching her. She wanted to strain closer, but resisted. His tongue delved into her mouth, possessing her completely. His hands swept down her back, holding her inches from him. Jessica felt them convulse on her ass, squeezing the tender lobes.

With her heels on, she was the perfect height to his tall frame. He slid his cock through her nether lips, coating himself with her moisture, causing her breath to all but stop. Heart pounding, she widened her stance. Abruptly, he spun her around. His hand moved her hair off her neck, one finger tracing the delicate arch of her neck, languidly down her shoulder and arm, taking her hand in his. Kissing her palm, he moved their joined hands to her breast.

Guiding her fingers, he held the heavy globe, moving so they both teased her nipple.

"Yes," she gasped.

Jessica hadn't realized he'd taken her other hand as well, holding it hostage so she couldn't touch either him or herself. Her fingers convulsed in his.

"Yes, what?" His breath was hot against her cheek.

Just as she was going to answer him properly, he moved their hands to her core, slipping her forefinger between her lips, letting her feel her wetness.

"Yes, what?" he demanded, harsher this time.

"Yes, Master," she gasped. Still holding her hand, he guided their middle fingers into her. "Oh," she moaned, trembling.

She swallowed hard, wanting to move. He refused her, and she could feel his grin against her shoulder.

Slowly, he moved their fingers in and out, her moisture coating them both. The eroticism of the movement had her orgasm washing over her. He withdrew their fingers and she moaned in disappointment, need still churning through her.

"Kneel," he ordered.

Jessica instantly did so, falling gracefully to the thick carpet. She felt him kneel behind her, hands spreading her thighs.

"Lean forward," he said, one hand on her shoulder to push her.

He slammed into her.

"Ah!" she cried, head falling down. Her hips jerked against his as he thrust into her several times, quick movements that tantalized more than assuaged.

Though she tried to draw him deeper into her, he refused, hands firm on her hips to still her movements. Then he completely withdrew.

Tears of frustrated passion in her eyes, Jessica looked behind her. His eyes were dark, unreadable in the firelight.

"Master?" she asked, her voice trembling from unfulfilled need.

The smile he offered was wicked, seductive. Jessica's eyes widened, and she moved backwards.

"Yes," she breathed, closing her eyes in anticipation.

She felt his hard cock at the entrance of her puckered rosette and push in. The sensations were exquisitely painful. Very slowly, he moved. Hot tingles of orgasm fired through her, and she pushed back hard.

With a sharp intake of breath, he pulled almost completely out and slammed back into her. Again, again, and suddenly she was coming, hard waves of desire colliding through her. Still moving against him, wanting the pleasure to go on and on, she forgot their rules and screamed his name.

"Kenneth!"

"That's it," her husband growled. "Come for me, baby."

She did, and felt his release, his hips slamming into hers as he came.

When she opened her eyes, much later, she was curled into him. The fire had burned down, and a thin blanket covered them.

"Hmm," she smiled, stretching in his arms.

"Merry Christmas, Jessica," he said, kissing her shoulder.

"Very creative this year, baby," she said, rolling to face him. "Saks?"

Kenneth chuckled, brushing her tangled hair off her cheek. "Twelve days every year for the eight years we've been married. Gotta keep you on your toes."

Jessica raised one leg, letting the blanket fall to one side. She still wore her red stilettos. "Hmm, yes," she agreed.

His hand caught her calf, and he leaned over to kiss it, gradually moving closer to her core, once more wet for him.

Thank God, their chalet was all theirs. Jessica pushed him back and straddled him. With a wicked smile, she guided him into her. "My turn," she whispered.

Shannon's Surprise

by Brandi Woodlawn

"I'm sick and tired of dating losers," Kelli said. "I'm about ready to give up on men entirely." She put another log on the fire while Shannon unloaded an armful of wrapped presents and arranged them neatly under the Christmas tree.

"Their loss will be my gain," Shannon said.

"You already have me," Kelli said as she hugged Shannon, resting her head on Shannon's shoulder. "How are you gaining anything?"

"Well, I wouldn't have to share you anymore," Shannon said as she brushed the hair away from Kelli's face.

"But I like it when you watch me with other people. It turns me on."

"I know."

"And you like to watch."

"I do."

"The moratorium on men will never last. Maybe I just need a moratorium on losers?" Kelli sighed. "All the good guys are taken."

"Maybe you're just looking in the wrong places."

Kelli broke the embrace. She bent down and picked up a medium-sized box wrapped in gold foil paper and adorned with a red bow. She shook it. "I don't suppose you figured out a way to fit a babe in a box?"

"No, but that doesn't mean Santa won't bring you one."

"Since when did Santa become an expert on finding a man? You're not . . . curious?"

The possibility piqued Kelli's interest. Shannon had always been so reserved. Maybe she was finally ready to come out of her shell.

"It would be cool with me if you wanted to do a guy. I'd watch. But I can't promise to stay on the sidelines."

"No. I'm not . . . curious. I'm not interested in men. I was just trying to be helpful."

"Oh," Kelli pouted. "So what do you suggest?"

"Well, there's this guy at work. I think you might like him."

"Is he a lawyer?"

"Yes."

"Ugh. I thought the point was to avoid jerks."

"This guy, Aaron, is not a jerk. If I hadn't told you he was a lawyer, you'd never know."

"I don't know . . . what does he look like?"

"He's totally your type. He's about five-foot-ten, a total jock. Strong arms, killer smile."

"If he's so great, why didn't you tell me about him before?"

"He's only been with the firm a few weeks."

"How do you know he'd be interested?"

"He just moved up here from Arizona or New Mexico or something. He's available."

"That doesn't mean he'd be interested in . . . us."

"I might have mentioned you already. I knew it was over with Brad. I figured you'd be down about that."

"Wow," Kelli said. "I know it's not easy for you to talk about our relationship, especially at work."

"Aaron's different. He's easy to talk to. He doesn't judge."

"It really means a lot that you'd put yourself out there like that."

"I love you," Shannon said. "I want you to be happy."

"I love you, too," Kelli said. "So when do I get to meet him?"

"Are you up for tonight?"

"It's Christmas Eve," Kelli said.

"You wouldn't want him to spend the holiday alone, now would you?"

"I've underestimated you," Kelli said. "You're just full of surprises."

"Look at all these guys trying to find last-minute gifts for their wives. This place is probably picked over by now," Kelli said. "We're crazy to be in the mall today."

"Aaron likes lingerie. If he's going to accommodate our kinks, shouldn't we take care of his?"

"I really hate wearing these frilly things," Kelli said as she held up a lacy black teddy. "And they're so expensive." She frowned in disgust.

"I forgot to mention one of the other advantages of dating a lawyer," Shannon said as she withdrew Aaron's credit card from her wallet. "He's buying."

"In that case, maybe it won't be so bad," Kelli said as she reconsidered her selection.

"Aaron isn't into lace," Shannon said.

"You sure know a lot about a guy who's only been in town for a couple of weeks."

"I asked for suggestions when he gave me the card. It

wouldn't be right to blow his money on stuff he wouldn't enjoy."

Shannon selected several negligees in an assortment of colors and prints, all of them silk.

"Those are kind of conservative, don't you think?"

"Those are for me," Shannon said as she set her choices aside. She went to the next rack and grabbed a hot pink Flyaway satin babydoll top, a black lace-up satin slip and a red sheer mesh halter top with the corresponding panties. "These are for you."

"The man has good taste," Kelli said. "I like him already."

"I knew you would."

Kelli stood in front of the mirror brushing her shoulder-length red hair while Shannon put the final touches on her makeup.

"I can't believe you're getting all dolled up for this," Kelli said. "You look great."

Kelli set the brush on the counter and grabbed Shannon's hand. She pulled her close and kissed her. "Thank you again for doing this. I'm sure you made Santa's 'Nice' list this year."

"You're welcome," Shannon said. "I don't think any of us will be disappointed."

The bell rang. Kelli squealed. "I'm not ready. Stall for me."

"You look fine," Shannon said. "Seriously."

"You sure?"

"Are you nervous?"

Kelli blushed, "A little."

"You are too cute. Aaron's going to love you. I'm sure of it."

Shannon dragged Kelli to the door. She opened it and stepped aside so Kelli and Aaron could make first contact.

"Aaron," Shannon said, "this is Kelli. Kelli, Aaron."

"Hi, Kelli," Aaron said.

The wind howled, sending a cold burst of winter air and a few flakes of snow across the threshold.

Shannon said, "Get in here before you freeze to death."

Aaron stepped inside and unzipped his winter coat. Shannon closed the door behind him. He took off his coat and hung it on the coat rack next to the door.

Aaron was just as Shannon had described. Tall, athletic. Dark hair, dark eyes. He was wearing jeans and a grey T-shirt that hugged the areas it covered in all the right places.

Kelli said, "Wow."

Aaron smiled and said, "You're not so bad yourself."

They made their way down the hall and into the living room. Aaron sat down on the couch and the girls flanked him.

"I like your Christmas tree," Aaron said as he gently flicked one of the colored balls. He looked up at the tree topper. "The angel is really pretty."

"Thanks," said Shannon. "I decorate the tree. Kelli bakes the Christmas cookies."

Shannon motioned to the plate sitting on the coffee table. Frosted snowmen complete with gumdrop eyes lined the plate in a neat row and were surrounded by an assortment of candy canes. "Help yourself."

Aaron selected the snowman with a green scarf and took a bite. "This is really good."

The trio talked for a bit over a few glasses of wine. Small talk, mostly. Where they'd lived, Kelli's job, how they'd all wound up in Chicago. Aaron finally had the courage to get down to brass tacks.

"You're everything Shannon said, Kelli. Smart, sexy. I really like both of you. What's next?"

"I . . . uh . . ." Shannon got a little flustered. Negotiating terms was not her favorite part of the encounter.

Fortunately, Kelli had a bit more skill in this area.

"I'm bisexual," Kelli said. "Shannon and I might play together while you watch. You and I might play together while she watches. Shannon doesn't do men. So you've got to respect that."

"Okay," Aaron said.

"Shannon and I have been together a long time," Kelli said. "If you decide you want to have a relationship with me, you need to know she's going to come first. We'll respect your boundaries. We don't fuck around with people's feelings. If you just want a casual thing, that's cool, too. Condoms are required, in any case. No exceptions."

Aaron said, "Understood."

"Is there anything else you want to know?"

Aaron laughed, "Who gets to kiss you first?"

Shannon said, "I do. But I'll be quick." She leaned over and gave Kelli a quick peck on the cheek.

"Don't rush on my account," Aaron said. "I'm kind of liking the view."

Shannon motioned to Aaron to scoot over. He switched places with her and watched as Shannon untied her robe and let it fall to the floor. Aaron didn't know what to focus on, the long blond hair cascading down her back or slim, tan thighs that were further exposed as Shannon straddled Kelli and kissed her properly. She leaned back and unfastened the belt on Kelli's robe, revealing the hot-pink get up. Aaron had seen the ensemble in the catalog and liked it, but seeing Kelli in the flesh almost left him speechless.

Aaron lost his words when the girls grabbed his hands, pulled him off the couch and led him to the bedroom.

Their bedroom was illuminated by light from scented candles. Vanilla and some sort of flowers, Aaron guessed. It was a very girly smell and it was welcoming. While he'd dreamed about the prospect of being with two women, he'd never actually done it. And though he knew Shannon wouldn't be an active participant, she would be watching. They worked together. Would it be awkward tomorrow? Aaron had to stop thinking about such things before irrational fears turned into performance anxiety.

Shannon likes you. She invited you here. It will not be weird tomorrow. End of story. After mentally repeating those thoughts a couple of times, Aaron's heart stopped racing and he began to calm down.

Shannon sat in an oversized armchair in the corner of the room. Kelli led him to the bed, pushed him to a seated position, and lifted his shirt over his head. He didn't know what he liked more, being manhandled or being spied on. His fantasies were coming true simultaneously and it was almost too much to bear.

Kelli brought him back into the moment. She ran her fingers through his chest hair and over his shoulders. Her right hand moved up his neck and she weaved her fingers into his hair. She tugged it firmly, bending his head back slightly, and kissed him.

"One more thing," she said. "Sometimes I like to play rough."

*

Shannon squirmed in the chair. Watching Kelli as she took control of Aaron really turned her on. The silky fabric of the negligee was clinging to the space between her breasts. As she listened to Kelli give Aaron his orders, she longed to take his place between Kelli's thighs. Soon the room was filled with the musky scent of her pussy and Shannon longed to taste her again.

Aaron was obedient, doing exactly what Kelli said without hesitation. When Kelli hit him with the flail, he winced but let out a low moan with subsequent blows. Shannon could see he was hard and since he'd been such a good boy, Kelli was certain to let him fuck her. It was getting harder to resist touching herself, but that was all part of the game. Shannon had to watch. Kelli had not given her permission to do anything else. Later, she'd be allowed her reward. And when it happened, the orgasm would be even more satisfying. Shannon would not have believed that delayed gratification came with such a benefit until after she'd tried it. Today, she wondered if she had the strength to wait.

Kelli was about to come when she put her hands on Aaron's head and said, "Stop."

He did as he was told, and for that she was grateful. She turned her head to the side and looked in Shannon's direction.

"It's not fair you're just sitting there all by yourself," Kelli said. "Come over here and join the fun."

"I thought she didn't do men," Aaron said, slightly confused.

"I don't," Shannon said. "Nothing's changed. No October surprises."

"Are you wet?" Kelli said.

"Yes," said Shannon.

"Do you want me to make you come?"

"Yes," Shannon said.

"How 'bout you, Aaron?"

"Yes . . . of course," he said.

"Aaron, I'm going to take care of Shannon. And if that's not too much for you to bear watching, then you can take care of me."

Shannon climbed onto the bed, and assumed her place over Kelli's head.

Kelli's legs hung over the side of the bed. She parted her thighs for Aaron's benefit.

Shannon and Aaron were facing one another. Shannon smiled at him, then said, "I'm ready."

Shannon lowered herself and shuddered as she felt Kelli's tongue probe her labia. She rocked her hips as Kelli's tongue fluttered over her clit.

Aaron took care of business with the condom, then gently thrust himself inside Kelli's slick, wet hole. He steadied himself by placing his hands on her hips, careful to leave the satin babydoll top within his fingertips' grasp. He loved the sensation of the fabric against his skin.

Kelli's moaning broke Shannon's rhythm. The short bursts of Kelli's breath tickled Shannon's thighs. Shannon shifted forward a bit and when she looked down, the only visible part of Kelli's face was the dimple on her chin. Shannon pinched her own nipples as Kelli sucked her clit. The scent of sweat and sex filled the air as Shannon came. She rested for a moment, then moved back to the chair, allowing Aaron the opportunity to finish.

Aaron continued thrusting. He and Kelli centered themselves on the bed. He tasted Shannon when he kissed her. He gave her breasts a gentle squeeze and increased the depth of each subsequent stroke as Kelli made her wants known.

When her thighs began to quiver, Kelli said, "Oh God, I'm going to come." She grabbed Aaron's ass, digging her nails into his flesh as she took his cock with all the force she could bear.

A few more deep thrusts and Aaron climaxed, whispering "fuck" as he collapsed on top of her. For a moment, their bodies were sealed together by the glue of hot and sweaty skin.

"That was . . . wonderful," Kelli said.

"Yeah," Aaron said. He kissed her again before breaking the seal and rolling to his side. He lay next to Kelli, stroking stray hairs away from her face. "What about you, Shannon? You good?"

"Never better," Shannon said.

"Come back to bed, baby," Kelli said.

Shannon curled up next to Kelli. Aaron lay on his back with his arms folded above his head.

"Thank you, Santa," Kelli said. She kissed Shannon on the forehead. "I really liked my present."

"Present?" Aaron raised an eyebrow.

"Good thing you weren't naughty," Shannon said, "or all you would've gotten was a lump of coal."

The girls giggled. Aaron smiled, shaking his head in disbelief.

Kelli turned to Aaron. "Whatcha thinking?"

"I've never been someone's Christmas present before. Nothing like this ever happened to me in Arizona."

"Aren't you glad you moved here?"

"I probably won't like the winters. But now I know why people call Chicago 'my kind of town'."

Christmas Pie

by Jesse Blair Kensington

My parents were coming for Christmas dinner. I was freaking out because I had never made a pie. You see, Christmas pie is a tradition in my family, and even though my mother had showed me a couple of times how to make the crust, I could not manage it. Even worse, my parents were footing the bill for culinary school. What they didn't understand is that you could be a really good chef and not know much about baking. Baking is a specialty. I shared my concern with my hunk of a teacher and he suggested I come to his apartment for a pastry lesson.

Well, of course, I had to take him up on the offer. Any culinary student who gets an opportunity for one-on-one instruction from a famous teacher would be a fool not to take it. I have to admit I was flattered that he paid any attention to me at all. I am short and waiflike and men tend to ignore me, although I really don't mind. I just want to cook, eat, and be left alone. Ben, my teacher, smiled when I told him that on one particularly grouchy morning in the school kitchen.

I was also curious about Ben. None of the other students had ever been invited to his campus apartment—at least not that I knew. I wanted to see how he lived. I mean, here he was, this gorgeous man who had written two cookbooks and was well on his way to fame and fortune. What kind of paintings hung on his wall? What books were on his shelves? And, I dared to wonder, what color were his sheets?

And we had all wondered. Watching Ben in the kitchen would turn anyone on, let alone a bunch of horny, food loving, twenty-somethings. One day we made meringue, and he carelessly licked his finger where the fluffy stuff had spattered on them, causing one of my colleagues to sigh out loud. I turned to look at her and she bit her lip, red-faced, and excused herself from the room. We didn't see her for the rest of the day.

We talked about it later. Joni admitted that she'd been having wild thoughts about him. "But my thoughts are nothing compared to Alexa's," she told her. "I think most of the class is having a hard time focusing because he is so fucking sexy."

I said a little prayer of thanks to the universe, because knowing I was not the only one in my class who was fantasizing about Ben helped a little. I was actually thankful he would be leaving next semester. I need to focus on the cooking, but a distracting sexiness just flowed from his every pore.

When he opened the door to his apartment, I almost melted. He was in a deep red, tight-fitting T-shirt and I could see his pectorals bulging. His blue eyes glowed and his dark wavy hair curled around his ears. It was the first time I'd seen him without his cooking cap or chef's toque. He smiled, revealing dimples that I wanted to touch, or even lick.

"Hi, Chelsea," he said, over the baroque Christmas music. "C'mon in." He walked over to his stereo to turn down the music.

"Hey, thanks, Ben," I said, walking in and glancing at the blank white walls. All blank, no kidding. Not one friggin' picture to give me a little insight into his character. There wasn't even a Christmas tree or menorah in the place.

He reached for my bags of groceries and placed them on the kitchen counter. "Okay, let's get to work."

The next thing I knew, my hands were in dough. The smell of flour hung in the air. The oven was already heating.

"They tell you to use a pastry cutter, but that's for amateurs," he said. "You really need to feel your work. The trick is to keep your hands cold and touch the dough lightly, as little as possible."

He grabbed my hands and held them, sending a rippled wave of excitement and fear through me. My chef-teacher was holding my hands, which were cupped in his hands with his long sensual fingers moving against mine. Our eyes met and I was sure I felt something give way deep inside. Was that a twitch between my thighs?

"Mmmm," he said. "You have such nice hands."

They were covered in flour and I was wishing I had cut my nails before the lesson.

"But they are too warm for the pastry." He continued to hold my hands as he led me to the sink, opened the faucet and let the cold water run on our hands. So cold. As he reached for the towel to dry our hands, he brushed up against my breasts. They are not that big and have never gotten in the way before, so I wondered if that was on purpose. I wanted to remain cool. You know, mature, like I knew what I was doing, like famous chefs hit on me almost every day. My nipples betrayed my pretend coolness and his eyes lingered on them, then moved back to my eyes. He lifted my chin—oh man, his gorgeous hands were so cold on my warm chin—and kissed me delicately, his tongue briefly flicking across my lips.

He pulled back. "I am sorry, Chelsea. I've just been watching you . . . do you mind my kissing you?"

I just shook my head. I could not have spoken if I tried. My mouth was still burning from his kiss and my knees felt rubbery. All I could think about was what was in his pants and had to stop my hands from reaching for it, unzipping him, and shoving his cock into my mouth or my pussy.

"Okay," he said. "I promised you a pastry lesson. Let's get the pie crust into the oven."

It wasn't as though I was a virgin, but there's something a little intimidating about making it with your teacher, an almost-famous chef at that. Most of the guys in my class were gay and I didn't have time to go out and look around for men. So I was kind of out of practice. When I had free time, I slept. Culinary school was painful—hard on your feet, shoulders, back, arms—well, just hard on both body and mind—even at the age of twenty-one.

I watched Ben manipulate the dough and tried to mimic him. His sinewy forearms were stronger than mine, but I was working on it. They were beginning to shape up and I was starting to look like a cook. He pressed the crust tenderly into the pie plate and I followed along. I was trying my best to concentrate, but all I kept thinking about was his tongue on my lips. The phone rang and he excused himself.

"Listen, Megan, I am kind of busy here," I heard him say into the phone. "I'll have a recipe to you tomorrow. I promise."

I didn't mean to listen, but he was right there and what could I do? I assumed it was Megan Matthews, his writing partner. I took a deep breath—she was gorgeous and I always wondered if they were a couple.

"I'm sorry," he said, after hanging up the phone. "Megan is always calling at the worst times."

"Shall we put the crust in the oven?" I said, pretending like I really didn't care.

He placed a bucket of ice on the counter and rubbed ice on the crust. "Just a little," he said, then opened the oven door. I followed his lead and slid the smooth ice over my crust.

I turned around to begin cleaning up before we started on the custard filling, and he came up behind me, pressed himself into me, and wrapped his arms around me as he kissed my neck. I could feel his warm breath and it made every hair on my neck stand up. My whole body tingled.

"Chelsea," he whispered to me. "I've been thinking about you. You're like a delicate flower, with all of these delicious little curves. Those pretty blue eyes . . . so sweet."

Was this really happening? I could feel such heat coming from his already-hard cock pressing on my lower back. His cold hands made their way up my shirt. I wasn't wearing a bra. I gasped at his cold hands and wanted to twist away from them, but he held me firmly in place. The cold of his hands, the heat of his cock pressing into me, the warmth of his tongue and breath on my neck, was melting my resolve. With one swoop of his chef's arms, my shirt came off, and my skin was dappled in goosebumps. He held me firmly in front of him, continuing to press into my back. His hands roamed, rubbing my shoulders and back, then his arms wrapped around me, he pressed hard into me, and he shivered.

He turned me around and lifted me onto the table. "Yes, just there," he whispered hoarsely. Beads of sweat trickled on his skin. My legs wrapped around him automatically. I just wanted to swallow him up. I was so swollen that I could feel my clit throbbing against the seam of my jeans.

Ben began slowly sliding ice cubes around on my nipples, which were harder and bigger than they had ever been before. "Ha," I breathed in. "Cold . . ." I gasped at the exquisite sensation. He loosened my jeans and slipped them off. I willingly lifted my hips.

He sucked in the air. "Oh, Chelsea, you're so hot. Look at your little wet pussy. So ripe."

"Mmmm," was all I could say. My breath was faster and hotter than ever before and I could feel my heart beating in my chest. I gasped and squealed—I never knew such noises could come from me—as he slid the ice all over my body, leaving cold wet traces. When he finally slipped to the hot mound between my thighs, I thought I would explode immediately. But he rubbed me with the ice and then pulled away, rubbed me, then pulled away. Finally, he shoved a cube inside of me and kept his probing long fingers there. The ice gave me a cool burning sensation that lit every pore in my body. Ben's tongue found my clit, where he swirled and bit in a pulsing rhythm. The push and pull of alternating warmth and icy cold, the sucking of his lips, and his gently probing fingers brought intense orgasmic waves shooting through me, and I bucked hard against Ben's face.

I stole a glance at him between my thighs and he was still intent on my crotch. He was going to kill me with that tongue. I reached for him and finally tore at his jeans. He laughed, gently. "Slow down, babe . . ."

But I didn't want to slow down. I had wondered long enough what his cock would feel like inside me. When it finally made an appearance, I opened my mouth. It was so long that I was surprised I could take the whole thing in my mouth and into my throat. I was beginning to think I'd choke when I heard him moan, and soon he jerked hard against my face, giving me a deep swallow of his salty juices.

Afterward, we cleaned up the table and I reached for my clothes.

"Please, don't get dressed," Ben said to me, reaching for me, holding me. "I love your sweet little body. Can we just make the filling for the pie? You know, ah, naked?" he grinned sheepishly at me.

I could not deny Ben DeFranco and wondered if any woman could.

So I stood naked in his kitchen, cracking eggs for the custard filling. And I felt okay about that. Surprisingly enough, it felt kind of good to be naked in the kitchen. I've never been embarrassed about my body. And he seemed to like it, so what the fuck? Every once in a while, while he was standing at the mixer, he'd reach out and touch me. Once he stroked my long red hair and looked straight into my eyes. *He was dangerous*, I thought. I could lose myself to those eyes, those hands, that cock.

He poured some wine after we placed the filled pies back in the oven. They smelled heavenly—the scent of cinnamon and nutmeg filled the air. The wine went to my head quickly. I hadn't had any breakfast or lunch.

"I always thought you were shy," he said.

I smiled and shrugged. "Well, I am quiet. Not shy." I swallowed the last bit of my wine.

He smiled, glassy-eyed, and looked me up and down. I felt his eyes caressing me and I placed my leg over his lap. He caressed it and I found myself moist again. His hard cock was pressing up against my thigh. He grabbed for a condom. "I want inside," he whispered and kissed my ear, sending prickling sensations throughout my body. I put the condom on with him gently guiding my hand. He pulled me on top of him. I straddled him, taking that long cock of his in me. His face was twitching with pleasure. I could feel him deep inside me, rubbing against my clit, with his fingers pressed gently on my ass. I milked him as hard as I could, squeezing myself around him, tasting cinnamon on his tongue.

I ran my fingers along the muscled ridges of his arms and fingered his nipples, then his balls, until he made me stop.

"Wait," he breathed. "Don't move. You are so smooth and tight . . . okay . . ."

Then he laid me down, his cock still inside me, placed my ankles on his shoulders and rammed into me. I cupped his firm ass in my hands as it moved in and out. I came in intense waves as he shot himself into me.

We lay in a sticky tangled heap on his couch. I was higher than I've ever been. I'd never felt like this in my life; all the muscles in my body were deeply relaxed. I don't know how many times I came. It felt like every part of me was melting and opening. The smoke snapped me back.

"Aw, shit! The pies!" Ben exclaimed.

I guess even when you know how to bake, it can still be tricky to make a perfect pie.

Home for the Holidays
by Ryan Field

Nathan Carmichael was a quiet young man who tended to avoid direct eye contact with most people. He owned the only video store in the small town of Martha Falls, Maryland, and lived upstairs on the second floor. And when an attractive man walked up to the counter to rent a video, he didn't just stare down at his lap and smile casually like he did with most people; he had to clench his fists so his hands wouldn't shake.

He wore thick black eyeglasses, plaid short-sleeved shirts and baggy, lifeless jeans that sagged in the back. Though he was six feet tall and had strong, wide shoulders, he tended to stoop forward when he walked. His reddish brown, curly hair fell to his neck in long chunks and he parted it too far to the right. His black gum-soled Oxfords were weathered and scrappy because there were no shoe stores left on Main Street in Martha Falls, and he hated shopping in large, crowded malls.

The only people who knew he had the naturally well-defined body of a swimmer were the men he met at the rest stop along the interstate. There were no gay bars in Martha Falls, and the only openly gay people he knew about were too outrageous to take seriously. So he kept his sex life simple and discreet and safe, but he didn't abstain from enjoying men altogether. When he needed a man, he cruised the rest stop on the highway or the glory holes in state park men's rooms. And there was always the adult bookstore twenty miles north. He kept a full supply of lubricated condoms in his car at all times—even though *he* was always the bottom—and never exchanged bodily fluids with strangers. It was furtive and dark in these places; you didn't have to look anyone in the eye and you could remain anonymous.

He liked his small video business and he was happy with his life for the most part, but Christmas was always so long and arduous. He hung little white lights around the entrance door and the front window, and placed a small, plastic Christmas tree—bought pre-decorated from the drugstore— on the counter. But he didn't go overboard with wreaths and ornaments like so many other shops in town did.

He kept the store open extra hours on Christmas Eve in case anyone wanted to buy a DVD to give as a last-minute gift, but few ever did. People rented DVDs earlier in the day to get them through the holidays, but by five in the afternoon, business slowed down to practically nothing. And cruising for sex on Christmas Eve was pointless: the rest stops on the highway were empty because the guys who normally would have been cruising were home with their families. Nathan didn't have any family left in town. He had one brother who lived in California, but he couldn't just pick up and leave the store once a year; he was the only one who worked there.

So it came as quite a shock one Christmas Eve a few years back when a good-looking young man tugged on the sleeve of his red plaid shirt and asked, "Do you have an adults-only section? I'm home visiting family for the holidays and I don't have an account here."

It was nine o'clock at night, and there hadn't been one single customer in the store since seven. Nathan had been so busy reading a new science fiction novel that he hadn't heard the man enter. He jumped back in his seat and dropped the book, then looked up to see an attractive young man with large blue eyes, dark brown hair, and a wide smile standing over him. He wore a sleek black leather jacket with a long red scarf. "There's a section in the back," Nathan said, and then pointed to a door with a sign that read, "Private: Adults Only."

"Do you have any private booths?" the guy asked. He leaned forward slightly to look into Nathan's eyes, but Nathan kept staring down at his own knees.

"Ah, well," Nathan said, "No. Just rentals is all." His voice became a bit harsh; he wasn't running an adult bookstore in the middle of town. But he did wonder how this guy was going to watch porn while he was home visiting his family. Did he sneak down to the family room when they all went to bed? Maybe he had a small DVD player or a laptop.

"That's cool, man," the customer said. But he stood there staring at him and rubbing his jaw. He tilted his head back and asked, "Do I know you? You look very familiar. What's your name?"

Nathan gulped and stared at the red scarf. "Ah, well, Nathan. Nathan Carmichael," he said. His voice was low and his hands felt a little shaky. The guy sounded a lot like someone he'd once known, but that was so long ago.

The guy smiled and shoved his hands into his pockets. "I thought so," he said. "Don't you recognize me, man? We went to high school together."

Nathan lifted his head slowly and stared at the guy's hand-some face and dark brown hair for the first time since he'd entered. He did know who this was, though his face might not have been the first thing Nathan remembered about him.

He had a flashback of his high school days, and he remembered this guy's long, floppy dick bouncing around in the boy's locker room. Nathan had attended a Catholic high school, and he'd worked late every Tuesday and Friday night after bingo with this person. Nathan was in the chess club and this guy was on the football team. They had nothing in common other than the fact that they were the guys who took down all the folding bingo tables in the school gym. Then one night, after all the tables had been folded and stacked, the guy asked Nathan if he wanted to get stoned in the locker room. One thing led to another, and Nathan wound up sucking dick for the first time in his life . . . big, thick football player dick, too. And all this continued on Tuesdays and Friday nights for the remainder of their senior year. It began with Nathan sucking him off, and by the time the school year ended, he was nailing Nathan into the locker room floor. It wasn't as if they became best friends and started hanging out. There was no talk of a relationship; this guy was dating one of the cheerleaders the whole time he was screwing Nathan.

"Lance Roberts," Lance confirmed. "We were in the same class, and we worked bingo on Tuesdays and Fridays."

"Ah, well, Lance Roberts," Nathan said. He reached out to shake his hand and smiled. Then it all came rushing back: the adolescent drama and excitement he used to experience when he saw Lance walking through the gym door in a pair of tight Levis on bingo nights, and the dread and disappointment he'd experienced when he watched him walking through the hallways with his cheerleader girlfriend on his arm. "It must be ten years, at least," he said.

Lance smiled and started to rock back and forth on the balls of his feet. "You haven't changed much at all, man."

Nathan wasn't sure that was a compliment. But he smiled anyway and said, "Neither have you." But Lance *had* changed, a little. Now he was even better looking; he'd filled out and gone from being a scrappy teenage boy to a strapping twenty-eight-year old man with a strong, wide jawline.

Lance laughed out loud and shook his head. "Of all the people to run into while I'm looking for porn on Christmas Eve," he said. "It's just that coming home for the holidays is rough since I came out of the closet. My family accepts me being gay, but there's this silence all the time, as if they don't know what to say."

"Ah, well, there you are," Nathan said. He wasn't sure how else to respond. The last thing he'd expected to hear that night was that Lance Roberts from high school was gay. He'd never kept up with *anyone* from high school. As far as he knew, he was the only one in his class to move back to Martha Falls after college. Everyone else had either moved to Baltimore or some other big city. "I guess that's family," he said, shrugging.

"Do you own this place?" Lance asked. He looked the store up and down for a moment. Then he stared at a sign that read: *Video Boutique*. "It's nice," he said.

"My parents died while I was in my senior year of college, in a car accident. And I decided to move back here and open a small business. Since there weren't any video stores, I figured I'd give the town something it needed. And here I am," he said. He quickly stared over the counter at Lance's jeans. They were tight and hugged his solid thighs. He remembered the salty taste of his cock after football practice on days when there hadn't been time to shower before work. Lance had always been so eager and needy, and Nathan had always been so willing to please him.

Lance told him he was sorry to hear about his parents, and then he went on to quickly explain that after graduation he'd gone to college in Baltimore, majored in criminal justice and become a state trooper. Then he said he'd been married for a few years and that he had a daughter who now lived with his ex-wife in Florida. He shrugged his shoulders and said, "One night, after we'd come home from a party, I just blurted it out. I told my wife, 'I'm gay. I'm sorry. I tried as hard as I could, but I can't do this anymore.'"

Nathan opened his eyes wide and asked, "What did *she* do?" He'd never actually come out of the closet to anyone. He'd figured it was no one's business after his parents died.

Lance smiled. "At first she was shocked, of course. But then, after she thought about it, she said it all made sense to her. We'd been having problems for a while, and there hadn't been much sex at all the last year of the marriage. It's not that we fought with each other. We lived like best friends, like roommates. I think she was actually relieved to know it wasn't her fault."

"Well, there you are," Nathan said. He'd heard a few stories like this while cruising for sex. Every now and then one of his tricks would open up and feel the need to purge. But he was starting to relax now. His hands weren't shaking anymore and when he spoke, he looked into Lance's blue eyes without thinking twice.

"Hey, why don't we go somewhere for drinks tonight?" Lance said, "What time do you close?" He pressed his large hands on the counter and leaned forward.

Nathan blinked a few times and tilted his head to the side; he smelled spicy and leathery. "I can close any time I want," he said, "but there's nothing open in Martha Falls late on Christmas Eve." But when he saw how Lance frowned, he added, "We could go upstairs, though. I live on the second floor."

Lance smiled and rubbed his palms together. "Cool, man. I'd like that."

When Nathan crossed from behind the counter to lock the front door and lower the lights, he brushed against Lance's black leather jacket by accident. He smiled and said, "Excuse me," but when he looked down he saw that Lance's tight low-rise jeans were bulging forward in the groin area. He remembered that Lance once wore a pair of red bikini briefs at Christmas, with the silly image of a black and white milking cow printed across his groin. The cow had a green Christmas wreath around its neck and gold balls hanging from its ears. When Lance walked around the locker room in that underwear, his dick was so large and his balls were so heavy the cow looked like it was jumping up and down.

Nathan felt a pull in his own groin and his dick began to grow. He wondered if Lance still felt the same way about him. Back in high school, though they never took any of it very seriously then, Lance couldn't wait to get his pants off. There had been nights when he'd been so horny he'd actually begged Nathan to suck his dick.

After the lights went out, Lance followed him to the back of the store, past the "Adults Only" section, and through a door that led to a narrow flight of pie-slice stairs. The building was actually an old Victorian house on Main Street that Nathan had renovated completely with money he'd inherited from his parents. The narrow, circular staircase opened up to an expansive second floor that had a loft-like feeling. Walls had been taken down and oak floors had been refinished with high gloss coatings. The walls were pure white now, and the few pieces of furniture were sleek and modern, with simple straight lines and solid angles. Nathan liked things precise and orderly, and he despised anything that reminded him of his grandmother's attic.

Lance looked around and said, "This is really nice. You've worked hard on this place. The floors are so shiny they remind me of the high school gym where we used to work bingo." And without being asked, he removed his leather coat and the red scarf and rested them neatly on the back of a brown leather club chair near the fireplace. "It's unexpected," he said. "It's all so modern."

Nathan smiled and shrugged his shoulders. "I hate old shit, is all," he said. "I wanted to live in a city loft but I didn't want to move to the city." He noticed that Lance was wearing a tight black sweater; his chest muscles rounded through the wool and the sleeves were pulled up to his elbows. He still had those large, solid forearms Nathan had always loved. There had been times back in high school when all he had to do was stare at Lance's forearms and he'd get an erection.

"But it's not very Christmassy up here," Lance said.

"I do my part for the holidays downstairs," Nathan said. Then he asked, "What can I get you?"

"A vodka martini," Lance said. He ran his palm across the arm of the soft leather sofa and smiled.

Nathan extended his arm and said, "Make yourself comfortable." He crossed the room to a long kitchen area and stood behind a massive center island that was covered with a highly polished slab of black granite. He reached for a remote control that was resting on another black granite surface behind him and turned on his favorite jazz station. It was the only station that wasn't playing the expected Christmas songs that night. They played a few jazzed-up holiday songs every hour, but it wasn't constant. He didn't have anything against Christmas songs, but he'd been hearing them since before Thanksgiving and he'd had enough by then.

When he returned with two martinis, Lance was on the brown leather sofa. He was leaning back with one arm stretched on a cushion and his legs open wide. He placed Lance's drink on a coaster already in place on a square, black marble coffee table and sat down at the other end of the sofa.

Lance's eyes grew wide when he leaned forward to get his drink. "Ah, I need this, man," he said. Then he raised his glass high and said, "To bingo."

"To bingo," Nathan repeated, raising his glass, too. But he wanted to say: *to boy's locker rooms and big dick*.

Nathan took a sip, but he saw that Lance swallowed back almost half the drink at once. He smiled and said, "You were thirsty."

Lance stared at him for a moment. A deep, intense stare; there was a half-smile on his lips and he raised one eyebrow. "Do you mind if I take off my shoes and get comfortable?"

"Ah, well . . ." Nathan said.

But before he could say anything else, Lance kicked off his shoes and stretched his long legs across the length of the sofa. Then he lifted his large feet and rested them on Nathan's lap and said, "Why don't you take off my socks?" His eyes were glazed now and he was smiling. "C'mon . . . for old time's sake. We don't have to worry about getting caught *now*. That is, unless you're married or have a lover."

Nathan lowered his head to Lance's large feet and sighed. "No. I live alone."

"I can't tell you how many times over the years I've

thought about our bingo nights in high school," Lance said, then he reached down and adjusted his dick.

Nathan remembered how much Lance had always liked to have his feet massaged, especially after he'd gone through a rigorous football practice. He used to stretch out on a locker room bench, naked, close his eyes, and moan while Nathan would rub and squeeze his sore feet. And by the time the foot massage was over, his dick was always rock solid and ready to be drained. Now, Nathan took a gulp of his drink, placed it on the table and slowly removed Lance's black socks.

Lance rested his head back and whispered, "Ah, yeah. That feels so good."

Nathan bit his bottom lip and began to massage his feet. They were large and strong, with small patches of black hair on the toes. He squeezed and rubbed for a while, and then Lance said, "Do that thing you used to do . . . please." His eyes were closed and his voiced was soft and deep. And between his legs, Nathan could see his erection popping through the denim.

Nathan knew exactly what he was talking about. So he leaned forward and started licking the bottoms of Lance's feet. He didn't have a foot fetish; he'd never licked anyone else's feet like this. But with Lance, he didn't give it a second thought. He'd always thought every part of his body was sexy. If Lance had begged him to lick and rub his earlobes instead of his feet, he would have done that, too.

"Ah, man," Lance moaned, "that feels fantastic. No one has done that for me since high school." He reached for his drink, swallowed it all, and placed the glass back on the coaster.

Nathan licked between his toes and all the way up to his instep. He licked gently with the tip of his tongue, and continued to massage the bottoms of his feet with the tips of his fingers. "Is this okay?" he asked, with his lips pressed against Lance's big toe.

"Yeah, man. But hold on for a second," Lance said. Then he unzipped his jeans and quickly pulled them off. He lifted his arms and pulled off his sweater, too. He wasn't wearing underwear and he was naked now. "Ah, man," he whispered, "Do it like you used to do it . . . please."

He didn't even have to say "please," because Nathan's man-hungry tongue was already licking his ankles and working its way up his strong, hairy legs. When he reached the inside of Lance's thighs, he opened his mouth all the way and sucked Lance's huge ball sack inside. His cheeks bulged with large, salty balls; he sucked and swallowed and took deep breaths through his nose. He could smell the damp, tweedy aroma of Lance's cock while he gently rolled his balls in slow, even circles.

Lance spread his legs wider and said, "Ah, man, yeah." Then he grabbed a handful of Nathan's hair and lifted his head up a little. "Get naked, man. I wanna see that hot ass again."

Nathan's head fell back and Lance's soggy balls slipped from his mouth. He stood up, kicked off his oversized shoes and stepped out of his baggy jeans. His dick was hard and jumped a few times. It wasn't as wide as Lance's dick, but it was just as long. His legs and his ass were shaved smooth because the guys he'd been with had always told him how much they liked that. And there was a small patch of hair, neatly trimmed and arrow-shaped, above his dick.

When he removed his plaid shirt, he kneeled down on the sofa again between Lance's legs. Lance smiled and said, "You look great, man. Now turn around and spread those legs so I can see that hot ass."

Nathan turned toward the back of the leather sofa and arched his back. He pointed his firm, round ass in Lance's direction and wiggled it a few times.

Lance reached forward and slapped it gently. Then he bit his bottom lip and said, "Suck me off now."

Nathan smiled and turned around. He remembered Lance had always whispered things like this under his breath, but he'd never actually been bold enough to talk dirty out loud. He pressed his palms on Lance's thighs again and opened his mouth. When he wrapped his lips around the head of Lance's dick, Lance moaned, "Suck it, man. Suck that dick."

Nathan took the entire shaft all the way to the back of his throat. He was a more experienced cocksucker now and he was ready to prove it. When he pressed his tongue on the bottom of Lance's dick and began to suck it in and out of his mouth, his cheeks indented. It was still as thick and meaty as he'd remembered from high school, and it still tasted salty and tangy. He took a deep breath through his nose and closed his eyes. He liked a man's dick to taste and smell like dick, not like soap or cologne. He knew Lance was ready to blow a load; his pre-come oozed and Nathan swallowed each sweet, clear drop.

When he finally released the big sopping cock, he reached down and massaged his balls a few times. "You want me to finish you off like this?" he asked. He didn't mind being submissive with Lance. That was what had always been so special between them: the lines between top and bottom were clearly drawn from the start. This was something he'd taken for granted in high school because Lance had been his first man, but when he'd started screwing around with other guys after high school, he was amazed at how boring sex can be with two submissive bottoms.

"I wanna fuck you, man," Lance said, "I want to open those legs and slam into that hole now."

He hesitated for a second, and then placed his palm on Lance's strong forearm. "I'm really serious about being safe, man." Then he lifted the lid of a small wooden box on the coffee table and pulled out a lubricated condom. He shook the small package a few times and said, "Is this cool?" His eyebrows went up and he shrugged his shoulders.

"I'm HIV-negative and disease-free," Lance said, "But feel free to put the condom on my dick. I think it's hot watching you cover my cock with a rubber." Then he grabbed his dick and banged it against Nathan's leg a couple of times.

Nathan smiled. Lance had always liked being treated like a king, like the man in charge, but at the same time pampered and babied and adored. So when he slipped the condom over Lance's dick, he did it gently and methodically, as if he were performing delicate surgery.

Normally, Nathan liked his sex fast and anonymous, but that Christmas Eve with Lance, it occurred to him that he wanted to be tender and articulate. There was something about the way Lance stared at his ass that turned him on so much that he wanted to fall on his knees and beg for dick. So when Lance slapped his ass again and said, "Can I fuck you now?" he nodded yes.

Nathan climbed on top and straddled the rock-solid dick. It was pressed up against his ass crack. He arched his back and licked his index finger, and then shoved his wet finger inside his hole and moved it around a few times. Even though the condom was pre-lubricated, he wanted Lance's dick to slip right in as easily as possible so that when the sensitive nerve endings at the head of Lance's big dick felt the inside of his soft, warm hole, Lance would gasp. Men always did that when they entered his ass; they raved about how soft and tight it was.

He pressed the tip of Lance's cock head to the pink opening and slowly pushed it past his tight anal lips. When the head was inside, Nathan arched his back and sat back slowly so the entire shaft could slide into his body. As Nathan had predicted, though Lance's eyes were closed by then and his brows were knitted together, when the big dick reached the bottom of Nathan's ass, Lance moaned and sighed out loud. "Fucking hot, man," he said, "I remember how fucking smooth and tight that ass is. Ride my dick, man."

"You wanna come inside?" Nathan asked. His teeth were pressed together and one foot anchored him on the floor. He never talked out loud during sex. This was a first. But he was so excited and so into Lance's dick, he couldn't help himself. "You wanna slam that fucking load into my hole?"

"Yeah, man," Lance said, "I wanna come inside. I wanna blow my load into your tight fucking hole, man." He grabbed Nathan by the waist and pressed down hard.

While Lance held his waist, Nathan slowly began to rock and rotate his hips in circles. He squeezed the lips of his hole and tugged on Lance's cock as if he were jerking him off with his hand; he went up and down fast so that each time Lance's dick slammed up his ass there was a loud slap. Lance started to buck his hips with the same rhythm Nathan used to ride the dick. In no time, Nathan was riding the big dick so viciously and with such intensity his head was turning in all directions and his eyes were rolling backwards. He couldn't seem to get enough; he backed into Lance's dick so hard, he had to grab the back of the sofa so he wouldn't fall off. He shouted, "Fuck me, Lance. Fuck me hard."

"I'll fuck that ass, man," Lance said. He bucked his hips harder and closed his eyes.

Lance began to wiggle his large feet and move his legs around, and Nathan remembered that's what he used to do right before he was about to come. So Nathan grabbed his own cock and started to jerk it off.

"I'm close, man," Lance shouted, "I'm fucking close . . . ready to blow soon."

"Go, Lance," Nathan said, now jerking his own dick so they could come at the same time.

Lance leaned forward to squeeze Nathan's round chest muscles, closed his eyes tightly, and shouted, "Fuck, man . . . here it comes . . . fuck, man . . . ride that dick." Then his entire body started to jerk around; his hairy legs stretched all the way out and his toes curled back. When he came, he bucked his hips into Nathan's ass and filled the condom. And Nathan hardly had to touch his own cock to come with Lance's big dick buried all the way up his hole. He shot a load over the arm of the sofa, past Lance's head, that landed somewhere on the wooden floor.

Lance grabbed his waist again and sighed. "Man, that's the best fuck I've had since high school." Then he bit his bottom lip again and slapped Nathan's ass hard a few times.

Nathan pressed his ass harder against Lance's dick and tightened his hole. He wanted to keep it inside as long as he could. "I needed that," he said. His hair was sticking up all over and his lips were swollen from cocksucking.

"Come here," Lance said. He reached forward and pressed his wide palm to the back of Nathan's head and pulled it toward his face so they could kiss. He stuck his thick, warm tongue all the way into Nathan's mouth and rolled it around a few times.

Nathan pressed his lips to Lance's and sighed while they sucked tongues. Even though they'd fucked all through their senior year, this was the first time they'd ever actually kissed. Lance's dick was still up his ass and he was moving his hips in slow circles; the big dick filled him completely.

After the kiss, Nathan slowly stood and Lance's dick slipped out and hit him on the stomach with a slap. Before Nathan crossed the room to get a clean towel and a warm, wet washrag, he leaned forward and slowly removed the used condom from Lance's dick. The towel was for cleaning up the come, and the washrag was for massaging Lance's empty balls.

A moment later, Lance said, "That feels really good." Nathan was kneeling on the floor beside the sofa, massaging his balls with the wet rag. His eyes were closed and his legs were spread wide. "I'm glad I stopped in for a DVD tonight."

Nathan smiled. "I guess you have to get back now," he said. Then he ran his other hand up and down Lance's hairy thigh and sighed.

"I'm a big boy," Lance said, "I can stay out as long as I want."

Nathan smiled and squeezed his balls a few times with the warm rag. "I'm curious. Do you still have the cow underwear? The red ones with the Christmas cow?"

He laughed and said, "You really liked them, from what I remember. All I had to do was walk around a little and you were down on your knees milking that cow with your mouth." He slowly rubbed Nathan's ass and said, "I threw them out years ago."

Nathan reached between his legs and grabbed his dick. It was soft now, but still a handful. "It wasn't the cow I wanted to milk. It was what was behind the cow that made me thirsty."

Then he opened his mouth, stuck out his tongue, and started licking the soft shaft. It was warm and spongy and smelled like his bathroom soap now.

Lance placed his hands behind his head and sighed. "If I sleep here tonight, I can give you a really good Christmas present in the morning."

Nathan looked up and his mouth fell open for a second. He'd expected Lance to do what he'd always done after fucking: put on his pants, pull up his zipper, and say, "Thanks, I needed that. See you next week."

"That is, if it's okay to spend the night," Lance said. He spread his legs a little wider and adjusted his position on the sofa.

Nathan pressed his lips together and squinted his eyes for a moment, and then he pressed his palm to his throat and said, "Of course it's okay to spend the night. Because I may have a Christmas gift or two for you."

Lance laughed and scratched his balls a couple of times. "I'll bet you do."

Bad Santa

by Jamaica Layne

I've never fucked Santa Claus before. And I wonder why not.

Because if what just happened here in the Macy's Ladies' Better Dresses department fitting room is any example, Santa Claus is the best fuck on this or any other planet.

Let's back up a bit.

It all started when I went to Macy's for their annual Fall Designer Sample Sale. I've always been a sucker for sample sales. My mom got me hooked on them back when I was but a wee girl growing up in Great Neck. Every spring and fall, Mom and I would take the commuter train into Manhattan for a day at the sample sales. We'd start out at Macy's, and once we'd picked Macy's sample stock over, we headed for Bloomingdale's to check out the next level up in merchandise. And then, if we had any energy or money left, we'd close the day out at Barney's. Alas, Mom and I only were able to afford to buy something at the Barney's sample sale one time, but it *did* turn out to be my senior prom dress.

After so many years scouting out sample sale schedules, picking through vast piles of department-store castoffs in search of that One Great Find—and my closet is full of One

Great Finds, from patent-leather Steve Maddens to well-cut broadcloth blazers by Laura Rowley to rhinestone-studded DKNY belts—I am an expert in All Things Sample Sale.

Well, an expert in all things save one, I guess. You see, I never expected to run into Santa Claus at the Macy's Fall Sample Sale. Let alone fuck his brains out in the Ladies' Better Dresses department fitting room.

When I arrived at Macy's at 8 a.m. sharp—they open the doors early for those of us lucky enough to have obtained a Fall Sample Sale VIP pass—the only thing on my mind was whether I could get my hands on the latest Michael Kors fall separates, maybe even a Jones New York black cocktail dress and matching black satin pumps, if I was lucky. I certainly wasn't in the market for nooky. Let alone nooky with Santa. After all, one doesn't usually equate "Santa" with "sex." Quite the opposite, in fact. The last time I even *thought* about Santa Claus was when I was nine years old and I asked the Santa at the Great Neck Mall if he would bring me a Cabbage Patch Kid for Christmas.

And twenty-odd years later, I'm *still waiting* for that damn Cabbage Patch Kid. Suffice to say that 1985 was the last year I believed in Santa Claus.

Until now.

Santa Claus came back into my life just as the Fall Sample Sale was winding down for the day. I'd just paid for my purchases—a green Diane Von Furstenberg wrap dress, black linen trousers by Michael Kors with matching blazer, and a pair of red-leather-and-cork wedgies by Ferragamo—and was heading for the escalator when I ran into Santa Claus.

Santa Claus came out of nowhere. I never saw him coming. It was almost as if he appeared out of thin air.

Hell, maybe he *did* appear out of thin air.

All I know is, one minute I had a wide-open path to the escalator down into the Ladies' Better Dresses department, the next I ran smack-dab into a belly like a bowl full of jelly.

Since I was wearing four-inch stilettos (on sale at Baker's last fall, $28.99) I lost my balance and ended up flat on my ass. And the floor of Macy's isn't exactly clean, either, so the seat of my seersucker Rafaella trousers was now ruined.

I looked up and stared into the most beautiful blue eyes I'd ever seen. Then I was shocked and disappointed to see those blue eyes belonged to a bearded fat man in a red velvet suit.

"I'm terribly sorry, miss. I wasn't looking where I was going."

I scoffed. "Yeah, I'll say. These are brand-new pants, you know. Now I'll have to send them to the cleaners and pay extra for butt-stain removal."

Santa extended a hand and helped me stand up. My shopping bags were scattered all over the floor; he gathered them together and handed them to me. "Allow me to make it up to you," he said in a voice that was a lot younger than he looked. "My name's Kris. Kris Kringle. What's yours?"

I couldn't help but be a little charmed. Those blue eyes were gorgeous, after all. And he *was* Santa Claus. Maybe I could still finagle that Cabbage Patch Kid out of him after all these years. "I'm Deborah," I said. "Deborah Manning."

Instant recognition flashed across Kris Kringle's pudgy pink features. "Ah yes. Deborah Manning. Originally from Great Neck, New Jersey, now living in a two-bedroom flat in Flushing."

My jaw dropped. "How do you know that?"

Kris touched a finger to his button nose and winked. "Oh, I have my ways. How's that new job working out for you, by the way? The one at the Water Department? Is your new boss still giving you trouble?"

Now I didn't know what to think. Obviously this guy wasn't your run-of-the-mill department-store Santa. This guy was the real thing.

Was he?

I guessed there was one way to find out.

"You know, Kris, since you're here and everything, I've been meaning to ask you a question for, like, twenty-three years now. Why didn't I get that Cabbage Patch Kid for Christmas '85? It was the only thing I wanted that year, but I ended up with a lousy old *E.T. The Extra-Terrestrial* doll from three years earlier instead."

He seemed to think back for a minute, then said "Aha! Yes, Deborah, I remember that Christmas very well. I did have you on my list for a Cabbage Patch Kid that year. But then I found out you cheated on a geometry test the week before Christmas, so I was forced to degrade your gift to one of my old overstock E.T. dolls. Let that be a lesson to you, Deborah: Santa always knows when you've been bad."

I felt my cheeks grow hot. I'd completely forgotten about how I'd cheated on my last fourth-grade geometry test of the semester by copying over my friend and math whiz Rachel Hanson's shoulder. I thought nobody knew about that, since I'd gotten away with it without being caught by anyone, not even by Rachel herself.

Anyone except Kris Kringle here, that is.

I hung my head. "I'm sorry, Kris." I said. "But I've always been really bad at math and I was afraid I was gonna have to repeat the fourth grade if I didn't pass."

Kris gives me a smile. "That's all right, Deborah. We all make mistakes. Myself included."

I shifted from one stilettoed foot to the other. Those pumps were killing me. I needed an appointment with Dr. Scholl. "I find that hard to believe, Santa."

"It's true, Deborah. Even Santa Claus isn't perfect. How do you think I ended up stuck here at Macy's during the fall clearance sales when I should be back at my workshop filling orders?" He paused, licked his lips. "I prefer to be called Kris, by the way. Santa is more of a title than a name."

"All right, I find that hard to believe, *Kris*. You're good and kind and perfect. You make all the little boys and girls around the world happy. The ones who don't cheat at math, anyway."

Kris's face wrenched into a nervous twitch, and he blinked twice. "You'd be surprised."

I raised an eyebrow. "What exactly do you mean by that?"

Kris cleared his throat and coughed twice. "I have certain . . . weaknesses."

I wasn't entirely sure, but I thought I saw Kris starting to undress me with his eyes. "Oh, yeah? And what kinds of weaknesses are those?" Though judging by the tent that was starting to form in Santa's red velvet crotch, I was beginning to have some idea.

"Deborah, why don't we take a walk and I'll explain." He took my arm and steered me over to the escalator. We rode it down into the Ladies' Better Dresses department. As Kris began leading me through a rack of silk-polyester blend knockoff Paris Hilton babydoll smocks, I began to notice a marked change in him. Gone was the fat bearded old man with a belly like a bowl full of jelly. A tall, strapping young man of twenty-five or so had replaced him, as if by magic. He was still in the red velvet suit, but instead of being baggy and lumpy, the red velvet clung to his lean, rippled body, emphasizing the chiseled outlines of his pecs and biceps. The long, snowy white beard was now a sexy stubble à la Orlando Bloom. "I have a terrible weakness for beautiful ladies such as yourself, Deborah. And there aren't a lot of beautiful ladies back at the North Pole. All I've got up there are a bunch of genderless elves. And Mrs. Claus, who by order of Saint Nicholas doesn't even have a vagina. So you can imagine I can get a little sexually frustrated. I pop into Macy's every year around this time looking for, well, you know what I mean. I think you and I could make some beautiful music together. Wanna fuck?"

I was speechless. After all, it wasn't every day that Santa Claus dropped into your life, looking like Orlando Bloom and wanting to fuck.

"You've been a pretty good girl this year, Deborah," Kris went on. "And if you don't mind, I'd like to grant your Christmas wish a little early this year. And I happen to know exactly what you wished for." He gave me a wink, and nudged his now-bulging crotch in my direction.

It was pretty obvious by now that Kris Kringle knew all I wanted for Christmas this year was a better sex life. I've been stuck in a dry spell since—well, I'd rather not say for how long.

And here was Santa Claus, offering to grant me that wish himself smack-dab in the middle of Macy's.

I'd say that more than made up for that damn Cabbage Patch Kid.

I sidled up to him, pressing myself against the bulge at Kris' crotch, and liking very much what I felt there. From what I could tell, Kris Kringle was about as well endowed as Ron Jeremy, and far better-looking. "We should probably find someplace private," I said.

Huzzah! I was about to fuck Santa Claus. And Santa Claus looked like Orlando Bloom. Hell, he looked *better* than Orlando Bloom.

Was today my lucky day, or what?

Now it was my turn to take the lead, so I took Kris Kringle by the hand and dragged him to the Ladies' Better Dresses fitting rooms. The gum-chewing attendant was too engrossed in her dog-eared copy of *Life & Style* to notice I was dragging a man who looked like Orlando Bloom in a Santa suit into the fitting room with me. Hell, I didn't even have any clothes to try on. After all, I was only going into the fitting room to get my clothes (and his) *off.*

I pulled Kris along behind me until we reached the last changing stall. I yanked him into the stall after me, latched the scuffed blue louvered dressing-room door shut, and began ripping off his clothes.

I was ripping *Santa Claus*'s clothes off. And he was *helping* me.

I could hardly believe it myself.

Before I could take another breath, Kris Kringle himself was standing before me naked in all his buff, young, rippled-muscle glory. I didn't care that it was all just an illusion, a bit of early Christmas magic designed to get me to fuck a fat old man who lived in the frozen wastelands of the North Pole. All my eyes saw was a drop-dead gorgeous man with a very erect penis.

A very erect penis he wanted to fuck me with.

Kris Kringle's hands roamed my body, peeling off one article of clothing at a time. First came my white cotton DKNY blouse, then my pink silk camisole by Victoria's Secret. Then off came my skinny jeans from Forever 21, followed by my black stilettos. My Miracle Bra was next. Kris threw it up in the air with a shriek of delight and it ended up suspended from one of the store's glaring overhead light fixtures. Last, but not least, was my black lace La Perla thong, which Kris eased slowly down my thighs, slipped off over my bare feet, then brought up to his mouth. He bit into their cotton crotch with a lion's growl, then started nibbling on my neck. The scent of my arousal filled the air, mixing with the floral notes of my Jessica McClintock perfume. He fingered my cunt, nimbly parting my folds and searching for my clit, which he found in less than a split second.

I spread my legs wider and squatted down, pushing my cunt into Kris's probing fingers. He explored me with all the dexterous skill of a Renaissance sculptor, bringing me to climax almost immediately. As soon as the last wild pulses of that first orgasm subsided, Kris grabbed me by the buttocks, flipped me over, and started fucking me from behind.

Kris Kringle plunged all eight-and-a-half inches of his bulging, throbbing, thick-as-a-tree-branch cock into my cunt all at once, stretching the walls of my vagina to the absolute limit. I had to bite down on my hand to keep from screaming as he fucked me, his cock ramming into my g-spot so hard that my teeth rattled in their sockets. I came again and again and again, my whole body experiencing a mind-blowing all-over orgasm. I could no longer contain my ecstasy, and began to groan and grunt aloud. I didn't care who heard me. I didn't care if a whole team of Macy's store detectives suddenly barged in and arrested us both for public indecency. The only thing I cared about was enjoying the hell out of this amazing fuck.

"Unnnnuuuhhhhhh," I said, bucking my hips up against Kris's like a brood mare in heat. "Unuh, unuh, unuh. Yeah. Yeah. Oh, *yeah!*"

Kris Kringle was enjoying it as much as I was. Not only

was he fucking me at mach speed—his cock was strutting up and down my cunt at a rate of approximately three hundred strokes a minute—he was showering me with the most incredible stream of dirty pillow talk imaginable.

"Oh, Deborah, you bad, bad little cunt. Oh, how I love your naughty little cunt. *Unuh.* Oh, yeah, baby. Give me some more of that cunt, baby. I love, love, love your pussy. You smell so good. Your cunt smells like honey, baby, and I want to eat you up. Give me some more of that beautiful pussy. Unuh, unuh, *unuh*, oh, baby, I love fucking you, Deborah. You've been such a good, good, good girl this year. Santa's gonna bring you a present . . . *unuuuuhhhuuuh!*"

With that, Santa Claus exploded into my pussy. His seed spurted into me so hard, I could practically taste it.

And Santa Claus tasted damn good.

I braced my body up against the Macy's three-way dressing mirror, my panting breath making a huge cloud on the mirror glass. I could see the reflection of Kris Kringle's cock penetrating my red, glistening pussy from three sides. Even with Kris collapsed over my back, groaning in exhaustion while his cock slowly deflated inside me, it was a beautiful sight.

"You've been a bad, bad boy, Santa," I sighed. "You won't be getting any toys this year. No siree."

"Baby, as long as I've got you, I don't need any toys," Kris sighed into the back of my neck. "Or anything else."

He spanked me lightly across the buttocks, and withdrew. "Deborah, I'm going to have to watch my back now that we've found each other. I can see myself being a very, very bad boy any time I'm within ten feet of you. Which doesn't bode well for the children of the world." He fell back onto the Formica dressing bench, began to pull on his red velvet suit. "Do you know that every time I fall prey to my weakness for beautiful ladies, Saint Nicholas adds another year to my sentence? At this rate, I won't be able to give up being Santa for at least another thousand years."

I was puzzled at this. "What do you mean, *your sentence*?"

Kris finished getting dressed and sighed. "I'll tell you a little secret, Deborah. I didn't *choose* to be Santa Claus. Being Santa Claus is a prison sentence. Saint Nicholas is actually an all-powerful evil overlord. Saint Nicholas forced me to serve as Santa Claus for five thousand years as punishment for sleeping with the Whore of Babylon back in biblical times. I've still got three thousand years left on my sentence, and every time I skip out of the North Pole and come down to New York for nooky, it just gets longer."

I was stunned. "Wow. I had no idea."

"Saint Nicholas doesn't like sex or people who like having it," Kris went on. "That's why he imprisoned me all those years ago, made the Whore of Babylon into Mrs. Claus, and then took away Mrs. Claus's vagina so we could never fuck for all eternity. The irony is, down here in the real world, people think Santa Claus and Saint Nicholas are the same person. Nothing could be further from the truth. And good ol' Saint Nick loves nothing more than to punish me for my libido. I'll never be my own person again at the rate I'm going. But I can't help it. I love to fuck, and I'm willing to keep myself imprisoned for all eternity to get what this body needs."

He pointed at himself. "*This* is what I really look like, by the way. Or what I *used* to look like, thousands of years ago when I was the randy boy about town back in Babylon. The whole bowl-full-of-jelly look and the white beard is all part of my punishment. And I'm sorry to say that I can't hold on to my real form for much longer. I'll be back to being fat and old before you know it, Deborah. I thought it best to warn you before it happens."

"Thanks for the warning," I said. "But no matter what happens, Kris, I'll always remember you just like this."

Kris smiled and gave me a gentle kiss on the cheek. Then a shimmering wave of light overtook him, and he was back to being good-old-fashioned fat, bearded, and old Santa Claus.

"Take care, Deborah. I hope we can see each other again sometime. Maybe right here at Macy's next year, after the Fall Sample Sale. Macy's in late November, just before the holiday season starts, will always be my favorite place on Earth." He leaned over, kissed me full on the mouth. "Keep on being a good girl, Deborah, and I promise your every wish will come true."

Kris tapped his pudgy little button nose twice. There was an audible *pop*, and he was gone.

I was sorry to see him go. But at the same time, I was happy I was able to bring a little joy into Kris's obviously very sad and lonely life. He sure as hell brought some joy into mine.

And you can be sure I'll be back at Macy's for next year's Fall Sample Sale. And I'll be on the lookout for Kris again too, right by the escalator to the Ladies' Better Dresses department.

Yes, Virginia, there *is* a Santa Claus.

And he sure as hell ain't a virgin.

Occupational Hazards
by Ginevra Ermine

Life-changing events come in many shapes and sizes. Some are easy to spot, like weddings, funerals, and experiences in a hotel room after the senior prom. Others sneak up on you on little piggie feet and blindside you. My life changed on an evening when I was doing something amazingly pedestrian: working.

It all began during the early shift at Tommy's Tasty Tail Town. I am a recreational performer . . . no, an exotic dancer . . . okay, I'm a stripper. That night, I went on for my first dance when the house was still very light. It was the week before Christmas, so I was wearing a red rubber bikini with faux fur trim and a matching Santa hat and G-string. My fire-engine red four-inch heels had sleigh bells stapled to them, so I was introduced as Prancer, though my stage name is normally Panzer.

Not because of my big guns, gutter-mind. It's because of my aggressive attitude.

So, I'm out there in the klieg lights strutting my stuff very effectively while sounding like damn Tinkerbell. But, hey, it's a living. In this business, BBB is not Bed Bath & Beyond, it's Boobs, Butt & Bend-over. Whenever facing the audience,

I bend forward to display my impressive, perhaps even awe-inspiring, cleavage. When facing away, I automatically project my ass forward (because of the heels) and, as often as possible, bend deeply at the waist to contort myself into a vulnerable, inviting position.

It ain't exactly subtle, but what's a girl to do? It works, as in it brings in the big tips. Of course, my voluptuousness, milky skin, shiny black hair, and button nose don't hurt either. Oh, and my legs. It's hard to turn heads properly on this stage without disproportionally long legs.

Tonight I was dancing to "Grandma Got Run Over by a Reindeer," which is a challenge Ginger Rogers never had to face. But as long as there is some sort of beat to shake your hips to, which song is playing isn't that important. I could disrobe to Chopin if absolutely necessary.

Most of the number I spent downstage right, playing to the biggest group of men in the audience. There were five of them, barely legal boys out on the town. They were newbies; their eyes dilated as big as dinner plates when I shimmied out of my bra and shook my breasts towards them. It was their first time in a strip club, I was sure of that, but they didn't skimp on their research: when I dip a hip at each in turn, they dutifully insert folded singles into the waistband of my G-string. I wordlessly flirt with them, smiling, smirking, and blowing kisses as they stare unabashedly at my tits.

Which is what they were supposed to do. I'd have felt insulted if they sat there pretending I was dressed, for gosh sake.

The song ended. I took a bow forward and backwards, gathered my bra and returned backstage to freshen up before I worked the crowd. Our dressing room had brick walls, bare bulbs, and cracked mirrors. Every expense had been spared in decorating our personal space. Four of my fellow dancers were there, making up, teasing their hair, or tucking silicone into Spandex. The tools of the trade, being readied for business. I dressed (well, put my bra back on and wrapped a hanky around my waist), checked my look and started to stride out to the floor. "What's the hurry, Pansy?" Jade asked me. She's a tall, skinny Asian woman with a surgically applied 32DD chest. In my opinion, this look didn't really work for her, but our profession wasn't really about aesthetics.

"There's an enthusiastic pack of Scouts out there. I don't want to keep them waiting."

"You lucky girl. Mind if I join ya after my number?"

"Fine with me, but don't dilly-dally. I'd say they're halfway home already." I jumped out of the way for Annie (stage name: Blaze), who was sprinting to the stage in response to her introduction. She was trying out a dominatrix act, so was squeaking past in a black leather unitard. I tried that once, when I first started in the business, and it was a disaster. Nothing is less comfortable under stage lights than black leather. I had a heat rash for weeks, and people are very intolerant of their strippers having rashes.

I walked around the stage as Blaze started cracking her whip to the classic Devo tune. The group I'm aiming for was sitting at their table, looking scared, apparently not very interested in either bondage or submission. Excellent, I wanted to monopolize their attention anyhow. I sneaked up behind the dude closest to me, a handsome boy with sandy hair and big brown eyes. I covered up those eyes with my hands and let my breasts tickle the back of his neck. "Hey there, sweetheart. How are you?"

He swiveled in his chair while standing. I was surprised to see he was a good head taller than I was, even with my tall shoes; men all look short from the stage. His boyish face makes me smile, especially the peach fuzz around his lips and chin pretending to be a goatee. He smiled and said, "Hello! We're so happy to see you!" His friends all stood up as well; if they were wearing hats, I'm sure they would be doffing them. This wasn't surprising—they were just acting like one of the two types of fans we strippers have. Type A treats us like princesses. They are complete gentlemen, and so very grateful for each view or touch of your grace upon them.

Type B treats us like whores.

So, I felt fortunate to be hanging with some Type As tonight. Most newbies are Type As anyhow, but these guys strike me as Type As for life. They all wore khakis, polo shirts, and loafers, which I appreciated. I like it when the customers dress up a little—it gives stripping a sense of occasion. We were still standing awkwardly and I realized I'd need to talk them through this process. "So, do you have an extra seat for a working girl?"

Upon hearing my words, they immediately scrambled into action, making room for me in the middle of their pack. I headed to my place and used both hands to smooth my micro skirt under my buns as I sat down. They all immediately sat surrounding me, their eyes never wavering from me for an instant. Was I the first woman they've ever seen or something? No, that was unlikely, but I may have been the first woman to sit down with them with so much exposed skin. I thought it was time to show them it's okay to talk to a lady, however she may be or not be dressed. I turned to the sandy-haired boy and said, "During the holiday season I'm known as Prancer, but the rest of the year I'm Panzer."

He stared at me with his intense eyes for a long moment and I was surprised to feel myself blush. He took my hint, though, and replied, "I'm Ben." I smiled at him warmly as he continued, "These are my friends Tom, Dick, Harry, and my roommate, Algonquin."

"Algonquin? Are you kidding me?" I asked with a smile to the last boy, sporting Kurt Cobain-ish stringy blond hair.

"No, ma'am," he replied with a straight face.

"Well, all right, Algonquin it is. I am pleased to meet all of you. Did you enjoy the show?"

In response to this question, they all broke out in bright grins. "Oh, yes," Ben told me. "You are an exceptional dancer. Will you be dancing again this evening?"

I was right; they were newbies. They think this is a strip club with two hundred dancers in it, so I wouldn't need to take another turn tonight. It made me want to laugh, but I control it. These were nice guys and I didn't want to make them feel bad. And even if I weren't such a sweetheart, they were guys who still had cash in their pockets. I couldn't afford to offend them. "Yes, I'll be on stage again in about an hour. But there's no reason to wait that long. If you want, we can go to a private room and I can dance for you right now."

Though I had their attention before, they were now really, really paying attention to me. I imagined I could hear their erections stretching out at the very thought of being in a room alone with me. Their enthusiasm was quite arousing. I liked newbies, I imagined in much the same way that men like virgins: they were non-threatening, you called all the shots, and there was the thrill of being the experience to which all others will be compared. This excitement on my part was not very professional of me, I knew, but when I was feeling it, I didn't try to stop it. Why would I? I was as human as the next woman. I knew what the next question of my new friends was going to be, and Ben finally works up the nerve to ask it. "Ms. Panzer, how much would that cost?"

I named my price and watched their mental arithmetic as they decided if they could afford my services or not. Their eyes flashed messages back and forth across the table, small nods and head shakes revealing their thoughts. I arched my back a little, making sure my assets were as liquid as possible, and saw boys who had been shaking start to nod. "We accept your offer," Ben said, stumbling over the words. Poor kid. It was hard to keep the higher brain functions working when your blood flow was so disrupted.

I don't know why I kept calling them "kids." I'm only twenty-four, probably no more than three years older than any of them, but I felt comparatively ancient. I agreed with the classic Indiana Jones line: It ain't the years, it's the mileage. All those years of loving, supportive childhood and family camping vacations really took their toll on a rebel like me.

I stood and smiled, giving them a come-hither finger so they'd follow. Soon I was a semi-clad pied piper, leading my charges away, never to return—or never to return quite the same, anyhow. I parted the curtains of the nearest orgas-ma-tron (as we ladies called the private rooms) and held the curtains out of the way for them to enter. It was very dim in here, so it was difficult for them to see where they were supposed to sit. Once they are all in and milling about in the center of the room, I closed the curtain and felt out the light switch, sliding the dimmer upward until I could see them all clearly, like a herd of sheep waiting for a dog to guide them. Wordlessly, I glided forward to each in turn, took their hand in mine, and led them to a seat. Ben squeezed my hand slightly when he had the chance. The layout of the room had love seats on each side except the one we entered from, so after I seated them there was only one spot left open, next to Ben. The men sat as far from each other as the love seats would allow; when guys are excited, they don't want to be too close to other guys.

"Okay, gentlemen. If we can take care of business first, then our performance can begin." They caught my meaning immediately and vaulted for their wallets, extracting wads of bills which they handed to their informal leader, Ben. He counted all the money and then nervously proffered it to me. I let him wait for a few seconds, slowly tiptoeing towards him and then caressing his hand before grasping the bills and taking them with me. I tucked them safely in my small purse and turned my back on the group as I walked to the stereo controls near the entrance. There I left my purse and chose some soft, slow music for this evening. I thought anything faster would frighten my charges more than excite them.

I started to dance, slowly, swaying just with my lower body. There was a language of exotic dance, messages the body passed on to the viewer as clearly as holding up flashcards. Hips, legs, and pelvis rotating slowly said, "I want you to be as excited as I am." Reaching out with the hands said, "I'm aching to hold you." Taking off the bra said, "Look here, stupid." Humping a pole (or a lap) said, "My feet are killing me; come already." So, I was rotating my hips and pelvis as I walked to the center of the room. I was performing in the round, so I needed to consider what the view was on three sides of me with each move I made. I noticed the guys were sitting in the same order as when I first met them, which wasn't intentional on my part but it made it easier to keep track of whom I was dealing with. I turned slowly towards Algonquin and approached like a cat stalks a mouse. I could see him swallow hard, his hands clamped on his legs to keep them from shaking. I moved close, but not too close. A lot of dancers made a mistake in lap dancing in forgetting that men are visually stimulated. If you got in too close, they couldn't see your breasts or derriere anymore and it wasn't as satisfying for them. So I stopped a few steps away and shook my breasts down towards his waiting face. He started to lean forward to meet them, but a quick shake of my head stopped him and he leaned back and just watched, as he should. I then rotated my way around and brushed against his lap with my cheeks and hips and heard him gasp. That made me smile. I looked from eye to eye of the remainder of my audience and saw in them the start of flight-or-fight responses, but each was up to the challenge. They held their ground and waited their turn.

I worked around the room without haste, giving each his due attention. I didn't repeat any move precisely, but I didn't do anything that different either; I mean, how many ways can you present your T&A? But I was a professional. I'd been playing this game for some time now, and I knew what I was doing. I thought I had them all feeling uncomfortably excited by now, so I backed away to a point where they all could see me and deftly removed my bra. I felt a little shiver go down my spine with this grand denouement. Talk about job satisfaction!

I danced my way closer to them, lifting my pseudo skirt out of the way from time to time. Watching their eyes tracking me, I was pleased to see I could direct their attention wherever I wanted it, on the headlights or the mud flaps, as I saw fit, and thought it was about time to bring this ship into port. I'm not supposed to play favorites, but I instinctively turned to and approached Ben, who seemed to be vibrating slightly in his chair, and just kept coming. I reached down, grabbed his legs, and slid him forward in his seat. Given this access, I slid onto his lap. I'm not supposed to touch too intimately, but tonight, I didn't care. I let my breasts touch both sides of his face and began my grand finale, working the hips. I felt the hard knob of him between my legs, telling me he was an overachiever in the important category of penile length. Ben was immediately past his point of no return and moaning. I cupped his face in my hand as his body shuddered and he continued to soil himself. His face, contorted in ecstasy, just moved me somehow. I smiled a genuine, happy smile.

I reluctantly slid off Ben's lap, figuring I'd have to go boy to boy at this point, but I noticed all of them were displaying their own sign language: hands cupped over their groins, the mixed pleasure and discomfort of climax and cleaning disaster. Damn, I was good! I was making men shoot tapioca from across the room.

I thanked them cordially as I re-dressed. I invited them to watch me again on the main stage as I departed, watching Ben watching me as I slipped through the curtain. I didn't really expect to see them, though, and I didn't. Once you'd climaxed in your shorts, the desire to clean up usually overwhelmed the desire to be aroused some more. The gentlemen were nowhere the rest of the evening, and I didn't think any more about them.

Until I got home that night. When you started considering a career in the erotic arts, no one warned you about a serious occupational hazard: getting hot and bothered and then going home alone. And it wasn't really possible to take your work home with you, if you know what I mean. First of all, you just didn't know where most of those men have been. And in the process of culling one from the herd, the rest of the herd sometimes got pretty pissed off. So I spent all that time arousing myself and others and then ended up watching late night TV solo, fishing around my bed for an erection that just wasn't there.

This phenomenon was particularly pronounced tonight. I had a soft spot in my heart, and in my head, for newbies. Especially newbies with kind eyes, impeccable manners, and prodigious erections. I really wished I had brought Ben home with me. I wasn't sure how I would have managed that maneuver, given Tom, Dick, Harry, and the ever-pleasant Algonquin, but I wished I would have given it some serious thought back when I had the chance. Maybe I could have . . . I didn't know. But here, in the dark, watching ads for chat lines and Extenze, my panties were as damp as a sponge and I was aching to be touched.

I hoped he'd come back into the club again and give me a second chance.

A week passed and I saw no sign of Ben. I danced, I collected money, and I went home thinking about only one man. I hadn't been this infatuated with someone since I was a Goth teenager and I couldn't stop thinking about Lon Chaney.

A young Lon Chaney, you perverts, not the dead Lon Chaney!

December 23 was a particularly long evening, punctuated by an old duffer with no hair and a huge turkey-wattle of a neck sitting in the front row all night hissing, "Sit on my face! Sit on my face!" After five hours of that, I had to get out of there. I changed into my faded jeans and a Metallica T-shirt and started for home. It was about two in the morning, but that was no reason to just go home, not in America anyway. In America, if I wanted to go shopping, I went shopping, clock be damned. There was a Wal-Mart Supercenter between Tasty Tail Town and my apartment, so I stopped in to do my weekly grocery shopping and try to forget about that very creepy old man.

I puttered around in the fruit-and-vegetable area for a while, not really sure what I wanted to buy. It was in this distracted state that I drove my cart around a display stand of apples and oranges and nearly crashed into a cart being pushed by Ben. "Oh, hey, hello!" he said, trying to act surprised to see me, but I wasn't recently off the turnip truck. The turnip truck and I have been down this road before, and it had never been a pleasant journey.

I instinctively backed up several steps, my fear and anger overwhelming my recent attraction. Bristling like a mangy dog, I barked, "Ben, you're a terrible actor. How long have you been stalking me?"

"Oh, no, I haven't been . . ." he started, then paused. "I . . . I followed you here after your shift ended. That's it."

"That's it!"

"But I just can't stop thinking of you!"

"You will when the bouncers beat the shit out of you the next time you hang out near our parking lot! Get it?"

I thought I was yelling or something close to yelling. But Ben looked like he'd already been worked over by the bouncers. My anger cracked and I just wanted to hug the little feller. He looked so scared after my tirade, but I didn't get a chance. He was ready to run and mumbled something I imagined was an apology as he abandoned his cart and headed to the exit. I wanted to call out to him, I really did, and Wal-Mart was empty so I really should have, but I didn't. Instead, I stupidly watched him jog away, again.

My heart just wasn't in shopping anymore. I went to the

checkout stand with my few items and, while unloading the cart, noticed a folded piece of notebook paper. I could barely pick it up. But when I unfolded it I saw ten digits next to that wonderful name: Ben.

I worked Christmas Eve, but it was a slow night. I barely made enough in tips to pay for the drinks I planned to have on the way home. But when the evening was over, and it was early Christmas morning, I just didn't feel much like drinking. I drove home and got ready for my day off. Not even Tommy's Tasty made me strip on Christmas.

Upon entering my apartment, I saw the unfolded piece of paper sitting in the middle of the dining room table. I hadn't called Ben yet. I wasn't sure why not. I was sure it was partially because I really should have learned my lesson by then about dating men I met at the strip club, but that wasn't all. This guy was scaring the heck out of me. I thought it was because he was a stalker. That was scary, right? But while eating Top Ramen out of the pan, I realized there's something else I was afraid of: not being willing to let him go again once I had him.

I slept fitfully. I finally dragged myself out of bed about noon, just me in my little apartment. Merry Bleeping Christmas, indeed. I saw the phone number on the table again. I'd memorized those numbers the first night I had them. I mooned around the house for a few minutes when suddenly I wanted to slap myself instead. "This is ridiculous!" I said to no one. The one thing I feared the most is fear. I refused to live being afraid all the time, especially of this guy. Was he a stalker or lover? I didn't know, but I dialed the numbers before I could change my mind.

It started ringing.

And ringing.

And ringing. I mean, this guy probably had someplace to be on Christmas, at home with the folks or out with the fiancée, something. I was about to hang up when I heard, "Hello?"

"Hi, it's Panzer . . ." I said as casually as I could.

"I was hoping it would be you," he said, and there was nothing left of me to protest anymore.

In twenty minutes, I was made up and at his place. He opened the door wearing a brand-new pair of black jeans and a loose sweater. I thought he looked good, but what did I know? I'd have thought he looked good in the Michelin Man costume right then. The second the door closed behind us, I was ready to vault on top of him even though it was the middle of the afternoon. It was always a good time for sex, after all. Some of my most screaming orgasms had been in the light of day. But I decided to control myself, at least for a little while. I wanted to give Ben a chance to make the first move. Guys liked that.

"Algonquin went to his parents' for Christmas," he said.

"I'm sorry I missed him," I lied.

"Would you like a glass of wine?" Ben asked sweetly as we sat down on the couch.

"No, thank you. I never drink and do it. You're too likely to become dehydrated. People should put Gatorade on ice instead of Champagne, don't you think?"

He smiled. "You're a very practical woman, aren't you, Panzer?"

"Yes, I am. But please, call me Emily."

"Okay, Emily." He leaned forward then. Thank goodness for that—a girl could only wait so long. He kissed me softly and dryly and started to pull back, so I wrapped my arms around his back and kept him trapped where he belonged. My tongue sneaked out of my lips and he responded in kind. Now we were getting somewhere! Our chests pressed closer and closer together. I started to throw a leg over Ben when he pulled back in earnest and said, "Emily, wait."

"Wait? Are you nuts?"

"I'm sorry," he said, panting, "but there's something I've got to tell you."

That phrase rarely portented good news. I uncoiled my hands from Ben's back and asked, "What is it?"

He took enough deep breaths to be ready to ascend Mt. Everest. But when he spoke, he didn't say he was married or dying or lactose intolerant. He said, "I'm a virgin."

I wanted to laugh, I really did, but I managed not to. I treated this situation with the seriousness that Ben thought it deserved. "That's great!" I exclaimed. This wasn't exactly the response he expected, I guessed. He was speechless, so I continued, "I couldn't be happier to be your first time. But I want to insist on one thing: we do it precisely the way you want to do it."

"I don't understand."

I smiled and leaned forward. "Ben, I promise I'll have numerous suggestions for activities we can do soon enough, but for your first time, it's definitely Virgin's Choice. It turns me on to try to recreate your fantasy vision of this experience as accurately as I can. So just tell me or show me what you want, and it's yours."

"Do you mean it?" he asked breathlessly.

That gave me pause. "As long as it doesn't involve beating the crap out of me, choking me, or anything else hazardous to my health, and as long as you wear a condom, then yes, I mean it. You have carte blanche."

Ben leaned over and kissed me. He wanted to tell me what he wanted, I thought, but decided it was more masculine to just do it to me instead. He reached out to my blouse and started to roll it up my midriff. He stopped kissing me long enough to roll it over my head, then continued with his very nice kissing. I was dressed in jeans and a peasant top, but anticipating this moment I was wearing my most expensive Victoria's Secret undies. They were lacy and absolutely, totally, unflinchingly black. Ben's hands reached down and started working the button and zipper of my pants. We kept on kissing and kissing as I lifted my hips to assist my partner in his goal of making me naked. He disengaged his lips long enough to take my pants off, staring at my lingerie as he went. He rolled the waist of my jeans as far as they were going to go, so he shifted me to my feet and pulled the cuffs of my pants to free me from them. He then offered me his hand and led me in my panties and bra wordlessly to his bedroom.

I was led to the bed and laid across it dramatically. I laid back and wriggled slightly, trying to invite him to keep doing what he was doing. He laid next to me and let his hands get in the game. He caressed me everywhere, head to toe, giving equitable attention to every part of me. His eyes were just as active as his hands, staring at me with a mixture of disbelief and fascination. "I'm really here, and I'm not going anywhere," I said.

"Good," he replied. "Are you ready?"

"Oh, yeah," I assured him. "I want you, and I want you now."

He took a moment to undress himself. The patience and tenderness of the living room was gone. He ripped off his sweater, kicked off his shoes, and pulled off his pants enthusiastically. The boxer shorts were the next to go, letting me see all of my new lover. Ben was no weightlifter, true, but he wasn't flabby either. His torso was nicely V-shaped and his legs were toned as hell. His penis was reaching out to me invitingly and, I noticed, already encased in latex. Talk about my big Boy Scout being prepared. I wanted to take his member in my arms and hug it, I wanted to take it in my mouth and kiss it, I wanted . . .

I wanted him all the way inside of me, now.

I arched my back and ripped off my panties, flinging them against the far wall. Ben caught this subtle hint and got right on top of me. Now, men, or at least young, inexperienced men, often have problems locating that one thing they're most aching to find. I wasn't going to take the chance that Ben might run into this issue. My hands were between our legs and I guided him home without delay. His penetration was enough to make me gasp. I was so ready. I thrust up to meet Ben and didn't think I could stop. I didn't want to stop. I looked up into Ben's eyes and saw only whites without the pupils.

Oh boy, I know what that meant. Ben was coming inside me already, his body shuddering and his chest heaving. He collapsed atop me, and I could feel his heart beating like Secretariat in the home stretch. I wrapped my arms around him and held him close while I clamped down on his penis like a vise grip. "I'm sorry, I'm sorry," he was gasping in my ear. "I tried to stop it, but . . ."

"Ben, it's fine. I'm going to tell you a little secret. Are you listening?"

"Yes?"

I continued in a calm, matter-of-fact voice. "All young men come like lightning. That's what you're supposed to do. But you also recover immediately and just keep on going.

You feel this?" I grasped his penis harder and squeezed it vaginally.

"Yes, I do," he answered.

"You're still in me, and you're still like a Louisville slugger. And now you've flushed your radiator so you're going to last like a stallion and rock my world. So, Ben . . ."

"Yes?"

"Whenever you're ready, fuck me like you mean it, okay?"

"Okay."

And then, all was right in my world. Ben was taking out twenty-plus years of frustration and depravation on my wide-open *labia minora*. And I was so filled up. I felt him under my stomach, and then pressing against my esophagus, and then reaching my brain stem as my mind and body exploded in waves and waves of pleasure that released the sexual energy I'd been storing up since I'd first danced on Ben a week ago. It went on and on, and somewhere in the midst of all this, I heard Ben's screams and gasps mingling with mine until he was again a dead weight pressing down on my chest.

Boy, howdy!

After a few minutes of deep breathing, Ben innocently asked, "Was it good for you?"

I liked that, when a man asked. "Ben, that was great. Truly. The best Christmas present I've ever received," I said as I removed his dwindling erection and the very full condom from within me.

"You're my best present too." He stared at me. I stare at him. Then, he suddenly gasped. "Oh, shit! I forgot to remove your bra!"

I couldn't help laughing at that. Ben laughed along with me, luckily. When laughing in bed, it's important to laugh *together*. "Don't worry, Ben, we can try everything you can imagine."

And just like that, my occupational hazard became my favorite feature of my chosen profession.

Snowbound and Gagged

by Morgan James

The snowstorm had been predicted for two days, but of course there would always be people who didn't listen, didn't believe it, or didn't care. Angie pushed a strand of straight black hair out of her eyes and stood at the front door of Delicious, Dangerous Delicacies, watching as the snow, which had been falling softly for the last hour, intensified into a whirling, howling, blizzard. It was hard enough to rattle the glass and made the wall shudder. The store's owner, Debbie, had left at two o'clock, telling Angie she was to keep the shop open until six, regardless of weather. It was only four days before Christmas, and that was when shoppers were the most desperate to find something quickly. And desperation was always good for business, Debbie liked to say.

Delicious, Dangerous Delicacies was a specialty lingerie boutique, offering the most expensive and desirable night-gowns, bras, panties, garter belts, and countless accessories for the sexually adventurous. Angie had worked in the shop only two weeks, starting at the beginning of the holiday shopping season. A quick study, she caught on immediately as to how to get women to buy more than they had originally intended and the men to imagine their women in this and that, thus ringing up large sales for a very pleased Debbie.

Yet Angie could not imagine herself owning any of the finery the store sold, much less afford it. Home from college for winter break, the minimum wage Debbie gave her was just enough to pay for gasoline, a couple gifts for her family, and a token rent to her older sister, Arlie, with whom she was staying until mid-January.

During an occasional lull in the number of customers, Angie would sneak a sheer robe or gown into the dressing room, slip off her jeans and sweater, slip on the lingerie, and then look at herself in the mirror. Shy since childhood, Angie wondered if someday she would have the courage to stand in front of a man in such thin fabric, her dark pink nipples clearly visible, the thick triangle of curly pubic hair peeking from between her legs. She would run her hands up and down her body with a touch of self-conscious embarrassment, as if someone might be looking. Then, before Debbie could realize what was going on, Angie would strip from the gown, slip it back on the satin-padded hanger, and replace it on the rack.

"It's getting pretty heavy out there," said one of two patrons in the store. Angie turned from the door to see a ruggedly handsome, medium-height man in his early thirties, with green eyes, short dark-blond hair, and a well-trimmed beard. He wore hiking boots, jeans, and a well-worn leather jacket. "I haven't seen a snow like that in years."

Angie nodded. "It's going to be a nightmare getting home."

The man chuckled and held out a set of crotchless red satin panties and matching bra in Angie's direction. "I have a new girlfriend. We've been seeing each other for a month. Do you think this might be a bit much as a first Christmas gift?"

Angie shrugged. She always felt a little uneasy with questions like that, though she was good at hiding her feelings. He had no way of knowing she was, as weird as it was in this day and age, a virgin.

"Well," said Angie, moving behind the counter and adopting her best confident-Debbie imitation. "Does she enjoy things on the wild side? Is she free with her body? Or are you just hoping she will be?"

The man shrugged. "I guess I'm hoping she will be."

"Then let me suggest pink satin rather than red. It is a color that hints at innocence while still giving her the message as to your desires. It's slightly less . . . direct."

The man looked at the panties. "Crotchless is pretty damned direct one way or the other, I guess."

Angie smiled and nodded. "I said slightly less direct."

A second man, the only other customer in the store, joined the other two at the counter. He held a pair of furry purple handcuffs and sheer babydoll gown in one hand and in the other, a long, black silk scarf. This man was quite tall, in his late thirties or early forties, with a good-looking but serious face, a thick head of curly black hair, broad shoulders, and dark, piercing brown eyes. He was dressed in pleated gray slacks and a long wool overcoat. He glanced at the blond man and then at Angie. "Can we ring this up quickly? The last thing I need is to get stuck out in this weather. My snow tires aren't very good and my wife will be pissed if I'm late."

"Sure." Angie rang up the items, scanned the charge, and placed the gown, scarf, and handcuffs into a special, sparkly green and red Christmas gift bag. As she slid the bag across the counter, the digital weather alert radio beside the register sounded a piercing beep.

"What the hell?" asked the blond man.

"Weather alert," said Angie, holding up a finger. "Shh."

A sputtering voice followed the beep. "A winter storm warning is in effect for the entire city. City officials are asking all citizens to stay off the streets as this white-out continues. Remain where you are. It is not safe to travel in any circumstances. Storm to continue through 3 a.m. tomorrow morning. I repeat, a winter storm warning is in effect for . . ."

Angie clicked off the voice.

Shit, she thought. *Am I stuck here until 3 a.m.? Or even later? There's a cot in the back but no way in hell do I want to spend the night here all by myself.*

The dark-haired man slipped the holiday bag over his arm, buttoned his coat, and slipped on a pair of kid gloves as the blond man continued to consider the red satin underwear. His brow furrowed thoughtfully. "Maybe she'd like the pink better. But she looks fantastic in red."

"Think it over," said Angie. *But not for too long. I want out of here! I don't care that Debbie said keep the shop open. I'm going home.*

Muttering a monotone "happy holidays," the dark-haired man pulled the front door open. He was instantly blown back by a powerful gust of snow-laden wind. He stumbled, then righted himself and slammed the door shut. Snow twirled around his arms and face then melted in the warm shop air. The man spun to face Angie, an expression of anger on his face.

"Damn it all! There is no way on earth we're going to get out of here until this is over. We'd just end up in a ditch somewhere. It's blinding."

And you want me to fix it how? Angie thought. "Sorry," was what she said.

The blond man dropped the red panty-and-bra set on the

counter and tried the front door himself. He was knocked back by the wind even harder than the other man had been. He threw his body against the door, shoving it closed.

"Yeah, you're right, man. We're not going anywhere."

The dark-haired man was already on his cell phone. He paced back and forth near the counter. "Liz, yes, it's me. I'm stuck in the weather and won't be able to get over there for who knows how long. We'll have to cancel our dinner plans. Yes, I know. Yes, I know. We'll do it another time." There was a long pause. Angie leaned on the counter, her hands up in her hair, wondering if she could just kick them out anyway so she could be alone in the store. She didn't know these guys from Adam. The idea of them being there with her for so long was unnerving. Although, as she let her eyes linger a moment on the blond, bearded man, she thought she wouldn't mind talking to him, finding out a little more. But he did have that new girlfriend. And Angie knew she herself was as ordinary as a girl could get, and could hardly compete. "Fine. Do whatever you have to do. Goodbye." The dark-haired man snapped his phone shut and shook his head. "Women!"

"Wife?" asked the blond man, one eyebrow up, trying to lighten up the mood.

"Ex-wife. Well, newly separated-from wife. I'm trying to get back together with her."

"So," said the blond man, scratching his beard and then looking from Angie to the snow visible outside the door. "Looks like the snow has gotten worse, if that was possible. Got anything to drink?"

There was a small employees' lounge in the back of the store, nothing more than a card table, a few folding chairs, a refrigerator, sink, and a coffee maker. Though still unhappy about having unexpected guests, Angie poured them mugs of coffee and offered them some of the doughnuts Debbie had put in the fridge yesterday morning.

They sat around the table as the walls rattled and the ceiling groaned under the blizzard's assault, the men eating doughnuts and drinking their coffee, Angie sipping at hers but having no appetite. She wasn't good talking to men. She had little to say. They had jobs and friends and lives. She was taking eighteen hours of art, history, and humanities classes. Her friends were limited to her roommate and her sister.

The dark-haired man was Gregory, a lawyer. The blond man was Colin, a freelance illustrator. After a good ten minutes of the men talking football, art, the stock market, and new cars, Colin nodded toward Angie and said, "You sure are quiet."

Angie shrugged, then self-consciously ran her fingers through her hair. "I don't know much about football. I don't own stock. And my car is thirteen years old."

"You own this place?"

"No. It's Debbie Younger's. I'm just a temp. I go to Regent College."

"Art major?"

"No." That was a curious comment. "Why would you guess art?"

Colin's brow arched. "You look arty."

Angie blushed, and then felt silly for blushing. Was being called "arty" a compliment or an insult?

"Arty girls are really cute," Colin continued. He unzipped his leather jacket, shrugged it off, and let it drop onto the back of his chair. "My first real girlfriend was a painter. We met in art school. Gorgeous black hair, a lot like yours."

"Oh. Well, thanks."

Gregory, who had already shed his wool coat, tipped back in his chair and put his hands in his trouser pockets. Angie could imagine him in a legal meeting, taking command with his body language. "Yes, I'd have guessed an art major, too. You're one of those still-waters-run-deep kind of girls, aren't you? Creative and mysterious."

Mysterious? Me? You've got to be kidding?

She felt both men's eyes on her as they waited for her reply. She didn't know what to say. And she blushed again, this time from nervousness. Her fingers fidgeted in her lap.

"You know," said Colin with a sudden, disarming grin, "I really want to buy that red bra-and-panties set, but I don't know what it would look like on a woman. Your mannequins are so unlifelike, so cold. You wouldn't want to try them on for me? Let me have a little look?"

Angie blinked. "What? No, of course not!"

Colin waved one hand. "I was just kidding. A man can dream, can't he?" Angie's eyes met his, and she couldn't help but grin back. Not only was he striking and rugged, but he had a twinkle in his eye that made her wonder how committed he was to his new girlfriend.

Gregory put his chin in his hand as if considering something important. Then he looked directly at Angie. For the first time since he'd entered the store, he smiled. But unlike Colin's, his was a sly, conspiratorial smile that chased a chill down Angie's spine. "I'm not an illustrator," he said, "but I agree with Colin. The mannequins in this store are lifeless. I would love to see my purchases on an honest-to-goodness female model. A living, breathing model who can show me if the gown hangs right, and if those cuffs fit slender wrists snugly."

"Ah . . ." Angie stopped. It took a full fifteen seconds

to find her voice again. "Are you asking me to model for you?"

"I can make it worth your while," said Gregory. He folded his hands on the tabletop and leaned forward. It was all she could do to keep from leaning back and away. "A girl like you, in college, working here over the holidays. I'm sure you could use some extra cash."

The words rushed out of her even as her heart began to beat a little faster. "I do all right. I make all I need, thank you. I'm just fine."

"Really?" said Gregory. "Fine enough to get yourself some nice things for Christmas? Fine enough to get a new computer for school, perhaps? Or just take a vacation somewhere?"

"What . . . what are you saying?"

Colin shifted in his seat. His smiled had faded. "Yeah, Gregory, what *are* you saying?"

"Just taking your idea and running a little farther with it, Colin," said Gregory. "Listen, we're here for who knows how long, without a fucking thing to do but drink bad coffee and eat stale doughnuts. I don't know about you, but I'd like a little entertainment to pass the time. So, Angie?" He tilted his head. "What do you say? I've got some . . . discretional cash I can part with. How about a one-woman fashion show with our choice of outfits from the shop? I'll give you three thousand dollars."

Angie stood abruptly from her chair, nearly knocking it over backward. Her heart was pounding madly now, and her throat had gone dry. "I can't do that."

"Why not? You're a beautiful young woman." He glanced from her face to her chest. "Although you're trying to hide them with that shapeless blouse, I can see you have fine, full breasts just aching to be shown off. Why not use your assets to make some good money?"

What would Debbie say? Angie thought frantically. *How would she handle this?*

"I'm . . . I'm not a prostitute," she stuttered.

Gregory reached over suddenly and caught Angie's hand. It was a large hand, muscular, with the back of it covered in dark hair. "I'm just asking for a little peep show. Some pleasant visuals to help make this bloody blizzard more tolerable."

"Hey, Gregory," said Colin. "I don't think she likes the idea. Don't push it."

Letting go of her hand, Gregory sat back and crossed his arms "Sure. No problem. I won't push it. No harm done either way. I can keep the cash; Angie can keep her lovely body a secret."

Angie walked to the door of the lounge, and then turned back. Her mind was racing. "Three thousand dollars. You have to be kidding." *I could do so much with that money!*

That smirking smile again. "Honey, I don't kid about things I want." With that, Gregory pulled out his thick wallet, removed a stack of hundred-dollar bills, and slapped them on the tabletop beside the remaining half of his doughnut. "Here it is. It's yours. Just for showing me what I'm getting for my shopping dollar."

"Okay." She couldn't believe she'd said it until she heard the words out on the air.

"Angie, don't let him push you into anything," Colin said.

"No, I'm not. I want to do this." She tossed her head to show her courage. "I could use the money, and, what the hell, it's only modeling. Could be fun."

"Could be a lot of fun," said Gregory.

"You mean it?" asked Colin.

"I mean it!"

She saw the pleased surprise on Colin's face.

Standing in the dressing room before the mirror wearing only her white cotton bra and panties, Angie took the babydoll gown out of Gregory's gift bag, held it to her chest, and tried to summon back the courage to go through with it. She'd never been intimate with a man; never had a man touch her; had never even let a man see her in her underwear. Why, her only bathing suit was a one-piece, and even then she was shy when going to the beach. She envied the beautiful, curvaceous women who strolled around the sand in their bikinis and thongs, their breasts pushing hard against the cups, their smooth, round asses bouncing proudly. But not Angie. She never thought her body was much to look at.

She took a deep breath. When she emerged wearing this gown, would Gregory laugh at her? Would Colin smile sympathetically?

What have I agreed to do?

There was knock on the dressing room door.

"Angie?" It was Gregory. "You've been in there a long time. Are you all right?"

"Yes."

"Do you need help?"

"No."

But the door swung open. Angie spun about and drew the gown closer to her body, as if the thin fabric could actually shield her from the lawyer's eyes. "What are you doing in here?"

Gregory closed the door and stood against it, nodding. "Just what I thought."

"What did you think?"

"You have a luscious body, a sweet body."

"I . . . I do?"

"Mm-hm. Turn back around."

Angie hesitated.

"I said, turn around."

She turned to face the mirror again, and watched in the reflection as Gregory came up behind her, so close his chest was pressed into her back. He reached around her with both arms, took the gown from her hands, and dropped it onto the floor. Then he put his arms around her waist. She shivered involuntarily with dread and delight as he drew her close. "Having trouble with your bra and panties?"

"No, I . . ."

"Yes, you are. Let me help you."

She gazed, unblinking, as Gregory put his cheek against hers—he smelled of British Sterling and an expensive pipe tobacco—and then moved his large, commanding hands up to cup her breasts. Startled, her spine stiffened and she reached up to push his hands away. But he said evenly, "No, Angie. Put them down. I'm here to help you."

His voice was mesmerizing, as was the powerful, raw sensation of having a stranger's fingers touch her where no one else had touched her before. She let her hands drop back down, every nerve beneath her skin at attention, waiting to see what would happen next.

"Good girl," he said quietly, soothingly, his warm breath against her neck. "Now, since you weren't able to get out of these clothes on your own, I'll just have to do it for you. You promised me a fashion show, but you can't do that until you've taken off your own clothes, right?"

She nodded, her breath coming in soft, ragged gasps.

With that, he squeezed her breasts gently, and then firmer, his thumb rubbing up and over her nipples, which had gone instantly hard beneath the fabric of the bra. "What are these sweet breasts doing in such a plain, cheap bra?" he asked. "They deserve something softer, something prettier. Don't you think? We can find something for you in the shop, I don't doubt."

She nodded, even though she wasn't sure why she was nodding. Her knees went weak but she locked them so she wouldn't slump to the floor. Between her legs she felt a rush of need, an urgent, electrical current gathering there, and she wanted to reach down and rub herself. But she couldn't do that. Not in front of this man, this stranger.

Gregory wriggled his fingers underneath the cups of her bra, positioning his hands firmly against her bare flesh. Angie arched back against him. Her nipples hardened even more as if begging to be squeezed and pulled. Reading her body's language, Gregory did just that, pinching with his thumb and forefinger, tugging and teasing, driving a liquid heat from her breasts down through her belly to her cunnie, which was now wet and on fire. Angie could no longer keep silent, and her gasps came out loud and sharp.

"That's a good girl," cooed Gregory as he kneaded and tweaked her nipples. Angie watched in the mirror, feeling equally detached from and a part of what she was seeing. She breathed through her mouth. Her face and chest were bathed in sweat. "You needed to be tended, to be cared for, didn't you? You said you wanted to give us a fashion show, but what you really wanted was for me to come in and pleasure you. Isn't that right?"

She truly hadn't thought of that. She had only thought how handsome Colin was and that she wanted to see him again, but now that she was trapped in the dressing room with the tall, demanding Gregory, all she wanted was for him to rub her and caress her in every place she had.

"Isn't that right?" he repeated.

"Yes," she whispered.

Without realizing she was doing it, Angie shifted her legs apart and whined, then reached for one of Gregory's hands to push it down to her sticky, soaking hole.

"Not yet," said Gregory. "You aren't ready." With that he let go of her breasts, unhooked her bra, and flung it aside. Then he cupped her breasts again. "There. They needed to be free. Such lovely mounds you have. They should be displayed for all appreciative men. Hiding them is a crime against nature."

There was a knock on the door. Colin said, "Angie, are you all right in there? Gregory? Is she all right?"

"She's more than all right," said Gregory. "Please come in."

Colin! I don't want you to see Gregory fondling me! she thought, and she squirmed to get out of his grasp. But Gregory jerked her hard and held her tightly. "No, he should see this. He will like it, and so will you."

Angie looked in the mirror as the door swung open and Colin stepped in. His eyes went wide and his fists balled up, and it looked as if he would take a swing at Gregory.

But then Gregory said, "Colin, look at our sweet little Angie. She wanted this so badly, I had to accommodate. Isn't that right, Angie?" He ran his left hand slowly down her abdomen where it held right above the elastic band of her panties. She knew he was waiting for the right answer, or else he wouldn't touch her there, where she was so anxious that he touch.

"Yes," she said, nodding vigorously.

"I suspect she is a virgin, though I haven't checked her little hole to be sure," said Gregory. "Angie, are you a virgin?"

"Yes."

"You've never had a man's cock in your cunt, have you?"

"No."

"Have you had a man's finger?"

"No."

"Only your own fingers, am I right?"

She nodded. "Yes."

"You've masturbated hard, haven't you, wishing it was a man taking care of that for you, haven't you?"

"Yes."

"Do you want us to teach you what it is to be with a man?"

She nodded even more anxiously, her pussy quivering and begging to be probed and fucked. "Yes!"

Colin walked around so he was between the mirror and the couple. He stared at her bare legs, her white cotton panties with Gregory's hand poised just above the elastic waist band, her bare breast held firmly, and the other untended breast. "Wow," he said in quiet admiration. "You are even more beautiful than I'd thought."

Angie liked the way he looked at her and knew in that moment that she really wasn't plain at all. She *was* beautiful.

"Are you ready to learn one of life's big lessons?" Colin asked kindly.

"Yes, Colin. I want you to teach me."

With that, Gregory nodded at the gift bag on the floor. "Get out the handcuffs, Colin," he said. "She's going to be sorely tempted to please herself while we instruct her. It would be natural, of course, but for now her hands would only get in the way."

Colin took out the fur-trimmed cuffs and secured Angie's hands behind her back. Then, as Gregory nodded affirmingly, Colin stood in front of her and pulled the cotton panties down from her hips, pausing for a moment to admire the thick bush of hair before pushing the panties all the way to her ankles. She immediately stepped out of them.

"I can't believe I'm doing this," she said with a little laugh. "If Debbie came in . . ."

But Gregory held up a finger to silence her. "Angie, you are not to speak now. You must be silent and obedient. You must watch and listen." With that, he took the black silk scarf from the gift bag. "Open your mouth."

She did. He worked the scarf securely between her lips and teeth, then knotted the ends at the back of her head.

Angie began to cough and had difficulty swallowing. But Colin took her face in his hands, smiled, and said, "Relax, Angie. Just relax." She closed her eyes and allowed her body to ease up, and then the gag wasn't so bad. In fact, like the cuffs, it heightened her sense of helpless expectation. Then she nodded. Colin brushed her breast with his thumb, then stepped back. Clearly he was going to let Gregory take the lead, since he was the one who'd gotten the ball rolling.

"Now," said Gregory. He rubbed his hands together and walked around Angie, looking her up and down, considering her firm ass, bare breasts, and flat stomach with the fine dark hairs that ran from beneath her navel down into her pubic thatch. "The first thing you need to know is how to take a man's finger. Open your legs."

Angie did. She stood, her legs straddled, while Gregory stooped before her. She began to tremble, her mind reeling, her body more alert than it had ever been before. She felt like a bound goddess prepared to be worshiped by mortal men.

"A man is going to want to touch and taste you. Like this." He touched the top of her bush with his index finger, then drew a line down and over her clit. She moaned as a red-hot charge fired in all directions from that erect pink bud. Then Gregory continued on to part her quivering wet pussy lips. He paused, looked up at her, and then plunged his finger deep into her hole. Angie threw her head back and her hips began to grind forward. Colin quickly moved behind her to hold her so she wouldn't fall.

"You see?" said Gregory. "That is how it works." He shoved his finger in and out of her hole. Angie felt the slippery, swollen walls of her cunt try desperately to catch and hold the finger. Then Gregory withdrew his finger, stood, and pulled the gag from Angie's mouth. "Here," he said, slipping the finger between her lips. "See how you taste? Isn't that delicious?" She nodded, savoring the taste of herself, and Gregory replaced the gag.

Kneeling down again, Gregory said, "Now we will try a few more." He plunged four fingers into her hole at once. The sensation was instant and overwhelming; she felt so full in her lower body she was suddenly afraid that something might come pouring out of her. Gregory seemed to know this. "Let it go if it must go," he said, nodding up at her encouragingly. "It's all beautiful and sexy."

Angie didn't know if she could, but then Colin touched her face from behind her and whispered, "Everything about you is beautiful. Let it go."

And so she let go, and the hot stream of urine flowed out and over Gregory's hand, down her leg, and onto the floor. She began to cry with embarrassment, relief, and release. Colin kissed her cheek. Then he stepped out of the room for a moment and returned with a warm, damp wash cloth and a dry towel from the shop's restroom. Gregory moved away as Colin gently spread her cunnie lips and washed her out, then swabbed her ass, and then her leg. Then, with the towel, he wiped the urine off the floor.

"Precious, sweet Angie," said Gregory. He smiled and nodded. Then he said, "The next lesson is pleasing a man. We love to put our cocks in your cunts, but first, you must ready us with your mouth."

Angie nodded, more than anxious to continue learning. The hairs on her arm were at attention and the blood at her temples throbbed.

Silently, Gregory sat on the dressing room bench and took off his shoes and socks. Then he unzipped and removed his trousers and his shirt. Angie could see the outline of a huge, angry organ against the front of his Jockeys. Staring at his crotch, she felt her own heat up even more.

"Do you want to see?"

Angie nodded.

Gregory stripped from his shorts, freeing his enormous, engorged penis. She gasped at its thickness. Gregory walked unselfconsciously to Angie, holding his dick in his hands. "A man wants his cock tended by your lips and tongue. It's important. It stimulates us and lubricates us, and causes your own pussy to become more lubricated as well. Do you understand?"

Angie nodded again.

"Colin?" Gregory turned to the blond man. "Will you help me demonstrate?"

Angie turned to look at Colin, who appeared at first confused. But then she saw the understanding in his eyes. He said, "I don't think I can do that."

Gregory laughed. It was a deep, throaty laugh. "My new

friend. What are our bodies but here for us to enjoy? It seems we've got two students today, and not just the one!"

With that he moved over to Colin, put his hands on his shoulders. "Will you help me show Angie how to love a man with her mouth? Who better to show her than one man who knows what is pleasurable to another man?"

For a moment Colin said nothing, glancing between Angie and Gregory's stiff prick. Then he said, "Angie, would you like to see this?"

Yes! she thought. And she nodded.

That was all the encouragement Colin seemed to need. He smiled and winked. Then Gregory guided Colin to his knees. "Watch, Angie," said Gregory. "This is what you do."

Angie watched as Colin took the other man's hair-covered balls almost reverently, and then pulled and squeezed them as tenderly as he might pull and squeeze an overripe fruit. Gregory drew in a sharp breath of air but remained still, one hand resting on top of Colin's head as if blessing him. Next, Colin grasped the base of Gregory's gigantic cock in one hand and leaned forward to draw his tongue across the shiny, purple head.

"You see?" said Gregory. "Slow at first. Savor it. Taste it. Lick it."

Colin began drawing his tongue up and down the fleshy rod, first the top and then the underside, leaving a glistening trail of saliva. Then he took the cock in his hand, slipped the dick head in his mouth and began to pump his hands back and forth vigorously along the shaft, the skin slipping wetly through his fingers. Gregory's hips shifted forward and he hissed through his teeth. "Yes, yes. See? This is what you do."

Angie nodded, fascinated and hornier than she'd ever been in her life.

Reaching around with both hands to grab Gregory's ass, Colin shoved his face clear up to Gregory's crotch, taking the entire cock in his mouth. Gregory groaned loudly. Colin pumped with his mouth, moving forward and backward with increasing speed, the swollen dick head making a wet popping sound each time it came out of Colin's mouth before he plunged forward to take it again. His cheeks puffed with the fullness and his hands clawed deep red divots in the other man's ass.

Suddenly Gregory pulled back and away. Colin wiped his mouth with his sleeve.

"I'm about to come, Angie," said Gregory. "Quickly, my dear, now it's your turn."

Colin untied the gag from her mouth, unlocked the handcuffs, and Angie gratefully fell to her knees before the dark-haired man. She knew what to do. She fondled his hot, soft ball sack, smelled him, kissed him, and licked him. As she did, she noticed out of the corner of her eye that Colin was stripping from his own clothes. As he kicked aside his own shorts, she saw, rising from a thatch of sweat-matted, curly blond pubic hair, his own thick and proud dick, anxiously waiting its turn. He moved to her quickly, presenting his cock for her oral ministrations. She leaned forward to kiss the dark little eye at the tip of his penis, and he smiled at her.

Then, one at a time, she licked, stroked, and sucked the two meaty, musky-tasting cocks, back and forth between the two naked men, pleasuring them as they blessed her, tugging, nipping, and pumping until, at the exact same moment, the dicks spouted forth furious streams of white, thick come that spattered her face and ran down her neck. She coated her fingers with the come from her cheeks and stood so the men could lick them clean.

Then Colin laid Angie on the floor, spread her legs, and licked and sucked her clit until she came so hard she thought she would split apart.

The blizzard was done. Gregory put his scarf, gown, and handcuffs back into the sparkly red and green gift bag and then, without another word, slipped out of the shop into the deep, drifted snow. Colin paid for the red bra-and-panties set, zipped his leather jacket, and walked to the door, red and green bag hanging on his arm.

And he turned back around.

"We never did get that fashion show," he said, one brow raised.

Angie leaned on the counter with her elbows. Her body was still humming with adrenaline and the rush of sex. "No, we sure didn't. But he still gave me the money!"

"I'm not so sure this bra-and-panty set would suit my girlfriend," he said, stomping his booted feet in anticipation of going outside in the cold. "In fact, I'm not really sure we're that great of a couple."

"No?"

Colin shook his head.

Damn, I really like this guy, she thought.

"If you want," he said, "you can give me a private fashion show later tonight, when you get off work. I can give you my address, since you're staying with your sister and we can't exactly go to 'your place.' How would that be?"

Angie smiled broadly. "That would be nice." Then she added, "But first you could buy me dinner. And I want to see some of your artwork. I'm not just any old part-time lingerie shop girl, you know."

Colin grinned. "Oh, I know. I know." He reached in his

pocket and gave her a business card. *Colin Dolan, illustrator. 1934 W. Riverside Drive. You name it, I'll draw it. Even if you don't name it, I'll draw it. Can't stop me. Just try.*

"Cute slogan," Angie said.

"I thought so. Tonight?"

"Tonight. What's a little snow?"

Angie spent her last hour cleaning up the dressing room, and, for the first time since she'd worked there, she didn't even mind.

Christmas Cruise
by Tricia Tucker

Dana Dash

He thrust his hips and it felt like my flesh was being stretched beyond its limit. But I enjoyed the feeling. He stopped suddenly, but my alarm didn't last long. He was readjusting the condom. Then without missing a beat, we were back at it again. I matched his moves, struggling to keep up. My nails dug deep into his tight, muscled ass, forcing him to go even deeper. Sweat from his perfectly sculpted body dripped all over me, but the wetness did very little to put out the fire.

"You like?" he managed, struggling to get his words out.

"Oh, yes, baby, yes. Yes, Yes, Yesss!" I cried. I didn't care who could hear. Good loving like this needed to be put on blast.

The good, hair-pulling, skin-smacking, heavy-breathing kind. Sheer electricity hung in the air, right along with the smell of raw hot sex.

Just when I thought the sheer bliss that had enveloped me couldn't get any better, I felt it. My eyes widened, and my mouth gaped as a tingling sensation shot from the very tips of my toes, through my veins, and bolted up my legs with lightening speed.

"Oh God!" I breathed.

"Good for you? You like it?"

"Yes, baby! Yes!"

I fell fast, unable to stop myself. I felt my body flinch. He kept moving, gyrating his hips, drilling me harder and deeper with each powerful stroke.

Warm and flowing ripples turned into crashing waves all the way up my thighs until my swollen clit exploded in delicious pleasure.

"Oh my God!" The voice cried in horror, startling us both, but not enough to make him stop.

"Uh, I'm so, I'm sorry," I heard Maxey's voice shriek. Then the door shut and we were once again alone.

Her timing couldn't have been worse. But Raven barely missed a beat. Soon I felt him jerk, his face twisted into a frown, and he released a belly-wrenching growl as he came hard.

"Damn, girl, that was the shit!" he exclaimed, tumbling off of me like he had no control over his limbs.

I rode my ecstasy to the fullest. Long after we were done, my body was still trembling. He had brought me to a shuddering, wriggling climax that left me with colorful stars dancing in front of my eyes and my head spinning dizzy.

Raven wasn't one to linger and I didn't even mind. With his six-foot-three-inch muscled frame, he was sexy on legs. He had a bewitchingly beautiful face, chiseled features, and thick black curly hair, giving hints to his mixed heritage. His mocha skin had reclaimed its full color as he dressed quickly and rushed out of the room.

Maxey had already tried to get into our deluxe penthouse suite aboard the Norwegian Pearl cruise ship. I knew Raven and I should've taken it into my bedroom, but we never made it that far.

Once we hit the door, we tore at each other's clothes, one thing led to another, and soon I was on my way to some of the best sex I've had in years, a mere few feet from the front door.

Can you say *oops*?

I finally regained the feeling in my legs and limped to the shower once Raven left. I felt awful about Maxey and what she saw, but I was sure she would probably understand.

I was in the shower when I heard movement in the living room of our three bedroom suite. Everything had been perfect during this divorce party Ramona and I had planned for our friend Maxey.

"Oh no, ma'am," I heard Maxey say the second I walked out of the bathroom later. We were supposed to be getting ready to go to the late night disco. Still draped in my thick terrycloth robe, I padded out to the living room where Ramona and Maxey were ready to hold court.

"Get to dishing, Ms. Dash," Maxey said, feigning an attitude.

Let me tell you about my posse. Ramona Hernandez is a dead ringer for the actress Penelope Cruz, except Ramona's dark locks are layered in a shoulder-length style, and where Penelope speaks with that thick accent, Ramona works in Hollywood doing voice-over work for commercials, large corporations, and a few other exclusive clients.

"We want to hear all about the naked wrestling that was going on in here earlier," Maxey teased.

Maxey, a possible Queen Latifah double, is less flashy and more on the quiet side. She has a heart ten times bigger than her waist, and is the most conservative of our trio. She had just officially ended a nasty marriage, and survived the even worse divorce.

The three of us had vowed to stick by each other's side after a drinking binge that consisted of bottomless 'tinis and cosmos ten years ago inside the Zeta Zeta Zeta Mu house at UC Dominquez.

Our friendship had grown at rapid speed. I'm an executive news producer for a local TV station, and Maxey is in nursing, so with no families to answer to, the cruise seemed a logical way to kill two birds with one stone: celebrate a major milestone in our girl's life, and spend Christmas living it up on the high seas.

I sat in one of the chairs and poured myself a glass of Eggnog.

"Okay," I sipped. "Where do I start?"

"Um, how about you start by telling us how the sexy cruise ship comedian wound up between your thighs?" Maxey asked.

"Well, ya know, a funny thing happened after we teamed up for that dance contest last night," I said.

"I guess that kiss was just that good, huh?" Maxey said.

She was referring to the awkward kiss Raven and I shared in the piano bar beneath the mistletoe. We'd been on the boat for three days at that point. He and I had been exchanging goo-goo eyes for most of those three days, so I knew there was something between us.

"No, but I knew then I wanted him to be my dance partner," I chuckled, pulling myself from the memory.

"Okay, but we go from dancing together, and what a dance it was," Maxey chuckled. "To, um, how should I put it?" Her cheeks were flushed.

"Oh, Maxey!" I yelled. "Loosen up. Raven was all of that

and then some," I couldn't stop laughing, all giddy like a schoolgirl.

"Hmm," Ramona said, as she eyed me closely.

And that's when the sinful thought crossed my mind. I was so excited I didn't know what to do.

"Ya know what?" I got up and started walking around the room. "I could go into all the juicy details. Tell you both how hung Raven is, how he completely ravished me, took me to such heights I nearly had an aneurism when I came hard. And how he left me feeling so good I was damn near brought to tears." I turned to see both of them hanging on my every word.

Maxey's eyes narrowed, but I could tell she was curious. Ramona simply smiled. I had read her without even looking at her. She and I were two of a kind—we loved great sex and the men who knew how to deliver. I figured Maxey had been trapped in a loveless marriage for so long, she didn't know what good sex was anymore.

"But I can show you a whole helluva lot better than I can tell you!" I said.

Ramona Martinez

The next day, we were slow to rise. The party inside the ship's disco lasted until the wee hours of the morning. We had gone there after leaving one of the bars where the bartender was explaining the rules to the game The Twelve Days of Christmas.

When I sat upright in bed, it was like the party was still going on in my head. It was one drink after another, partying with all the other night owls aboard the ship. I had seen Dana talking to that hulky comedian of hers.

I figured we'd order room service and I'd crawl back to bed. But Maxey and Dana said they were going out. I went back to bed.

I pulled my mask over my eyes and begged sleep to come quickly. How I could still be drunk the day after the party was a mystery to me. But I figured I'd just sleep it off.

Knocking jarred me from my blissful sleep. It felt like minutes, but it had actually been hours.

"Who the hell . . ." I muttered as I walked to the door, wiping sleep from my eyes. "Okay, okay, I'm coming," I yelled. I pulled the door open without even checking the peephole.

"You must be Ramona. Dana sent me," he announced. My eyebrows shot up. The sexy sound of his voice made my legs feel like water. I stumbled back a bit, struggling to maintain my balance. I prayed I had removed all the sleep from my eyes.

"My friends call me Raven, or they simply just call when they need me," he said.

My eyebrows nearly touched my hairline, "*Sh-she* sent you?" I questioned, not really understanding what he was trying to say, yet taking in this heavenly sight.

"She did. Said you need some *'special attention'*." He smiled casually as he used his fingers to do air quotes.

His body was a mass of chiseled perfection. A Santa hat sat atop his head, and he wore dark denim shorts that hugged him just right, with a white T-shirt. Despite being fully dressed, I could tell he was cut in all the right places. In addition to his outfit, he wore leather sandals and carried a duffel bag.

The sight of his perfect lips temporarily held me hypnotized. *Were they calling to me?* I shook naughty thoughts from my mind and realized we were standing there, me with awe in my eyes and drool probably running down the side of my mouth, and he looking just as delicious as ever.

"Can I come in?" he asked.

I cleared my throat, and glanced around the hall, "Um oh, yeah, yes, of course you can come in. Dana sent you, right?" I was nervous and warm with embarrassment because of the sinful thoughts I was thinking about Raven and his magnificent body. As I led him into the suite, the phone rang. I rushed to get it. It was Dana.

"I know he's gotta be there by now," she said without even a *hello.* I turned to look at Raven, sitting on the sofa, his long legs extended under the coffee table.

"What in the hell were you thinking?" I whispered into the phone.

"Girl, I was thinking about you, that's what the hell I was thinking. I told you how skillful this man is. Well, I figured in order for you to really understand where I was coming from, you had to experience him for yourself!"

"Are you crazy?" I whispered. "I mean, are you for real?" I started thinking about what she was saying. It had been so long since I had been with a man other than Adrian, my longtime boyfriend who'd been caught cheating again just before we set sail.

"*Am I for real*? Is Raven's sexy ass sitting there in your room?"

"Um, yeah," I answered, stealing another glance at him.

"Girl, you can sit here on the phone with me if you want, but I suggest you sit on his face! 'Cause that's the only way you'll really understand what he's capable of," she said, chuckling.

The moment I hung up with Dana, I approached Raven.

"Would you like a massage?" he asked in his deep baritone, allowing me to momentarily shake doubtful thoughts from my head. This time, the sound of his voice was enough to make me start creaming instantly.

"Ah, a massage sounds nice," I managed, feeling my nipples stiffen. Raven extended his hand for me to take.

"I can do it here, or you can follow me to the bed," he informed me.

I was prepared to follow him straight through the gates of hell if he'd only ask.

"Ahem." He stood, and motioned toward me before I took another step.

"What's wrong?" I asked.

"You gotta lose the robe."

"Oh, um, the robe, yeah, right," I looked down at the robe, then pulled the tie at my waist and it fell open. Raven's eyes rolled up my legs, took in my hips, my taut breasts, then stopped at my face.

He smiled approvingly before he walked over to his bag and removed a couple of small bottles. Then he followed me into the bedroom.

I stepped out of my robe but left on my red thong and matching bra, both with white fur trims. It was what I had worn beneath my clothes to last night's festivities.

"Would you like a drink?" I asked Raven.

"No, I'm good," he answered, "I like to keep a clear head when I'm working." He removed the Santa hat from his head.

When Raven's strong hands touched my skin, all of my problems and thoughts of Adrian seemed a world away. I felt like I was in heaven once I decided to let myself go and climbed onto the bed. I closed my eyes and allowed the oil and his hands to mix into an almost surreal and magical sensation.

Before I knew what was happening, I turned over and pulled him closer. I could no longer resist, and the sweet agony was driving me crazy.

Without hesitation, Raven opened his mouth and sucked at my bottom lip then my tongue. I kept my eyes open so I could see this beautiful man at work. I felt drunk all over again, but this time with passion.

"Are you wet?" he asked, pulling back a bit.

"Emm hmmm," I managed.

"Good," he said. "That's real good." Raven eased his hands between my thighs, moved my thong to the side, and slipped his thick fingers into the depth of my core. He jammed his fingers deeper and massaged and worked my flesh like he knew me well. He did this while ripping open a condom wrapper with his teeth.

"Ooooh God!" I shrilled, wide-eyed, rocking my hips and moving to a beat only I could hear. I began to explore his glorious body with my own hands. I ran my fingers along the ripples of his six-pack, then down to his waist, and was surprisingly shocked when I could barely fit my hand around his throbbing cock. From the moment I first saw it I felt it had been screaming out to be touched.

Raven moved between my thighs, allowing his muscular chest to graze my face. He had a sweet scent, some cologne masking a cocoa butter-based lotion, if I had to guess.

"I want you," I whispered softly. "I want you badly."

"You'll let me make you feel good then?" Raven asked in a husky voice that told me he was ready.

I eased back so he could slip my thong over my hips. He pulled my legs over his arms, allowing them to spread and touch my ears. He dipped his head between my thighs and sucked me with such force that my legs began to tremble.

After doing enough work to make my toes curl twice, Raven looked up, my wetness still glistening on his face, and he smiled at me.

I couldn't believe Dana had sent me a *fuck*, but that's exactly what she had done. And I was a better woman for it. I couldn't be more appreciative.

Maxey Barber

Late one afternoon after lunch, Dana and I made our way back to the room. We'd been sitting around for nearly an hour when Ramona came strolling in.

"Let's go out to the pool," Dana suggested.

We grabbed some snacks and cocktails and headed out to the pool in the private courtyard reserved for the suites. It was December, but in the waters between L.A. and Mexico, it might as well have been mid-July. It was a balmy Saturday afternoon and the evening promised the same with just a touch of humidity. I was glad we decided to take the cruise. If someone had told me years ago that my marriage would've ended and I'd be celebrating its collapse on a cruise, I would've thought they were lying. But here I was, and here we were.

Once we settled in our respective lawn chairs overlooking the sparking pool and with views of the Pacific, I eased back on my chair and closed my eyes.

Dana turned to Ramona and said, "Okay, spill it!" She snapped her fingers, and I opened my eyes.

"*Chica*, you know you were wrong," Ramona began, traces of a smile at the corners of her lips. That got my eyes open.

Dana started cracking up. Soon I was looking between the two, wondering what I was missing.

"What'd I do?" Dana cocked a provocatively arched eyebrow.

I brought my straw to my lips, watching them.

"You were *so* out of order for turning me on to that fine-ass Raven!"

Ramona shifted toward me and started telling it all.

"This one here." she motioned in Dana's direction with a

slight nod of her head. "She sent a sight to behold up to the suite after you guys left. Girl, the things that man does with his tongue should be against the law! Do you hear me?"

I was eating up every word.

"Can I get a witness?" Dana held her hand up in the air, and Ramona reached over to slap her palm.

"The man is undeniably perfect. I came so damn hard, I thought I was gonna die for sure."

"Wow, he's that good?" I asked with wide-eyed wonder.

"Girl, yes, just talking about it now, hours after the deed was done, it's giving me a shiver of arousal. Just thinking about *it*, about *him* . . ." she testified with a neck twist to boot.

"Okay, that's his tongue, but what about the other tools?" Dana questioned.

"Lemme just say this. What he's got should be classified as a lethal weapon. He's all that and then some!"

I hung on Ramona's every word, and grinned with curiosity.

"Girl, after all this time, the area between my thighs is still alive, probably wondering when Mr. Wonderful is gonna come hit it again," she added.

"That good, huh?" I asked meekly.

Dana turned to me and said, "See, you need to shed that shy persona and let your hair down. See what's really out there." She snickered.

I didn't say a word. I just listened as Ramona continued to rave about just how talented this man was between the sheets.

When I couldn't take it anymore, I turned to Dana and said, "So lemme get this straight. This was *your* man"—I pointed a manicured finger at Dana— "but you shared him with Ramona when you were done. What kind of craziness is that?" I wrinkled my face like a foul smell had invaded the air. Then I eased back in the lawn chair and waited for her answer.

"Look, I've already told you," Dana said. "Men have been passing women around for years without as much as a second thought. That cock is nothing to me but a guaranteed good time. Why not share with my girls?" She shrugged. "Shit, we share everything else: good gossip, good drama. Why not some good cock?"

I looked at her like she was speaking Portuguese.

"You didn't feel funny having sex with her man?" I turned to Ramona.

"Her man?" Ramona nearly choked on her drink. She gathered her composure and said, "You heard her. That's just some good cock, and I'll be the first to admit he comes correct. He turned it out!" Ramona confirmed with conviction. Then she leaned toward Dana, hand in the air for another high-five.

"Good looking out, girlfriend. Really good looking out!" She winked and grinned.

"Hey, what did we agree on?" Dana asked.

I rolled my eyes.

"What happens on the high seas in international waters, stays right out here with the whales and the sharks!" she and Ramona sang.

They were drunk, I decided as I lay back, put my earbuds in and tried to relax. But I had to admit, thoughts of this sexy man and his so-called skills danced around in my mind.

But I was done with men, or at least for a while anyway, and I had the *official* papers to prove it.

Dana Dash

For the rest of the evening we ate, drank, and talked about the good times. And although we were enjoying each other's company, I could tell something was wrong with Maxey. She was a bit more reserved than usual, and she wasn't saying too much. I knew she wasn't thinking about that low-life ex of hers—she was thrilled to be free of him. She had told us so many, many times.

Ramona, on the other hand, was on cloud nine. I noticed when she moved, she did so now with a smooth saunter in her hips. *That*, I told myself, is what a good *fuck and suck* will do for a woman. And right then, I knew just who to turn my secret weapon on next.

"We're gonna go walk around a bit. You coming?" I asked Maxey.

Ramona rose nearly instantly.

Maxey never removed her shades, but she shook her head from side to side.

"Okay, see you in a bit," I said.

Every area of the ship was spotless. We happily explored all the lounges, dining rooms, and public areas. The entire boat was decorated from top to toe with Christmas and Hanukkah decorations, right down to live poinsettias in all the restrooms.

"Dana, are you having a good time?" Ramona asked as we approached one of the deli counters.

"Let's see, it's two days before Christmas, I'm on a *fabulous* cruise with my *fabulous* girls. I couldn't be better!" I exclaimed.

"Good," she said. But it was Maxey I was worried about. This was *her* divorce party and, so far, it looked like Ramona and I had lost all inhibitions while Maxey clung to hers with clenched fists.

We ordered our sandwiches and found an empty table near the pool. There were fliers taped to the table with a list of the holiday events.

"Oooh, look," Ramona said. "I see there's something here for everyone. Man, look at all these Christmas Eve activities, including a Christmas Show in the theater, open caroling in the Atrium Lobby, and even late-night Church services offered in two locations."

I bit into my sandwich and thought more about my plan.

"So, would you do Raven again?"

"In a New York minute," Ramona exclaimed between bites of her own.

"Well, I wonder what you think about me turning him on to Maxey."

Ramona stopped chewing and looked at me.

"To do what?"

"You know," I shrugged. "To do what he did for me, then for you," I said, beaming from the memories.

First a look of concern washed over her face, then she broke into a wide grin.

"I'd like to be a fly on the wall when that goes down," Ramona joked. "What do you think she would do?"

"I'm not sure, but we'll find out soon enough," I said.

Ramona removed her shades and looked at me. "You're serious, aren't you?"

Maxey Barber

Monday was Christmas Eve. We did the buffet for breakfast. I had a fresh omelet and waffle, which were very good. Ramona and Dana opted for scrambled eggs and bacon. Since we could get room service, we didn't really get out much around meal times. But I was glad we did this morning. The weather was perfect, in the eighties, and that led to the usual chair issues on the main deck, but it worked itself out.

"So what's on the agenda for today?" I asked, just because it was too quiet at our table. There was no doubt we were all having a good time. Some of us more than others, but still, I had no complaints.

Even though I had been separated for almost two years, when the divorce finally became official, my girls really wanted to celebrate in a big way.

"We're gonna go play holiday bingo," Dana said.

I looked at her, then Ramona. They had to be joking. Bingo? As in bingo. Like, bingo for old people?

"You wanna go?" Ramona asked.

"Nah, I'm gonna have to pass on that. Maybe I'll go back to the room to relax for a bit. You guys can come for me after bingo," I said.

"Okay, cool."

We finished eating and I made my way back to our room. I heard the clanking sounds the minute I rounded the corner. I didn't remember any problems in the room. So I picked up the pace and quickly opened the door.

"Hello?" I called out.

"In here," a baritone answered back. "At the sink. I think I found the source of the leak."

When I walked into the kitchen area of our suite, I wasn't

prepared for what greeted me: a mocha-hued washboard stomach with pecs and bulging biceps.

"Yeah, I think I've got it."

"Um, excuse me, but what are you doing in here?" I realized how stupid the question was as his half-naked torso hanging from beneath the sink made the answer evident.

"I'm Raven. Dana said some pipes were clogged in here," he said, pulling himself into an upright position.

Up close, he was even better looking than I remembered. I ignored the heat flash that washed over me. My eyes glazed over him. His shirt hung open, showing off that spectacular chest, and his short-clad muscular thighs looked delicious. Just the sight evoked feelings I thought had died long ago in me.

"So you're the plumber and the comedian?" I asked, getting more suspicious by the second.

He chuckled.

"I guess you could say I'm a jack of all trades." He sat upright on his bottom.

"I'll bet," I muttered.

Before I knew what was happening, I was following him back into my bedroom. It was sickening, the way he led me back like an obedient little puppy.

No words were necessary after I locked the door behind me. He pulled out the condoms but I thought it was me who made the first move. Raven knew why he was here and so did I. That damn Dana, I cursed as I accepted his hot lips on mine.

After nearly an hour, my insides tingled, my heartbeat increased, and my breath was caught in my throat. Electricity danced from muscle to muscle, vessel to vessel, through my veins. I felt my skin burning.

His sex was the perfect combination of pain and sheer bliss. I was hungry for more. I spread my legs wider; my muscles tightened and gripped him, pulling him in deeper.

"Oh! Yes! Right there!"

"That's good?"

"Yesss, ooooooh, God, yesss!"

I dug my nails into his muscular back, then I felt it. Shockwaves flooded my clit. My walls tightened, released, then throbbed. I felt him jerk, and I tightened my walls.

"Oh, shit," he moaned.

I held him tighter. When he exploded, I felt an intense sensation, such power. It had me teetering on the edge of pleasure and pain.

Dana Dash

On Christmas, we had an easy and relaxing day. We stayed on the ship and enjoyed quiet time by the pool. We slept in to catch up on some rest after four days of non-stop partying and other activities and excursions.

I stretched out on the lawn chair and waited for Maxey to start talking. But it was obvious she wasn't giving up anything.

Ramona leaned forward on her seat and finally said, "Okay, so what happened with Raven?"

Only then did Maxey bolt upright. She removed her shades and smiled.

I considered that to be a good sign, a sign of satisfaction, to be exact.

"Oh, my dears, I don't kiss and tell!" She smiled. "But I will say this. Raven and I are talking about spending more time together, for at least the duration of the cruise."

She leaned back, and as an afterthought, added, "Or maybe even *after* the cruise."

My eyes widened as I looked at her. I shook my head. She couldn't be serious. This good time was just that, a good time, nothing more and certainly nothing serious.

Oh God! What had I done?

I didn't want to rock the boat, no pun intended, but I had to ask.

"Um, Maxey, you do know that Raven is just um, like . . ."

"A man whore," Ramona interjected nonchalantly.

"Um, I was kind of going for something a little less descriptive, but okay." I nodded.

Maxey looked at us like we were aliens who were just dropped from the sky above.

My heart started racing. What had I done? I thought

having a little fun while we were out in the middle of nowhere would be just that, fun. She had just gotten out of a rotten marriage. Now she was already looking for something to get into? Didn't she know cruise ship romances never left the cruise ship?

The shock became evident on Ramona's face before it registered on mine, but I was hoping I hadn't started anything crazy by turning Maxey on to Raven. I just figured passing him around was a sure way to ensure we had a blast.

"Are you for real?" Ramona questioned with a frown.

"Yes! We're looooove," Maxey sang, and crossed her hands on her heart as if to drive the statement home.

Ramona and I exchanged strange glances. This couldn't be. It was only supposed to be a good time, something for us to look back on and laugh about once we were back at home.

Silence hung in the air. The only sound was seawater slapping against the side of the ship.

"I'm just kidding!" Maxey sang as her face broke into a huge grin. "You were right! He was all of that and then some!"

I didn't know if I should believe her, but Ramona didn't hesitate to reach her hand up and turn her palm outward.

"Gimme some!" she sang.

When I saw her and Maxey slap palms, I sighed with relief.

"Whew!" *That was close*, I thought. "You know what?"

When I had their attention, I said, "Maybe we should make this Christmas cruise an annual thing."

"Only if we're booking it on Raven's ship," Maxey said.

"Amen to that," Ramona added.

And I smiled as I lay back on my chair to enjoy the sun. The boat was on its way back to L.A., and, to me, the remaining three days meant we each had at least another session with the cruise ship comedian. Yeah, we'd definitely be able to laugh about this later, I finally decided.

Memorable
by Isabel Roman

Chapter One

She didn't remember.

Jozette Bellerose remembered very little since waking in the hospital a week ago. This wasn't the hospital. This was an unfamiliar bedroom. Everything was unfamiliar, from the face in the mirror to the faces surrounding her in that hospital.

Vague impressions of things and people was all she could recall. They'd said she'd been in a crash. Her private plane went down in the Northern California forests. It was a miracle she'd survived. They were all strangers. Telling her who she was, what they wanted from her. It had been an incessant barrage of information.

Until he arrived.

Looking around now, the first thing she really noticed was the roaring fire in the fireplace several feet in front of the bed. She sat up, allowing the covers to fall to her lap. Frost clung to the window panes, snow covered trees beyond.

"You're awake."

Jerking at the sound, she saw a tall man enter, carrying a

tray. The aromas of fresh bread mixed with those of rosemary and basil wafted to her, causing her mouth to water.

"Where am I?" she demanded. "Who are you?"

"You're in our house in Maine," the man said. He stood closer now, and Jozette could see his eyes were blue, contrasting the dark brown of his hair. Handsome, too. Broad shoulders, strong chin, muscles. Lots of muscles.

Something was different about this man. Off, odd. Not like anyone she'd seen in the hospital. There was a stillness to him even as he moved.

"Our?"

"Yes." He set the tray on a table, turned, and approached her. Taking a seat beside her on the bed, he reached out to caress her cheek. Jozette jerked back. His hands were cold.

"Our house. I inherited it, but you decorated. Christmas, it was all about Christmas. You wanted to celebrate the holidays in an authentically New England setting. You have a thing for sleighs and skiing."

His grin was infectious, and Jozette briefly smiled before lowering her eyes. "I don't remember skiing. Or this place, or anything."

"I know, darling." The way he said the endearment flowed over her in warm waves that had nothing to do with the fire. "Your memory will return."

"Here," she stated with a nod around the room. She didn't take her eyes off the man before her, however. Jozette couldn't have said why but instinct had her watching him. "My memory will return *here*."

Suddenly feeling self-conscious, Jozette crushed the cover to her chest. "In the hospital, you said you are my husband."

She didn't remember undressing, only leaving with him. And she definitely didn't remember going to Maine. Curious as to the truth in his words, Jozette had dressed and followed him out of the hospital. The cool California night had felt good on her skin, and she breathed in the freshness of it. It was the last thing she remembered before waking here.

The irony was not lost on her.

"I am," he replied firmly, his smile replaced by a piercing stare.

She felt as if he saw more than just her. Saw straight through her to things she didn't know.

"No one mentioned you," she accused. "Why weren't you at the hospital when I woke up? Why didn't any of the nurses, doctors, or investigators mention you? Why did you come for me in the middle of the night? *How* did we get here? And why bring me to Maine?"

He touched her hand and sensation raced up her arm. She closed her fingers around her palm. She didn't remember anything, but she knew that kind of feeling couldn't be faked. Not on her part, at least.

"What's your name?" she asked with a shy tilt of her head.

"Nicholas, my love." He kissed her fingers. "Nicholas and Jozette Bellerose."

"Do we have children? Other family?" She watched him carefully, every gesture, the movements of his eyes. A sense of urgency rose inside her but it didn't warn of danger. Her senses were drawing her closer to Nicholas.

"No, we have no children, no family of importance beyond each other." His cool hand squeezed hers. "Only you are important to me."

He pulled her into his arms, into a tender embrace. Her heart raced as she pressed her body into his arms. Again, she had that feeling of stillness from him. It was disconcerting even as it was surprisingly comforting.

When he released, her long moments later, a sense of loss washed over her.

"What now?" Jozette asked. Wanting to remain near him, feeling as if he told the truth, she leaned back, confused by her own feelings.

"Now you eat and dress. I've laid out clothes for you in the dressing room. When you're ready, come downstairs. I have a surprise for you."

An enormous tree decorated with tiny white lights and dozens of red bows was centered in front of the large picture window. The entire great room evoked Christmas. Holly adorned the garlands bordering the doorways and the red poinsettias strewn throughout the space.

"It's gorgeous," Jozette blurted the moment she could speak again.

Nicholas wrapped his arms around her from behind, and pressed his cheek to hers. This, too, was cool in the warm room. Had he gone outside? Maybe for more firewood?

"This was always our time," he whispered.

"It feels . . . right." Jozette placed her hands over his, leaning back.

She had a vague impression of doing this before, of standing before a Christmas tree in his arms, enjoying the . . . room? Season? She couldn't tell what. But the image was there, and she knew it belonged. She belonged there. Here. For the first time in weeks, the confusion she lived with gave way to instinct.

Nicholas caressed her skin, running his hand up and down her arm as she leaned her head onto his shoulder. He kissed her temple, and she closed her eyes.

Turning in his embrace after a breath, she looked up at him and murmured, "I've so many questions."

His forehead pressed against hers for a long moment. So still. Jozette couldn't feel his breathing and glanced into his eyes. The heated stare in them made her blood race. Moving his hand from her arm, Nicholas traced the neckline, over her breast.

"There's time enough for that," he rasped. "I've missed you so much. I need you now."

Nicholas kissed her, taking complete possession of her; he drank her in. Before she realized it, her sweater and bra were gone. His fingers toyed with her nipples and they grew harder, tauter under his touch.

Jozette's breathing sped up, excited. Her body reacted to his touch, yet she was also frightened. He was her husband and she believed that. But he was still a stranger until she remembered. They continued to kiss with passion, with urgency and desire. Jozette found herself caught up, lost in his overwhelming need and fervor. In her own body's need for and reaction to this man.

He kissed her deeply, kissed her cheeks, her jaw, her neck and that small hollow. She squirmed, and felt him chuckle against her skin. He continued to bestow attention to that spot on her throat, and Jozette thought she'd explode from that alone.

When his teeth scraped her neck, her orgasm crashed through her. It was hard and fast, over before she could fully enjoy it as he built her toward that delicious peak again.

Dipping his head to suckle her breast, his hands were cool and steady on her. Jozette's knees buckled.

"Your body remembers me, darling."

Though she couldn't deny it, she said nothing in reply. She

couldn't. Nicholas picked her up then, and her legs wrapped around his waist. Through their clothing, she could feel his erection. Moving her hips, she couldn't help the groan of pleasure.

Laying her on the floor before the fire, he kissed and sucked his way up her body. Wrapping her arms around him, she lifted her hips as he pulled her pants off. Her eyes half-closed in passion, she leaned up on her elbows and watched him strip.

Oh, was he gorgeous.

Pale skin, very nicely defined. Jozette was positive not an ounce of fat graced those beautiful muscles. His chest was still, eyes bright with a dark passion she was drawn to. Her gaze wandered up his body, and she felt herself growing wetter. Yes, her body knew this man.

His cock was stiff and thick, and her legs opened wider at the sight.

With a growl, Nicholas kneeled before her, fingers teasing her slick folds, teeth scraping her clit.

"Nicholas!" she gasped.

Her body shuddered, but it wasn't enough. She needed more. Needed to feel him move within her. He pressed his body against hers, and she felt his rock-hard arousal at her entrance.

"Yes," she panted, hips jerking. "Yes, please."

He cupped her head in his large hand and kissed her. She could get lost in his kisses. His cock slid up and down the valley between her soft nether lips, and her skin tingled with arousal.

Jozette arched backwards as Nicholas entered her. She came instantly. Her mouth opened in a silent scream and she felt herself near fainting. Nicholas hadn't yet moved, she could feel him watching as the orgasm enveloped her.

Limp, sated, she felt more than heard him growl. It was only then he began moving. Winding her arms around him, the cool granite of his back, she matched his pace. Each movement of his hips was well controlled, slow and deep. When she opened her eyes, her gaze locked with his. There was no control there.

The fingers of one hand drifted down her body, and she shivered again, already anticipating another orgasm, welcoming it. With sure strokes, as if he knew exactly where to touch her, Nicholas brought her to a peak once more. Matching his rhythm, Jozette felt as if she couldn't tell where one began and the other ended.

When she came this time, she felt as if she finally found her home.

Chapter Two

Nothing in his existence had ever compared to the feel of his wife against him.

As Jozette dozed in his arms, firelight shadowing her features, Nicholas knew nothing ever would. For two years he had dreamed of this moment, of recapturing what he once had. His obsession with her, his consuming desire for her, once drove him to the breaking point. Confined as he was to the estate, he'd tried to forget even as he tried to remember.

Nicholas wanted to purge his passion with hellfire or take complete dominion over it once and for all.

They'd taken him from his life, stolen his future. Two years was nothing to some of his new family. To him, it was an eternity.

Now all he wanted was who was lying in his arms, the rapture of her embrace and the ecstasy of desire returned. His hands caressed hers, lifting her fingers so he could see the indentation of her ring. They'd taken it off her at the hospital. He'd have to send someone to retrieve it from their safe.

She opened her eyes and tried to move away. Holding her to him, he fanned his fingers below her hand. Up, down, up down. Though he purposely did it to see if she remembered, it used to be an unconscious gesture.

Jozette didn't move her hand, allowing him this pleasure. He wondered if she knew how much such a small sign meant to him. "You're cold," she said, turning away. "Um, why don't you warm by the fire?"

"I'm fine," he said, but allowed her to move away. He planned on telling her, but not so soon after making love. "Here, wrap up."

She took the soft red chenille blanket and did so, hiding her body from his gaze. Nicholas shrugged and tugged his pants on, needing her relaxed.

"We must've had an exceptional life," she said, her eyes roaming the room. "This place is beautiful. You're beautiful." She faltered, but met his gaze and demanded, "Tell me about it."

"The first time I saw you, you were riding Athena, your horse." Smiling at the memory, he watched her for any reaction. She continued to listen, but nothing more. "I was walking the border of our properties when I saw you, you had no idea I was there. From that moment, I was captivated. Took me weeks to work up enough courage to join you for a ride."

"You stalked me," she said, but a smile lit her face.

"Absolutely," he said, laughing. "I was the older man by all of six months. Had to make an impression."

"How old were we?"

"Why do you ask?" he countered.

"I don't know," she said, shrugging. "But how old were we?"

"Sixteen," he admitted. "After college, we married. Big lavish wedding, two hundred people I didn't know. Lots of food, even more wine."

Jozette cocked her head and then slowly asked, "Where? Where was the wedding?"

"In the vineyards." He waited for more questions, wanted to pull the memories out of her, but was reluctant to do so.

Everyone said the patient was supposed to remember on her own. Nicholas didn't much care for what *everyone* said. He needed her to remember their life. Remember him.

"In a vineyard?" She seemed surprised, but he pushed back his disappointment.

"Yes, ours. Your grandfather's vineyard borders my family's."

"Grandfather. I don't remember my grandfather visiting me."

He stepped closer, hesitating for a moment before lifting her into his arms. Though he couldn't feel the coldness, he knew it had to be seeping through the thin blanket she wrapped herself in. He sat her on the couch and knelt next to her on the hardwood floor.

"He died five years ago," he said. "I'm sorry."

"Oh," she said weakly. "Me, too."

"You inherited it, and we joined our brands."

"Ah. I see." She didn't look like she did, but he let it go. She was silent for so long he wondered if he'd rushed this.

When she started to speak again, he assumed it was to ask about her parents, dead since she was eight, but she surprised him.

"Where were you that it took two weeks to get to California?"

Nicholas blinked. "That's unimportant. What's important now is that I'm here and we're together."

"I think it's *very* important. No one mentioned you. You didn't come during visiting hours, and we left without telling anyone." She folded her arms across her chest and waited. "And you still haven't told me how we got from California to Maine without me remembering. So. Where were you?"

Nicholas stood and strode to the Christmas tree. He looked beyond it to the snow-covered lawn. She loved the house because of the view from the picture window. She said it was right out of a Currier and Ives painting. He heard her stand and wander the room. Her breathing was soft, a reminder of the stark differences between them.

There were several pictures on the mantle, ones from previous Christmases here. Jozette moved to them, and he detected a change in her.

It was now or never.

"Ever since you brought me here," she said into the silence, "I've understood there's something off, something . . . different about you."

He felt her stare burn into his back, and he turned. She faced him without fear. Some part of him was proud at that.

"Not this place, not the hospital. You, Nicholas. I don't need my memory to understand that." She paused, calm in her stance. He sensed no anxiety about her, saw none in her eyes. Jozette faced him with the same cool determination she'd always had. "What is it you're not telling me?"

"You're not prepared to hear it," he whispered.

Jozette hesitated, watching him. Then she took a step forward, another until she was only about a foot away. "I may not remember you," she said, "but I know you."

He caressed her face, the softness of her cheek. "All you need to know is I love you. I always have. Let's just enjoy these few days. They're a gift; you don't understand."

"Then tell me." Her hand captured his, twining their fingers together.

Nicholas jerked his hand away, desperately trying to suppress the rage that boiled inside him. He didn't want to lash out at her, but at the years stolen from them. "I didn't want to leave you," he ground out. "I'd never leave you."

"What happened?"

Turning to face her, Nicholas confessed. "There are things in this world that are dangerous. I'm one of them."

She did jerk back then, but in confusion not horror. "You're . . . what? An assassin?"

"No," he snorted. "Jozette, please believe I love you. I always have. I'd have come to you sooner, but wasn't allowed to."

"Allowed?" she whispered but he ignored her.

"They took me. Changed me in the middle of the night, refused to let me see you." His hands curled into tight fists, nails digging into his palms. What little blood he had in his body seeped from the wounds, and he growled at the scent.

Frustrated, angry, he longed for her. All of her.

"Can't we ignore it for now?" he demanded. "I only just got you back."

Slowly, she nodded. Without a word, Nicholas turned and left the room, terrified he'd lost her before he truly got her back.

Chapter Three

Tucking the blanket securely around her, Jozette followed Nicholas out of the great room. He was nowhere in sight. How had he disappeared so quickly?

"Nicholas?" she called. Her voice echoed along the high ceilings. "Where the hell did you go?"

She wandered through the many rooms on the first floor, calling out his name. They all seemed familiar, vaguely so. Not in the way the great room did, that drew her in ways nothing but Nicholas had. The kitchen seemed most familiar and Jozette wondered if she'd cooked.

Maybe they did together. Christmas breads and cookies, ham for dinner with sweet potatoes. It sounded delicious, but she couldn't remember how to make sweet potatoes. Maybe just cookies, then?

Wandering back through the house, she called again. It seemed empty, but she couldn't shake the feeling that he was close by.

"Nicholas!" His name echoed with no response. A sudden feeling of dread snaked through her as she walked barefooted back to the great room.

"Nicholas, I know you're here. Show yourself. This isn't funny!" Jozette scanned the room. He wasn't there, but she could feel him as if he was.

The fire was dying. She went to the fireplace, pressed the button that popped open the side door containing the stacked wood, grabbed a log, and tossed it onto the fire. Turning, she scanned the room. Nicholas was there, yet there were no shadows deep enough for him to hide in.

Moving around the room, something caught her attention about the Christmas tree. Something was missing.

Tightening the blanket around her, Jozette walked closer, examining it.

Where were the cork ornaments?

"He left them in his office again, didn't he? I can tell him a hundred times to pack them but unless I go get them myself..."

Jozette stopped. Her heart pounded in her chest, her lungs hurt, and she tried to remember to breathe. Fingers numb with shock tightened further around the blanket.

"Oh God."

"Jozette, I'm sorry. It's very hard to explain," Nicholas stated as he instantly appeared before her, blocking her view of the tree. "I—"

"You forgot our little cork ornaments," she whispered. "The ones with the crests." She stared through him, still seeing the tree minus the ornaments. "The ones you like to keep in your office, with the first crest we designed together. The only thing..."

Tears streamed down her cheeks. Staring at her husband in disbelief, her voice cracked. "You died. Two years ago."

Nicholas reached for her but she stumbled backwards. Furiously swiping her cheeks, she looked at him. Standing perfectly still, unreadable, he watched her back. Unchanged from the last moment she'd seen him, leaving for a business meeting in New York. She was to follow him a week later.

He'd vanished. She'd spent millions searching for him, never believing he was truly dead. Worse, that he'd leave her. Her cousin, Richard, insisted Nicholas was gone and she needed to get on with her life. Jozette hadn't, convinced her husband was alive somewhere. Waiting.

"When your plane went down, I was afraid you'd die," Nicholas said. "I'd been at the hospital since you arrived.

Lurking. When I heard you lost your memory, I thought maybe this was a chance. Maybe you wouldn't be so frightened."

"Of what you are?" Jozette stared at him. She swallowed and composed herself. Her husband stood before her. She didn't care why. "You spoke of being turned. I'm guessing vampires are real and you're one of them?"

"Yes," Nicholas responded. "I wanted to come for you sooner. I wanted to tell you sooner. I wanted . . . but I'm not a good thing. You are. I'm evil and you aren't. I didn't want to pull you into the darkness."

"I see." Jozette lowered her gaze. His voice flowed over her, and she had to shake herself. This was real. It wasn't a dream. She wanted to jump into his arms and forget the past two years. "And now?"

"I won't harm you," he answered.

"Harm me?" She choked out a harsh laugh, glaring at him. "You destroyed me, Nicholas. You left me when you promised you wouldn't. You were alive for the past two years and didn't tell me. You didn't want to pull me into the darkness? There's been nothing *but* darkness since I lost you."

Frustrated, angry, her fingers tightened further on the blanket. "You have *no idea* what that did to me. You didn't lose your memory—*you* remembered *everything*. Did you think I would just accept you were gone?"

She opened the blanket covering her, let it fall to the floor. "Did you remember how much I love you?"

Approaching him, she ran her fingers over his bare chest. It didn't move with breath—he had none. But it was still him. "I have you back. Take me any way you want to take me. I can't lose you again."

He lifted her up, crushing her lips under his. Leaning forward, he drew a nipple into his mouth, one hand smoothing up her torso to roll the other between his fingers. Jozette gripped his shoulders, legs winding around his hips. Placing a light kiss along his temple, she reveled in his touch once again.

A small mewl of pleasure escaped her as his fingers traced the veins rising along the areola. Smoothed over the head of the nipple before slipping down between her thighs. His fingers ran along the edge of her sex, enjoying the moisture coating the passage between the lips. He slowly moved a large finger into the honeyed valley. Urging him on, she moved her hips, but Nicholas wouldn't be rushed. He placed his thumb on the head of the bud, and she gave a deep, erotic moan.

"Yes, oh yes."

Nicholas suckled harder on her breast, taking into his cool mouth the sensitive nerves and reddening the area. He increased the pressure on her clit and Jozette's body tensed, her nerves assaulted by the intense pleasure. Shuddering, she fell limp against him as she reached and passed a quick peak. She needed more; it wasn't enough to assuage the ache of two years alone.

Releasing her breast, Nicholas removed his hand from her soaking sheath and laid them on the floor before the fire. Positioning her under him, legs about his hips, he pressed his body to hers. After kissing her eyes, cheeks, and the tip of her nose, he found her mouth and Jozette let him dominate her, knew he needed this as much as she.

With one smooth thrust, he entered her. Settling into a slow rhythm, he built her up again, talented fingers playing over her body. His mouth paid homage to her, fingers teasing her until she screamed his name. Even as he moved within her, Jozette wanted to taste him, wanted to explore his beloved body.

There'd be time enough for that.

They made love until each was so overwrought that a mere breeze on the skin turned slightly painful. When Nicholas finally exploded within her, Jozette curled into him and instantly fell asleep.

Nicholas tossed another log on the fire. It sparked and flared in the early morning light. A snowstorm blew in while he watched Jozette sleep, and a fresh layer blanketed the ground. He wondered if she'd be up for a walk later, to re-explore the grounds.

"Who took you?"

Turning to look at her, so beautiful on the floor, the firelight making her skin glow, he wondered how he survived these last years.

"I didn't mean to wake you."

"You got up," she said, smiling. "I missed you."

Stretching, she propped up on one elbow and beckoned him back to her. Unable to resist, he complied. Gathering her to him, he tugged the blanket over her back. The chill didn't affect him but he worried about her.

"Who took you?" she repeated.

"His name is Xavier. He needed an heir and wanted me. I was chosen," he said bitterly, "taken and given no choice. I spent the last two years learning the ways of the Family."

"And me?" she wondered. "How do I fit in?"

"You're my wife," he said. "That's all that matters."

"What happens now?" she whispered into his shoulder.

Nicholas pulled her closer. "I can't leave you. Not again. The past two years were hell for me, too."

"I'm not letting you go," she promised, holding his gaze.

"I just found you again. I don't care what you are, vampire, demon, bluebird. I don't care. You're mine."

Catching her lips with his, Nicholas raised her slightly so she could see how important his next words were. "We'll figure it out. There's a lot about me you still don't know. My status, my responsibilities." He kissed her again, settling her over him.

He easily slipped into her body, warm and hot. This was home.

"Still don't care. I love you, Nicholas."

She rocked slowly, body illuminated in the firelight. Taking him deeper.

"We'll figure it out," he repeated. "There's fresh snow on the ground," he murmured, kissing her stomach.

"Can you walk in the daylight?" she asked, arching back, breasts moving tantalizingly before him, nipples hard peaks.

"I can do a lot of things," he said, teeth closing over one hard peak. "We'll discuss it later."

Alone Again for Christmas

by Stacy Brown

We stuffed Karen's already overstuffed suitcase into the hatchback and tied her skis to the roof.

She kissed me quickly, and whispered, "I love you for this, Mom." She ran to the front of the car, where her boyfriend of a year was sitting in the driver's seat anxiously waiting to get the hell out of New York City and home to his parents in Connecticut, where he could really begin to unwind and celebrate Christmas.

Josh and Karen had stayed with me for the first day of their Christmas break in my two-bedroom co-op in the West Fifties, sleeping in what I still considered her room, but was now my office-slash-guest room. She had shown him her childhood Christmas of Macy's windows, skating in Rockefeller Center, FAO Schwarz, and Radio City, but I could tell he was more than ready to take her away to his suburban countryside for a holiday of skiing and fucking. *Like mother, like daughter*, I thought.

As the Honda pulled away, leaving me completely alone on Christmas Eve for the first time in my entire life, I knew that I would have done the same thing in her high-heeled boots—and I really was glad to see her so happy with a guy her age who seemed to be a lot of fun and really into her.

But I had made absolutely no plans for myself. And it was just too late to start calling around to my other single friends to see if someone else was home alone.

I went back into my building, acknowledging the doorman, whom I had already tipped for the season, and let myself into my now subdued apartment.

I plugged in the Christmas tree and turned on the TV, hoping to find some old classic that would pull me in and help me forget that Karen and I had spent every Christmas Eve together since I left her dad a decade ago. We'd done the Disney Christmas cruise, we'd gone out West, and one year we even went to Paris. Seven hundred channels and there was still nothing on, unless you wanted an ESPN Christmas or A Headbanger's Christmas Eve ball.

The sun was just starting to set, so I turned on a light even though I loved the glow of the Christmas tree lights in my darkening apartment. I looked though my assortment of DVDs, hoping I'd find a gem I'd forgotten, but I felt like I had seen most of the holiday ones already.

And then I remembered that there was a box of VHS tapes in Karen's closet that had a bunch of really old and quirky Christmas specials I hadn't seen since Karen was a kid—and some from my own childhood. I was hoping that *A Very Brady Christmas* was in there somewhere.

I hadn't even taken off my coat, but I was really inspired to find that trove of Christmas crap, so I opened her closet and rummaged around until I found the box at the back of the closet and pulled it out. The force of my tugging made its cardboard seams burst, and the tapes spilled on to the floor. *A Scooby Doo Christmas, A Rugrats Christmas Special.* And then, my heart almost skipped a beat—*Alone Again for Christmas*, starring Mark Stevens.

I grabbed the box and hurried into the living room, where we still had a player for both DVDs and VHS.

I just couldn't believe that I had forgotten about this nugget from my childhood—actually, my early teenage-hood. I had been in love with Mark Stevens from the age of twelve until fourteen, when I gave him up for a real, live boy named Lenny Schmidt.

I pushed the tape in and sat on the living room floor, and was immediately transported back to my youth. I knew every word of the lyrics to the theme song, which had been a Billboard hit because not only was luscious Mark Stevens the teen heartthrob of the year, but he was also the front man for a made-for-TV band that cranked out pop hits. I had every single one of his albums—yes, albums—and they, too, were tucked away somewhere in Karen's closet.

This movie had entranced me as a young girl. I had seen it six times in the movie theater with equally mesmerized girlfriends when it first came out. My best friend, Susie, had actually bought me this VHS tape when it came out years later as a token of our long and strange friendship. The last time I had seen it was with her when we were in our twenties, right before I got married.

The plot was as cheesy as they came, but I loved it. Stevens played a college freshman who scrapes together enough money for the bus ride home for Christmas as a surprise to his warring parents, only to find they have gone away on a second honeymoon. Hilarity ensues as he finds himself home alone with no food, and he doesn't even know how to turn on the heat or boil water. He blows the power, and is miserable, but is rescued by his now-grown-up and suddenly beautiful next-door neighbor (who he remembers as an awkward girl with braces), who invites him to stay with her family. And he does. Forever. They marry in a few years on Christmas Day.

I finally took off my coat and sat on my couch, curled under the Christmas throw that I had only put out for decoration. This was comfort nostalgia for me. I was in heaven, as Mark counted his change in his unbelievably tacky clothing from the eighties. Did men ever really wear that layered shirt and pastel sweater look? He had short long hair—that style that signaled the beginning of the Reagan years—just long enough to cover the ears and show some counter-culture inclination, and he had this really endearing way of sort of tossing his mane . . .

I put the movie on pause and decided I wanted something festive to drink. It was too early in the day for eggnog, so I decided on peppermint schnapps. I loved peppermint. I had candy canes strategically placed throughout the Christmas tree, and ate one every day when I came home from work until I either took the tree down or ran out of them.

Sipping my drink and snuggling with myself, I momentarily forgot it was Christmas Eve, until Mark reminded me of my own aloneness with a well-turned phrase from the movie. "It's never a good idea to be home alone for Christmas." It made me cry.

I sat there with hot tears streaming down my face, watching a memory of an imaginary lover from my adolescence, and thought to myself, *This is pitiful. I should be eating ice cream.* A fat tub of Godiva or Haagen-Daz was what was missing, so I turned off the movie, grabbed my coat and headed to the local Food Emporium to overpay.

The place was empty, and that made the store-employee

decorations of red and green look that much more forced. Horrible Christmas muzak played in the background.

I strode over to the frozen food section and stood staring at the wealth of choices, until I saw the pink swirl of the Edy's Peppermint Stick container at the top of the silver case. I knew I had to have it.

But I couldn't reach it. Even with my three-inch-heeled boots, I couldn't manage to get to the top of the case. I stood on the lower rung of the freezer, holding the door open and freezing my ass off, but I still couldn't get to it.

Of course, there wasn't an employee in sight. But there was a rather tall man ogling the yogurts, so I walked over to him and interrupted his quandary over Yoplait versus Dannon.

"Excuse me," I said. He turned around, a little startled to be interrupted. He was surprisingly handsome, in that way that older men who were once the hot high school jock had of aging to perfection. His hair was blond turning white, but almost reached his shoulders, and he still had a light tan, even in December. I felt like I knew him—probably from around the neighborhood.

"I can't reach something. Could you help me?" He must have been six feet tall, although everyone seemed as though they were at least six feet tall to me, because I was five feet tall in my stocking feet.

"Of course," he said, suddenly really seeming to look me over. I immediately wondered if I still had any traces of lipstick on, and whether I had slurred my words or smelled of peppermint schnapps.

I led him over to the freezer, opened the glass door and pointed to the pink container, "Could you please get me that Edy's Peppermint Stick ice cream?"

He reached in and handed it to me in one fell swoop.

"Is this any good?" he asked, looking at the container.

"Oh God, yes," I said, reaching for it.

He chuckled. "Anything that can make a woman respond that way is worth remembering." He handed me the ice cream.

I blushed, and then tried to cover my tracks. "I just love peppermint."

"I do too, but obviously not as much as you do. I wish they made peppermint yogurt. I could go for some of that now."

"Why don't you get some ice cream?" I asked.

"I'm staying in a hotel, so I just wanted something light." I realized that I probably didn't know him from the neighborhood if he was staying in a hotel, which meant I would probably never see him again.

"Well, thank you for helping me," I said. And then added, because I was the kind of gal who could just never stop offering her two cents, "The Yoplait Boston crème pie is pretty good, and so is the white chocolate with raspberries."

"Thanks," he said, and ambled off to the yogurts again.

I turned away from him, but instead of going directly to the cash register, I found myself heading to the candy aisle. When I got to the check-out, I also had some peppermint bark in my hand, but I swore I didn't remember picking it up.

And he was right in front of me in line.

"Oh, hello, again," he said, smiling. "I took your advice." He pointed to the white chocolate raspberry yogurt. "This looks pretty good."

In the brighter light of the check-out aisle, I could see just how handsome he was—movie star handsome—in a navy blue (I guessed cashmere) coat and light blue checked scarf.

I was in mom clothes—Gap jeans and a black long-sleeved T-shirt (thankfully with a V neck), and a shapeless black quilted coat that kept me warm on my way to and from the university, but made me look—well—shapeless.

I smiled back.

"Well, I hope you'll enjoy it, and think of me when you're eating it."

He smiled again, the lines around his rich, brown eyes almost sparking, "Likewise," he said, pointing at my ice cream.

Now it was my turn to laugh.

He waved his hand at me and headed toward the automatic doors.

I handed the cashier my Food Emporium customer card and she looked at me like I was an elf. "What's that for?" she demanded, rather than asked.

"For my purchase," I said.

"Oh," she said. "The gentleman ahead of you already paid for you."

I was stunned, but not too stunned to grab my bag and run after him.

He was on the corner waiting for the light to turn green. I reached for his coat—it *was* cashmere—and he turned around.

"Hey," I said. "That was really nice of you."

He looked surprised to see me there.

The light changed, but he didn't cross. "Well, I just wanted to give you some Christmas cheer."

"You did," I said. And then added, "Hey, I live around the corner. Would you like to try some of this ice cream?"

He smiled, and I could tell he was thinking it over, but then he said, "Thank you, but I wouldn't want to intrude on your holiday."

"I would love to share this with you." I said.

"Okay," he said, "but aren't you afraid I could be a serial killer?"

"Not in that coat," I said. And then I added, "But I could be."

He smiled that beguiling smile and took my bag. "Lead on!"

I told him about how my daughter had just left to spend this part of the holiday with her boyfriend, because I wanted to prepare him for the state my apartment was in. He told me he was recently divorced and that his daughter and her mother were in California. He told me he was wishing for snow, as it had been years since he'd seen any.

The doorman seemed surprised to see me with a man when I had obviously just run out for something, but he was courteous when he opened the front door for us. "Merry Christmas, Miss Sommers," he said, as though he hadn't seen me less than an hour ago.

As I turned the key in the lock, he said, "Well, it's a pleasure to make your acquaintance, Miss Sommers."

I interrupted him, and said, "April. Just call me April."

He shook his head. "You're April Sommers? Dr. Sommers? My ex-wife read all your books."

"Well, I'm impressed."

He took off his coat, and I hung it in the hall closet. It was soft and very heavy.

When I turned to lead him into the kitchen, he tossed his hair, and for a moment I knew who he reminded me of.

"Has anyone ever told you that you sort of look like . . ." I trailed off. It was just too embarrassing to even think that this hunk in front of me could be . . .

"Mark Stevens, at your service."

We both laughed. It was too funny.

"Come on," I said, pulling him by the equally soft cashmere of his sweater. "Let's get some of that ice cream!"

We sat at the kitchen table and I served up heaped helpings of semi-melted peppermint stick ice cream. It was delicious.

And I found I could talk to him as though he was a long-lost friend, but that might have been because I really knew the outline of his life. I knew about his first disastrous marriage to co-star Sarah Blain, and their messy divorce that led to his cocaine and DWI arrests. I knew about his father's suicide and his second marriage to his casting agent, who got him back on TV in bit parts throughout the networks and cable channels (he'd been on *Law & Order* enough times to be almost a regular), and how that marriage had just ended because all her energy was now going into her daughter's Disney Channel TV show.

And he knew enough about me to comment that he liked me better with longer hair (the photo on my first book jacket was the only time in my adult life that I had allowed myself short hair) and he had seen me the one time that I'd been on national TV, on a now-canceled show (he'd been home sick that day).

Somehow we moved into the living room, where the bottle of peppermint schnapps was sitting on the coffee table. I poured some into the one glass nearby and took a swig and passed it to Mark. He drank the rest and then just stared at me. I was hoping he was going to kiss me, but he reached over me on the couch and grabbed the video cover of *Alone Again for Christmas*.

"You weren't kidding when you said you were a fan. Should I be worried that you're going to keep me chained to your bed?" I knew he was referring to the movie version of *Misery*.

I leaned over him, so that I was practically on top of him, and said, "Yes. I'd be very afraid if I were you," and then I kissed him. I kissed him hard. I practically attacked him. It was as though I had thrown every bit of pent-up unrequited desire of my entire life into that one kiss.

He was stunned, but he didn't resist. He actually pushed up against me to meet my desire, and then seemed to give in to it. Our tongues were entwined. And he tasted so delicious with all that peppermint. He smelled so damn good, too.

I was like a wild teenager filled with lust. I pawed at his clothes, rubbing up against his crotch, dry-humping him in a way I hadn't done since I was in the back seat of a car. His hands were under my shirt, running along my back. My bra popped open and his fingers found my nipples. I did the same, running my hands over his chest and tweaking his nipples. I put my mouth to the left one, and he let out some sort of moan. I kissed him to shut him up. And then I tweaked the right one, and he groaned into my mouth, which was unbearably sexy.

I pulled at his belt and opened his fly. He had taken off his shoes when he came in, so it wasn't hard to pull his jeans down. He was wearing these form-fitting boxer briefs, and I could see the 'shroom of his cock bulging up against them. I stroked it through the flimsy material, and he groaned into my mouth again.

His hands had found my zipper, and his fingers were

inching their way into my lips, which were already slick with juice. When he got his finger inside me, I was stunned at how aroused my clit was. I was on fire.

My jeans were gone and I rubbed against him. We were only separated by the material of our underwear.

Suddenly, he pulled away.

"I'm sorry. I don't have a condom."

"I do," I said, and quickly scurried beneath the tree, where I found the gag gift my darling daughter had given me for Christmas—candy cane condoms.

I slithered out of my underpants, and pulled his off of him. I put the condom in my mouth and rolled it onto him, just as I had practiced decades before. It was like riding a bicycle.

And I just slid right on to that engorged candy cane of his. We were rocking and bucking in astounding rhythm. His cockhead was the perfect size to reach my G-spot, and I was getting that double sensation of clit and G-spot stimulation. I knew I wasn't going to last long.

He seemed to know exactly where to hit me, and when to accelerate and when to change the tempo. I was on the verge. And through it all, he managed to continue to kiss me and stroke my nipples and my hair. I licked his neck. He smelled of peppermint.

He groaned, and thrust deep and hard into me, and I knew he was coming. I felt as though he had burst through a dam inside me and I was off. It was like an internal waterfall had been unleashed. I rode that wave and almost felt as though I was blacking out.

I came to in his arms, on the floor, under the blinking lights of the Christmas tree. Mark Stevens, the man of my teenage fantasies, kissed my head.

"That was amazing," he said, kissing my hair again. "And so unexpected."

"Well," I said, "who expects to find—literally—the man of her dreams in the frozen food section of the Food Emporium?"